To Joe!
I hope this is
one of many books
you read this year.
You are a wonderful
human who
deserves wonderful
stories!

-N. Dominic

Contents

Dedication

To Chris, for loving me.

And to Seth, for always inspiring me to step out of my comfort zone.

Thank you.

Acknowledgments

I have to start by thanking my husband, who spent the last ten years telling me to write this book. I finally listened, Chris! I hope you're happy! Thank you for inspiring me while also driving me absolutely insane – this book wouldn't exist without you.

I want to thank my dad and brother, both of whom read this book in its many pre-published pieces. They were my sounding board, my encouragement, and my ego boost when I needed it most. I appreciate every red markup, every discussion, and every little note you gave me. I am so thankful you both thought I had something worth reading!

Thank you to all my other family and friends who supported me throughout this exciting experience. I know I probably annoyed you all at one point or another, but you stuck with me. Thank you to Jillian and Olivia, who read random morsels as I sent them; your feedback was so important and appreciated. Thank you to my mom, sister and sister-in-law, who listened to me agonize over random details and panic over the fact that I was publishing. Thank you for listening! Thank you to Ellen McGee, Eugene Engrav, and George McIlvaine, who all posthumously gave me character inspiration and quotes to use in this story.

A huge thank you to Murphy Rae, who took the time to work with me despite her own busy schedule. It means more to me than you'll ever know.

Finally, thank you to the team at KDP, who guided me through the process of writing and publishing my first book.

About the Author

N. Dominic lives in Wyoming with her husband, daughter, two dogs and seven chickens. She loves words in all forms, unless they appear in the form of public speaking, in which case she loathes them entirely. Her formative years were spent obsessing over the Lord of the Rings, Harry Potter and the Golden Compass; providing her with the foundation to appreciate characters in all shapes and sizes. Although she no longer does her hair like Legolas, you can still find her reading these three series repeatedly.

N. Dominic has a Bachelor of Arts in English from the University of Wyoming and currently works full time for the state.

Introduction

She was numb. Unfeeling. His hand was limp in hers, but she continued to cling to it. Vaguely, she realized the clamor around her. She should stand. She should fight.

All she could do was sit and try to will life back into that beloved face.

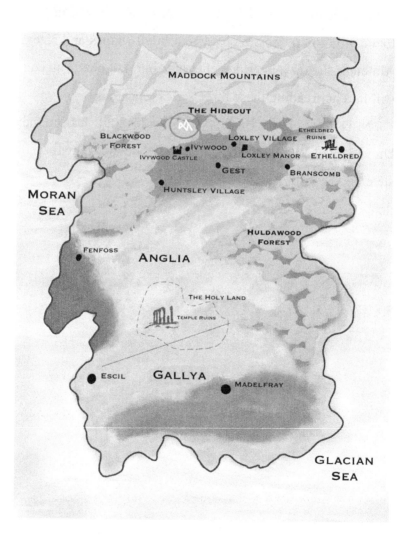

Chapter One

"Shit, shit, shit!"

Moira knew better than to be out like this, but here she was, skirting along the edge of the castle, trying to get back through her window in time. She was close but not quite there. Sweat collected on her brow and started to drip into her eyes. Her flats were not the right shoes for this. Her dress was a poor choice as well, but thankfully she was in one of her less substantial skirts. She quietly prayed that her natural clumsiness would not kick in, otherwise, she'd be a goner.

"*Shit!*" She whispered to herself, wishing she could scream it. She carefully inched a little farther to her left, keeping both hands flat on the wall, her arms splayed out, attempting to keep her balanced. Her ankles began to ache as she continued to keep her feet sideways to fit along the narrow edge of stone around the castle wall.

Ahead of her, much to her surprise, Hanna popped her head out of Moira's window. Her eyes bulged at the sight of Moira inching along the narrow ledge.

"What fresh hell are you up to, girl?! Get inside!" Hanna scolded.

"Yes, Hanna. Thanks. Thought I'd just relax out here a while longer!" Moira huffed through gritted teeth as she took the last few side shuffles to her window. Her fingers gripped the window ledge as tightly as she could. Hanna's hand clamped down around her forearm, a small assurance she might not fall to her death.

"Stow the attitude until you're safely inside, Moira." Hanna snapped while helping with the final heave through the window.

Once inside, Moira collapsed in a most unladylike manner, splaying her legs out in front of her and fanning her face with both hands. She was sweaty and tense from the exertion. She lifted the hem of her skirt and used it to dab at her forehead. Thankfully, only Hanna was in the room, although she looked far from pleased.

Hands-on her plump hips, Hanna stared down at Moira with her deep blue eyes, slightly creased at the outer corners, and tsked before speaking. "Catherine Hammersmith fell to her death leaning too far out of a window, you know. Do you have any idea how lucky you are?" She asked and said, "Care to fill me in on why I just pulled you in through a window, or shall we just get ready for dinner?"

Moira arched a brow. She had no idea who Catherine Hammersmith was, but it was common for Hanna to be full of cautionary tales.

"I'll say dinner, thanks, Han. I'm not feeling terribly verbose at the moment!" Moira said with a dramatic exhale and an exaggerated smile. With a rather uncouth grunt, Moira hoisted herself up and stood - with a little hop and flourish at the end - which earned her a sharp look from Hanna.

Even though Hanna looked annoyed, you could see a flash of amusement in her eye. She was more than a little bit curious about where Moira had been. As her lady's maid, it was Hanna's unofficial job to keep Moira in line as much as possible, but it was a task easier said than done. Tall, thin, and perpetually clumsy, Moira was always knocking something over or bumping into things. It was a task to refit dresses to the appropriate length and an additional job to constantly mend the little rips, snags, and tears she managed to create while doing things such as climbing castle walls and stuffing herself into windows. Moira also had a terrible habit of speaking out of turn, being horribly sarcastic, and cursing at every possible opportunity. Hanna had to step on her toes, nudge her ribs, and flat-out shush Moira several times since she had moved into Ivywood Castle and settled under Hanna's purview.

Moira's first few months living in Ivywood had been one big blur. There was a thick veil of grief wrapped around her after her father's death and it did not go away when she started her new life. While there were many who hoped the change in scenery would be beneficial, Moira felt like she'd been pulled away from everything she knew and loved right when she needed it most.

"Really, Han, if you deep sigh at me one more time, I'm just going to have to throw myself back out the window! Honestly, you're becoming an old fuss budget. I am fine, and I do believe I have time to read a bit before dinner," Moira said while snagging a book from the table and flopping down onto her favorite chaise.

Before she could even crack the book, Hanna snatched it away, declaring, "You absolutely do not! I refuse to hear from Lord Leofwin about your state of dress *one more time*. He believes he is betrothed to a proper lady, not a street performer! Do not subject me to his complaints again, or I will send the village witch to curse you. Now, wash up."

Moira rolled her eyes at the mention of Lord Leofwin, her *betrothed*. She loathed the word as much as the stifled future it held for her. Lord Leofwin, ten years her senior, was the most average man one could possibly imagine, but the match had been made before her parents died, and now there was no going back. The Lord was still reasonably young, just past his thirty-first birthday, but Moira knew there had to be a reason he'd never married before, and she was not too keen to find out firsthand what that reason was.

With only slight grumbling, Moira submitted to Hanna's scrubbing, primping, and tutting. She sat on a small footstool in order to be the right height for Hanna to do her hair in intricate braids piled on top of her head. As Hanna braided, Moira reflected on her surroundings. She lived in a

4

comfortable suite on the west end of the Ivywood castle. Prince Lyric, likely soon to be King Lyric, had graciously allowed her residence here when she was summoned to court by Lord Leofwin. The suite included a sitting/entertaining room, her bedchamber, and a separate bathing chamber, which was a true luxury to Moira. Although she'd grown up as a lady in Huntsley Village, not too far from the town of Ivywood, she felt a world away from her early life. The castle contained so many rooms she frequently got lost in her first few months.

People here expected her to dress and act like a proper lady, whereas back at home, she was used to training with her brother and the other young men of the village. She helped care for the livestock, learned to use a bow and arrow, and generally ran around like the true wild child she was. Her village lacked the clear caste system that existed in Ivywood and in the castle. Her father supported the non-traditional training Moira received and her mother had died in childbirth, so there was no major female influence in her upbringing. While she was loosely versed in lady-like pursuits thanks to a few overbearing aunts, her true devotion had lain elsewhere – archery and the Blackwood Forest.

Although Moira was not yet married to him, she already felt the harsh smothering presence of her life as Lady Leofwin.

Moira had been in the castle for a year now and was continually relieved that the lord seemed to be in no hurry to get married. She spent very little time with him other than evening meals and the occasional castle event. For this, she was grateful. Most of her time was her own, and, despite being under Hanna's watchful eye, she managed to get away with a little bit of mischief when she felt so inclined. As far as Moira knew, Hanna did not have any family nearby, and she spent nearly all of her time in the castle. She was sweet to Moira, but she also had a steely streak that Moira undoubtedly knew to avoid. Hanna's hair was long and graying but mostly a deep brown. She always kept it in a tight bun at the nape of her neck. Moira had yet to see her in anything other than the same three dresses and aprons. In short, Hanna was no-nonsense on the surface, but Moira felt she had a fun person lurking somewhere. She was determined to bring it out.

Hanna interrupted her thoughts with the declaration that she was "as good as she was bound to get" and was shuffled to the mirror to see for herself. As usual, Hanna had done a wonderful job, yet Moira still felt ridiculous in her current outfit. A cheery pink dress with soft green trim and plenty of lace made her look practically comical. She was already quite tall for a young woman, so she wore flats. Never heels, which suited her lack of grace and balance just fine. She would admit that with the reddish hint to her dark blonde hair, a green dress would have suited her better. However, she rarely had the opportunity to select her own wardrobe. With a nod to Hanna, she was sent out to greet her older brother, Amis, who was waiting for her in the hall.

"Ah, there she is!" Amis said, clapping his hands together lightly. He, of course, looked impeccable. His slightly shorter stature worked well for him. He had the same hair and facial structure as Moira did, but she was the one stuck with an unusual height. Amis knew how to dress in a colorful and stylish but not ostentatious manner. He always wore a little bit of facial hair but never a full beard, and he kept his hair longer on the top and shorter on the sides, but always well-groomed. Compared to Moira, he was stunning and stylish. She felt like a towering pink loon next to his quiet elegance and good looks.

"Do not pretend the way I look is visually appealing, you fool. We both know I look utterly absurd," Moira stated with a serious look of self-deprecation.

"Breeches and a tunic suit you better, but it isn't what's called for here, and you know it, Moi. Let's just get through one more droll dinner, and I promise to get you out of this castle and into the woods soon. That outlaw rascal and 'happy men' haven't been seen in a fortnight or more now!" Amis said.

"'Merry men,' Amis. Merry, not happy." Moira corrected him.

"I cannot be bothered to care what adjective a group of grown men prefer to use while hiding out in the forest for years on end. Can you imagine what they must smell like? 'Merry' my fine ass! I would wager they're disgusting and dying for a bath. Not to mention some female companionship!" As he went on this tirade about the local fugitive and outlaw, Roman Loxley, Amis led Moira down through the castle to the dining hall. Although she was a few inches taller than him, she had accepted his elbow and was attempting to walk at his comfortable pace.

Moira suppressed a laugh at Amis's latest comment just as they entered the hall, and she braced herself for yet another formal and uneventful dining experience. Complete with Lord Leofwin, of course.

Chapter Two

Moira tossed her book to the side and gave her most dramatic sigh while looking over at Hanna. Her companion gave no indication of having heard her, so she sighed again while picking the book back up and dropping it to the floor, just for the added effect.

"How may I be of service to you, my Lady?" Hanna asked sarcastically, with her own sigh.

"Enough with the 'my Lady.' No one else is here. I'm bored, Han! I want to get outside. I want to move!" Moira said, with a note of petulance in her voice.

"I'd say your extra excursion the other day - which you still haven't explained, by the way - should be movement enough for you. Or would you like to try exiting your room through the chimney today? Mix things up a little." Hanna responded.

"This is one of those times where it's best if you don't know the details, Hanna. Trust me. It's dead dull what I was up to anyways," Moira said while picking at her fingernails, hoping that action helped disguise the badly attempted cover-up.

"If your father w-" Hanna started.

"Right, well, my father isn't here, so let's just not, shall we?" Moira interrupted her, not wanting to hear what Hanna might say about her father, who Hanna had not actually known. "What're you working on over there, anyways?" she said, deflecting.

Hanna looked at her skeptically, then said, "The usual mending, Moira. How on earth do you get so many snags and tears in each article of clothing?" Moira started to answer, but Hanna continued, "Don't actually answer that, girl. I saw you trip and fall getting out of bed this morning. Not to mention last week when you fell while standing still. It's no real mystery." She gave Moira a soft smile, indicating that the harsh words were only said in jest and not in any true frustration.

Moira returned her smile before saying, "I'm off to the library, I think, Hanny. No, no!" she said in a rush as Hanna started to set down her mending and stand. "I don't need any company and it's within the castle, so no escort is necessary. Amis doesn't need to be summoned!" Moira acted quickly before Hanna could protest. She slipped her feet into her nearest flats, grabbed her book bag, and half ran to the door before Hanna could fully respond or act on the sudden decision.

Moira threw her empty book bag over her shoulder and wandered through the castle. She really could go to the library, she supposed. Prince Lyric, wildly self-centered as he was, had very kindly allowed her full access to the castle's expansive Athenaeum. Although she heard many conflicting rumors about his mood swings and general mean nature,

Moira had not personally suffered at the hands of Prince Lyric. She often wondered if what she heard from the people of her village and in the castle were all wrong. Lyric had only been on the throne since his older brother, King Leo, went to fight and disappeared during the Anglia Crusades. The Crusades were a religious war between Anglia and its neighboring country, Gallya. Both countries wanted control of the Holy Lands that lay in the middle of the continent. While the innerworkings of the Crusades were beyond her, Moira did know that the fighting lasted two full years. There were multiple known cases of disappearances and fatalities on both sides. Moira's own father and uncle disappeared during the many battles.

In Moira's limited time living in the castle, the prince had been very accommodating. This was most likely due to Moira's engagement to Lord Leofwin, one of the prince's favored lords, but she was thankful to have access to the library regardless. Books were her greatest comfort.

Moira continued down the castle steps into the main hall when she overheard two men shouting. She picked up her skirt and rushed toward the sound as quietly as possible. As she approached the prince's trophy room, she realized two men were inside, with the door slightly ajar. Moira briefly considered continuing on her way to the library, but temptation got the better of her. Before she knew what she was really doing, she inched closer to the trophy room door and attempted to follow the heated conversation.

"-and he mustn't be found, you fool!" Stated the first man, still audible but no longer shouting as loudly.

Moira noted his voice was familiar but while it was laced with so much rage, she couldn't place it.

"I do not agree, your Highness! He must be found in order to return balance to the kingdom. Can you not see that this limbo we are in is detrimental? Be the hero and bring him back in an elaborate show of brotherly love," the man said with clear desperation. He paused before he continued, "Don't even get me started on the issues in Loxley Village! Do you understand the impact of your giving away that estate to the *sheriff*?"

Moira deduced that the first shouting man was Prince Lyric – no one else would be called "your highness". Who was the other man? And was this man really indicating that Prince Lyric knew of King Leo's whereabouts…there was no other brotherly love she would think of.

"Silence!" demanded Prince Lyric.

The prince lowered his voice, causing Moira to inch a little closer to the door.

"My brother will remain hidden. I will ascend the throne. The timeframe for him to reclaim the crown is quickly running out. Stay the course, Greggory. I will not be foiled by your weak constitution when we are so near our goal," Prince Lyric snarled the last few words.

Moira knew then that the second man in the room was Greggory Maddicot, the Prince's most trusted Lord. They were very often together, along with Lord Leofwin and a few others. Since moving into the castle, Moira had seen Lord Maddicot on his own only a handful of times; he was always at Prince Lyric's side.

"But, your Excellency – ," Lord Maddicot started to speak again, but Moira heard a loud slap followed by incoherent mumbling.

Moira was shocked. Lord Maddicot was one of Prince Lyric's highest-ranking and most trusted Lords, yet she was certain the prince just struck him. She heard stories of the prince's violent rages but had yet to witness one herself. Her heart raced, and she suddenly grasped the reality of what she was doing. Spying on the prince probably came with a punishment she'd rather not experience. Moira turned on the spot and practically ran back down the hall toward the staircase that led to her room. The library would have to wait. There was no way she could calmly peruse the shelves now.

Chapter Three

Moira rushed through her chamber door and closed it quickly behind her. She was breathless from her full sprint up the stairs and then down the last stretch of the hall. When she reached the top of the stairs, she experienced the distinct feeling she was being followed and she sprinted until she reached her door.

Hanna was startled when Moira threw open the door. She set down her mending and looked at Moira with one eyebrow cocked. She said nothing, waiting for Moira to explain herself.

Moira took a gulp of air, then, with a forced casual tone, said, "This castle is so strange and haunted at night." She gestured with her thumb to the hallway behind her and gave her best casual expression.

"It's only late afternoon, Moira. Not quite the witching hour, is it?" Hanna replied skeptically.

"Far be it for me to explain the complexities of the spirits confined within these walls!" Moira said dramatically as she hung her still-empty book bag back up and flipped off her shoes. She turned and started to walk toward her bed chamber.

"If you don't tell me what has you tied in knots, I will make sure your bath tonight is ice cold, girl," Hanna said in a soft tone full of warning.

Moira turned and stared at Hanna. She had begun the task of untangling her braid, so her arms were up and bent at the elbow.

"You always did know how to drive a hard bargain, Han," Moira said with a sigh. She gave up on her braid before sitting down. "I was venturing to the library when -"

Hanna held up her hand. "I need no embellishment or flowery language, Moira. I will not have the wool pulled over my eyes while you weave me one of your narratives. I am not Lord Leofwin, entranced by your every dramatized word. Tell me *plainly* what just happened." Hanna sounded so serious that Moira heard herself audibly gulp.

"On my way to the library, I overheard Prince Lyric and Lord Maddicot having a heated argument about the concealment of King Leo and their future plans to take the throne once the timeframe of his reclamation has passed," Moira said.

She rattled it off in one quick breath and then felt herself deflate. There was significant relieve to Hanna forcing the story out of her, because she had no idea what to make of it on her own.

Hanna looked at her in silence for several seconds. Moira could see she was running through the deluge of information.

"Are you sure of what you heard and who you heard saying it?" Hanna finally asked.

"Yes, Han. Absolutely sure."

Hanna paused another beat. "You will not bring this up again. Not to me and certainly not to Amis. Gods know what he would do with this information. I need time to think."

"I can't keep anything from Amis. He'll know two seconds after seeing me that I'm hiding something. What am I to do with this, Hanna? I haven't heard of any uprising or issues in Loxley Village either. What's going on that people aren't telling me?"

"Uprising? Loxley Village? What on earth, girl?" Hanna asked. She looked frustrated as she stood up and walked over to the chaise where Moira sat. She stared down at Moira intently.

"Oh well, that was all part of the discussion, too," Moira began weakly. "Lord Maddicot said Prince Lyric's actions have negatively impacted Loxley Village. Something about him turning over an estate to a sheriff?"

To be entirely honest, that part of the argument hadn't been as intriguing to Moira at the time. The part where King Leo was alive, and Prince Lyric might be concealing his whereabouts was far more interesting to her. It gave her the utterly foolish hope that her own father and uncle were not killed in the Crusades but had simply gone missing under mysterious circumstances.

"Moira Ellyn Finglas, I need you to sit here, be still and recount every detail, every *word*, of the conversation you

16

overheard. Now. Don't you dare behave like Thomas Warby, who repeatedly kept secrets until he was finally so overcome with the guilt of it all that he threw himself off Pierre's Bridge and drowned!"

Moira could sense there was no messing with Hanna right now, despite the easy to laugh at and bizarre anecdote she threw into the mix. Moira recounted, nearly word for word, what she overheard. When she was done, Hanna was silent again. Moira began to fidget with her hair, just for the mere appearance of not being completely freaked out.

"Are you certain you were not seen, Moira?" Hanna asked after her beat of silence.

"Absolutely sure. The halls were entirely empty. I'm not even sure the library was occupied, but I never made it there."

Hanna nodded, then sat on the end of the chaise, giving Moira's feet a little tap to get her to move them. Although she was comfortable, Moira acquiesced and adjusted, tucking her feet under her as she sat a little straighter.

"Moira, there is a lot of upheaval in the kingdom right now. King Leo's death -," Hanna started to speak. Moira opened her mouth to interject, but Hanna shook her head, indicating she would not entertain interruptions. "His *disappearance* has prolonged Prince Lyric's time on the throne far longer than many noblemen and subjects would prefer. You need to understand that there are forces at work here much bigger than you can imagine."

Moira nodded but did not speak. She was unsure if Hanna would continue her explanation or not. There were at least ten questions Moira was dying to have answered right now, but something told her Hanna would entertain none of them right now.

"I will summon the maids for your evening bath," Hanna said as she heaved herself out of the comfortable embrace of the chair. "Speak of this to no one, as I said earlier. We will not discuss it again," Hanna said this, gave Moira's arm a gentle pat, and immediately left the chamber.

Moira sat and wondered what on earth just happened. As she sat and dissected the conversation between Lord Maddicot and Prince Lyric again, there was a new element to her curiosity. What would Hanna do with the information and why was she not allowed to bring the topic up again? Her life in the castle suddenly was taking on slightly darker meaning.

Chapter Four

The following morning, Hanna behaved as if Moira had not divulged the prince's secrets to her the previous day. She helped Moira get ready and then disappeared, as usual, to do whatever it was she did during the day. Moira couldn't help but wonder, for the first time since her arrival at the castle, just what it was that Hanna did to occupy her time. She decided to wander around the castle a little and see if she could find her.

Moira rounded the corner on the first floor nearly bumped into Amis. They both took a few startled steps back after nearly walking right into each other.

"On a mission today, Moi?" Amis asked. He wore his usual cheerful smile and seemed to have a little extra bounce to his walk.

"Not particularly. Just sort of looking for Hanna," she replied distractedly as she peered around his shoulder to look down the hallway.

"Sort of?" He asked with his head tilted back slightly as he looked at her.

"I am rather curious about what Hanna does during the day. I rarely need her unless there's a formal occasion, and so I was going to find out where she goes." As Moira said it, she realized it made her sound both mildly insane and incredibly bored. Who spent their day wondering what their lady's maid did without them?

Amis chuckled, probably thinking the same thing about her mission as she did. He had a much better alternative in mind.

"Fancy a stroll in the forest? Don't worry about your dress as long as you've got your boots on," he paused as Moira lifted her skirts just enough to show off the fact that she was indeed in boots. He continued, "Excellent! I've got a great bow and arrows stashed away in a secret spot. I've been dying to let you try them out. Let's go!"

Moira needed no further convincing. Too much time had passed since her last foray into the forest, and it had been even longer since she had the opportunity to practice her archery. If she went much longer without any practice, she would lose her ability altogether. Without a moment's hesitation, Moira followed Amis. Her fleeting curiosity about Hanna's whereabouts was entirely forgotten.

Chapter Five

A full week had passed since Moira overheard Prince Lyric and Lord Maddicot arguing. The Autumn Ball was to take place that night, and Moira was dreading it. She was lounging on her chaise, book in hand, as the dread grew with every passing second. The ball would be another opportunity for Lord Leofwin to show her off while she feigned delight over their engagement. Moira wished she could say no to the impending wedding entirely, but without her father, she felt trapped with Leofwin and powerless to make her own decisions. Amis seemed settled and happy with their new life, so she didn't feel comfortable asking him to risk both their futures simply because she wished to be free of Lord Leofwin.

Moira sighed and dug herself out of her pessimistic spiral. Just as she propped her book up and was ready to dive in again, Hanna called from the dressing room and informed Moira it was time to get ready for the festivities. With a sigh, she set her book down and went into her bedchamber.

Several hours later, Moira was stuffed into a gown she hated slightly less than the pink and green gown from the other night. Hanna dressed her in a gold-toned gown tonight, so she felt far less foolish. She was laced into the usual tight corset that was so fashionable at court, despite the extreme discomfort it provided. Moira would never understand fashion trends. If it were up to her, she would wear leggings and a tunic every day. Although the color of the gown was better, it was still difficult to breathe and impossible to carry any sort of weapon. Although, she rarely carried a weapon on her person, Moira found herself wishing she could. Hanna was persuaded to leave Moira's hair down, on the grounds that Moira could not endure another screaming headache halfway through the night from all the pins digging into her skull from an up-do. Overall, Moira felt that tonight's ensemble was a mild success.

Once she was deemed ready, Moira went downstairs to join the frivolity. She was tucked tightly into the side of Lord Leofwin, or as he'd just asked her to call him, Conor. She stopped herself from wrinkling her nose at the mere thought of using his first name. The intimacy of being on a first name basis was too much to stomach. Unfortunately, being forced to have physical contact with him left her spirits in the gutter. She felt legitimately ill when she imagined calling him Conor, so Moira began to imagine ways to avoid addressing him at all.

Lord Leofwin was fine if you didn't look too closely at how his teeth sort of fanned up and outward. It was as if he spent entirely too much time sucking his thumb as a child. The upper row of teeth never connected quite right with his bottom row of teeth. He did, she realized, look something like an overgrown blonde baby with an abnormally long face. She was willing to admit he had lovely green eyes, though. He was tall, she supposed, but at the same time he had an oddly short torso and an obscenely large head, if one was being entirely honest. Moira was very entertained by her assessment of him and found her spirits climbing as she lost herself in possible ways she could insult Lord Leofwin if ever given a chance.

"Did you hear me, pet?" Lord Leofwin asked, pulling her from her thoughts and using a nickname that made her gag.

"No, sorry, my Lord. The grandeur of the room briefly overwhelmed me," Moira replied, sugar-sweet and subtly sarcastic.

"Call me Conor," Leofwin said with a slight edge. "The overwhelmed feeling is understandable, pet. It is quite glamorous if one isn't used to it."

Moira chose to ignore the dig at her less-than-sophisticated upbringing and instead plastered on her best smile. She could hear Hanna in her head saying, "If you don't have anything nice to say, keep your mouth shut, for the love of the Gods!"

"Come along. I wish to show you off," Leofwin said with a light tug.

She considered, ever so briefly, what it might feel like to hold a knife to his throat and ask him to kindly shut the fuck up. The thought alone calmed her wave of annoyance. Once again, she chose to say nothing and let Leofwin tote her around the room as if she were a prized trophy. She wondered who was left to show her off to after the year of doing nothing else but decided not to challenge their long engagement since she was in no hurry to marry this dolt.

****

Moira was pouting, and she knew it, but she'd be damned if she would spend the entire Autumn Ball trapped on the arm of Lord Leofwin. Just a jewel for him to display. No, fuck that. Instead, she left the ballroom at the earliest possible chance, completely unnoticed by Leofwin.

There was peace in a deserted alcove off the great hall. Before her escape, Moira made sure to get a plate of the evening's dessert (a towering slice of honeyed spice cake). She even remembered to grab a fork but found she was not interested in eating. This alarmed and annoyed her as dessert was one of her favorite things. First, that bastard Leofwin treated her like his personal possession, and now he'd robbed her of her appetite. She leaned against the wall and sighed. She was lost in the tangle of her self-pitying thoughts when she realized that she had failed to notice a man standing in the shadows to her left.

Rather than show her apprehension, Moira stood straight and said haughtily, "It's impolite to lurk."

"It's even more impolite to sulk, miss," the man replied in a mocking but playful tone. "Lost in a mental thicket?" he asked.

She hated to admit it, but she felt drawn to his voice and his teasing tone.

"Don't call me 'miss,' or I'll be forced to stab you with this tiny dessert fork," she said, brandishing the fork dramatically.

The man in the shadows chuckled softly but remained where he was. She wanted him to move closer.

"I see I've miscalculated. A fierce beast stands before me," he said jovially. After a pause, he continued, "Not a moping, weak lady of the court," he replied with a surprising edge when he said *lady of the court.*

Moira noted once again that he remained in the shadows.

"Excuse me?" she asked with a biting tone. She felt offended by his slight shift in manner. She attempted to step closer to see him more clearly, but he stepped back, further into the shadows.

The sound of laughter invaded their alcove, and Moira heard footsteps coming down the castle's stone hallway. She turned to see who was coming.

"Until next time, Beastie," the man said mysteriously.

"What?" Moira asked as she whipped around, but he was gone.

She walked closer to the doorway where the man had stood, but he was nowhere in sight. Did he call her *beastie?*

As Moira stood in the doorway, Amis and Lady Lucia appeared. She noted their intimate proximity to one another and quietly snuck away before her presence could be noted.

Moira walked down the hall and found solitude in the prince's trophy room. The room gave her the creeps, but at least she could no longer hear Lady Lucia's flirtatious giggles. She stood frozen for a second before realizing she still held the small fork in her right hand with the dessert plate still on her left. She set both down on the prince's large writing table and decided she was ready to go to bed. She didn't particularly feel like tempting the fates into making the night any more interesting than it already was.

Chapter Six

Moira desperately wanted to be tucked in her chaise with her blanket and book, but on her way back through the castle, she was distracted by some overheard conversation coming from the ballroom. Despite her desire to avoid the crowd and Leofwin, she couldn't resist entering the great hall.

"He was here, in the castle!" Exclaimed a portly man she didn't recognize.

The bird-like woman next to him replied, "Surely not! Loxley wouldn't dare after-"

"What about his band of ruffians?! Where are they?" Another woman interrupted her.

Lord Leofwin found Moira as she stood there, listening to the group rumble about the outlaw. Everyone in attendance was in an uproar about the easily infiltrated castle. Moira wondered how the band of outlaws had managed breaking and entering so easily.

"Is it true?" She asked, being sure to avoid using any variation of Leofwin's name or title. "The outlaw infiltrated the castle and wandered into the Autumn Ball festivities?"

"'Wandered into' isn't accurate, pet. More like robbed us bloody blind while one of his henchmen stirred up a distraction!" Leofwin huffed.

Leofwin stuck his chest out a little further and straightened his back as if posturing would keep any lingering outlaws away.

Moira stared with what she knew was ill-disguised disgust at this fool she was expected to marry. Just when she thought she might cave and shove Leofwin over, she heard Amis half-shout, "Moi! Are you ok?"

Amis made his way over to her, attempting to get through the thick crowds gathered to gossip. Behind Amis, Moira saw a rather disappointed-looking Lady Lucia.

"I'm fine, Amis! Did you hear -" Moira started to reply.

"Of course, Moira is fine," Leofwin huffed. "She's with me, isn't she?" Leofwin pulled her to his side and threw his arm around her waist.

Moira immediately disentangled herself from Leofwin and hugged Amis, whispering, "Get me the hell out of here!"

Without missing a beat, Amis announced he would be taking his sister to her room to retire for the night. Leofwin, whose attention rarely stayed on Moira, had already been distracted by the continuing commotion around him. He nodded his approval without looking at them and gave a distracted wave as he spoke to several men.

Once in the hall, Moira asked Amis if what she heard was true. Amis had the good graces to blush ever so slightly before admitting he had not been in the ballroom for quite some time, so he'd missed all the action. Moira rolled her eyes and chatted with Amis as he saw her safely to her room.

As soon as Moira entered her room, Hanna undertook the task of undressing her. Moira's mind ran over the night's events. She could sense Hanna's growing frustration as she failed to adequately answer a single question about the ball. Finally, she told Hanna about Loxley and his band of fugitives. She noticed that Hanna worked a little quicker after hearing this news. She excused herself from Moira's room as soon as her dress was off. Curious, Moira thought, as she grabbed her book and settled in.

****

Moira lay in her bed. The oil lamp flickered on the table beside her as she held a book in her lap. She was not actively reading as she lay there, despite her best intentions. Instead, her mind swirled around the man from earlier, the man in the shadows. She was convinced he was Roman Loxley, yet she had no concrete proof. The women at court all said Loxley was a large and attractive man, but there was no way to confirm that about the man when she hadn't seen his face. She scoffed at herself, noting that Roman Loxley couldn't possibly be the only large, attractive man in Anglia, and these two traits did not guarantee he was who she spoke to in the alcove.

Moira thought back to her short conversation with Amis on the way up to her room earlier that night. She had inquired

29

about the outlaw as nonchalantly as possible after Amis admitted to missing the excitement. After the quarrel between Prince Lyric and Lord Maddicot, her interest in Loxley was piqued, even though she was loath to admit it. Amis told her that Roman once owned Loxley Manor, which the village of Loxley was named after. His family had been there for generations, all belonging to the court in some fashion or other. Amis said that as far as he knew, Roman had done something unforgivable in the Anglia Crusades, which resulted in Prince Lyric stripping him of his lands and title. Roman didn't find out about this until he returned home to find the old Sheriff of Ivywood running his family estate. Apparently, Roman was given the boot rather unceremoniously. Although Moira wanted to know more and she desperately wanted to know what Roman had done in the Crusades, she knew if she continued to ask questions that Amis would want to know why. She couldn't answer that for herself, let alone answer Amis. She let the subject drop and said goodnight.

In a moment of desperation, Moira had considered asking Hanna what she knew about the outlaw; however, her brain caught up with her before she asked. Hanna would dig the reason for her curiosity out of her like a bloodhound on the hunt. What could Moira even say to her? That she'd met an intriguing stranger in the shadows earlier that night and thought it might have been the outlaw? No, best not to even start that discussion.

Moira faded into sleep. As she drifted off, she thought about how badly she wished she could say she hated the whole interaction with the man in the shadows. Rather than hate it, she felt excited and intrigued by the man. It was the first time a courtly event had not completely bored her to death.

Chapter Seven

With the Autumn Ball behind them, the castle and village were abuzz with the upcoming archery competition. This was another annual fall tradition that always came one month after the ball. Moira looked forward to the competition, even though women never competed. Even in her childhood, her family had traveled from Huntsley Village to watch the event. Her father usually participated, as did Amis once he was old enough. The competition used to be open to any man who wanted to compete, but she'd heard this year that interest was at an all-time low thanks to Prince Lyric's unpredictable behavior.

Moira was desperate to get out of the castle. Despite Amis's promise to get her into the forest soon, he was nowhere to be found. Their last adventure felt like it was ages ago. She decided would get out on her own if her brother could not be relied upon.

Although she wanted to wear trousers and a tunic, she opted for one of her less formal dresses. It was essentially a brown sack, but there was no restrictive corset, and it lacked the multiple skirts that so many dresses had these days. It would also allow her to get through the castle and surrounding area without too much speculation, an advantage that trousers or a fancier gown would not provide.

Hanna was once again nowhere to be found, which made escape all the easier. Moira slipped on her plainest pair of boots, grabbed her book bag and Hanna's cloak from the peg by the door, and headed to the first floor of the castle toward the library. Thankfully, she was not intercepted by anyone until she made it into the library itself and realized that Lord Maddicot was seated in one of the reading chairs near the entrance.

In order to avoid an in-depth interaction with the lord, Moira knew she needed to be chipper. Lord Maddicot hated loud chipper women. He clearly preferred the silent and meek type.

With her widest smile and bounciest step, Moira approached Maddicot and said, "Lord Maddicot!"

Moira executed a flourishing curtsy, which may have been too much, but she couldn't stop now.

"How are you on this fine autumn morning?" she asked cheerily. She gave no time for the lord to respond as she kept chattering in her sweetest sing-song voice. "I have to say I sleep so much better when I'm not suffocating from the stifling summer heat. I feel rested and ready to tackle a large tome!"

Moira maintained her obscenely cheerful smile and held his gaze.

Maddicot looked at her with an eyebrow arched and his mouth set in a firm line. He said nothing and resolutely returned to his book.

"Have a lovely day, m'lord!" Moira trilled exuberantly.

Moira hid her triumphant grin and walked further into the library, past a few shelves. As she looked at the books, she wondered if Maddicot could really read or if he was planted here for some other reason. She decided exploring that question was not worth her time today and went about her business as quickly as possible.

Moira left the library with two books shoved into her bag. She did not want to linger for fear of rousing Maddicot's interest, so she grabbed the first two books that seemed even remotely appropriate for her plan.

Once out of the library and free from Lord Maddicot's scrutiny, Moira made a short stop in the kitchens. She snagged a pastry on her way out the back door of the castle, practically skipping once she was outside.

Moira ate the pastry as she hummed to herself and headed toward Ivywood Village. She opted to take the longer route so she could walk along the edge of the Blackwood Forest.

Chapter Eight

Moira did her best to make sure the hood of Hanna's cloak was up all the way. The hem was laughably short on her, but her own cloaks these days were far too garish to wear into the village. The bag she carried held the comfortable weight of the books she'd taken from Prince Lyric's library. She had a temporary pang of guilt over the theft but quickly reminded herself that she always returned the books. It was not truly stealing but merely an extended form of borrowing. All but one book she'd ever taken from the library had been returned.

Moira tucked away her guilty feelings and instead focused on getting through the streets of Ivywood to her destination. She was always surprised to see signs of growing poverty all around the village, no matter how many times she visited. Very few children were wearing shoes, and most were dressed in tattered clothing. Moira wondered how they would fare when winter came. She felt a new wave of guilt as she wished she could help these people, but without any money of her own she felt useless.

Before the crusades, Ivywood had been one of the nicer and wealthier villages. As far as she could tell, none of the financial struggles in the village echoed in the palace, and she wondered how Prince Lyric could do so well while the people closest to him seemed to be doing so poorly.

When she finally arrived at Taylor's cottage, she tapped lightly on the door and stepped back to wait. Moments later, the door was opened by a young girl in her early teens. She had long dark red hair and the brightest eyes Moira had ever seen. She was small for her age, but she made up for it with spirit. Like many of the other children, she wore no shoes; however, her father earned a decent living as the village tailor, so she remained decently dressed, albeit in a dress with mismatched patchwork.

"Hello, Meggy!" Moira said fondly as she ducked a little and stepped inside the cottage.

"Hi, Moi!" Meggy said.

Meggy closed the door behind her and said, "I wasn't sure when I'd get to see you again! Fresh bread if you're interested." She gestured to the wood stove.

Moira hated to take a single crumb from the Taylor family, who were doing better than many in the village, but still not flourishing. She scolded herself for not grabbing more food from the castle kitchens when she'd taken a pastry earlier. Regardless, she knew it would be painfully rude to turn down the offer of food.

"I'd love a thin slice, but not too much, Megs. Really!" Moira responded.

"I'll even add some honey! I know it's your favorite." Meggy said with a smile.

Moira and Meggy sat at the table kitchen stove and ate their bread in companionable silence. The room was comfortably warm. The table was worn from generations of use, but Moira found it soothing – it was as if she briefly belonged to the family. Once they were both done with their bread, Moira pulled out both books she smuggled from the castle library. She worried that one might be too advanced for Meggy, but she hadn't had time to be picky.

"I'm not sure this one will work for you just yet," Moira said, gesturing to the slightly thicker book. She picked up the other book and continued, "This one, *The Inkwell and the Witch,* should be just about perfect. Maybe a bit remedial, but better than too advanced." She opened it up to the first page.

"Wait, Moira!" Meggy exclaimed as she reached out to cover the book with her hand. "I love to read, and you've helped me to learn so quickly, but you can't just dive in and deprive me of the opportunity to hear the castle chatter. I know the Autumn Ball was the other night, and from what I hear from Ma and her rambling friends, I know there was some sort of excitement! Tell me! Please!!"

Meggy put her hands together and made her best pouty face.

Moira sighed. She hoped to avoid this exact conversation by diving right into the new book. On a typical day, Meggy could barely contain herself before reaching into Moira's bag and taking out the first book she touched. Of course, gossip of the Autumn Ball reached the town. Several of the minor lords and ladies lived in Ivywood, so they would have spread the word. Not to mention half the castle staff or more lived in the village. Moira wondered how many versions of the story Meggy had already heard.

"Why don't we make it a little easier and start with you telling me what you already know, Megs," Moira said with a sly smile. She set the book down and leaned back in her chair.

Meggy did the opposite, moving to the edge of her seat and leaning forward, so her elbows rested on the table.

"I heard that the outlaw Roman Loxley and his men stormed the castle! They committed multiple murders and robbed half the palace. Tilly next door said that he took all the riches back to his manor in Loxley Village, but Ma reckons that can't be right since he's been kicked out of his estate. I think he's building his own castle in the woods," Meggy said barely taking a breath. She paused and took a sip of whatever was in a mug on the table. She continued, "But get this, Moira, my friend Alaine swears that her Gran has found copper and silver coins on their kitchen table two times in the last few months. Alaine's family has been real poor ever since her father disappeared in the Crusades. Her Gran claims the coins are from Roman's gang and that they give the gold they steal back to the people. Can you believe that? Can it get any more romantic?"

Meggy placed her hand on her forehead and gave a fake swoon, then giggled.

Moira scoffed, "Romantic? Meggy Taylor, please enlighten me as to which part of that messy and wildly untrue tale is romantic!"

"The part where a daring, handsome stranger steals from the rich to give to the poor, Moira!" Meggy replied, looking at Moira as if she was disappointed that she did not inherently agree with this.

"I see," Moira said with a small smile. "Well, I can't say what Alaine and her Gran have experienced, but I can tell you with certainty that no one at the Autumn Ball was murdered. As far as I know, killing is rarely on the agenda for Roman Loxley and his band of men. I did hear that they robbed several of the nobles in attendance at the ball. Not sure what they do with that gold once they've got it," Moira shrugged and then reached again for the book.

"Whoa!" Meggy slammed her hand down on the book, knocking it from Moira's hand and holding it firmly on the table. "You *heard* they robbed several nobles? Weren't you *there*, Moira?"

Despite her best efforts to remain casual, Moira felt her cheeks flush. She tried to hide it by propping her elbows on the table and setting her face in her hands while giving Meggy an exasperated sigh.

Meggy did not let it go and slid the book to the side of the table before scooting her chair around the table right next to Moira.

In a demanding tone, Meggy said, "Tell me, Moi. I can sense a story seeping out of you, so let's have it! Ma won't be home for a while yet, and it won't kill you to spend *one* afternoon gossiping with me instead of furthering my puny education."

Moira sighed in resignation. She dropped her hands and hung her head slightly, then said, "Gods, why am I telling you this story? I need friends my own age."

"I'd be insulted by that comment if I wasn't thrilled you're going to tell me. Quit delaying!" Meggy said all too eagerly.

"I am unable to confirm the details of the night because I was not in the ballroom when it all unfolded. I was down the hall in one of the alcoves having some peace and quiet. Believe it or not, being at these balls and castle events is not quite as titillating as you'd like to imagine. The part I know you're dying to hear," Here Moira paused and held up her hand as she looked sternly at Meggy, who had opened her mouth to speak. Moira gave her friend a little smirk and continued, "The part I know you'll find far more interesting is the bit of intrigue involving a conversation with a mysterious man who stood in the shadows while I hid in the alcove."

Meggy squealed and leaned back in her chair before leaning forward again and stomping her feet on the ground while she remained seated and clapped her hands together. Moira said, "Please never make that sound again."

Meggy laughed. "I promise not to if you tell me about the mysterious shadow man. Who was he? What did he say? What did he smell like?"

Moira started to respond, but then the last question registered and she looked at Meggy with skepticism.

"What did he smell like? Meggy Taylor, what kind of question is that?"

Moira and Meggy both broke out into a fit of laughter. The ridiculous question brought forth a merriment that Moira hadn't felt in a long time. Rather than stifle her laughter, she enjoyed the moment with her friend.

"Okay," said Moira as she gathered herself. "To answer your first two questions. I don't know who he was, at least not for certain. I never saw his face - he purposefully stayed in the shadows. As for what he said," she shrugged, "...not much, to be honest. He teased me, mostly, but there was no real substance to the conversation. Now that I say it out loud, I have no idea how or why he found me and why he even bothered to speak to me."

Saying this out loud got her thinking more seriously. Why hadn't she really considered the man's motives before? If Amis and Lucia hadn't shown up, what would have happened? Was Roman Loxley there to harm her? Moira's mind reeled. All she had that night to protect herself was the dessert fork she threatened him with. At the time, she'd been joking, but now she wondered how she might have used it had she needed to.

"Moira? What happened? You just went far away, and the look on your face is making me anxious," Meggy said, seeping concern. All traces of the laughter just moments ago were gone.

"I'm so sorry, Meggy. I got off on a mental tangent and worked myself up. Bad habit. It's getting late, and I bet your Mum will be back soon. I don't want to get caught again and face her lecturing. What do you say I leave *The Inkwell and the Witch* with you, and you do your best, eh? Read it to the others if you can, and I'll return next week."

Moira stood up and tossed the other book into her bag. She slung the bag over her shoulder and pushed her chair under the table.

Meggy looked disappointed, but the mention of her mother and guaranteed lecture if they were caught again was enough to mollify her. Her mother, unfortunately, did not approve of her daughter learning to read. Particularly when it came to the "trivial nonsense" that Moira brought with her from the royal library. Meggy stood and tucked in her chair. She motioned toward the front door and lead Moira out.

"Thanks, Moira. I know you're busy, but it means the world to me that you visit and bring stories." Meggy said with utter sincerity.

Moira gave Meggy a quick hug.

"You are the best part of most of my weeks, Megs. Take good care of that book, yeah?"

At the cottage gate, Moira turned and waved goodbye to Meggy, who was still standing in the doorway. Moira turned, flipped the hood of her borrowed cape back up, and made her way back to the castle.

She didn't want to waste any time. She realized how long she spent at Meggy's and was immediately antsy to get back to the castle. Moira didn't want to risk the dangers of being out after dark or the even greater peril of facing an irate Hanna if she got home late. While she walked, she hoped Meggy wouldn't get into too much trouble for ignoring whatever chores she was supposed to have done today.

Chapter Nine

"Shit!" Moira exclaimed, dropping an especially heavy and timeworn book to the floor after she fumbled with it on the shelf above her head.

"That's not a terribly lady-like language, Lady Moira!" Lady Lucia said playfully from behind her.

"Oh, my Gods!" Moira exclaimed, hand to her heart as she whipped around at the sound of Lucia's voice. "You scared the soul out of me, Lucia. I had no idea anyone else was even in here!" Moira wiped her brow a little and took a few deep breaths. She was sweating from the effort of retrieving the heavy tome, but the scare did nothing to improve her physical state.

Lady Lucia gave a small giggle, probably to hide her discomfort over Moira's continued improper language. She returned to her usual seriousness and said, "Sorry to have startled you. It was not my intent. I was searching for your brother but stumbled upon you. I only meant to come to ask if you've seen him, but it appears you are very occupied."

Moira blinked a couple times. She was still regaining her equilibrium and realized the large book still lay on the floor where she dropped it. She bent to grab it and noticed the hem of Lucia's gown was filthy. It had a thick layer of mud on the bottom few inches, which was very unlike her. In the last year that Moira had never seen Lucia with a single hair out of place. Her fair complexion was always clear, her nails always clipped, her gowns were always clean, and her hair was always brushed. She was walking perfection…until today.

"What did you say you need Amis for?" Moira asked, dragging her gaze back up to Lucia's face.

Lucia looked down, saw her dress, and blushed. "I should have gone to change. Shame on me. Please accept my sincerest apologies, Moira. I won't bother you any longer."

"No, please! Your dress doesn't bother me at all. It surprised me is all. You are normally perfectly put together, so I was taken aback. I'm not offended in the least. Look," Moira held up the hem of her dress a little. "I left my room without putting shoes on." She shrugged, wiggled her toes, and smiled, hoping this would put Lucia at ease.

Lucia looked giddy over Moira's barefoot revelation. She laughed and visibly relaxed. "Oh, Moira. I have no real need for your brother. I know that you saw us together at the Autumn Ball, but that was the last time he spoke to me. I've been left wondering if I did something or said something wrong. I know the vile outlaw showed up, and there was quite a commotion, which rather ruined our moment, but I did expect him to seek me out after things calmed down. Now here we are, over a week later, and nothing." Lucia's pretty face practically crumpled before Moira's eyes.

"Oh, Lucia. I'm so sorry to hear Amis has behaved badly. I wish I could be more helpful, but I've barely seen him myself since the ball. He's made some unkept promises to me lately, mostly in the form of time in the Blackwood, but I can sympathize with your disappointment. I'd be happy to find him and tell him he's a right git for ignoring you if you'd like."

Lucia grinned and looked at Moira thoughtfully. "I'm sorry to have put all of this on you unexpectedly. I have never been particularly welcoming to you, Moira. I'm sorry for that. When you came to the castle, it seemed as though you did not belong. But now I think I may have misjudged you."

Moira was taken aback. She couldn't be sure if Lucia was being complimentary or insulting. It was an odd comment to make, but she decided she'd take it as a compliment since she realized she did not want to belong in Ivywood castle. No one outright treated her poorly, but they were also not her people. Plain and simple.

"Well," said Moira, hoping to shift the focus away from herself, "it also helps that I have an attractive and enigmatic brother who can get along with anyone, anywhere." She gave Lucia her kindest smirk just to make sure she knew she was joking.

Lucia laughed. "Yes! Speaking of him, I suppose I'd better go change and see if I can find him." She started to turn but stopped and said, "Also, Lord Leofwin was looking for you not too long ago. He said he'd checked in here, but I imagine him checking the library included him looking through the door and moving on when he didn't see you. Has he spent any time at all getting to know you?" She shook her head in dramatic exasperation and left, not waiting for Moira's response.

Moira laughed at Lucia's parting comment. No, Lord Leofwin had not spent a single second getting to know her. Something she was equal parts annoyed with and grateful for. It was easier to keep him at arm's length if he essentially remained a stranger to her. He didn't know her habits or preferences, and she didn't know his.

Now that she was alone again, she went over to the nearest table and set down the large, ancient-looking book she'd worked so hard to get down off one of the higher shelves. Thankfully, it didn't appear to be damaged after she dropped it. The title's text was faded, but it was just what she was looking for, *Anglia: A Heritage. The Historical Lineage of Villages, Towns, and Estates.* She hoped the information was broken down alphabetically, but she quickly realized that she was hoping for too much. The book was written chronologically, so she had to give it a rough guess and then flip through while she searched for one name: Loxley.

After what truly felt like an eternity (so many little villages had come and gone in the country's existence), she finally found it. Loxley Village. It cropped up not long after Ivywood Village. Roman's thrice great-grandfather, Robert 'Robin' Loxley, had been the first lord of Loxley. The estate stayed in the family and passed down the male lineage ever since. Roman inherited the estate from his father, Royce, just a few years before the Crusades.

Moira was satisfied so far with what she read. Finally, she was gaining some additional perspective into Roman Loxley. There was one looming question remaining; one she was unlikely to find the answer to in one of these books. How on earth had he lost his lands to the sheriff of Ivywood? What the hell happened in the Crusades that caused Prince Lyric to take Roman's blood right from him? She turned the page, and then a hand came down on her shoulder - she screamed.

"Hush, Moi! Holy honey cakes, it's just me!" Amis said, stepping back with his hands in the air in total surrender.

"For fuck's fresh sake, that is the second time someone has scared the soul out of me in this library today!" Moira nearly shouted, unable to contain herself after the absolute fright Amis gave her.

Amis laughed, "'For fuck's fresh sake?'"

Moira took a breath and then laughed, too. "Well, it's better than 'holy honey cakes'! Care to explain that?"

They both laughed but regained their composure instantly as Lord Leofwin appeared, almost specter-like, from behind one of the shelves.

"I thought I heard merriment coming from back here! Wherever Amis and my pet are, laughter is sure to follow!" He said with the most obscenely goofy grin on his face.

Moira almost felt bad for the poor sap, who clearly had no idea how much he did not mesh with the two of them. If she had not vowed to abhor his very existence, she might pity Lord Leofwin completely.

Amis took a big step closer to Moira and tossed one arm casually around her shoulders. With his other hand, he reached behind his back and deftly shut the book on the table now behind them. Moira realized immediately what Amis was doing and smiled broadly at Lord Leofwin. Thankfully, all he needed was that smile to continue rambling.

"I have had quite the search for you, pet. Why I've scoured the entire castle at least twice and found neither hide nor hair of you until now. This will teach me to look deeper into the library when you cannot be found!" He grinned with an almost threatening intensity and continued to look at Moira and Amis.

Moira realized they were all just standing there. Amis gave her the smallest squeeze on the shoulder, nudging her to speak.

"Whatever did you need me for, Lord Leofwin?" She said, proud she could manage even that much when she was torn between curiosity and disgust. Mainly she really wanted to tell him to get lost.

"I fancied a walk before dinner, but now I fear it is too late. Might I escort you to your room? I assume Hanna is ready to help you dress for the meal."

Leofwin's tone remained light while his expression stayed shadowed. He offered his arm to her.

Amis gave Moira a slight shove. "She would absolutely adore that. Moira loves nothing more than being escorted through the castle! You'll have to excuse me while I reshelf this unusually large volume on -," he paused, glanced at the title, made a fleeting face of utter confusion, then continued, "land wars in Askia. Yes. I do love to read about things. See you both at dinner."

Moira took Leofwin's arm and practically shoved him out of the library. She turned her head back and gave Amis a slight glare for banishing her with Leofwin, even though there was no way out of it. Amis gave her his biggest smile and a goofy wave. Moira turned around and suppressed her laughter over the wave, and the false subject Amis came up with. He had the world's quickest and weirdest wit. She'd give him that.

Chapter Ten

A few days later, Moira was sneaking out of the castle again. She was still elated after finally finding information about Roman Loxley. She had a couple of books for Meggy and wanted to deliver them as quickly as possible. It was already later in the day than she normally preferred to go to the village, but she knew Meggy would be ready for new reading material, and she had nothing better to do with her afternoon.

On her usual pass through the kitchens, Amis stopped her. He was leaning casually against the back wall, with one leg tucked up behind him.

"Where are we headed off today, my little ray of sunshine?" He asked her, taking a bite from the apple he held.

"Out for a walk, Amis. What about you? Hoping a kitchen maid takes notice of you and lets you tumble in her sheets?" Moira taunted. She regretted saying it instantly, as two young kitchen maids walked in, and both scowled at her. She grimaced and started to say sorry, but they turned and left immediately.

"You have such a way with people, Moira," Amis said with a little laugh. He didn't have a harsh tone, but the comment still stung. She hadn't meant to upset anyone.

"I'll find them and apologize later. I'm going for a walk, Amis. Please don't start to hound me as everyone else does. Even Hanna doesn't grant me a moment's peace unless I'm dead asleep!" Moira tried to keep a whine from entering her voice, but the truth was she was utterly desperate for a moment alone. She was counting on the walk to Ivywood Village for that moment.

Amis gave her a quick once over and looked a little hurt, which surprised her. He said, "Alright, Moi. Keep your knickers on. Sneak out, but come back before dark, alright? I'll say I haven't seen you since the midday meal."

She could have cried with relief. "Thanks! I promise I'll be back plenty early."

Amis smiled and said jokingly, "As Hanna would say, 'staying out too late will get you eaten by a ghost at midnight' or some such nonsense. She'd know someone it happened to, at the very least!"

Moira smiled back and gave him a peck on the cheek before she hustled out the door and down the well-worn path to the village and to Meggy.

Chapter Eleven

Moira made it to the Taylors' cottage in good time but felt like she was too late to visit. It was late afternoon, and she usually tried to visit before lunch or shortly after. Meggy did not answer the door when she knocked, but Moira found her out back hanging up the family's washing.

"Hey, Megs! Sorry, I'm so late. It's been a day for me," Moira said, trying to sound as if nothing significant was on her mind.

"Moira! That bag looks full. Let's have a look! I whipped through the last one you left, and all the girls loved it except for Alaine. She said her Gran wouldn't approve of her reading a story about witches, but she never did quit coming until we reached the end, so I reckon it didn't really bother her." Meggy rambled.

The books were exchanged, along with some quick catch-up. Moira was feeling antsy and insisted on keeping the visit short. She promised Meggy to return, gave her a quick embrace, and walked around to the front of the cottage.

Moira stepped out of the gate, turned to make sure it latched, and was walking down the street when she was grabbed from behind. She attempted to scream, but a large hand covered her mouth and nose. She was hauled up against a massive man's chest. Her feet were off the ground, leaving her dangling. Before she could twist her head around and see who held her, a sack that smelled utterly foul was thrown over her head, and she was carried away before anyone could notice her abduction.

Chapter Twelve

Moira stood in a dimly lit room inside an unknown cabin, held against her will.

There were three men in the room with her, one of which wore a mask concealing his identity. He was incredibly tall and well-built, dressed in a deep green tunic and dark trousers that both looked rough for the wear. His dark brown hair was long, tangled and tied at the nape of his neck. A bushy, lengthy unkempt beard dipped down just below his collar bone.

Moira held her chin high as the man circled her. Chest heaving and hands bound, it was the only thing she could do that made her feel remotely in control. Which, of course, she was not. Thankfully, the foul sack had been removed, which did wonders to improve her mood, despite the abduction. Amis was going to kill her…if she made it home.

Moira decided to break the silence and gain a little control. She stated with as much strength and attitude as she could muster, "Well, do you have a plan, or do you just intend to circle me thoughtfully all night, Roman Loxley?"

She hoped her guess was correct and that they wouldn't detect the faint catch in her voice. Her nerves were frayed and close to overwhelming her. She forced herself to take some discreet deep breaths before she descended into full panic.

A small, round man in the corner stepped forward, vehemently stating, "Watch your tongue, lass! For all you know, our plan is to slit that soft, pretty throat!"

Moira bristled at the threat. She rolled her eyes and fixed her stare upon the small man. She was already sick of his male bravado, and he'd only just begun. The man was much shorter than her and had watery, morose-looking eyes. He wore plain but tattered clothing. His head was entirely bald, and he appeared to have nicked himself several times while shaving his face recently. Moira was certain if it came down to it, she could knock him over without issue.

"Cut the ties, Pew," Roman said from where he stood while he looked intently at Moira. There was not an ounce of feeling in his voice. He turned his back to Moira, stepped to a basin in the corner, removed his mask, and splashed water on his face.

"But Ro cut the -" the man called Pew started to protest.

Roman interrupted him. "I said cut the ties, Pewsey. Do it." He gave the order without turning around.

Pewsey grumbled audibly but slouched over to Moira and cut the too tight binding. Her wrists tingled and throbbed as the blood rushed back to her hands. While distracted by her wrists, Pewsey wrapped an arm around Moira's shoulders, across her chest, and pulled her tightly against him. He put the tip of his blade to her ribs and whispered,

"Careful, lass. It's sharp. Try anything, and you'll see just how sharp firsthand."

Moira cringed at his proximity and turned her head away from his hot breath. Whoever Pewsey may be, whatever he may do, she already knew that she hated him. There would be nothing to convince her otherwise.

Pewsey stood on his tiptoes just to be able to put his arm around her shoulders. This was an advantage Moira recognized immediately. As quick as she could, with his arm still around her, Moira slammed her right elbow back and directly into Pewsey's diaphragm, earning both her freedom and a satisfying groan from the vile man.

"You bitch!" Pewsey exclaimed as he grunted and let go of her.

The other man, a giant brooding creature who barely moved and hadn't spoken at all, stepped over to restrain her. He had a wild mane of dark blonde hair and the beginning of a beard that was, quite uniquely, red. Moira gave no struggle when the brute restrained her, but she wore a satisfied grin, despite her efforts to suppress it.

Roman approached her slowly. He wiped the remaining water from his face using the sleeve of his shirt and stopped directly in front of her. He gestured for the man restraining her to let go and then continued to stare at her. Moira noticed that, despite the dim lighting, she could see Roman's features clearly. He was just as good-looking as the women of the court said he was. She noticed they stood almost eye to eye, with Roman's gaze just an inch or two above her own. Despite the gritty conditions in which he seemed to live, it looked like he attempted to stay somewhat put together. While both his hair and beard were wild and long, both appeared to be relatively clean. Moira thought back to Amis's statements about the possible stench that must come with forest living, but she couldn't detect any overwhelmingly foul odor. Maybe, she thought, the mongrel had some standards after all.

"Are you done, Beastie?" he asked, pulling Moira out of her head.

"Done?" She asked, blinking and looking up at him. Her brain was whirring at the confirmation that Roman Loxley was the man in the shadows on the night of the Autumn Ball. No one else would use that ridiculous nickname.

"Yes. Done assessing me. Done assaulting and injuring my men. Done making that ridiculous look of revulsion you've plastered on your face to try and hide the fact that you're nervous." He cocked his head to the side before asking, "So, are you done?" His tone didn't hold any threat, but it did have an undercurrent of amusement. Was he toying with her?

With a spark of annoyance, Moira said, "First of all. Do not call me 'beastie.' Secondly, I only assaulted your man because he gave me no choice. If threatened, I will not cower!"

Roman chuckled, his dark eyes dancing as he answered, "It's good to know you felt threatened by Pewsey. Not many people have that reaction to him!"

Pewsey, who stood off to the side still massaging the spot she'd elbowed him, simply said, "Bugger off!"

"All in good fun, Pews," Roman replied, looking at his friend. He returned his gaze to Moira and said, "I can only assume you would have tried to wallop Wilhelm, too, if I hadn't intervened. I must say, that's a fight I'd like to see, given he is nearly twice your size."

"Wilhelm?" Moira asked, but she flushed as soon as she'd said it, realizing there was only one possibility of who it could be - the colossal man who restrained her after she'd lashed out at Pewsey.

Roman chuckled. "I can see you've worked that one out for yourself. It's just a shame we don't have Bobby in camp tonight to really make things interesting. Now, let's move on to the reason we brought you here - "

"Abducted me. I think 'abducted' is the proper word. I was not invited, nor did I come here of my own volition. One second, I am visiting a friend in the village. The next, I'm blinded, bound and taken off into the woods. Let's not pretend, outlaw, that you are a gentleman."

Moira glared at the man standing less than a foot away from her. She was trying her damndest to pretend she wasn't beginning to sink entirely into her curiosity about why she'd been abducted.

"I take offense, Beastie! I consider myself a gentleman, as did the prince and court once upon a time. That's a story for another day. Let's focus on your choice of word. 'Abducted,' you say? Well, if you feel as though you are being detained against your will, then I'll tell you right now you can leave whenever you like. No one will stop you. Not me. Not Pewsey, poor fellow. And not Wilhelm. No one outside this cabin will stop you, either. Do you wish to go?"

Moira was immediately skeptical. This felt like some sort of trick. A test of sorts, but she couldn't figure out what Roman and his men stood to gain. She wanted to leave, yes. Despite her curiosity, she harbored no desire to stick around this hovel. However, she also knew she was in an unknown location somewhere deep in the Blackwood Forest. Although she and Amis spent much of their childhood and even adult years in the forest, it was not going to help her leave and find her way back home if she had no idea where she was. Blackwood Forest was massive...she could be anywhere.

"Ah," said Roman. "I see you've worked out that you don't know where you are. I could tell you you're in what we call the hideout; however, that's not exactly a location you've seen on any map. Why don't we strike a bargain?"

She scowled. "A bargain hardly seems wise for me when you hold all the power in our current situation," Moira spat, feeling like a cornered animal.

"Not true, my dear Beastie. You happen to have something that we are very much lacking," Roman said enthusiastically.

Roman ticked one brow up at her but also backed away several steps, giving her more space. Moira needed that more than she realized as she felt some of her building tension evaporate.

"Care to shed light on that, outlaw, or do you plan to continue being an enigmatic bastard?" she quipped.

"The mouth on you, Beastie! While I always appreciate sarcasm and an expansive vocabulary, I fear we may need to start over. Did we bring you here under rather unrefined circumstances? Yes. I sincerely apologize for that," He stated, with his hand over his heart and a slight bow at the waist. He stood straight again and continued, "It could not be avoided. Do you think, ever so briefly, we could set that uncouth behavior aside and talk about why you're actually here?"

Moira sensed that Roman was slightly agitated and growing impatient, but not aggressively so. She wasn't particularly concerned about his feelings, but despite the conditions that brought her here, Moira had to admit she didn't feel like she was in any actual danger.

"I am willing to set the unpleasantness of my abduction aside for now, but rest assured, I reserve the right to bring it back up at a future date I deem appropriate," Moira responded, almost annoyed with herself over her petulant tone. She was not ready to let the abduction go. She added, "Is there anywhere to sit in this shanty, or must I stand all night?"

Roman clapped his hands and exclaimed, "Of course! Another oversight and accidental rudeness. Let's go sit at the table, and I'll see if we can't get some tea. Pews, please ask Gwin if she will help," He prattled almost too quickly for her to follow. It was clear excitement bubbled in him, and he couldn't suppress it.

Moira stood still and waited. Roman made to grab her elbow, most likely to guide her through to wherever the table was, but Moira moved away and glared at him. He grinned, nodded, and gestured through a rounded doorway.

As she made to walk through the arch, Moira noticed she really had no business calling the structure they were in a hovel or shanty. It was a decent hunting cabin. Wide wood planks covered the floor with stacked log walls surrounding her. A fire must be going somewhere because it was pleasantly warm. The lighting was dim, yes, but they were deep in the forest. Light would be a commodity and only truly illuminating at certain times of the day. A large, threadbare rug covered a good portion of the room she stepped into, with a surprisingly large dining table to the side. Mismatched but beautiful chairs were set out around the table, and Wilhelm was lighting multiple candles along the fireplace mantle, with the ones down the center of the table already lit. There was no roaring fire, but the embers smoldered with plenty of heat. Near the fireplace were two worn, but comfortable looking armchairs and one of the largest, deepest looking couches Moira had ever seen.

"Rethinking those insults, Beastie?" Roman asked with a wicked grin. "Don't answer that. I don't feel like wasting time with a stubborn response. Choose a seat. Before I share my side of the story, I want to know what you were doing in Ivywood Village unescorted."

Roman looked intently at her. There was neutrality to his expression now that she seemed to be cooperating. He settled into a chair across from her.

"Where am I?" She asked, ignoring his question. She wanted to gain some sort of footing for herself before answering any of Roman's questions.

The outlaw looked at her a beat longer. After a moment he sighed and said, "You are deep in the Blackwood Forest. Specifically, our hideout, as I said earlier. I cannot tell you where exactly; however -," he held up a hand, already sensing she was about to argue. When Moira closed her mouth and glared at him, he continued, "However, if you answer my questions and hear what I have to say, then I promise to tell you exactly where we are…if you agree to work with me."

Completely taken aback, Moira took a moment to stare at Roman in shocked curiosity.

"Work with you?" she asked skeptically.

"Yes, Moira. Work with me," he said, more serious than she'd ever heard him.

"You used my name."

"Is that a problem?"

"No, you've just never said it before."

Moira didn't want to admit it, but his use of her real name and not the annoying nickname he'd been using, indicated to her that the stakes were high. He was no longer playing, and she wanted to know badly what on earth he could possibly need her help with.

"No, I guess I haven't. What were you doing in Ivywood, Moira?" Roman asked patiently.

"First, I'd like to know what happens to me if I don't want to work with you."

This small detail and twinge of uncertainty nagged at her.

Roman looked surprised. He held her gaze and said very seriously, "If you do not want to work with us, we will return you to the castle. Blindfolded but unharmed. I'm not interested in hurting you, Beastie." He put a little extra emphasis on the nickname, trying, she thought, to put her at ease.

Moira inhaled deeply as she bobbed her head in thought; momentarily lost in an internal debate. She was about to share a secret that no one knew. Amis didn't know, nor did Hanna, though they both likely suspected.

"I like to smuggle books out of Prince Lyric's library. Once a week, more when I can manage, I go to the village with the books. I take them to Meggy Taylor. When the timing works, I have been teaching Meggy and several other village girls how to read."

Moira realized her arms were crossed, and her body was tense. She uncrossed her arms, took a breath, and looked at Roman. The expression on his face was unreadable. The candles on the table top flickered and cast weird shadows. Although she did not know Roman well, if Moira had to guess, she would wager he was a little bewildered by her answer.

"Why do you steal books to teach village girls how to read?" he asked.

"I never said I steal books," Moira snapped, leaning forward slightly in her chair. "I answered your question. You never said this was to be an inquisition. I've told you why I was in the village. Now, you tell me why you took me, Roman Loxley."

Again, Moira glared at Roman. Was this the only expression she'd ever make at this man? It was beginning to feel like it.

"You're not what I expected, Moira Finglas," Roman said quietly. "Alright. I need you to gather information from Prince Lyric and share it with me so that my men and I can take back what is rightfully ours," he said a little too casually.

Moira stared at him; lips parted in surprise.

He tucked his hands behind his head and pushed back in his chair, tipping it away from the table slightly.

"In other words, Moira. I need you to be my spy."

Chapter Thirteen

Moira continued to stare at him from across the table. The candles flickered, and the cabin made the usual settling noises, but otherwise, there wasn't a sound.

"Just like that, we went from insults and threats to total and complete silence. I must say, not at all what I expected," Roman said with his now-familiar smirk.

Wilhelm and an older woman that Moira assumed was Gwin appeared. Moira noted Pewsey did not return with them. Wilhelm carried a wooden tray with some sort of biscuit on it. Moira chuckled to herself at the image of the brutish giant serving biscuits. Gwin worked quickly, setting down the teapot, cups, and saucers from the tray she carried. As she watched her work, Moira realized Gwin was humming softly to herself. She was maybe in her late fifties and had a messy, frazzled, and distracted air about her. Despite this, Moira could sense she was kind. She smiled at Gwin in thanks as the woman poured tea for her and Roman before disappearing out the door she entered.

Wilhelm settled into a chair at the other end of the table. No biscuit or tea in front of him. He joined their silence with ease. Moira briefly wondered if Pewsey would reappear but decided she didn't really mind if he stayed out of the conversation.

Moira wasn't sure what to say, which had to be a first. She was blindsided by Roman's request. She reached for her biscuit and started to crumble it into tiny pieces just for something to do.

"Moira?" Roman asked with the vaguest hint of concern in his voice.

"I'm thinking, Roman. To be entirely honest, I am still attempting to figure out how I went from a dirty sack thrown over my head to being asked to be your spy. I shared a fairly significant secret with you, a stranger, and now I've been invited into a cadre of treason. Let me have some time to gain one speck of stability," she said without any heat or venom in her voice. She was still intrigued by everything unfolding, but she was also acutely exhausted.

Roman laughed a little. "Cadre? Is that what the people call us?"

He looked over to Wilhelm, who shrugged a little but smiled. The first time, Moira noted, that she'd seen Wilhelm do anything other than a scowl.

Roman continued, "I must once again argue over your choice of words. 'Treason' is technically what you're already participating in by supporting *Prince* Lyric," He said the word 'prince' as if it was the foulest curse word. "Lyric has usurped his brother's throne illegally. He was never meant to be the permanent ruler of Anglia. He has taken lands, estates, and people's entire livelihoods just to ensure he is the richest ruler Anglia has ever seen. He has raised taxes to such a steep level that many people have lost everything. He is a false ruler, and the people in this camp, and many others spread throughout the kingdom, have no plan to allow him to continue like this."

Moira could see why Roman amassed a following. He spoke with clear conviction.

"So King Leo *is* alive?" Moira asked, incredulous. She looked briefly at Roman, then back down at her hands. She dusted the crumbs off her biscuit back onto the plate in front of her, wishing she had kept her mouth shut.

It was Roman's turn to look shocked. He asked, "What exactly do you already know about King Leo? You are full of so many surprises this evening."

Roman leaned forward a little farther. He reached across the table and moved the crumbled mess that was once her biscuit off to the side. Roman grabbed Moira's hand in his, which surprised her enough to look up at him.

"Moira, please. Tell us what you already know. I have no desire to harm you. It has become increasingly obvious that we need someone within the castle, someone in your exact position, to help us."

Moira maintained eye contact with Roman but slowly removed her hand from his. It wasn't that she disliked the contact. It was quite the opposite. She was barely able to form coherent thoughts when he looked at her the way he was right now, let alone while he held her hand. He didn't seem hurt by her withdrawal but merely drew his hand back and relaxed a little further into his chair.

"If you are continually surprised by me, why on earth did you bring me here in the first place? If you imagined me to be a typical lady of the court, why the hell would you waste your time abducting me in the hopes that I would help you?" She asked bitingly. A wave of her usual attitude washed over her unexpectedly. Not a bad thing, as the negotiations for their partnership still seemed a little uneven to her.

Roman sighed. "I promise to be completely honest with you, B. However, I must warn you that you may not like everything you hear."

Moira scoffed a little over the shortened nickname and the attempt at scaring her. "You say that as if every part leading up to now has been my wildest dreams come true." She sat back and crossed her arms. "Continue, Roman. No need to hold anything back now just to spare my delicate feelings. I'll already be in heaps of trouble for not returning before dark, and despite your efforts with the tea party, this has not been an enjoyable interlude in my usual routine. You may as well make it worth my while."

Roman's eyes twinkled, and he smiled at her before shifting and returning to business. "I will tell you my unpleasant truth if you then promise to tell me what you already know of the *possibility* that King Leo is still alive. Do we have a deal?"

Without hesitation, Moira said, "Yes, we have a deal."

"The 'cadre' and I have infiltrated the castle several times in the last year. Usually, Pewsey and Bobby are the ones going in, in some level of disguise. Sometimes I'm there, too, although it's a little harder to hide my identity as many of the nobility know me. They have come to know me with the wild beard and long hair thanks to several wanted posters, so hiding is a challenge. I digress. To answer your question, we knew we wanted to talk to you because we've been watching you."

Roman let that sink in for a minute. Moira's mind raced. They had been watching her. Watching her do what, she wondered.

"We have not been watching you every second of every day. So, before you let your imagination run wild with that, let me explain. We have watched you closely at social gatherings. Events. Balls. You are betrothed to Lord Leofwin, are you not?" He asked.

Moira cleared her throat, then said, "I am."

"But you dislike him." A statement, not a question.

"It is not a love match if that's what you're wondering," Moira answered stiffly.

Roman laughed.

"I feel that's putting it mildly. You look at the man as if you'd love nothing more than to shove him from the nearest turret."

Moira smiled, maybe a little wickedly, before saying, "What's your point, outlaw?"

"My point is that you are engaged to one of the prince's favored lords, but you seem to give him no loyalty. That's a powerful position. One we'd like to exploit," Roman responded gleefully.

A light flickered to life in Moira's mind. It was all clear now. They wanted to use her relationship, if you could call it that, with Leofwin to get information. For a moment, she thought she might feel insulted, but she quickly realized she loved the idea. Her engagement was such a sour point in her life, something that drove her down to her darkest thoughts about her future, that she found it wildly uplifting to find a way to use it to her advantage.

Roman continued, "At the Autumn Ball, you left his side as soon as politely possible and went to pout in an alcove -,"

She interrupted him, "I was *not* pouting!"

"A difference of semantics. I must work on that. Regardless of what you were doing in the alcove, you chose to leave Leofwin's side and the festivities altogether. This was not the first time we took notice of this. As I was in the castle that night, I decided to risk it and take advantage of the opportunity to talk to you. Just to feel you out. I was as surprised by you that night as I am tonight," Roman said, a softness in his tone as he spoke the last few words. He stopped talking and looked at her.

Of course, Moira thought of their interaction often over the last two weeks. Especially after she shared the story with Meggy and started to truly wonder why he talked to her in the first place.

"I find no joy in my engagement to Lord Leofwin," Moira said, deciding she had nothing to hide. "It was arranged long ago by my father. He disappeared during the Crusades, along with my uncle. I was so wrapped up in my grief that I didn't fight it when Leofwin summoned me to court a year ago. Amis, my brother, came with me to ensure I was safe. I would be lying if I said I was entirely happy. It has been a great relief to realize Leofwin appears to be in no rush to get married."

Roman nodded but didn't say anything.

Moira looked down at her hands, then back up at Roman. She knew what he was waiting for.

"I overheard an argument between some men in the castle. It was implied that King Leo is alive, and the prince knows where he is," Moira said.

"Between which men?" Roman asked.

Moira paused, then decided she had nothing left to lose and answered, "The discussion was between Prince Lyric and Lord Maddicot."

Roman cursed and slammed his fist down on the table.

"Can we trust you?" Wilhelm asked, startling Moira. She forgot he was there.

Moira looked at Wilhelm. She held no animosity toward him, but she did dislike the way he asked whether she, the one abducted and held (somewhat) against her will, was trustworthy.

"Can I trust *you*? I think we are both in the position of not knowing the answer to that right now. My loyalty is to myself and to Amis. If you and your mission mean a better, happier future for us, then yes. You can trust me."

Wilhelm nodded at her.

Roman sighed and rubbed his face then spoke again, "It's late. Later than I thought we would be, I must admit. There remains a lot to discuss, but I think we better get you back to the castle. Am I wrong in assuming that you agree to work with us?"

Moira hesitated, but she wasn't sure why. She said, "Yes. I'm not sure why, but I agree to help you."

With a huge grin, full of mischief and excitement, Roman said, "Excellent! I still want to hear more of that overheard conversation, but it can wait. The time for discussion tonight has passed. Let's get you home."

Roman stood and held his hand out to her. Moira surprised herself by placing her hand in his. She let him lead her out of the cabin and onto the back of a waiting horse.

****

"This is as far as we can take you," Roman said as they reached the edge of the forest. The castle was in sight, just through the trees.

Moira bobbed her head. "How will I know what you need? How will I get the information to you? Roman, it suddenly feels like we didn't cover nearly enough of what matters tonight." She could feel herself spiraling into panic. She'd agreed to be a spy, but she had no idea what she was doing.

"Don't worry, B. We will contact you when we need something. You'll know what to do when the time comes. Will you be alright getting into the castle?" Roman asked.

She paused and frowned at him, halfway off her horse. She scoffed, then set her feet on the ground before dusting herself off. She gave her horse a light pat on the neck.

"There I go again, saying the absolute wrong thing," he said as he chuckled. "Good night, Moira Finglas. I am very much looking forward to working with you."

Wilhelm urged his horse forward to take the reins for Moira's horse. Roman doffed his hat, then turned and left her at the edge of the forest.

Chapter Fourteen

Once again, Moira found herself tumbling through her window, but this time she didn't have Hanna's help. She managed to get through on her own and land on her feet, which she was feeling quite pleased about until she turned around and saw Amis.

"Mothers above!" She exclaimed, stepping back and grasping the windowsill for support.

"Where the hell have you been?" Amis asked. No room for joking tonight, Moira noticed. She also took note of the empty glass on the table. She hoped he hadn't been sitting here all night drinking and stewing in his own frustrations.

"Amis, it's late. How long have you been sitting there?"

"I am asking the questions, Moira, as I'm not the one who swore to return 'plenty early' and is instead crawling through her window after midnight. You sneak out of the castle at every opportunity and go Gods know where, but normally you're back before the castle locks up. What was different about tonight? Were you pushing the limits because you were frustrated I tried to stop you?" Amis asked, the volume increasing with each additional question. He stared at Moira in a way that made her squirm. She felt like a child who misbehaved.

Amis took her silence as an opportunity to keep talking. "You used to tell me everything, Moi. When did I become the boring older brother and not the best friend who you included in all your adventures?" His tone and question struck Moira right in the heart. She hadn't realized, but Amis was right. Somewhere in the last year, she cut him out of huge chunks of her life.

Hanna wandered out of Moira's bedroom, looking rather like she'd just woken up from an unexpected nap. Moira was almost relieved to see her, as Amis's last question very nearly brought her to a full emotional breakdown, but then Hanna threw an ominous look her way and the relief evaporated.

"Thank the stars above. You're back! Daft girl. Where on this green earth have you been?" she demanded. Hanna's hair may have screamed nap time, but her face glowed with frustration.

"Oh, joy. A double interrogation! Fantastic. In case the two of you have forgotten, I am a grown woman. I do not require constant supervision!" Moira retorted viciously. She was tired and had roughly two thousand things to sort through in her brain. The last thing she wanted tonight was another long discussion.

Hanna eyed her. "You came in through the damned window again, didn't you? Did the story of Catherine Hammersmith mean nothing to you?"

"Again?!" Amis nearly shouted.

"Thanks for that one, Han," Moira said, exasperated, as she rubbed her eyes.

"In her defense, the last time was much earlier in the day. I would wager a strong pint that the first time was because she opted for the window over an interaction with Lord Leofwin," Hanna explained, looking at Amis with a knowing smirk.

"That wasn't the first time," Moira mumbled, unable to stop herself from pointing out the small discrepancy. Although there really was no way for Hanna to have known, considering it had been the first time she helped.

Amis looked at Moira sharply. She could have sworn she detected something else, but she couldn't quite read his expression. It was late and one of the stranger nights of her life.

"I'll add climbing castle walls and sneaking through windows to the list of new and weird shit you're pulling these days, Moira," Amis said, striving for humor, but his tone was still strained.

"Please do, Amis. I'm going to bed. Make whatever lists you want!" Moira said, turning toward her room.

"Moira, wait. Please," Amis said. He sounded exhausted, too. "We just want to know that you're alright. Hanna and I both know that Leofwin isn't exactly your first choice in marriage, and we worry about you. You disassociate at every social event and flee at the earliest opportunity. Tell us you're fine, and we will drop this. For tonight, not forever."

Moira felt as if she stood at the edge of an emotional precipice. Hearing the concern in Amis's voice and seeing it etched into his face nearly made her sob. She took a deep breath and said, "Yes. I'm fine. I think, for the first time in a long time, I feel good."

Amis nodded, grabbed the empty goblet he left on her table, nodded to Hanna, and left Moira's room without another word.

"He's right, you know. We are worried about you. Your brother may be willing to overlook a lot of things, but you staying out alone half the night is not one of them. Be prepared for another round of questions tomorrow, girl," Hanna said while shooing her into her bedroom.

Moira nodded and walked into her room. She noticed her bed looked a little ruffled. She turned to Hanna and asked, "Did you sleep in my bed, Han?"

For the first time since she set foot through her window, Moira felt a little giddy and laughed.

"Oh hush, wicked thing! Yes, I did, although it wasn't on purpose. One moment I was waiting for you to return, and the next thing I knew, I heard voices in the living room and woke up in here." Hanna shrugged it off, but there was a faint blush on her cheeks.

Moira said nothing else and let Hanna get her ready for bed. Her mind was reeling. Both Amis and Roman had given her plenty to think about. So, Amis and Hanna noticed her tuning out at social events. Amis also noticed her leaving the castle so often. She didn't know what to make of this. It had been easy to feel like she was invisible once she moved into the castle, but clearly that was not reality.

Chapter Fifteen

Moira felt like the walking dead the next morning. She never fully calmed down enough to fall into a deep sleep and had instead spent the night either rehashing the conversation with Roman or agonizing over what Amis would say to her the next day. It was entirely unrestful. She pulled on her tattered but warm housecoat and blundered out to her living room, pulling her hair up into an untidy bun as she walked. To her absolute horror, Amis was already there. To her absolute delight, he appeared to have carried up a breakfast tray with him, complete with a large, steaming hot coffee.

"Curse you!" she said, "And bless you!"

Amis smiled and looked at her with his usual steady gaze. Even with his obvious frustration from the night before, Moira was happy to see Amis maintained his composure and style. He may not have slept much last night, but you wouldn't know it by looking at him. Moira curled her left leg under her and sat down at the table, wrapping her robe around her and settling in. She figured she might as well be comfortable for the morning inquisition.

"Coffee and breakfast first, Amis. Please?" She said earnestly, pulling a cup of the life-reviving liquid toward her.

Amis nodded. "Coffee and breakfast first, Moi."

They ate in companionable silence. It surprised Moira at first, and she remained coiled, tensed, and ready for a fight. However, after a few minutes, she tucked into her meal and felt comforted by Amis's presence. Moira felt a wave of nostalgia as they sat and ate together; reminiscent of their youth and all the mornings that were spent just like this, but in a very different place. Back then, Amis was her partner in mischief. They'd done everything together, and she desperately wanted that back. She didn't know when it happened for sure, but at some point, that dynamic shifted. Moira didn't want Amis to feel like the parent or responsible guardian in their relationship. That wasn't his job, even if their parents were gone.

Once she'd set down her utensils and drained her second cup of coffee, Amis cleared his throat.

"Moira, do we need to make a run for it and return to Huntsley? I can leave word that the engagement was a mistake. This marriage was arranged so long ago, and I cannot imagine Father would want this for you if he could see Lord Leofwin and the empty life you currently lead."

Moira was stunned. For the second time in less than a day, she felt at a loss for words. The feeling was disorienting. She looked down at her empty coffee cup for a beat and then looked up at Amis. Despite the risk, Moira wanted to be entirely truthful with Amis.

"Amis, before I can answer that, I want to be completely honest with you, but -," she started to say.

Amis interrupted. "Moira, if you ask me not to be mad at you, I'm not going to do that. It's the world's worst promise to make, and nobody is ever able to keep it." He sighed and shook his head before continuing. "I will promise to support whatever hair-brained idea brought you back to life last night. You have life back in your eyes, Moira. Tell me what happened. I will listen. And I will do my best to contain my frustration, fury and flogging."

Amis sat back and put his hands in his lap. He looked at her expectantly.

"Flogging?" Moira asked curiously.

Amis shrugged and responded, "Maybe not the best word, but it sure flowed nicely, right?"

Moira laughed softly and nodded. She appreciated his lightheartedness. It was a welcome distraction from the nerves threatening to overwhelm her.

"While in the village yesterday, I was…," Moira started, but trailed off, unsure of how to explain the abduction in a way that made it sound less intense than it had been. She summoned a chipper voice and said, "I was taken by surprise after visiting with a friend."

Before she could continue, Amis interjected and asked, "Does 'taken by surprise' literally mean you were taken?

Physically taken?" He had one eyebrow cocked, and she almost laughed at the familiar expression.

"Umm. Yes. I was literally taken, in an unplanned manner, by some gentlemen I did not know until later that night." Moira nodded and smiled at him.

Amis frowned at her. "Moira, excuse my directness, but it sounds a hell of a lot like you were snatched off the street against your will." He stared at her in a way that made her think she'd better get to the details of the story quickly.

"Funny you should see it that way! I did, too. Then Roman and I had a nice long chat, and I felt better about it. Although it was technically still an abduction, I guess you could call it an abduction with good intentions," Moira explained, rambling before Amis could interrupt again.

A coffee cup was knocked over as Moira gestured wildly as she explained. She rushed to stand it back up and accidentally flipped her fork onto the ground, sending egg remnants onto the rug. Moira felt like a bungling fool. She placed her face in the palm of her left hand in a sign of mild defeat. This was already not going the way she had planned. Maybe she should have started with the bit where she smuggles library books to give to the village children...Too late now.

Amis's frown deepened. He asked, "Roman? Do you mean Roman Loxley?" He kept his gaze on her as he bent down and grabbed her fork, then set it back on the table.

Moira still had her head in her hand, but she nodded, albeit a little sheepishly.

"You were taken against your will by Roman *fucking* Loxley, and then you had the gall to climb a trellis in the middle of the night, inch along the castle wall, tumble back into this room through the damn window, and then act as if nothing ever happened?" Amis kept his voice disconcertingly even, which Moira decided was most definitely worse than if he started yelling at her.

She lifted her head and looked at him.

"Correct," she said, putting on her best *this is no big deal*, face.

Amis stared. He sat in silence, scowling at her, and silently seethed. She could feel his frustration coming off him in waves. Moira let him have a moment and then continued her story.

"I'd like to remind you that I did not leave the castle yesterday with the intention of being abducted. That's all part of the definition of an 'abduction.' Generally speaking, the one being taken isn't in cahoots with the abductors," Moira said with a little more bitterness than she meant to. She leaned forward and pointed at Amis. "So, before you focus your anger and rage on me, let's remember that I left here planning to visit Meggy Taylor. I had zero intention of interacting with Roman Loxley or any of his men."

Her tone still held more acidity than the situation warranted; however, she would not be blamed for something that was entirely out of her control. Before Amis could barrel over her, Moira continued, "Now, would you like to hear the rest of what happened, or are you content chafing over the first upsetting thing I've told you?"

Amis surprised her by laughing. He bent forward, rested his elbows on his knees, and rubbed his eyes with the heels of his hands. Moira watched him silently. She did not want to keep lying to her brother, her one true friend and ally in this castle, but she also couldn't continue with her story if he wouldn't allow her to speak freely. Moira found herself hoping that, by some miracle, Amis would support her decision to be a spy for Roman. At the very least, she hoped he would not try to stop her.

"Tell me everything, Moi. I'll sit here, still as a stone, and listen to you."

Amis sat up straight, crossed one leg over the other, and tucked his hands behind his head.

By some miracle, Amis was as good as his word. Although he made many faces and came close to interrupting her, he refrained. She told him everything, and she immediately felt better once it was all out in the open. Once she was done speaking, they both sat in silence again. It was clear Amis was attempting to process everything, and Moira was tempted to wish him good luck. She had spent all night going over things and still felt like she had a lot to work through.

"I have two questions for you," Amis finally said.

Moira took a deep breath and nodded.

"What do you hope to gain by working with Roman?" he asked.

She thought about this herself after Wilhelm asked her if she could be trusted. She had an answer, if not a fully formed one.

Moira hesitated briefly, then gave in to the vulnerability she felt and said, "I want something better for us, Amis. This life here in the castle doesn't feel real. It's like a strange, surreal break from whatever we are meant to do. Helping Roman and his men feels like the right way to get back to where we are meant to be."

Amis smiled softly. He said, "I understand. And I agree with you. It's like an interlude in reality." He paused, thinking for a moment before he continued. "My second question is the one I asked earlier. Moira, do we need to make a run for it and return to Huntsley?"

Without a moment's hesitation, Moira answered, "No. That's not what I want. Not now. If you'd asked me that yesterday when you stopped me in the kitchen, I would have said yes. In a heartbeat, I would have been ready to leave. Something big is about to happen, Amis. I want to be a part of it! I don't want to be passive anymore. I don't want to be a smiling lump on the arm of Lord Leofwin forever!" She felt Roman's conviction now. She may not have the same motives as he did, but she understood now where his passion came from.

Amis gave her a devilish smile. She could do nothing but return it while clapping like a giddy child.

"Let's use that asshole for all the intel we can, Moi!" Amis said enthusiastically. "I have wanted to punch him square in the face for months now, but I've held back for your sake. I have no idea how I can help you, but we'll figure that out as we go. I don't assume a good spy operates entirely alone. It's about time the Finglases have a little adventure and cause a little mayhem!"

Moira couldn't help herself and let out an excited shriek, which she immediately hated herself for. This was quickly followed by some tears of relief and happiness. Amis stood and motioned for her to do the same. He gave her a tight squeeze before pulling back and holding her at arm's length.

"Silly Moira! Can you imagine a scenario where I don't support you wreaking a little havoc?" He asked jovially. "Thank Gods you don't want to marry Leofwin. What a lumpish, foot-licking dolt! I was positively dreading spending every holiday until I die with him!"

Moira laughed, wiped her eyes, and gave Amis another quick hug.

Hanna bustled in through the chamber door, carrying a basket of mending as usual. She looked surprised to see the two of them standing there, probably looking both giddy and exhausted. Moira smiled at her, which earned her a wink before Hanna continued through to Moira's bedroom without any commentary.

Chapter Sixteen

After she finished talking with Amis that morning, Moira immediately took one of the greatest naps of her life. She was curled up in bed with the curtains drawn when Hanna came in to wake her because Lord Leofwin wished to walk through the castle grounds before dinner. Moira rolled her eyes and groaned, but Hanna took no excuses as she pulled the covers back and dragged Moira from bed.

Freshly bathed, slightly primped, and feeling barely conscious, Moira found herself walking along through the castle grounds while tucked into Lord Leofwin's side. He was droning on about his preparations for the upcoming Archery Tournament, which did at least mean Moira only needed to add in occasional affirmative sounds to ensure he continued speaking. She noted that Leofwin looked rather like a shoebill stork, with his oddly long face and rather pronounced chin. The bird was not native to the area, but she'd seen a drawing in one of the library books and couldn't get it out of her mind now that she realized it. He was wearing a light gray jacket and was all puffed up as he talked about himself, only solidifying the image. Moira was overcome with laughter and had to turn her face away before Leofwin caught sight of her.

Leofwin lead Moira into one of the larger gardens behind the castle. There were many large trees in this portion of the grounds. The garden was not the most lively this time of year, but since it wasn't too late into the fall, there were still plenty of trees with colorful leaves, and a handful of flowers maintained the last of their blooms. Moira loved autumn and found that she did at least enjoy the pleasing scenery if she could not enjoy the current company. Several other members of the court and village were strolling among the grounds today, soaking up the last of the mild weather.

Lord Leofwin steered Moira over toward Lady Lucia and her father, Lord Dayben. Leofwin immediately struck up a conversation with Dayben, and Moira found herself people-watching while Lady Lucia stayed politely tuned into the men's discussion. Moira noted that Lucia was a much better lady than she was, and she'd be sure to let her know the next time they were alone. For now, however, she enjoyed the opportunity to watch the other people weaving in and out of the gardens.

Off to one side, Moira noticed a noblewoman who looked vaguely familiar walking around with her young daughter. The child seemed to be interested in picking every remaining flower as her mother stayed dedicated to the task of ensuring she did not succeed. Moira smiled and continued glancing around. There was a nice walking path that weaved throughout the garden and grounds, allowing for plenty of entertainment as people walked by.

As Moira scanned the far corner, she nearly convulsed at the sight of Wilhelm strolling along the path, hood pulled all the way up, casting a shadow across his face. Despite the hood, Moira knew it was Wilhelm thanks to his large stature and the cursory hand gesture he gave her, indicating she should follow him.

Moira reestablished her neutral expression and looked back at Lord Leofwin, Lord Dayben, and Lady Lucia. Nobody seemed to have noticed her moment of shock, thank goodness. Without a clue what they were talking about, Moira interrupted, stating, "Do excuse me. I need to just go look at a tree over there."

She gave no room for a response but gave Leofwin a huge smile before she untangled herself from his arm and walked determinedly toward the corner where she saw Wilhelm disappear.

Moira repeatedly told herself not to run. Damn her general impatience. As she rounded the corner into a private copse of trees, her toe caught an exposed root, and she flailed through the air before slamming into Roman's chest. She let out a very unladylike grunt and attempted to straighten herself. Roman put his hands on her shoulders and gently helped her regain her balance. His eyes were crinkled at the corners, and she noticed they were the color of whiskey in sunshine. Moira shook her head slightly, wondering why the hell she would think something like that.

"Are you always this graceful, Beastie?" Roman asked. She detected a hint of barely contained laughter in his voice.

"As a matter of fact, yes. I'm well known for my inelegant blundering through life. However, you'll find I'm quite agile while sitting and reading," she said with a smile and dramatic curtsy.

Roman and Wilhelm laughed and immediately suppressed the sound. It made her want to hear them both laugh freely without the constraint of secrecy. She had a feeling under different circumstances that she might genuinely enjoy the company of these two. Not Pewsey, she thought. Something about him made her think of a soggy, rank wool blanket.

"I didn't expect to see you so soon after agreeing to work with you," Moira said, blabbing what was in her mind before she could catch herself.

Roman smirked and said, "Acta non verba, B. We don't have time to waste."

Acts, not words. Of course, he'd have a Latin motto. She refrained from rolling her eyes.

"So, what are you doing here?" Moira asked with a glance behind her. She couldn't see back around the corner, but she assumed her freedom away from Leofwin was limited.

They were in a fairly private pocket of the grounds. Heavy shrubbery covered the area, some of the bushes up to her knees, and there were many trees and thick foliage concealing them from all but an aerial vantage. There was a

94

small bench off to the side and only one path leading in and out. If they needed to make a quick escape, then Roman and Wilhelm would have to weave through the trees until they popped out on the other side. Moira didn't like that and immediately wished they'd found a different spot to talk to her.

"We attempted to find you in the castle, but your brother -," here, Roman paused to give her a pointed look.

Moira assumed from this look that Roman had interacted with Amis. She originally wanted to let Roman know she told Amis everything, but it seemed that ship had sailed. Rather than give him an answer, Moira gave Roman a tentative smile and small shrug.

Roman continued, "Amis told us you were out for a walk in the gardens. I don't normally risk my own presence here, but I heard Prince Lyric is gone for several days, so it seemed mostly safe."

Roman leaned back against a huge, thick tree trunk. His feet and arms were crossed as if he always held covert meetings in the castle gardens.

"Mostly safe?" Moira asked with a look of skepticism. She didn't want to waste time delving into how or why Roman and Wilhelm were in the castle, let alone how Amis managed to come into contact with them.

Moira glanced over her shoulder again, still fretting about when Leofwin would appear looking for her.

"We tend to operate in the range of mostly safe to utter disaster. There's not much else in our line of work, B." Roman pushed off the tree and straightened before he turned to Wilhelm and said, "Go have a peek at the Lord. I can't get Moira to focus on what we need if she's constantly worried about when he will come to find her."

Wilhelm nodded, pulled his hood back up, and went down the short path and around the corner. Moira wondered if the hood really helped disguise his identity. It seemed to her that a hood drawn up on a day like today was more likely to draw attention to Wilhelm.

"Better?" Roman asked her.

She nodded, thankful that Roman picked up on the source of her anxiety.

Roman continued, "Prince Lyric left the castle two days ago and has not returned. Do you know where he went?"

"No, I don't. I honestly didn't even notice he was gone. I don't see him daily," she replied with a shrug.

Roman nodded. "That's ok," he said. "I need you to find a way to inquire about his whereabouts with Leofwin. This is your first official task as my spy, Moira. I don't want you to get too swept up in the novelty of it because that's only going to make you act foolishly. Keep a level head and ask whatever questions you think you can get away with. We need as much information as possible."

Roman looked at her intensely. He did not break eye contact and spoke with even more ferocity than the night before. Moira felt a shiver run up her spine and realized there was a difference between agreeing to aid a band of outlaws and actually acting upon that agreement. Although she felt the weight of that decision settle upon her shoulders, she also felt a spark of excitement and purpose bubble up in her.

Moira smiled and said, "Don't worry, Roman. I'm going to be good at this."

He smiled back at her, full of roguish enjoyment, and was about to speak when they heard several footsteps coming up the path toward them. In an absolute panic, Moira stepped forward and gave Roman the biggest shove she could muster. He was unprepared, so he easily fell backward into a bramble of bushes. Part of his deep brown cloak stuck on one of the branches, and he was making some sort of groaning noise. She tossed the last bit of cloak over the bushes and hissed, "shut it!" before going to sit primly on the small bench.

Moira took one giant gulp of air, straightened her skirts, and pulled one bright orange leaf off the nearest tree just as Lord Leofwin came into the secluded area. He looked a bit disheveled, which Moira thought was unusual for him. Following behind Leofwin were Lord Dayben and Lady Lucia. They also looked worried, but not nearly as much as her betrothed.

"What on earth is going on?" Moira asked, using her best confused damsel voice.

Leofwin was slightly out of breath, which made Moira scowl ever so slightly. He hadn't been running, and the ground was flat, so it wasn't as if he'd had a steep incline to walk up. Why on earth was he near hyperventilation?

"Thank goodness you are unharmed! One of the outlaws made himself known. We were all worried you'd been taken!" Leofwin stepped closer to her.

Moira laughed nervously, averted her gaze and sent a silent prayer to the Gods that Roman would stay completely still in the bushes next to them. The irony of Leofwin's concern was not lost on her and she needed a moment to make sure her amusement did not show on her face.

Something must have happened to cause Wilhelm to make a scene. There would be time to ask about it later, but for now she had a part to play. Moira stood and went over to Leofwin, entwining her arms with his, and angled him back toward the path that would lead them back to the castle.

Moira gave her best smile to Lady Lucia and said sweetly, "What sweet friends you are to be concerned about me! I was entirely safe in this lovely little clearing. I just adore the autumn leaves. I'm sorry to have worried you."

Practically dragging Leofwin along, Moira started walking down the path. The sooner they got out of this clearing, the sooner Roman would be able to make his escape.

Lady Lucia gave her a questioning glance but then grabbed her father's arm and started leading him down the path. Moira was suddenly grateful for Lucia and her courtly ability to know when not to question someone's behavior.

Moira glanced over her shoulder and saw Roman's face in the shadows. If she hadn't known where to look, he would have been easily missed. She gave him a small nod, then turned to face forward and begin her first mutinous mission.

Chapter Seventeen

Moira was seated to Lord Leofwin's left at one of the long tables in the least formal dining hall within the castle. The room was full to bursting with various nobility, all dining on the small feast provided most nights to those in the prince's favor. This hall held three long rectangular tables with plain wooden chairs. A deep purple runner ran down the center of each table, and large candles flickered down the middle. The room was elegant but cozy, despite its size. Moira preferred dining in this room compared to the great hall. She looked around the room and noticed that Lord Maddicot was seated where he normally was, along with a few other lords, but the prince was nowhere to be seen. This was at least the third night that he was gone, and Moira knew that what Roman told her was true - the prince was not in Ivywood.

"Is Prince Lyric unwell?" Moira asked Leofwin, her right hand placed gently on his forearm to ensure he knew she was speaking to him.

Leofwin turned to her from his discussion with the man to his right and said, "Not at all. The prince is quite well, pet." After he answered, he turned away from her again.

She squeezed his arm to pull his attention back to her.

"I have not seen him in days, m'lord. Is he quite busy? Surely you, as one of his most trusted lords, know what he's up to."

Moira wasn't sure where to start with her questioning, but Leofwin was proving she would have to work hard and rely on flattery to keep him engaged with her. Typical, she thought. He was a selfish pig, after all.

Leofwin turned to her once more with a bit more self-importance, glanced around the table, and then said in a low voice, "Naturally, I know his whereabouts, although many do not. Prince Lyric has business elsewhere and will return once he's finished. Are you familiar with a place called Etheldred, pet?"

Moira was surprised at how easily Leofwin shared this information after one simple, flattering comment that she barely cared that he spoke to her as if she were a child who needed appeasing. She had seen Etheldred on a map but knew nothing specific about it.

She answered, "I'm afraid my geography is lacking, m'lord. Is Etheldred a lovely place to visit?"

Leofwin chuckled and again looked around the table. He seemed to be ensuring no one was listening to them. He was fine sharing things with his young, unintelligent fiancé but did not want the entire table to know what he was telling her. This suited Moira's needs just fine. The fewer people who heard her asking these questions, the better. She plastered her most innocent smile and leaned in closer.

Roman better appreciate this, she thought to herself.

"Etheldred is not a lovely place to visit. A large castle ruin sits outside the city limits, which is said to be horribly haunted. The city itself is a dark place, full of nefarious individuals. Common criminals all the way up to corrupt courtiers who were exiled from Gallya rule the populace. No one goes there for relaxation, pet." Lord Leofwin smirked at her as if she were an utter fool for not knowing this. "It is not my business to share what the prince does there, but I know he will return two days before the Archery Tournament."

Moira was about to respond when Amis appeared out of nowhere and loudly said, "There is an absolute downpour outside right now!" He made pointed eye contact with her as he sat down across the table and said, "It's pouring outlaws and rascals out there!"

Amis threw his head back and laughed in an exaggerated, nearly maniacal manner. Moira furrowed her brow, suddenly worried about Amis's wellbeing.

"Pouring outlaws? What an outrageous way to talk about rain, Amis!" Lady Lucia said as she gave him a playful swat on the arm. She then executed the most perfect courtly giggle Moira had ever heard.

Moira briefly wondered if Lucia was catching on to more than she realized or if Lucia was just a really good player of the courier game. Moira made a mental note to ask Amis about Lucia later. First and foremost, she needed to figure out what the hell he meant about it "raining outlaws and rascals". With a glance at Leofwin, Moira realized he had quickly given up on their discussion and had returned to focusing on his neighbor. She rolled her eyes and sighed, once again frustrated and grateful for Leofwin's clueless and selfish conduct.

"Moira," Amis said seriously and waited for her to look at him. "If you're done with your meal, I think I should escort you upstairs. You're looking rather pale."

"Amis, what on earth are you -," she started to ask, but stopped as Amis glared at her and widened his eyes. Finally catching on, Moira said loudly, "Oh, yes. Now that you mention it, I don't feel all that well. I think an early night is exactly what I need."

Without wasting another second, Amis gestured for her to meet him at the end of the table near the doorway. Moira glanced at Leofwin, who remained ignorant of her existence. She'd be annoyed if he wasn't making her life easier with his lack of attention.

"Yes, feel better, Lady Moira," Lucia said with almost believable sincerity.

Moira smiled and walked toward the door where Amis waited.

Amis grabbed her elbow tightly and led her out of the dining hall and up the stairs at such a brisk pace Moira worried someone might stop them and ask what was wrong.

Once they reached the top of the stairs and appeared to be alone, Amis stopped, turned to Moira, and said, "Loxley is in your rooms. Possibly injured. I'm not sure. Poor rascal was climbing the castle walls when the torrential downpour began, and he slipped. Damn near landed right on top of me as I hurried to get inside. Shame he didn't manage to land on someone important and really stir things up!" Moira gave him an elbow to the ribs, mostly playfully, at that last comment. "I'm only joking! I managed to haul him up to your rooms undetected, but it was a chore. Thankfully, most of the castle was either in the hall eating or preparing the castle for evening life."

"Why the hell did you take him to *my* room, Amis?" Moira seethed. She was pissed and her mind also reeled. She had no idea what to do with Roman if he was injured.

"Good Lord, my apologies for helping *your* outlaw! I'm not exactly the gilly on this expedition, am I?" Amis asked with so much carefree frivolity she wanted to punch him.

Amis grabbed her elbow again and gave her a little tug. They were once again hustling in the most reserved manner possible and quickly arrived at the door to her room.

Moira turned to him, speaking through clenched teeth, "He is not *my* outlaw. Amis, what on earth do you expect me to do with a possibly injured man in my room?"

Amis chuckled and waggled his eyebrows at her, which made Moira blush. Before he could speak, she said, "Do not make this some sort of crude joke! Come in here with me!" She nearly stomped her foot but decided that was not the best tactic. As Amis pointed out, she was the one who agreed to aid and abet the outlaw now hiding in her rooms.

"If I stay up here and do not return to the hall, that busybody Lucia is going to come find me. Where would we be then? All I said I was doing was escorting you to your rooms. I must get back to the hall, but as soon as I can, I'll come back up here and help. Good luck, Moi. Being a rebel is already off to a roaring start, eh?" He gave her a playful nudge before turning and rushing back down the hall toward the stairs.

Moira stood there utterly dumbfounded. Had Amis seriously stashed a known fugitive in her rooms, possibly wounded, and then pranced back downstairs to dinner? With her hand on the doorknob, Moira took a calming breath and walked inside her room, where she found…nothing. Not a thing was out of place, and there was no dead man lying on her floor.

Moira closed the door behind her and whisper-shouted, "Roman?" She paused and said a little louder, "Roman Loxley, if you jump out and scare me, I swear I'll kill you!"

There was no response. Moira walked through to her bedroom, where she found Roman lying unconscious on her bed. He was lying flat on his back, covered in mud and muck. His boots were especially filthy, but thankfully his height meant his feet hung just slightly over the edge of the bed. She groaned audibly at the sight of him, which caused Roman to stir. He opened his eyes slowly and looked at her.

"Oh, thank Gods you're alive! I would have no idea what to do with your body if you were dead!" She blurted out, relieved.

Roman chuckled softly, then emitted a very loud moan before saying, "I'm afraid I may have a broken a rib or two. Can you take a look at this gash on my head, Beastie?"

He started to sit up but struggled until Moira stepped over to him, grasped his hand, and gave a heave.

She stepped back as soon as he was sitting up. He turned as he sat and now his legs hung over the edge of the bed, feet planted on the floor.

Moira cringed and said, "There is definitely a gash on your head."

The gash was over his left eyebrow, with a steady stream of blood dripping out of it and down the side of his face. The hair above his left temple was matted and red from the blood that had seeped into his hairline while he was laying down.

"Simply amazing determination. Not sure what I'd do without you. Care to get within even a foot of me to actually *look* at it?" His words dripped with sarcasm.

"To be honest, no. I don't want to get any closer."

To prove her point entirely, Moira took another step backward.

Roman looked at her quizzically and took a big breath, clearly preparing himself. He winced and took another, shallower breath. After this, he stood up. Roman swayed dangerously, and Moira felt she had no choice but to go over to assist him. She lifted his left arm and put it around her shoulders. She weaved her right arm around his waist but was careful not to grip his ribs. He leaned on her a little, but not as much as she expected. He looked down at her, and she looked up at him.

Her breathing hitched a little, and she blurted, "Well, your pupils are the same size. I'm pretty sure that's an important sign that you aren't damaged in the head."

Roman gave her a goofy, off kilter smile. Then he faced forward with a look of pure determination.

Once he was vertical and somewhat steady, Moira glanced down at her bed.

"Ugh!" Moira nearly sobbed, unable to stop herself.

Roman looked down at her with concern. "What?"

"You got blood all over my pillows!" Moira grumbled.

He gripped her shoulder a little tighter and wrapped his other arm firmly around his chest as he laughed. After several seconds, Roman gathered himself enough to say, "Begging your sincerest apologies, Miss Finglas! I'll be more cognizant of where my blood gushes out of my skull the next time I'm injured and in your bed!"

Moira scowled at him and said, "I would hope you are never injured in my bed again!" Despite her efforts to remain serious, she broke into a fit of giggles. "I'm so sorry!" She exclaimed. "I really am no nursemaid. As you can see, my priorities are a little skewed. Can I get you into the bathing room? There are at least towels in there, so you can get cleaned up."

"I take it I'll be getting myself cleaned up then, Beastie?" Roman asked with an arched eyebrow.

Moira rolled her eyes.

"Based on your mental acuity, you're more than capable of cleaning up your own face, outlaw."

With a slight shake of her head, she started to guide Roman into the small room connected to her bedroom. Now that she knew he was alive, she was beginning to panic about how the hell she'd get him out of the castle and back to the hideout.

Chapter Eighteen

Roman balanced himself on the edge of the deep copper tub that was in Moira's bathing chamber. It was an immense luxury to have at her disposal, and Moira did her best not to cringe at the grime and blood that oozed into the basin. This was easier said than done and she was doing her best not to look directly at Roman.

"Quit worrying about the bathtub, B," Roman commanded as he grimaced slightly. He dabbed at the gash on his forehead with the corner of a towel. "I'm sure it'll clean up just fine, and you won't even remember all this," Roman grumbled, not unkindly as he gestured at himself.

Moira scoffed. "Oh please, outlaw. I'm certain I won't forget the time my brother stashed an injured fugitive in my room."

"I won't be forgetting it anytime soon either," said Hanna, standing in the doorway.

Roman and Moira's heads jerked up at the surprise intrusion. Moira's mouth dropped open, and she found herself gaping at Hanna dumbly. Moira looked back at Roman and realized he was smiling broadly at Hanna.

"Ms. Ashdown," he said cheerfully, "I was beginning to wonder if I would see you."

Hanna chuckled and beamed at Roman. Beamed. Moira had never seen her look at another human being with so much admiration before. She could do nothing other than continue to stare, totally dumbfounded.

"I was beginning to wonder if I'd see you, Roman," Hanna answered endearingly. She curtsied slightly and continued, "Moira seems to be doing the absolute bare minimum here. Can I step in and assist before you yield to death entirely, thanks to lackluster care? It's precisely what happened to Artemis Thomas when he had an ill-attended head wound."

Roman chuckled at Hanna, then looked at Moira. She could have sworn his gaze softened as he held her gaze. He maintained eye contact with her while speaking to Hanna, stating, "I have a feeling Miss Finglas is preparing an excellent argument about just how well she's doing. Aren't you, B?"

"As a matter of fact, yes!" Moira responded a little hotly. She looked at Hanna and said, "How the hell do you know Roman?"

Moira threw a look of accusation and betrayal Hanna's way, which was returned with a look of outrage and mild entertainment.

Roman spoke before Hanna could answer. "Hold on. Bleeding from the head, here. I do love a good story, and I'd love to be present for all of this, but I would adore the ability to talk without blood running down my face." He gestured to his still-open wound.

Moira glanced at Roman and shrugged, stating, "Looks like it's gushing a little less to me." She turned to Hanna and said, "Hanna, let's hear it! I need the full story."

Hanna huffed and started bustling about, pulling items out of the tall cabinet in the corner that Moira never noticed was there. She set a dark brown bottle of something down next to Roman, then gathered gauze and wrappings from yet another corner of the cabinet. She used the ewer in the opposite corner to rinse off her hands, dried them on her apron, and turned back around. Before she spoke at all, Hanna shooed Moira away. She then grabbed Roman's chin to tilt his head up, down, left, and right, the whole time assessing the wound on his forehead. She tsked and tutted a couple of times, then nodded and got to work. She grabbed a new cloth and pressed it to the wound. Roman grimaced a little, but Hanna paid no mind. She grabbed his hand and placed it on the towel she held to his head, stating, "Hold that there, firmly." She wiped away the blood that had dripped down Roman's face. Moira stood in the corner and watched with rapt fascination. Part of her wondered if every bathing room in the castle had these supplies or if Hanna stashed them here for a specific reason. Something told her it was the latter.

"One of these days, girl, you will have to learn these skills. If you plan to be a rebel, and a good one at that, it's going to be about more than gathering secrets," Hanna said to her. "Hand me that bottle, please. We are going to put some honey on this before we bandage it. Ideally, the honey will help stave off any infection."

Moira handed her the bottle that she'd set on the floor and continued to watch.

"Are you specifically ignoring my question about how you know Roman?" Moira asked, somewhat annoyed.

Hanna scoffed. "I would have thought that was obvious."

Hanna gently put honey on Roman's head wound, which had nearly stopped bleeding after he held the towel to it for a few minutes.

As Moira watched Hanna work, she noticed Roman was watching her. She met his gaze and saw way too much merriment for a man with broken ribs and a head now slathered in honey. She stuck her tongue out at him before she could think, and he chuckled.

Hanna turned to look at her. With a sigh she said, "Always fooling around. Hand me that wrapping, Moira."

Hanna gestured to a long stretch of the fabric when Moira did not immediately do what she was asked. When Moira grabbed it, she realized it was an old sheet torn into thin strips. She handed it to Hanna, who immediately wrapped it around Roman's head, securing the honeyed gauze she put over the wound. Moira possessed no medicinal background, but she wondered how on earth this sticky looking mess would help Roman heal.

Moira admitted that Hanna's ministrations seemed to bring normal color back into Roman's face. His hair remained matted and bloodied, but his skin was returning to a normal color instead of the rather worrisome gray that appeared when he stood up from her bed. She let out a relieved breath and realized she had been more worried than she wanted to consciously admit. Roman gave her a knowing smile, so she threw him her best exasperated look.

Hanna dusted her hands, looked at Moira, and ordered, "Out."

Moira looked at Hanna, bewildered. "Out?"

"Yes, girl. Out. His ribs need binding. Go sit in the parlor and wait. You are no help to me now, and I can only imagine you'll be worse once I've got his tunic off."

Hanna turned Moira around and gave her a gentle shove toward the door.

Moira couldn't help but turn around to give one last look at Roman. She felt compelled to make sure he was comfortable with this arrangement. Roman smiled encouragingly and nodded at her.

"I'm alright, B. You did a remarkable job verbally berating my injured ass, but I think Hanna can finish things up from here. After all, I don't want to end up like Artemis Whatshisface."

Hanna laughed and gave Moira another nudge. She begrudgingly left the room.

****

Moira stood in her bedroom for a moment and wondered if she should go back in and demand to help. Her dismissal from the situation did feel like one of her own creation since she was useless in terms of medical assistance. However, it was her agreement to work with Roman that led them to this point in the first place. She turned and was about to barge back in when she heard Roman emit a loud, pain-filled moan. On second thought, she decided she would be more useful sitting out in the living room.

She stepped into the living room and was startled by a large figure that said, "Can't find anything useful to do in there, huh?"

Moira nearly screamed, stepped back into the doorframe and slid slowly to the ground, hand on her chest.

Wilhelm stepped out from the shadow of the bookcase and, with a huge, mocking grin, said, "You are fascinating! One moment you show immensely reckless levels of bravery, and the next, a mere whisper sends you to the floor."

114

He moved closer and held out his hand in offering. She grasped it and let him help her stand, her heart still racing from the surprise.

"How did you get in here?" she asked once she was standing.

"Secrets of the trade. Being an outlaw and rebel has its required skill sets. Sneaking into this exact castle happens to be a specialty of mine," he said rather arrogantly.

Moira rolled her eyes. "Listen, if you came in through that window," she said, gesturing to the large window that opened into her living area, "Then just know that I have also entered that way. Multiple times. So, no need to let your ego get any larger." She walked over to her chaise and plopped down without an ounce of propriety that a lady of the court should show.

Wilhelm smiled and sat on the settee where Hanna usually sat.

"How's our guy doing in there?" he asked seriously.

Moira looked at him skeptically and asked, "*Our* guy?"

Wilhelm nodded. "Is it serious? I never did make it back to him when I left you two in the gardens earlier. After being forced to show my face, I escaped, and I waited at our usual meet-up spot. When he didn't show, I got nervous."

As he spoke, Wilhelm settled further into the couch and propped one leg up on the small, low table in the center of the room. He looked almost comical; his large form squeezed onto a rather small couch. No wonder he needed to spread out and utilize the table.

"Make yourself comfortable, Wilhelm -," Moira started to say with a snort.

"You can call me Wil," he interrupted.

Moira looked at him and found that she felt a little warm and glowy over the request. If he was asking her to use a nickname, maybe she truly belonged in this band of odd but strong people she stumbled upon. Or really, had been abducted by. Semantics, she told herself with a smile.

"Don't go all gooey on me over it. Wilhelm is a mouthful, so the group calls me Wil. No need to make a fuss," he explained. He looked wary, as though nervous Moira was about to cry.

"Is Wilhelm your first or last name?" She asked, hoping it wasn't rude to ask a personal question.

He looked at her for a moment and then said, "First. My last name is Clarke."

"Wilhelm Clarke," she said, just to try it out.

"That's me. Wilhelm was a family name, but I believe I'm the only one to have it as my first name. Used to be a last name on my ma's side. But I really shouldn't divulge so much information to a newcomer," he said with a shrug and teasing grin.

Moira nodded. "I'll get us back on topic. Roman will be fine, as far as I can tell. He was as loquacious as ever, despite a gash on his head and some potentially broken ribs. Unfortunately, or maybe luckily in Roman's case, I am not much of a nursemaid. Hanna showed up and took over. She should be finishing up with him anytime now." She relaxed further into the chaise.

Oddly enough, Wilhelm's presence made her feel far more comfortable than it should have. Getting Roman back out of the castle was no longer her sole responsibility. She had Wilhelm, and even Hanna, to help her solve the rest of this huge problem. She felt confident they'd be able to figure something out together.

"Oh, I'd wager my left foot that Roman would rather have you in there taking care of him, no offense meant to Hanna. She's right wonderful, but she's near twice his age." Wilhelm said without any hint of teasing.

The teasing made Moira slightly uncomfortable. No matter what banter existed between her and Roman, she wasn't ready to admit any of their feelings were real. They were simply two stubborn people who happened to enjoy giving each other crap as much as possible.

"How is it that you two even know Hanna?" Moira asked, easily changing the focus away from her and Roman.

"Did she not explain that to you herself?" Wil asked.

"No, she didn't. She seemed offended that I'd even ask before Roman got patched up, and then I got the boot before I could really push it."

Wilhelm started to pick under his nails with a small knife he pulled out of his boot. "Ah, there's the catch then. I can't tell you Hanna's story. You'll have to wait until she tells you herself."

Moira was surprised by this. Maybe she'd spent too long in the castle, where every single person here was willing to tell anyone and everyone someone else's story. All the courtiers were the worst gossip hounds she'd ever encountered; however, it led to her learning a lot about everyone very quickly when she'd first arrived. Despite how badly she wanted to know Hanna's involvement in all of this, she felt Wilhelm's refusal to talk about it showed his strong character. She could already tell he was someone she could trust implicitly.

She didn't say anything else but nodded at Wilhelm, an acknowledgment that she would wait until she could speak to Hanna directly. They sat in companionable silence, with Wilhelm picking at his nails and Moira drifting off. It took several more minutes until Hanna came into the living space. Wilhelm stood up immediately, but Moira simply sat up a little straighter. Both looked expectantly at Hanna. She wiped her hands on her apron before she spoke.

"He'll be fine, Willy. No need to look so concerned. I've got his ribs wrapped nicely, but he's going to need a day or two of strict rest. He's ready for whatever it takes to get him home, but after that, it's bed. I'm trusting you to make sure that happens," she lectured sternly.

Wilhelm nodded so sincerely as Hanna spoke that Moira realized Hanna's involvement must go much further back than she'd originally thought. The use of "Willy" and the school-mistress tone made her wonder if Hanna had known Wilhelm since childhood. She continued to watch the two of them intently.

"Yes, Ms. Ashdown. I'll sit on top of him if I must. He's not one for rest, as you know. He has a lot to prepare for, but I'll do my best."

Hanna nodded, gave Wilhelm one of the sweet smiles she'd given Roman earlier, and stepped forward with a "come here" type motion. Wilhelm bent down and allowed Hanna to give him a soft peck on the cheek, as well as a quick embrace.

"It's so good to see you, lad," she said tenderly, going a little misty-eyed.

Moira was astonished once more. Hanna was never unkind or cruel to her, but Moira never received such warm, loving affection from her either. It was fascinating to watch. Hanna always held onto a strict air of formality around

Moira, no matter how casual Moira herself started to get around Hanna.

Hanna pulled away from Wilhelm and turned to Moira. "As for you, girl," she said as she shook her head slightly. She stepped closer and put her hands on either side of Moira's face, then said, "Thank you for helping Roman."

"I – I uh -," Moira struggled over what to say. She hated having her face touched, so forming coherent thoughts was a challenge. Hanna sensed her discomfort and let go. Moira said, "It's no problem, Han."

"What the hell is wrong with you tonight, Moira? I swear in the full day I've known her and all the time I've watched her, I've never seen her so tongue-tied and peculiar," Wilhelm said, watching them.

"I'm fine! Good grief, am I not allowed to have a single moment to adjust? In case no one has really noticed, I've gone from abduction victim to secret spy for a gang of outlaws to impromptu nursemaid and more, all within less than two days. My ability to sarcastically and verbally respond to every little detail is beginning to wear thin, you ass!" Moira seethed at Wilhelm in one long breath, then sat back with her arms crossed.

Wilhelm clapped, "There she is!"

Hanna turned and smiled at Wilhelm.

"I thought we ironed out the whole abduction misunderstanding?" Roman asked, standing rather unsteadily in the doorway to Moira's bedroom.

It looked like Hanna managed to clean some of the dried blood out of his hair and off his face. Despite his wild mane and still matted beard, Moira had to admit he looked a right sight better than when she'd last saw him.

She looked him in the eye and said loftily, "If you'll recall, I maintained the right to bring it up at a later point. That point is now."

Roman smiled at her, then looked to Wilhelm. "How'd you find me, mate?"

Before Wilhelm could answer, Moira waved her hand over her head in a casual gesture to the window and said lazily, "He shimmied in through the window over there, but he's going to lead you to believe he did something far more mysterious and dangerous."

Wilhelm opened his mouth to speak, but Hanna said, "As much fun as the verbal sparring match is, let's focus on the issue at hand. I don't much care how you got *into* this room, but I care greatly about how we are going to get both of you *out* of it."

No one spoke. Hanna seemed to have pointed out the issue no one had resolved yet. They all looked around the room at each other.

****

Moira begrudgingly gave up her spot on the chaise to Roman, but only after ensuring he was no longer oozing and leaking blood. After sacrificing her pillows, she was not about to risk sitting on a blood-crusted chaise to read the next day. Hanna gave her a pointed look when she asked Roman if he was still bleeding, but Moira could handle a good glare or two if her favorite chair was safe.

"Have we got any secret tunnels at our disposal?" Wilhelm asked. He was leaning forward on the settee, elbow resting on his knee with his hand out flat, palm up as if he held before him their salvation.

Moira stared at him incredulously.

"I'm sorry, Wil, but weren't you just telling me all about how being an outlaw requires special skill sets, including getting in and out of this exact castle?" Moira asked, her voice dripping in sarcasm.

Wilhelm gave her a disparaging look and replied, "My skills are far more specific to large events. Causing a quick scene, distracting mass amounts of people, picking a couple of rich pockets, and then disappearing into the night. I'm afraid my skills at sneaking out of a lady's room are quite limited!"

Before he could retract what he said, the room erupted into fits of laughter. Even Hanna seemed unable to resist laughing at the self-deprecating comment Wilhelm made about himself.

Roman said between gasping laughter, "I'll teach you how to get in and out of a lady's room some other time, Wil! You inexperienced bastard!'

Wilhelm was flushed but remained good-natured about his slip-up. He shrugged and teased, "Well, if you're so practiced at it, *Lord* Loxley, let's hear your plan to get us out of *Lady* Moira's rooms, then!"

Unfortunately, it didn't have the effect he hoped, and the laughter didn't immediately die down. The group was still giggling when the door to Moira's rooms started to open. Moira gave an odd squeak of surprise and grabbed the blanket she kept at the foot of her chaise out from under Roman's feet. She flung it open and down on Roman's head and torso before squeezing onto the side of the chaise lounge in an attempt to shield him from view. Wilhelm flopped down onto the floor, did a surprisingly agile tuck-and-roll maneuver, and ended up crouched halfway behind the settee he'd been sitting on. Hanna simply stepped closer to Moira and turned to see who was entering.

Amis tip-toed backward through the door, carrying with him a large and bulky bundle. He had his back to the room, seemingly to keep an eye on the hallway. He shut the door, flipped the latch (which, Moira realized, she should have done upon her arrival earlier), and turned to face the group. He seemed absolutely stunned by the sight before him. He took a moment to look and then let out a loud guffaw.

"Good gravy, what on earth was this meant to look like? Someone's legs are hanging out at the end of the chaise, while Moira offers a poor disguise for his blanket-covered upper body. Meanwhile, a wild man is hiding in the corner, crouched like a beast ready to spring." He laughed again and turned to Hanna, then continued, "I assumed you ran a tighter ship than this, old gal! Simply stupendous! I cannot wait to see how the rest of this night turns out!"

At some point during Amis's speech, Roman removed the blanket from his head and torso. It lay bunched in his lap, no longer hiding any part of him. He tucked his head onto Moira's shoulder, his face right up against hers, and said, "We await your rescue, good sir! I'm afraid times are quite dire!"

Moira jumped at Roman's initial contact, but due to his recently gushing head wound, she resisted the urge to shove him away. She let him say his bit, and then she gently shifted away before standing up. She looked down at him, raised her finger in mock warning and stated, "Proximity, outlaw!"

He gave her a goofy grin and said, "What's a man to do when a lovely damsel attempts to suffocate him with a blanket before sitting in his lap? Mixed messages, B!"

Roman then he had the gall to look at her as if she had offended him.

Moira rolled her eyes and said, "That's the last time I will try to rescue you! And I did not sit in your lap. I merely sat incredibly close to your lap."

"Do you swear not to rescue me anymore?" He asked earnestly.

Everyone in the room watched them closely.

She stared daggers at him and said through clenched teeth, "Oh, I swear it, Roman!"

"Thank the Gods!" He exclaimed, throwing his arms up before wincing and bringing them back down. "It's just that earlier, 'rescuing' me involved shoving me rather aggressively into an unforgiving bramble. I can't even call your nursing abilities 'rescuing,'; although you did a great job scolding me for bleeding. Then there's this most recent 'rescue,' and I must say, I am not sold on your methodology."

Roman gave her a small shrug and settled back into the chaise, this time pulling the blanket up tightly while tucking it around his shoulders.

Moira stared at him. She fumed silently. Wilhelm stood from his crouch and now had his back to her, clearly stifling laughter.

Whipping around to face Amis, Moira said, "I hope you have one hell of a plan, Amis. Otherwise, I have half a mind to alert the castle guards and have these two hauled to the dungeons."

Amis gave her the biggest grin she'd seen on his face in ages.

"Funny you should mention guards, Moi…," he said as he reached down and pulled up the lumpy bundle he'd been carrying when he arrived. He dumped the items down onto the table, and she realized exactly what they were. Three guard uniforms.

Chapter Nineteen

"There's only two of us, mate," Roman said, leaning over the chaise to look at the gray and blue uniforms piled on the table.

"Nothing escapes you," Moira said mordantly.

Amis waved his hands dramatically and said to Moira, "You are exhausting, you know that?" She looked at him with a 'who me?' expression, and he shook his head. He turned to Roman and explained, "I know there are two of you; however, neither of you knows the best way to get out of the castle in the middle of the night. I do."

Everyone stared at Amis. Moira's heart seemed to stop at the thought of Amis risking his life to get Roman and Wilhelm out of the castle. She knew when she told him the truth that he might end up in some level of danger, but he was already exceeding her expectations, and it hadn't even been a full day. While she knew the outlaws needed to get out of the castle, she suddenly resented the fact that her actions had placed Amis directly in harm's way.

Moira was drug back to the conversation by the sudden silence; everyone was looking at her expectantly. Wilhelm, in particular, looked at her as if he was truly concerned for her mental stability.

"What did I miss?" she asked.

Roman and Amis sighed.

Wilhelm spoke up and said, "We asked if you had a better idea or if we could just move ahead with whatever your brother has concocted. I'd also like to point out that I still don't fully understand how the spritely lord got looped up with us in the first place. Care to explain that one, Moira?" He looked at her expectantly.

With everything else happening at this exact moment, Moira was annoyed Wilhelm would even ask to explain Amis's involvement. She reminded herself that she had been asked to be their spy and, to her general understanding, spies were not meant to discuss their work. It was fair of Wil to want answers, even if his timing was shit.

Moira sighed and said, "We can get into the meatier details of that later. Suffice it to say, I'm a young woman in the court, and I felt that Amis's understanding of what I agreed to do would only aid the cause."

Moira shrugged and looked around the room. Hanna gave her a reaffirming nod.

"I can speak to Amis's ability to help. He is well-liked but not intimidatingly high ranking. This puts him in an uncommon position. Moira may have the arm of Lord Leofwin, but Amis can flit between many groups of people without raising suspicion. He can do things like sneak a wounded fugitive into a room and not have people really wonder what he's up to." Hanna gave Amis a soft squeeze on the arm before turning to Roman and saying, "You would be an ignorant ox to turn down help from Amis."

Roman held Hanna's gaze for another beat before looking at Amis and giving him a firm nod. One simple bob of his head, and then he was back to business. Roman turned to Moira and said, "I'm open to other suggestions, but it looks like the best option we have right now is whatever your brother cooked up. It's now past midnight, and we need to get out before the early servants rise to get the castle ready for the morning. The clock is quite literally ticking on our escape."

Wilhelm stepped forward and started going through the uniforms still lying untouched on the table. He sorted out three cloaks with the royal emblem, three habergeons, three pairs of trousers, and three kettle hats. He held up one hat and said, "Oh, hell no. I will not be putting this on." He then held up the trousers and said, "These aren't going to be long enough for me."

Amis stood there, his left hand on his hip while he rubbed his eyes with the right. He pursed his lips, looked at Wilhelm, and said, "Listen. I grabbed what I could find. The trousers will have to do. It's late. Most of the castle is unlit. If they're a little short, you'll live."

"Ideally…," mumbled Wilhelm, but everyone could hear him.

Amis glared. "I do think we can get away without the kettle hats, *except* for the fact that we need to hide our faces. We need the shadow the brim will cast. The perfect scenario has us walking the halls like we own the place, getting out through the kitchens, and then changing at the edge of the forest without being seen. You two will be on your merry way, and I will put these items back before returning to my own room for the night."

"Hold on!" Moira said. "That plan leaves Hanna and me to just sit and wonder if everything went well. I don't like it."

Hanna spoke up quickly, saying, "I can go down to the kitchens shortly after they leave. I can wait to help Amis put things away, then return here to report to you, Moira. After that, we all need to go about our day tomorrow as if nothing happened. A break in routine will be what gives us away. You're a very routine-driven lady, Moira." Hanna said the last bit almost as a critique. Moira wanted to argue but realized they really did not have the time.

As if through some unspoken agreement, all three men began to put the guard clothing over the top of their own. Hanna stepped in and assisted Roman with the habergeon since his rib injury was an added challenge. The cloaks the two outlaws normally wore were stuffed down the front of their guard shirts, giving them pot-bellied looks. Moira admired that this unplanned effect added to their legitimacy.

None of the guards in the prince's employ were in top-tier shape. Amis caught her gaze and smiled. She knew he was attempting to reassure her, but she could tell that he was also feeling the weight of their decision to be involved with the outlaws. She sent up a quiet prayer to the old Gods that this whole thing would truly result in a better life for the two of them.

****

All three men stood near the door, fully dressed as guards and ready to go. Hanna gave one last look over and nodded. She pulled Roman and then Wilhelm in for a quick embrace, which made Moira roll her eyes and Amis say with a dramatic pouty face, "What, no love for me?"

"I should be seeing you in roughly seven minutes, clodpoll. I'll give you a hug then if this whole thing works!" Hanna said exasperatedly. She shook her head and then said to Roman, "I'll keep doing what I've been doing. Give my best to Gwin when you see her."

Roman nodded solemnly. "Thank you, Hanna. I will. You can count on it." He turned to Moira, who stood awkwardly off to the side. He said, "Don't worry about us too much, B." He winked and started to turn.

"Wait!" she said. She remembered the conversation she had with Lord Leofwin earlier - before her whole night went sideways. "I spoke with Leofwin about the prince!"

Wilhelm groaned. "Good heavens above! We sat around yacking for nigh on twelve years, and you bring this up now?! As we are *literally* leaving?"

Moira immediately took the defensive. "You utter ass, Wilhelm Clarke! I had shit to do! Do you want to hear what Leofwin told me, or would you like to keep harping on about my incompetence? Regardless of what you think of me tonight, the information is good." She looked at Roman and decided she would ignore Wilhelm for the foreseeable future.

Roman took a step toward her eagerly and said, "Share quickly, please. I didn't expect you to talk to him about where Prince Lyric has been so soon."

"You were right," Moira said excitedly. She hurriedly filled him in on the rest. "The prince is gone and will not return for quite some time. He's in Etheldred. Doing what, I do not know. If Leofwin knows, he drew the line at sharing that information with me."

Roman's eyes held the now-familiar sparkle of excitement. He grinned broadly at her and said, "Did you happen to learn when he'll return?"

She gave him her biggest smile. "As a matter of fact, yes! He will not return until two days before the Archery Tournament."

"You were right, Moira. You are good at this," Roman said, granting her a genuine smile.

Even with the ridiculous kettle hat and ill-fitting guards' uniform, Moira couldn't help but admit she was wildly drawn to Roman Loxley.

"Good work all-around, troupe! Let's go!" Amis said, starting to show his impatience.

Moira knew the longer they stood around dressed and ready to leave, the higher Amis's anxiety would climb. She looked away from Roman and nodded to Amis.

Amis opened the door to her room and looked out into the hallway before saying, "Clear as air." He turned to Roman and Wilhelm, then said seriously, "Remember to walk in formation behind me. Stiff legs. Slow pace. It's how they patrol the corridors at night. No speaking. Tap my shoulder if you need me, and I'll find us a spot to chat. Yes?" The outlaws nodded solemnly.

Amis turned to leave. Roman turned back to Moira and looked at her. She felt like there might have been a purpose to the look, but he simply took one deep breath before touching his fingers to the rim of his hat, then turning to leave.

"Be safe," she said, almost imperceptibly. She hoped he heard her.

Wilhelm followed behind Roman as the support in case anyone came up behind them. Roman might be able to get back to the hideout, but they knew he was not in fighting shape.

Hanna closed the door behind them, slid the latch into place, and then slumped against the door. "Now, the hardest part, girl. We wait."

Chapter Twenty

If she could wear a hole through her floor just by pacing, Moira felt like she was about to do it. Hanna left nearly twenty minutes ago to help Amis wrap things up, and she had not returned. This left Moira with entirely too much time on her own to wonder, worry and torture herself over the events of the night as a whole.

While she paced, Moira worked herself into a lather of self-loathing about her inability to help Roman with his injuries. There were times in her life when she or Amis had been injured, and she stepped in to help their parents or whoever was fixing them up. It was not her passion, so to speak, but she was more than capable of assisting when needed. When it came to overseeing Roman's care tonight, however, she found that not only was she far too anxious to help, but she was also hesitant to be physically close to him for a prolonged time. The magnetic pull she felt from Roman was too new and bewildering for her to push its limits.

"Better stop that thought in its tracks," she mumbled to herself.

There were people in her life whom she trusted, but typically those people were family members. For whatever reason, Moira found herself jumping into Roman's cause headfirst, without much thought or doubt that what he said was true. She had whiplash from how quickly she allowed herself to go from trusting Prince Lyric and those around her to doubting them entirely. Despite the incredibly fast pace at which her life turned around, Moira did have to admit to herself that it felt right. For whatever reason, she trusted Roman Loxley implicitly, and she knew his cause was just. Amis was right. This whole thing brought her back to life in ways she didn't even know she needed.

Another few minutes passed, and still, Hanna did not return. Moira was beginning to wonder if she should throw on her shoes and cloak to go down and investigate. It was still too early for the castle to be waking. Most had only been in bed a short time, so Moira felt like the chances of being caught were slim…but also not zero.

Moira walked over to the door, paused, then made up her mind. She was going to go look for Hanna. She decided not to wear shoes, as she wanted to sneak effectively through the castle. She opened the door and was immediately pushed back into her room by Hanna rushing in.

"Can you not follow a single detailed plan, Moira Ellyn Finglas? I swear, if something takes two seconds longer than you expect, you throw the plan out the window and decide to do what's best for yourself," Hanna fumed as she shook her head and rubbed one eye while glaring at Moira with the other. She sighed and said, "I'm sorry, that was unkind. I've been the one left waiting before, and it's enough to make the toughest person crack."

Hanna pulled Moira into a quick hug before walking over to the chaise and flopping down in a most Moira-like manner.

Moira, still a bit shocked from the sudden appearance and backlash from Hanna, stood rather dumbly where Hanna left her. She took a moment to gather herself before asking, "Well, I would guess since you're just about to fall asleep in my chair that everything went as planned. Would you like me to just wait until morning to hear about it?" She had a little acidity in her tone, but she couldn't help it. She did her waiting, and now she needed to know how things ended.

Hanna scoffed. "You surprise me, girl. Way more mischief in you than I expected and a lot more gumption than I would have originally expected from the sad, silent, clumsy thing that arrived here a year ago. You remind me of Elmira Payne."

Moira was so exhausted she couldn't even summon the energy to ask Hanna who on earth Elmira Payne was. She stole a pillow from behind Hanna on the chaise, dropped it on the floor near the base of the settee, and laid down on the floor. The settee was not long enough for her, and this at least allowed her to relax while still looking up at Hanna. She tucked one arm behind her head and settled in, allowing herself to relax just a little under the assumption that Roman and Wilhelm escaped, and Amis was tucked safely in his room.

"They're all where they are supposed to be, Moira. You did well tonight," Hanna said softly.

Moira found herself releasing a huge, heavy breath of relief at Hanna's words. She hesitated then said, "I feel like a fool tonight, Han. I froze when Roman needed me. I don't regret saying I'd help, but I did not expect so much to happen so soon."

Moira sniffed and wiped her running nose on her sleeve, surprised at the weighty emotions she felt admitting that.

Hanna looked at her knowingly. "Roman is an easy man to care about. I'm sure you know why?"

Moira was surprised Hanna easily pinpointed what she was emotional about but realized she shouldn't be. Hanna was always more perceptive than anyone seemed to want to give her credit for, Moira included.

"I can guess why, but I still want you to tell me," Moira said quietly.

"He's easy to care about because he cares in return. If you have not noticed already, Roman cares greatly about his people, about King Leo, about the cause he's fighting on his behalf, and, most importantly, Roman cares deeply about those he counts as family. By agreeing to aid his cause and join that core group, you are now counted among his family."

Moira inhaled deeply and looked at Hanna. She held her gaze, let her breath out and said, "I've noticed that. He's an all or nothing type of person. Everyone in the court is so self-centered that I think I forgot what it felt like to be part of something bigger. Something that might create a better world. A better outcome for those involved. Something more than just caring about how I look and what everyone thinks of me." She felt her face flush, but she wasn't sure why. Maybe just the simple fact that she never talked so openly about something so personal like this with Hanna. They were crossing into a new realm of their relationship. One that felt raw and new right now but not uncomfortable.

Hanna was about to speak when Moira had a revelation. She sat bolt upright, then said with a little more ferocity than she intended, "Hold on, Hanna *Ashdown*. I have yet to hear how on earth you know Roman and Wilhelm in the first place." She glared a little but felt it was overall ineffective.

Before she started speaking, Hanna sat up and leaned down to tuck a runaway strand of Moira's hair out of her face. Moira felt affection well up inside her chest at the small but comforting action. Her previous surge of annoyance evaporated.

Hanna sat back into the cushions and said, "I owe you the longer version one day, but I don't want to delve into that tonight. I used to serve Roman's parents when they were Lord and Lady Loxley. They were the most wonderful people, beloved by the entire estate and surrounding village. When Roman's mother, Elmira, died, I did what I could for the young lad, although he was quite fortunate to still have his father. I served Roman when he became Lord Loxley right up until he lost the estate during the Crusades. And before you can ask, no. I do not know what happened," she said sternly as she gave Moira a pointed look. "Once the prince took the Loxley lands and estate and turned things over to Ivan Odril, the corrupt sheriff, I got out of the village as quickly as possible."

"How did you end up here?" Moira asked, gesturing vaguely to their surroundings.

She was willing to continue to wait and find out what happened with Roman in the Crusades. However, Moira couldn't help but wonder aloud how a trusted lady's maid in the Loxley estate could have been allowed to work in the castle.

Hanna gave her a devious smile. "I lied, of course. How else would I have accomplished it?"

Moira smiled and laid back down on her floor pillow.

Hanna continued, "Until tonight, have you ever heard anyone use the last name 'Ashdown' in reference to me? No, you wouldn't have. Here in the castle, I am Hanna Kale. As far as Prince Lyric understands, I do not come from Loxley Village, nor do I have any association with that estate. I trusted that one day Roman would return and need help to get back what was rightfully his. Here I stayed until he made his presence known. As soon as I could make contact, I did. I have been making sure his camp stays fed and clothed whenever they need assistance."

They both sat in silence for a moment. Moira heard Hanna's breathing get a little slower, a little deeper, and she wondered if she had fallen asleep.

Feeling like she'd finally gained a little understanding, Moira relaxed back onto her pillow on the floor and settled in. She felt like Hanna had given her a lot to think about, and she still didn't have the full story. As she started to drift off, she felt Hanna lay a blanket over her.

Moira whispered, "Thanks, Hanny."

Moira's last conscious thought was to wonder if Elmira Payne was the same Elmira as Roman's mother in Hanna's story…she briefly considered waking Hanna to ask just before she fell into a dreamless sleep.

Chapter Twenty-One

Moira was seated at the worn kitchen table in the Taylor's cozy cottage once again. Several uneventful days had passed since Roman and Wilhelm were hidden in her rooms. While she did not know how Roman was doing, she felt confident that no news was good news.

On her way to Ivywood Village, Moira passed through the castle kitchens and filled an entire basket with freshly made pastries to share with Meggy. They both had steaming cups of tea in front of them as they ate pastries and chatted. Moira brought two more books with her, although so far, they hadn't delved into her book bag.

Meggy brushed a crumb from the corner of her mouth and asked Moira, "Do you believe that Roman Loxley and his gang would leave money for the poor people of this village, Moira?"

Despite her surprise at the sudden topic change, Moira regained her composure quickly and said, "I'm sure I have no idea, Meggy. Why do you ask?" This topic was not new, but Moira had not expected it to come back up again so soon.

Meggy remained silent, but her face indicated she was wrapped up in her own thoughts. Moira sat quietly and let her think, curious about what her young friend was going to say next.

Meggy kept her eyes on the pastry in front of her, which she was picking apart slowly. "Well, Alaine *swears* that her family has been given money from the outlaw on multiple occasions now. It just makes me wonder if it really is Loxley or someone else. And if it is Loxley, why on earth is he helping the poor of this village when his own village surely needs the aid just as much?" She took a deep breath before looking up at Moira and continuing, "Why does Prince Lyric paint Roman Loxley to be some sort of villain if what he's doing is ultimately helping those who need it most?"

"Meggy..." Moira started but realized she had no idea how to answer any of her questions without giving away her newfound involvement with Roman and his company of questionable motivations. Not to mention the mere topic of Prince Lyric could be considered treason.

Meggy continued, "I don't think Alaine is lying, Moira. That's the thing. Her family needs that money and I know it has made a huge difference for them. Her Gran has said the same thing to anyone who will listen in the village." Meggy looked at Moira with such earnestness and trust. "Other families have mentioned aid from the outlaws as well. It appears overnight or while they aren't home. Nobody is ever seen delivering the money. Some people say they will support him whenever he really starts the uprising."

"Meggy, I want you to listen to me. I mean, really listen, got it?" Moira said, leaning forward and reaching for

Meggy's hand. She squeezed Meggy's hand gently once it was placed in her own and said in her most serious tone, "What you are talking about has a greater risk, one that you cannot even begin to understand. Speaking of a rebellion so openly to the wrong person could lead to trouble for you and for your family." Moira maintained eye contact with Meggy and gave her hand one more squeeze before she let go and sat back. She took a deep breath and said, "I personally have no reason to doubt what Alaine and her Gran are saying." Moira paused again, still questioning how much she wanted to tell Meggy. "Do you think what you've heard about Loxley is false?"

Meggy thought for a moment. She stirred her tea with her fingertip and twirled a lock of her hair aimlessly with her other hand.

"I think what Prince Lyric says is wrong," Meggy finally said. She spoke clearly and with a surprising amount of determination. "I think he's lied to us all about Roman Loxley and his motives." She sat up straighter, as if taking a physical stance while she spoke.

Moira smiled at her a little sadly, suddenly aware that her young friend may be tiptoeing into the rebellion. "I think you may be right, Meggy."

Meggy raised her eyebrows so high they practically disappeared into her hairline. Her piercing eyes looked at Moira in total surprise. A little breathlessly she said, "I didn't expect you to agree with me! I thought you'd tell me to grow up and not believe in ghost stories...or outlaw stories, in this case."

Moira laughed. "You're a bright young woman, Meggy. And you're one of my only friends. I don't want to treat you like a child. You've got a sharp mind and if you keep your wits about you, I don't think telling you the truth will do any harm. Besides, I'm the one who brings you the ghost stories in the first place. I most definitely want you to believe in them!"

Meggy beamed at her, and Moira smiled warmly back.

"I don't know that I can tell you much more than what I've already said. I don't know much myself, other than the fact that I've been in a similar position as you. There has been a lot happening lately to make me question what Prince Lyric tells his people." Moira said with a small shrug. She reached forward and brought her teacup to her lips. The tea was finally at the perfect temperature, allowing Moira the chance to sip it and giving her an easy task to keep her hands busy.

"Thanks, Moi," Meggy said, still beaming at her friend across the table. She picked up what was left of her shredded pastry and took a large bite before gulping down her tea. "You have no idea how much that has been weighing on me! I can't *actually* talk to Alaine because she is a total gabbler. She works in the castle and will tell anyone everything she's ever heard." Meggy gave Moira a dramatic look and took another bite of her pastry.

Moira laughed and said, "Yes, I know the type. The castle is full of them!"

The friends giggled together and finished their food. Moira decided it was time to pull out the books she'd brought along and get to work. Thankfully. Meggy did not push the issue and seemed to feel content with what had been said about Roman Loxley and Prince Lyric. Moira was glad she didn't have to say more than she had. She longed for a female friend her own age, and she worried that if pushed, she may give Meggy too much information for someone still so young. Moira needed someone she could trust entirely with everything going on in her life now. She had Hanna and Amis, of course, but it was different than what she really longed for these days.

Another hour passed in companionable reading. Moira was continually impressed with how quickly Meggy picked up new material. One of the books that Moira brought along this time was more advanced than anything she'd brought before, but Meggy tackled the challenge with relish. It brought a genuine smile and a sense of pride to Moira. Her heart felt full to bursting as she listened to Meggy read along without struggle. Even if she was unable to truly help Roman's cause, she felt sure that at least in this one small corner of the village, she made a true and important difference.

Chapter Twenty-Two

Moira said a quick goodbye to Meggy, having stayed a little too long as usual. As she walked through the village, she couldn't help but notice new "wanted" signs were posted on the front of several shop windows. One even hung loosely on a fence post. All of them had a very well-drawn likeness of a now-familiar face: Roman Loxley. It was clear that at least one person had seen him recently, for the posters included his shoulder-length hair and scraggly beard. Underneath the illustration of Roman's face was the message:

Wanted:Roman

Loxley

High Treason, Theft, Debauchery, and Public

Indecency

Reward:

Two Tower Pounds

As surreptitiously as possible, Moira pulled the sign off the fence post. One less for people to see and one for her to laugh at back in her rooms. Two tower pounds was a significant reward. Three times what most of the villagers made in a year. She had a feeling the prince knew exactly how tempting that reward would be for the people who lived in Ivywood Village, no matter how much Roman might try to help them. She hoped fervently that none of them was ever foolish enough to believe the prince would pay that sum, Roman Loxley in hand or not.

Chapter Twenty-Three

Moira was taking the scenic route back to the castle, walking along as close to the forest's edge as she could get. It added around thirty minutes to the journey, but she liked to be close to the wildness she felt within the trees. They were all an almost black shade of green and smelled better than anything she'd ever known. It was a mix of moisture, soil, and foliage that she had never encountered anywhere else. Paired with the overcast sky and chilly air, Moira felt like the walk was almost perfect.

Moira took a deep inhale with her eyes closed as she walked along, but she suddenly felt herself flying through the air after tripping over something on the road.

"You really shouldn't walk with your eyes closed like that, lass," said an all-too-familiar voice behind her.

Moira started to straighten herself out when she froze in realization. She stood, dusted herself off and said, "Pewsey." Until she learned what he was doing here, she would say nothing else to him.

"I can tell from your tone that you're just as tickled to see me as I am to see you," Pewsey sneered. "Let's let our mutual disdain simmer in the background so I can deliver my message, aye?" He looked at her out of the side of his eyes. His body remained sideways to her as if he was literally keeping one eye on the path.

Moira nodded stiffly and said, "I assume Roman sent you. What news?" She held her head high and maintained a look of boredom, hoping it would encourage Pewsey to keep things short.

Pewsey looked directly at her then. He gave her the meanest glare she had ever seen before saying, "I'd ask you not to use his name so openly here, lass. It's not the wisest move when we don't know who may be around."

"Don't talk to me as if I were a fool, Pewsey. I walk this path regularly and it is not one with frequent guard patrols. I guarantee that if we do not see anyone, then there is no one watching. Quit prolonging this vile interaction and tell me what I need to know."

Pewsey spat on the ground, thankfully in the opposite direction from Moira. She was relieved it wasn't directed at her but disgusted all the same. The man looked no different than the night he abducted her. He wore the same dour clothing without the appearance of having washed at all. His skin had a thick layer of grime, and his fingernails were nearly black. She held her face in check, not wanting to offend him so much that he refused to deliver the message.

"He asked me to tell you that the information was good, and he wants more."

Moira stared at him. "That's it? He sent you out here for that? I knew that much without being told, thanks." She did her best to make sure each word dripped with disgust.

Pewsey scowled again. "No, he ruddy did not send me here for just that. There's more to the message, it's just that I don't enjoy being a carrier pigeon for nonsense."

"Good of you to drag it out then. Makes sense for something you hate. How did you even know where to find me?" Moira asked, knowing that she was prolonging their interaction, but she was curious all the same.

"We watched you for months, lass. Do you not remember? This is your preferred path when you return from the village.," he said with a sneer, knowing full well that the reminder would set her off balance with discomfort.

Moira rubbed the spot between her eyebrows with her right hand, holding the empty book bag and pastry basket with her left and took a deep breath. She wondered why Roman hated her enough to send Pewsey to deliver his message.

"I remember," she said icily, "Tell me the rest of the message. *Please.*"

If she delayed too much longer, she knew Amis would come storming down this path to find her and while he now knew what she was up to, she didn't want him to suffer the displeasure of meeting Pewsey.

Pewsey gave her a meanspirited grin, showing her that he was missing several teeth. Moira imagined his breath must be terrible. Here was the walking example of what Amis predicted when talking so animatedly about Roman and the "merry men." She felt like it was a lifetime ago when it had only been a matter of weeks. Moira realized she had no idea what made the villagers call Roman or his men "merry" when she could not assign that specific adjective to a single one of them.

"Gods, you are one to let your mind wander, aren't you?" Pewsey said with mild disgust. "Roman wanted me to tell you that when you're done worrying about him and thinking about the way he bravely handled his injuries, you could try to find out what Lord Leofwin knows about King Leo and his possible whereabouts."

Moira couldn't help but note the mocking undercurrent to Pewsey's voice. He did not expect her to be successful.

Knowing how much Pewsey must hate delivering that message, Moira gave him her largest, brightest smile. She rolled her eyes internally because Roman was certainly still full of himself if he imagined she was thinking and worrying about him.

She brushed one more time at the front of her skirts and said, "Thanks, Pews. I'll go ahead and do that. Send Roman my best!" She turned as she finished speaking and started walking toward the castle again, not wanting to give Pewsey another second of her time.

She heard him grumble a little behind her but eventually heard him start walking back toward the forest. After several minutes and with the castle in sight, Moira realized that

Pewsey must have been the one to trip her as she walked with her eyes closed. She made a mental note to pinch him as hard as she could the next time she saw him. For whatever reason, she felt like that would be both demeaning to him and satisfying for her. She'd stab him if she could, but she imagined Roman wouldn't be particularly happy with her if she did that. Such a shame.

Chapter Twenty-Four

Moira entered the castle her usual way, through the back door of the kitchens. It was always pleasantly warm, especially compared to the chilly autumn air in which she'd been walking. There was the satisfying sound of things cooking and women chatting, which she found comforting. She returned the basket to the corner where she'd grabbed it from earlier, smiled at the women who were preparing dinner, and walked into the hallway. As she rounded the corner to the stairs, she was grabbed roughly on her right upper arm. Moira was led aggressively down the hall and shoved her into one of the many studies on the main floor of the castle.

"You're hurting me!" She shouted.

Lord Leofwin was the one who grabbed her, but she was unsure why. Knowing his distaste for causing a scene, Moira felt being loud was the quickest way to get his hands off her and she was right. He let go as soon as she shouted.

Leofwin turned his back on her and shut the door to the room. Moira attempted to slow her breathing, but her adrenaline was pumping, and she couldn't calm down. There was a writing table and two wooden chairs in the room. She often forgot there were several of these quiet studies in the castle.

She started to walk toward one of the chairs when Leofwin grabbed her again and said, "No. You will stand right here and listen to me."

Moira looked up at him, realizing his words were slightly slurred and his tone was different than normal. His eyes had a manic look about them and they were slightly pink and glossy. He reeked of alcohol, and she knew instantly that he was heavily intoxicated. In her time in the castle, Moira had not seen Leofwin drunk. She cringed away from him, unable to suppress the need to put distance between her body and his. He held tight to her arm and took another step closer.

He could not loom over her, given their similar height, but he did try to. Physically, he was stronger and stouter than her and he stood nose to nose with her.

"Do not move away from me, *pet*. I am your betrothed. I think it's time you start acting like it," he taunted, this time speaking clearly.

Leofwin pressed his lips violently against hers. Moira was initially shocked, but that quickly changed to a desire to scream. She tried, but he held his face firmly plastered to hers. Her scream came out muffled and muted. Moira felt Leofwin's tongue pressing against her lips, and she recoiled in a wave of fresh revulsion. Her arm remained tightly in his grasp, and he used his other hand to hold her head pressed into his. Several feelings rushed through her at once, primarily disgust, but surprisingly she felt the sting of shame and embarrassment, too. Tears sprang into her eyes, and she tried again to break away from him. She twisted her body away from his as violently as possible. Leofwin, whose lips moved from her lips to her cheek as she twisted, emitted a strange guttural growl of frustration.

Although trapped in an awkward half-kiss, half-forced embrace, Moira's lips were at least free from his assault. Leofwin pulled his face away from hers. They were both breathing heavily.

Moira shouted, "Stop it, Conor. Stop this now!" She said it as loud as she could while continuing to twist and pull away from him. She fervently hoped someone was nearby and would come in to find out what was going on. Her heart raced, and she broke out in a cold sweat as true panic settled into her stomach. As the knot of fear settled in her stomach, she didn't know what to do if no one heard her shouting.

Leofwin still had a firm hold on her, but she started to pull away again. Moira yanked with all her might. She gave a heaving tug, which he gave in return, yanking her back toward him. She used the momentum of his own pullback to slam into his unstable form. His intoxication worked to her advantage, and as soon as she slammed into him, he fell backward into the table, letting go of her. She teetered backward but didn't fall.

As she backed further away from Leofwin, rubbing her throbbing arm, Lord Maddicot barged into the room. He had one hand on his sword, which was still sheathed at his side. Moira couldn't help but scoff, noting that Maddicot hadn't been too concerned about what he heard in this room if he couldn't be bothered to come in with his sword drawn.

Moira was about to speak up when Amis came running into the room and nearly slammed into Maddicot's back. His eyes went wide as he took in the scene of Moira, clutching her arm, while Lord Leofwin lay crumpled on the floor in front of the desk, breathing but not entirely conscious.

Teeth clenched in rage, Amis said to Maddicot, "I'll trust you to handle Leofwin while I get Moira up to her room."

Amis put his arm around Moira's shoulders and led her out of the room without another word or backward glance. Leofwin moaned loudly from the floor, and she heard Maddicot say, "Oh shut up, you mangy mutt!"

Moira felt herself starting to shake and registered in the back of her mind that it was probably the shock of what happened finally hitting her. She allowed Amis to lead her while she retreated somewhere deep inside herself,

Chapter Twenty-Five

The next thing Moira knew, she was waking up in her bed, bundled up with several blankets. She felt suffocatingly hot and started to thrash around in a wild attempt to get untangled. Amis, who had been dozing off in a chair in the corner, stood up and hurried over to help her.

"It's alright, Moi. Calm down," he said reassuringly.

"I know it's alright, dimwit, I'm just fucking hot!" Moira responded a little more aggressively than she intended to while throwing the last of the blankets off her legs.

Amis laughed and sat at the foot of the bed, clearly relieved. "Hanna insisted on bundling you up like that. I knew you'd hate it once you woke up."

"Where is Hanna?" Moira asked, wondering if she'd appear from the outer room after hearing the commotion.

"She went down not too long ago to let the kitchens know you'll be taking dinner in your room tonight. I believe she was also going to get word to Lord Leofwin that you won't be joining him for dinner, although I can't imagine it will come as a great surprise to him. I'd be surprised if he's even conscious at this point, the drunk bastard," Amis said, a touch of hostility in his voice at the last comment.

Moira sat up in bed and leaned back against the headboard. She curled her legs up to her chest, wrapped her arms around her shins and rested her chin on her knees before saying feebly, "He was glazed drunk, Amis. I've never seen him like that before."

Amis crawled up from the foot of the bed and sat next to her. He put his back to the headboard and although he kept a little distance between them, reached out and put his hand on her shoulder. He gave her a gentle squeeze. Moira turned her head toward him and laid it back down, her ear resting on the top of her knee. She looked at Amis but said nothing. They stayed like that for a while, looking at each other with his hand comfortingly on her shoulder until they heard Hanna come in through the main door. Amis removed his hand and hopped off the bed, going out to help Hanna set up dinner in her living room.

Moira stayed where she was, allowing tears to spring to her eyes. She was grateful for Amis, who seemed to understand that she did not need or want words right now. His presence was comforting enough. She brushed away the moisture from her eyes, took a calming breath, and headed out to the main room. Despite herself, she found she was incredibly hungry and hoped Hanna came bearing something hot.

Chapter Twenty-Six

After dinner, Moira soaked in her giant copper tub. There was a large blue and purple bruise blooming on her right arm. The bruise formed just above her elbow, where Leofwin grabbed her earlier. If you looked closely, there were a few spots you could practically see the imprint of his fingers. She found herself staring at it blankly, wondering if she was watching it grow imperceptibly larger with every passing minute.

Hanna appeared in the doorway and watched her for a few moments before saying, "Staring at it won't make it disappear, I'm afraid."

Moira gave her a half smile, unable to summon a full one. "I know, Han. I'm wondering how on earth I'll hide this bruise for weeks."

"It's cold enough out we can dress you in long sleeves, not to worry," Hanna said bracingly.

Hanna continued to stand in the doorway and Moira realized that she might be witnessing the first time that Hanna did not know what to do.

Moira said lightly, "I'm fine, Hanny. He plastered the nastiest kiss on my lips, but that's all that happened. Swear."

It didn't make Hanna smile or relax the way Moira thought it would. Instead, a deep, serious frown formed before she said, "The fact that he forced himself on you at all is a bad sign, Moira. If he's willing to do it at all, in any way, it means he's willing to take it farther. Maybe not sober. But there's always alcohol available to the lords. I'm worried about you, girl, in a way I haven't been ever before."

Moira noticed Hanna's chin wobbling a little and wondered if she was holding back more emotion than she was showing.

Moira suddenly found her eyes burning. She held back the tears that threatened to escape and said quietly, "I know." She looked at the bruise again and said, "The worst part is that I shall have to carry on as if nothing happened. We need Leofwin."

Hanna's face crumpled. She closed her eyes and shook her head. She kept her eyes closed as she said, "No, Moira. This is not what Roman would want." She opened her eyes and looked at Moira beseechingly. Her voice wobbled as she said, "I know that for a fact. He would not want you in danger like this. The information is not worth it."

"It is worth it, Hanna. How is this danger any different than the potential danger I'm already in by agreeing to help in the first place? I am next to nothing to Roman without my connection to Leofwin! He does not know me, not truly. I am his spy and nothing more. If I am unable to gather the information that he needs, then I am no longer his spy. If I am not his spy, then I am nothing." She found her voice quivering and full of despair. It surprised her how much the thought of not helping Roman broke her heart and she didn't want to hear Hanna's arguments or logic.

Moira's breathing grew heavy. She sucked in a deep breath and ducked her head under the water. She hated that small outburst at Hanna. She'd done nothing to deserve it, but Moira felt strongly that what she said was true. If she couldn't get use Leofwin and his knowledge of Prince Lyric's inner circle, then she truly had no role in the band of outlaws. She felt unmoored when she imagined her life without this purpose. Even though she had not been involved for very long, she knew if she gave it up, she would sink into a deep pit of melancholy.

A couple of air bubbles floated to the surface, and Moira decided she couldn't hide here forever. She resurfaced and found Hanna waiting with a large, warm drying sheet.

Chapter Twenty-Seven

The Archery Tournament grew ever near and to Moira's great relief, Lord Leofwin seemed to be using it as an excuse to avoid her. She had not seen him since the incident, which was now several days behind her. She did receive a note stating that her betrothed would be focusing on his archery for the time being. Her bruise remained hidden from view throughout the day under long sleeves and Moira was happy to note that it seemed to be fading to an ugly yellow very quickly. Only a few darker spots remained.

After ensuring there was nothing she officially needed to do today, Moira decided to sit in the castle gardens, soaking up the calm, chilly autumn air. She was seated on the bench in the same secluded spot where she'd shoved Roman into the bushes not that long ago. The memory of that moment made her smile. She had particularly enjoyed Roman flailing around as he tried to regain his balance.

There was the sound of crunching leaves and people chatting as they walked the paths in the surrounding area. So far, no one ventured down the path that led to her now-favorite spot. Hopefully, no matter how long she sat here, she could maintain this sense of peace. She was feeling overwhelmed recently and was thoroughly enjoying the tranquil moment to herself.

For the first few nights after Leofwin's assault, Moira and Amis dined in her rooms. It was a blissful change in routine if Moira was being entirely honest. She found herself enjoying the easy interactions with Amis and did not miss the prying eyes of the court. At first, she wondered what everyone would say about their absence, but Amis squashed that concern by saying, "Oh, who gives a good fuck what they think, really?" It made her laugh and allowed her to remember that the one true opinion she cared about was that of the eccentric but caring man sitting across the table from her. As long as she had Amis, she really could not bring herself to give a good fuck what anyone else in the castle thought.

Although it was mostly overcast, the clouds parted briefly, allowing Moira to enjoy a moment of soft sunshine on her face. She closed her eyes and enjoyed the conflicting sensations of the cool air and warm sun before the clouds shifted again, and the sun was gone. Moira kept her eyes closed and allowed her mind to wander. She began to work herself into a light panic again, fretting over how she was going to gather any useful information about Prince Lyric if Leofwin was actively avoiding her. A large part of her wished he would call off the engagement entirely, thanks to the utter shame she liked to imagine he was roiling in. However much she enjoyed the fantasy of a canceled engagement, Moira knew deep down it would never happen.

Moira let out a loud sigh and finally opened her eyes. She leaned forward to rest her elbows on her knees, put her head in her hands and turned to look into the trees surrounding her. She zoned out before she realized what she stared at. Looking out from the mass of tree branches and brambles was a man's face. Heavily bearded, with wild hair surrounding his head. Leaves, twigs, and dirt covered him almost entirely. Moira choked on her scream, knowing it would only cause her problems if she drew attention to herself. The face in the trees gave her a wicked grin and stood before he started walking toward her. He was nearly silent somehow despite all the mess surrounding him.

Moira stood up, crossed her arms, and cocked her head. She glared at Roman as he fully emerged from the trees.

"Aren't you literally a fugitive? For someone who should be in hiding, you show up at the castle of your sworn enemy an awful lot. If I didn't know better, I'd worry that fall resulted in some sort of brain impairment," She taunted.

Although she spoke with a tone dripping with derision, Moira found herself oddly elated to see him. She had not seen him since the night he had to sneak out of her room in disguise.

Roman shook his head like a wet dog, flinging bits of twig and leaves all over while simultaneously making the matted mess even worse by lodging certain pieces further into the thicket of hair. Moira held up her hands to shield her face as Roman moved closer to her. He finally stopped and looked at her with a gleeful expression.

"You are an absolute animal!" she said in mock disgust.

He grinned at her again, looked down at himself, and shrugged, then said, "I'm relieved to hear your affections remain true, Beastie. Whenever I find myself wanting a kind word, you are the first person I think of."

Moira found herself returning his grin, despite her best efforts not to. She took a step back, adding a little more distance between them, and said, "How are you, Roman? Healed, I hope, considering you'll have to sneak out of here."

Roman stepped closer to her almost as soon as she'd stepped away. He gave her that damned smile again, confirming her suspicion that he knew he was putting her off her axis. "I am capable of escaping, B. No need to worry about me hiding out in your rooms again." He paused here and raised an eyebrow. "Unless you want me in your rooms again. Then I'd be all too happy to oblige."

Despite her attempts to keep her wits about her, Moira could feel a hot flush creeping up her neck and into her cheeks.

"I'll have you remember I'm betrothed, outlaw." She hated herself a little then for bringing up Leofwin, even indirectly, but she was out of her element.

The twinkle left Roman's eyes immediately. His gaze turned dark, and Moira suddenly felt like her stomach was tying itself in knots. Did Roman somehow know already

167

about what happened? She wasn't sure how it was possible, but he did have other sources in the castle. Hanna could have told him. Moira folded her hands in front of her and twisted her fingers around themselves, waiting for Roman's response. She fervently hoped that he would not tell her that her work for him was done, so she decided she'd speak first. His features remained menacing, and he looked as though he was struggling over what to say.

"Roman, I can still gather information from Leofwin. I'm not going to let this stop the entire mission. It's a setback. A minor one, even. I promise you, as soon as I can, I will get more of the story on why Prince Lyric is in Etheldred." She spoke quickly and stepped closer to him this time, making them only inches apart. She continued, "I was even thinking I could try and approach Maddicot. I don't think he's terribly fond of me, but perhaps if I play the dumb lady role, I could…," she trailed off, as Roman reached out and grabbed both of her hands in his. Her breathing hitched. She looked down at their clasped hands, then back up at him.

His features softened again. He looked at her with concern and tenderness, which surprised her.

"Moira, please do not think so low of me as to imagine that I would expect you to continue working with the man who assaulted you." Roman was looking at her so intensely that Moira was certain his stare was drilling into her very soul.

"I do not think lowly of you at all, Roman. Even though you have abducted me in the not-so-distant past. But no matter how gallant you feel about the incident with Leofwin, I remain his betrothed. There are not many ways to end that without significant turmoil for me and Amis."

Roman squeezed her hands and she gave him a squeeze in return before stepping back and pulling her hands away from his grasp. She rubbed a hand across her forehead and turned away from him briefly.

"I do not want to marry Leofwin. In fact, I have no plans to actually go through with it should the time come," Moira said as she turned around to face him and saw a look of pure relief before he composed his features again. "If I am stuck in this engagement, for whatever length of time remaining, I want to use that for something good. I *want* to do this." She mustered as much conviction as she could, despite the tumble of nerves that came with it.

Roman considered her for a moment. She wondered what might be bothering him, considering he had no skin in the game of her engagement. Moira was also slightly annoyed with everyone. What Leofwin did was wrong. But it wasn't as if she hadn't already prepared for some level of personal danger by agreeing to spy in the first place. It just so happened that the risk came from an unexpected origin.

"I will let you do this on one condition," he said.

Moira scoffed and said, "*Let* me?" She crossed her arms and gave him her most condescending look.

The smile finally returned to Roman's face. "There I go again with the wrong word choice. Semantics." He waved his hand casually as if it didn't matter.

Moira smiled a little and tilted her head, indicating she wanted him to continue speaking, but she kept her arms crossed.

"I would *ask* one thing of you," he corrected. He gave her a questioning look. She nodded, agreeing his word choice was improved. Roman continued, "If another incident occurs and you find yourself in that same position, or Gods forbid, an even worse one, then I need you to do something, Moira."

She blinked at the use of her name. It may never sound quite right in comparison to the ease with which he said that obnoxious nickname.

"Knee him in the groin and run?" she asked with an exaggerated smile, making sure he knew she was at least mostly joking.

He dipped his head, returning his features to a more serious look, and said, "I would very much like for you to kick his ass. Or allow me to."

Before she could stop herself, Moira let out a barking laugh. Roman stepped forward and gently covered her mouth with his hand. Moira stepped back immediately and said, "I'm sorry! I forgot myself for a moment, but please, for the love of all things holy, stop touching me with your filthy hands! Hanna will kill me if I come back covered in muck!"

This time Roman stifled his laughter as he held his hands up in mock surrender. "I would hate to invoke the ire of Ms. Ashdown."

"Precisely. I sincerely appreciate your understanding of the gravity of the situation." She paused and shook her head a little, realizing she completely derailed their conversation. "My ability to defend myself may not be up to the standard it should be, but I promise to give him hell if anything happens again. And -," she paused, considered for a moment, and said, "Thank you for encouraging violence. Not enough people in my life do that for me!"

"We can build up your fighting skills easily if you'd like to improve on those violent tendencies," Roman said.

This offer intrigued Moira, but she decided to redirect the topic. There was no feasible way right now that she could think of accomplishing something like fighting lessons.

"Why did you come here today?" She asked, with another small step back.

He gave the briefest of pauses, taken aback by her quick change of subject.

"For this," he said while gesturing between the two of them.

"This?"

"You are one of my - what did you call us? Cadre? You are one of my cadres, Moira. A part of the coterie. A member of my pack." He gave her a grin and continued, "Call it what you want, but you and your wellbeing are important to me. Not just the potential information you could gather - although I like that very much, don't get me wrong...." Roman stopped and made an odd face as if he were annoyed with himself. "The point is this is what I came for. To find out if you were truly okay and to learn how you wanted to proceed." He shrugged, but she noticed a slight reddening of his neck.

Moira found herself giving Roman a genuine smile, which he returned magnificently. For a moment, they both stood there smiling and saying nothing until Moira realized felt like an utter buffoon.

"Well, if I'm to continue spying for you, I need to go and get ready for the big return to dinner on Lord Leofwin's arm," she made a mildly disgusted face just to keep their mood light. "I need to strategize on how to work it, but I imagine I shall have to accept some poorly worded apology and go on as if nothing happened." She spoke flippantly as if this didn't bother her, but she knew it was going to be a tremendous strain for her to willingly be near Leofwin again.

"Don't be false with me, Moira." He stepped close again as if the proximity helped him drive home the point that he cared. "I know it will be difficult for you, but remember you don't have to go through with it if you find yourself unable to. I happen to know an absolute shanty of a hideout where you and Amis are both welcome if you realize that the courtly life is no longer for you." Roman smiled at her, knowing she would appreciate his use of the word she'd used to describe his hideout. He then started to back away a little more, inching ever closer to the trees.

Suddenly, Moira was acutely aware of just how long they had been chatting. She looked around her and sent up a silent prayer of thanks that they had not been caught.

"I will remember that invitation, outlaw," she said with a dramatic, slightly off-balance curtsy. "Now, please try to get out of here without nearly killing yourself. I would like to have a few peaceful days before the Archery Tournament next week!"

Moira did not wait for his response but turned and walked determinedly toward the castle. If she planned to get down to dinner tonight and pretend everything was normal, she'd need Hanna's assistance. She groaned, wishing that her job as a spy could just once include a nice pair of trousers instead of a corset and gown.

Chapter Twenty-Eight

"I don't like it, Moira," Hanna fretted.

"Me either, but…," Amis started.

"Nobody has to like it. I am wide open to suggestions, ideas, and alternatives! Please, give me something. Anything to get me soundly out of this situation while still aiding Roman and King Leo. Do either of you have anything to say other than sharing your feelings?" Moira asked as she stared them both down, hands on her hips.

Moira was trussed up in one of her most tolerable gowns. A beautiful emerald green dress that seemed to always be moving, even when she held still. She liked the effect as it made her feel far more graceful than she really was. The fabric was lighter than most, but there was still a corset. It was a trade-off she'd make tonight because she knew she looked absolutely fantastic in this particular dress. She felt like she'd need to rely on her looks more than normal tonight to ensure things went smoothly. The only downside to the gown was that the sleeves were short. She was attempting to remedy this by hiding the bruise with a shawl draped carefully around her shoulders and down her upper arms. If she could keep it in place all night, no one would see the marks Leofwin had left.

Her feelings regarding the incident had turned from embarrassment and shame to icy resolve. Lord Leofwin might have caught her by surprise once, but Moira vowed she wouldn't let him get away with it again. She would play the courtly game as long as she needed, but she would make sure Leofwin eventually saw her true strength.

"Yes," said Hanna, a little haughtily. "You two get the hell out of here. Meanwhile, I will remain in the castle and do my best to gather whatever snippets of information I can. Flee to the hideout, go back to Huntsley, or go somewhere entirely new! Just get out of here. You owe Roman Loxley *nothing*. And I don't say that lightly. He and the cause mean something to me personally, but you have no obligation to stay."

Moira gaped at Hanna, more than a little stung. "I have given my word, Hanna. That matters to me. Not to mention the fact that Roman and the cause have become important to me! Going anywhere in Anglia will still mean being under Prince Lyric's false rule, and you know it." She whispered the last bit with as much fierceness she could muster without speaking at full volume. She was trying to be careful about what she spoke out loud within the castle, even while in her own rooms.

Hanna pursed her lips and paused for a moment. Moira started to speak again, but Hanna shook her head.

"You're right. I'm sorry. It's clear that Roman and the cause he fights for have grown to mean something to you," Hanna acceded.

"We really shouldn't forget that this whole venture started out as dangerous." Amis reasoned. "Did we expect that total ass Leofwin to become *this* type of danger? No. He caught us by surprise with this complication; however, we didn't agree to join Roman with the expectation of safety. At least not immediately."

Amis leaned against the bookshelf. He had both arms loosely crossed and looked so relaxed Moira could have smacked him. Only he could make this topic seem like a laid-back interlude.

"Exactly. Thank you, Amis," Moira said. She looked at Hanna for a long moment and said, "I'll be careful, Hanna. It's not as if Leofwin is pissed drunk on a regular basis. I've been here a year and have not had a single interaction like that with him. If we keep discussing this, we will be late for dinner."

Hanna gave her a weak smile before she reached out and gave Moira's hand a gentle squeeze.

"Just don't end up like Coraline Lane, and I'll be happy," Hanna said softly before leaving the room.

Moira looked at Amis, who shrugged.

He said, "She's grown fond of you, Moi. I'd wager you're the closest thing she has to family here. Give her a little grace while she grapples with the fact that you're not just her easily looked after ward any longer."

"Wise words coming from someone who only recently stopped flashing the world his buttocks whenever the chance arises!" Moira teased, laughing at Amis and the *oh so wise* tone he used.

Amis looked at Moira with mock affront, then said, "You've wounded me, dear sister! Whoever said I was done mooning people? I hope to never leave that *behind* me!" He gave her a wink and then offered his arm, ready to escort her down to dinner. She rolled her eyes and gave him a slight pinch on the arm before she took it.

Amis wondered aloud as they left Moira's rooms. "Do you ever wonder who all the poor souls are? The ones Hanna speaks of. She's got a person with a terrible outcome to reference at every turn!"

"Poor Coraline Lane…and Catherine Whatsit…and all the others. Whoever they are, they've never known happiness!" Moira said with false solemnity. Half of her always wondered if Hanna made these people up. Amis shrugged and gave her a tug.

Full of trepidation, Moira allowed Amis to lead her downstairs to the smaller dining hall. They were not dining in the great hall again, as Prince Lyric had not returned to the castle. If what she heard from Leofwin was true, the prince would not be returning for another few days. Her mind started churning on how she could get some more information tonight, but part of her wondered if this dinner would be wasted on regaining their footing with each other.

Chapter Twenty-Nine

As Moira feared, dinner was a collection of awkward interactions between her and Leofwin. He started off stiff and formal toward her but progressed quickly into his usual method of generally ignoring her entire existence while speaking to everyone else around them. She found herself, as usual, equal parts relieved and frustrated by this behavior. Amis made sure she was looped into conversation with him and Lady Lucia, which was possibly just as much for his benefit, considering Lucia seemed a little icy toward him.

Lord Leofwin excused himself as soon as Lord Maddicot rose from his seat further down the table. They both disappeared from the hall at the same time, which Moira felt was a little odd. She looked at Amis, who arched an eyebrow at her. She shrugged and took another bite of her dessert – spice cake that she drowned in honey. Amis gave her a light kick under the table and stared intently at her until she made eye contact. Once she was looking at him, he nodded his head in the direction of the door. Moira stared blankly at him before it dawned on her that she should have followed the two lords when they left.

She felt like a total dolt, but she didn't want to give up her dessert. In an unladylike display of gluttony, Moira shoveled the remaining bites of cake into her mouth at once and quickly made her excuses. Her mouth was so full of cake, she doubted anyone understood a word she said. Amis had his hands covering his face while his shoulders shook in silent laughter. Moira stood up and left the hall, chewing furiously. Amis gave her a look that said he was definitely going to give her a hard time about this later.

Once in the hall, Moira choked down the last of the cake she'd shoved into her mouth and realized she had no idea which direction the two lords went. She dusted crumbs from her face and wondered briefly if they would have gone to one of the small studies like the one Leofwin pulled her into the other day.

Moira stepped away from the entrance to the dining hall, leaned back against the stone wall, and took a breath. Once she took a moment to think, she realized exactly where the two men had gone - the trophy room. It always seemed to be where the dark and shady discussions happened. She gathered up her flowing, endless skirts so she wouldn't trip and hurriedly walked down the corridors, attempting to look as casual as possible in case she ran into anyone.

Both sliding doors to the trophy room were closed. Moira pressed her ear to the spot where the doors met and strained to hear if anything was being said in the room. She caught the faint sound of voices but she couldn't be sure it was Leofwin and Maddicot. Many of the lords seemed to favor the room for its privacy.

Moira admitted the trophy room was pretty perfect for any sort of covert conversation. The room contained wall-to-wall shelving on two of the four walls, which were covered in books and curiosities. All other wall space was dedicated to stuffed and mounted animals of all kinds and various weapons. All these items helped to soundproof the room and give off an impressively nefarious atmosphere. Along with the shelving, the room also contained a massive, ornate and intimidating writing table - behind which was a rather oddly mounted suit of armor that looked as if it was coming out of the stone wall. At the other end of the room was a gargantuan fireplace, several thick rugs, a comfortable lounge, and two well-stuffed chairs. The room practically invited corrupt plotting or a really good nap.

Unsure of what to do next, Moira found herself loitering in the corridor outside the room. She couldn't manage to confirm who was in the room, but she knew it was occupied. When not in use, the double doors to the room were always open. There was an external window she could possibly peak into, but that would require going outside and not being seen. She felt like this would be a substantial challenge due to the cold weather and her overall lack of talent when it came to staying unseen. Not to mention the fact that the window would give her a visual, but she'd still be left without any auditory option to know what was being said. Deep down, Moira knew her spy abilities came from a more direct approach and less from sneaking around and staying hidden.

This train of thought gave her an idea, and before she could think it through any further, she flung both doors wide open and walked into the trophy room as if she belonged there. The maneuver gave her exactly what she wanted: the element of surprise. Not only were Leofwin and Maddicot in here, but so were Lords Dayben, Godberd, and Owen. Moira knew the last two just enough to identify them. This must be the core group of lords who supported Prince Lyric unquestioningly.

As Moira pretended to be utterly shocked at finding people in the room, she caught Lord Godberd shoving multiple items into an ornate wooden box. He stood behind the writing desk. She couldn't tell what the items were, but he locked the box quickly before shoving it onto a shelf behind the writing table. Before anyone could notice she saw this, Moira walked over to Leofwin, who was standing near the fireplace and looped her arm through his.

"Might my betrothed like to escort me on an evening stroll?" Moira asked, attempting to behave as though she had a little too much to drink. She let her shawl drop a little on the left side but kept it up on the right. Showing her bruise would likely not do her any favors in this situation.

Leofwin looked at Moira in stunned surprise. Moira continued to look at him as if no one else were in the room, but she could feel their stares.

Leofwin cleared his throat and said quietly, "Perhaps you should return to your room, Lady Moira. It appears it is time for you to retire."

He gave a hand that was on his arm a gentle pat. She found it curious that he used her name rather than calling her "pet," but she didn't have time to analyze that now.

"Shall I call for her brother to escort her, Conor?" Lord Dayben asked as though he couldn't wait for her to be gone.

Moira frowned and looked at Lord Dayben. "I can find my own way back, Lord Dayben. No need to call for an escort."

She looked back at Leofwin, who gazed at her as though she sprouted an extra eye in the center of her forehead. She gave him a massive grin and then pranced away toward the door. In her sweetest voice she said, "Nighty, night, gentlemen!" Then, in an effort to ensure they found her entirely non-threatening, Moira gave a curtsy and left with a high-pitched giggle.

Moira continued her whimsical walk down the hallway until she heard the trophy room doors close behind her. Moira couldn't help but hear the distinct sound of the latch, too. She laughed to herself. It appeared the group of lords realized that the door should be locked when they were having secret meetings.

As she walked down the hall at a normal, slower pace, Moira worked through what she'd managed to see. Although disappointed she hadn't learned more specific information, she was still certain that reporting the lords within that room would be helpful to Roman. Until now, she felt like there was ambiguity surrounding which power players in the castle truly supported Prince Lyric in his mad plan. Each one of those lords held different areas of influence and talent, which made Prince Lyric a stronger leader in this game she was slowly becoming more aware of. Lord Godberd came from Fenfoss. Moira read about his family when she perused the book on Anglian nobility. Lord Dayben held influence in Gest and, some said, with the criminals that lived in Etheldred. Moira wasn't sure where Lord Owen's influence came in, but she knew his tastes veered more into the realm of evil than all others combined. With lords like these supporting Prince Lyric, his hold on the throne would grow stronger the longer King Leo stayed away. Or rather, was kept away.

Amis came up behind her and wrapped his arm around her shoulders, giving Moira a start before she realized who it was. He put a finger up to his lips, indicating he didn't want her to say anything. Amis turned her around and led her quietly back toward the library, which was at the front of the castle, and back in the direction of the trophy room. She kept silent and allowed him to steer her. Once in the library, Amis weaved in and out of the shelves, leading her to the farthest back corner. Moira noticed everything here had a thick layer of dust, including the table and chairs, indicating no one came back here on a regular basis – not even her.

"I'm not sure I've ever been to this particular corner," Moira said, looking a little closer at what titles were on the shelves.

"Yes, yes. Books are great, lots of undiscovered texts back here. I'm sure you'll have time to explore later, Moi," he quipped and grabbed her gently on the wrist "Where did you go, and what did you learn?" he asked excitedly.

Moira beamed at Amis and said proudly, "I didn't gain tons of insight, but I did manage to get a little something!" She explained what happened, from reaching the closed door to bursting in and what she'd seen. He nodded in excitement and smiled with pride when she was done.

"Well done, Moira! I have to say, bursting in and playing a little tipsy is quite fun when you think about it! I'm sure Leofwin was nearly wetting himself out of sheer nervousness. He likely had no idea what to do with an intoxicated lady, considering what he did while drunk last week. Well played. I think you're right - Roman will find the tidbits you've gathered to be very helpful."

Amis pulled out one of the dusty chairs from the ancient table, sat down, and tipped it back with his feet propped up on the tabletop. The chair creaked in protest. "I happened to get a little intel, myself," he boasted casually.

Moira looked at him in surprise. She moved to the table, pulled out a chair, and grimaced. Normally getting a dress dirty wouldn't bother her at all, but since she liked this one, she thought better of it. She pushed the chair back in and looked at Amis again. "Is there anywhere else we can go where I can sit without getting filthy? What's wrong with my rooms?"

Amis shrugged and said, "This felt far more clandestine, don't you think?" He pulled his handkerchief out of his pocket and tossed it onto the table. "Clean up the chair a bit and sit down. I like having a covert meeting place that isn't your parlor, Moi."

A little begrudgingly, Moira grabbed the hanky and did her best to clean up the chair. At least the seat and back were better off than before.

"This happens to be the only gown I enjoy wearing." Moira groused. "You talk as if this is some sort of game, Amis. I think it's arguable we are far safer in my rooms than we are in the library."

"It is a bit of a game, isn't it? There are just far higher stakes than we usually have while playing cards. Don't take it all too seriously, Moi. We're pawns in Roman's game, no matter how much you may like the chap. Don't get your knickers in a twist, either. I like Roman, too," he said, seeing she was about to argue the point of her liking Roman. Which, of course, she did. She was just loath to admit how much she liked him. "Now, clearly, no one comes back here, and if anyone gets close, we will hear them coming. So, I think we are safe here."

"Fine! I'm settled. Tell me what you learned tonight."

Moira was not very comfortable, but she didn't feel like arguing the point.

Amis looked out one of the tall windows next to the table. The tops of the windows were stained glass, but lower down, it was clear. They were in the near pitch black, having only lit a few of the wall sconces on their way through the library, which allowed them to see into the darkness outside. There was a full moon in the sky, casting a pale glow upon the castle grounds. It was a little eerie, but Moira supposed it suited their motives tonight.

"It seems Lady Lucia is paying more attention than most are giving her credit for," Amis finally said.

Moira turned away from the window and looked at Amis with a mix of surprise and concern. She said, "I wondered if she was more aware than I want to give her credit for. I haven't had any proof, though. You haven't mentioned Roman to her, have you?"

Moira didn't need to talk to Roman to know he would hate having another person added to the inner circle without his approval. While she'd been willing to loop Amis in without Roman's permission, there wasn't anyone else Moira was willing to break that trust for.

"Oh, no! Absolutely not. She may be willing to trust me with bits of knowledge, but that is not a reciprocated feeling," he answered adamantly.

Amis removed his feet from the tabletop, plopping the chair back down onto all four legs. He turned slightly, so he was fully facing Moira. "Lucia let it slip that her father and many of the lords will be gone for two days in order to meet and escort Prince Lyric home. They leave tomorrow to ensure that the prince returns in time for the Archery Tournament."

This piqued Moira's curiosity. She wondered if Leofwin was one of the lords going and, if so, why he had not mentioned his impending absence. Then again, there had been many occasions in the past when he did not share his plans with Moira, so it wasn't too far out of the norm. They weren't exactly on the friendliest of terms right now.

"Did she mention where they are meeting the prince?" Moira asked.

"If she knew, she did not say. I would be surprised if Lord Dayben gave her that much detail, even if she is his favorite daughter. My guess would be they'll meet the prince in Gest or Branscomb. Etheldred is a long journey, but either of those locations makes a decent halfway point of sorts." Amis shrugged a little as if the finer details weren't of consequence. "I think the main point of this is the fact that we will have several days without the usual oversight in the castle." He looked at her pointedly.

"Your point being?" She asked, unsure where he was going with this.

"My point being that it is highly likely Leofwin goes on this excursion. Maybe all five lords in that room tonight will be gone, which is exactly who we want to go to if we are to enjoy a few scrutiny-free days. Think about it, Moi. We could practice archery to your heart's content, wander the forest...hell. We could go to the hideout if we can manage to learn where it is!" Amis's eyes sparkled with delight.

Moira had to admit Amis had a great point. A few days without the encroaching presence of Leofwin and the other lords would be lovely.

"Alright, you master plotter. Let's confirm that Leofwin will be gone, and then we can determine our course of action!"

Amis laughed a little and rolled his eyes. "Of course, we mustn't have fun without first having a plan!" He stood up and reached for her hand. "Come, I'll escort you to your rooms like the delicate bloom you are. Tomorrow we can finalize our plotting after I get the knowledge you desire."

Moira threw her hand up to her forehead in her most dramatic fashion, stating, "Yes, I'm simply too delicate for words!"

They both laughed, and she allowed him to lead her out of the library.

****

Moira lay in bed that night feeling buoyant and hopeful. She was proud she managed to grasp at least a small amount of new information, which left her feeling accomplished. She drifted off to sleep while imagining archery practice, a visit to the hideout, and the opportunity to learn more about Roman Loxley.

Chapter Thirty

Through the inner workings of castle life, Hanna was able to confirm that Lord Leofwin was accompanying Lords Dayben and Maddicot on their journey to meet Prince Lyric on his way back to Ivywood. She also learned that Lords Godberd and Owen were leaving the castle, but they were going somewhere else, unrelated to escorting the prince. Despite her best efforts, Hanna was unable to get the details of where they were going but did learn that all five lords planned to return on the same day.

Moira couldn't help but feel overjoyed. Freedom. Well…freedom adjacent. The bulk of the castle oversight that cared about where she was and who she was with would be gone. As long as they were careful, she and Amis should be able to fully enjoy the next few days.

"I let Gwin know first thing this morning," Hanna chirped while sorting through Moira's wardrobe. "She said to plan on meeting someone at the edge of the forest at nightfall. They will escort you and Amis to the hideout."

Moira had yet to get out of bed but was propped up on a few pillows. She rarely had the opportunity to lounge in bed and she was taking full advantage this morning.

She looked at Hanna quizzically. "You let Gwin know?"

"Yes, I did. Have you got cotton in your ears this morning, girl?" Hanna retorted, holding up an article of clothing and scrutinizing it.

Moira made sure to let out an exaggerated sigh before saying, "Allow me to rephrase. How did you manage to already tell Gwin all of this when the sun is not yet warm, and I am not even out of bed?"

Hanna scoffed. "You may not start your day until the sun is warm, but many of us are up and working well before there's even light on the horizon. And by 'many of us,' I do mean Gwin and myself."

Moira flopped her head back and stared at the ceiling in frustration. "Hanna. How is it that you've managed a lecture while still not answering my question?"

"Before dawn on every third day, Gwin comes to the kitchens to get supplies. It worked well that I was able to get the information you needed prior to Gwin coming by. It made passing things along very easy."

Hanna pulled out one of the dresses Moira brought with her from Huntsley, frowned, and tossed it into a brown sack.

"Satisfied with that answer?" Hanna asked as she looked pointedly at Moira.

Moira responded with an enormous grin, threw back the covers, and hopped out of bed. She said, "Yes! Hanna, I have no idea what on earth I'd do without you, but I'm certain I don't want to know!"

"Ha!" Hanna said, tossing a tunic and trousers at Moira's head. "Wash your face at least, girl. I'll braid your hair before you run off to play outlaw with Amis!"

****

Moira could not remember a day in the last year when she felt so fulfilled. She and Amis embraced their roles of playing outlaw.

Amis packed a picnic feast (Moira assumed he had help from the women in the kitchens) and brought it along to their spot in the forest. It was a small clearing just outside the castle walls where Amis liked to keep a bow and arrows stashed in a small crevice of rocks. They weren't very close to the Maddock Mountains, but Moira noticed that the Blackwood Forest tended to contain rocky patches spread throughout. It made for some very odd forest terrain, but perfect for hiding things. The two of them had taken turn after turn with the bow and arrow. Moira was out of practice at first and sour about her poor performance, but after warming up, things turned around, and she was shooting well again. She mourned her lack of practice time more than once, to which Amis always had a smart-ass response. They ate lunch and napped in the clearing.

Amis nearly drug Moira back to the castle just long enough to clean up and eat dinner. They wanted to make an appearance for whichever remaining courtiers were there to report to Leofwin. Thankfully, it seemed the other members of the court were embracing their own freedom. Dinner that evening was sparsely attended, and no one seemed to notice Amis and Moira shoveling their food in at an alarming pace before jumping up and exiting the hall in record time.

Moira returned to her room long enough to change back into trousers and an old shirt of Amis's. It was so much more comfortable, and she didn't want to spend time on horseback riding through the forest in a dress if she could avoid it. Hanna escorted her down to the kitchens where Amis was waiting. Hanna bid them good night with an air of mischief and promised to stay in Moira's rooms until she returned later that night.

Thankful that they didn't intercept anyone on the way to the forest, Moira's ebullient mood was only slightly spoiled by the sight of Pewsey just inside the tree line. Her smile returned when she saw Wilhelm towering behind Pewsey, a little further in the shadows of the trees.

"You must be Pewsey. Amis Finglas, nice to finally meet you!" Amis said, his hand outstretched to Pewsey.

"I don't shake hands," Pewsey snarled, then turned and spat into the forest.

Amis turned to Moira, cringing, and said, "You're right. He is the least merry of them all!"

Wilhelm let out a somewhat contained laugh while clapping Amis on the back in greeting. "You haven't met Bobby yet, so you may want to hold off on announcing the title just yet."

"I'm growing old and ugly. Let's get moving," Pewsey growled, starting to move further into the forest, where Moira saw they had horses waiting.

"*Growing* old and ugly?" Moira asked sarcastically, unable to help herself.

Pewsey let out an indecipherable grumble but started walking toward the horses. Wilhelm gave Moira a huge grin and waved for her and Amis to follow.

"Follow me. Keep up or don't. I can't be bothered to care," Pewsey hollered as he climbed onto his horse and started riding into the forest.

Wilhelm rolled his eyes and said quickly, "Ignore him. We're all excited to have you back in the hideout, Moira!" He swung up onto his horse, clicked his tongue twice, and turned to lead them back through the forest.

Chapter Thirty-One

The forest was dark, but calm. A companionable silence fell over the group and Moira enjoyed the serenity of a nighttime ride through the trees.

After nearly an hour of riding, they arrived at the hideout. Moira thought it looked almost magical, glowing in the deep darkness of the forest. The main cabin was aglow from the inside, with a small puff of smoke wafting idyllically from the chimney. Surrounding the cabin were several large canvas tents, also glowing from the inside. In the center of it all was a roaring fire pit with several people sitting around it. Overall, there was an air of relaxation, which surprised Moira. She expected to find the camp on full alert, no matter the hour of the day.

"Sentries are posted throughout the forest. Before you ask, everyone in camp can relax and unwind because we've got people on the lookout. We passed three on the way in," Wilhelm told her as he hopped down off his horse next to her.

It amazed Moira that he managed to guess where her mind wandered.

"Three? Really? I didn't even think to look for any guards," Moira answered, surprised.

She got down off her horse, as did Amis. Moira looked around and realized she lost track of Pewsey. *Good riddance*, she thought. The less she interacted with him, the better.

"Roman runs a tight ship around here," Wilhelm explained. "Although, he also relishes the opportunity to embrace downtime when the rare chance arrives. With you two in camp tonight, he's declared that it's a minor celebration."

Wilhelm gestured to the hideout and gathering of people with broad smile.

"Why would he do that?" Moira asked. "I assume when one is leading a secret rebellion, there is quite literally *always* work to be done."

Wilhelm gave her a curious look and said, "I would have thought it was obvious." When Moira just continued to look at him in confusion, he sighed and said, "He's welcoming you, Moira. He wants you to meet people and feel comfortable here. It's a welcome celebration."

Moira was astonished but pleased. She smiled at Wilhelm and realized it was just the two of them standing and chatting. Amis already approached the group at the fireside and was enjoying himself thoroughly. He held a pint of ale in one hand and was gesturing wildly with the other. Moira briefly envied him and his easy social ability. She saw Roman sitting at the fireside, watching her. She froze briefly, unsure of what to do. Wilhelm gently touched her elbow and led her over to the fire. Introductions were made, and before she knew it, Moira was also laughing along and telling stories.

After sitting around the fire and smiling so much her face hurt, Moira was struck by the sudden feeling of belonging. It felt almost foreign to her, having never been part of a group like this one. During her childhood in Huntsley, she and Amis existed peacefully enough with the children from the village, but there had still been an element of otherness. No matter how dirty she got, how well she shot, or how welcoming she was, Moira had always been the young lady of the Huntsley estate. Moira felt an almost magical atmosphere around this group, ebbing and flowing as they shared and laughed together. There was no need to put on a show or pretend to be anything but herself.

As she listened to the conversation around her, Moira felt overwhelmed by an unexpected realization: *She never wanted to leave.*

Roman sat across the fire, watching Moira closely. She met his gaze and smiled, enjoying the way the firelight cast a warm glow on his face. Warmth permeated her being as Moira watched Roman turn and laugh at whatever tale Wilhelm pulled him into. Amis wrapped his arm around Moira's shoulders, and she turned to listen as he told a familiar story of their first time away from home.

Chapter Thirty-Two

Moira sat on the floor of the cabin, close to the fireplace, with her feet tucked up under her as she sipped on spiced tea. The fire crackled in that rustic, pleasing way with lots of snapping and popping. There was still plenty of raucous noise outside, but inside the cabin, it was peaceful, which was exactly why she'd come inside.

Amis's laughter carried in through the partially open windows, and Moira was once again delighted with how quickly he made friends here. He always did manage to fit in wherever he went.

Moira leaned her head back against the cushion of the lounge behind her. She thought briefly of getting off the floor and sitting on the comfortable settee but couldn't bring herself to move. Something about the floor was just right tonight. She held her teacup, resting it gently in her lap as she closed her eyes and relished the solitude.

A moment later, she opened her eyes and realized Roman had come into the cabin, completely silent, and sat on the floor across from her with his back against the other settee.

She smirked at him and asked, "How do you do that? No one your size should be able to move so silently. It's unnatural." She brought her cup up to her lips and took a sip of her tea while she continued to look at Roman.

The flickering firelight cast a shadow over one side of his face, but she still caught his smile. He looked at her with an expression she'd never seen before. It tied her stomach in knots, but not in an unpleasant way. It made her feel a little giddy and very nervous. His hair was pulled back at the nape of his neck, but his beard was still free and wild. The shadows from the fire, paired with the flickering light, made his beard almost dance on his face.

"You looked too peaceful to disturb, so I took my boots off when I came in," he explained while stretching out his legs and wiggling his stocking-covered feet in her direction.

Moira couldn't help but laugh and said, "That was very kind of you, outlaw. I hate to admit it, but I find your shanty of a cabin to be entirely too comfortable!"

She shifted a little and faced him, stretching her own legs out alongside his. The fire continued to crackle to her right, and the noise continued outside, but she and Roman looked at one another in silence, smiling softly.

"Tell me something I don't know," Moira said lightly. There was a building pressure filling the space between them and she wanted to ease a little of the tension she felt.

Roman scrunched his face a little and looked at the fire while he thought. She didn't want to rush him, so she pulled her legs back up and tucked them into her chest. Her now empty teacup was set off to the side, and she rested her chin on her knees while she looked at Roman and waited.

"I hate chickens," he said as he looked back at her.

She arched an eyebrow and looked at him as if he spoke in a foreign language. "All that thought, and all you've got to tell me is that you hate chickens? Ultimate disappointment."

Roman pulled his legs in and mimicked her pose, his chin resting on his own knees. He looked at her another beat before saying, "This cabin was built by my great-grandfather. He built it in secret so he could sneak away from my great-grandmother. I'm told she was a formidable woman, and he found he needed somewhere to hide every so often." He smiled softly and returned his gaze to the fire. He continued, "I didn't even know the cabin existed until my father brought me here a few years before the Crusades. I was so angsty back then, and I think he sensed I needed a place to get away from things. He said he'd never used it but knew of its existence. It's been something of a secret kept by the men in the family." Roman's smile grew wider as he reminisced.

He reached up behind him and grabbed a large quilt from the settee behind him, which he tossed gently toward her. She caught it as the blanket tumbled out of its fold and cascaded down onto her head. As Moira unfurled the blanket, she straightened her legs out again. While the cabin was cozy with the fire going, she was starting to get chilly as the night got later. How Roman caught onto this, she couldn't say, but she appreciated it.

"Wilhelm and I used to come here when we felt the pressures of growing up a little too acutely," Roman said, clearly fond of the time they spent here. "For a long time, he was the only one who I told about it."

He paused for a long time, looking at his hands. Eventually, he continued, "When I returned from the Crusades, and everything had...changed, I knew this would be a safe place to bide my time. You might not realize it because you've only ever been here at night, but we are backed up against a small rock formation, which makes us entirely hidden from anyone approaching from the north. If needed, we can get to the Maddock Mountains easily enough and hide there. It's a great place, really...," Roman tapered off, leaving Moira with the sense that a lot went unsaid.

"It's a great place, but it isn't home," she said, hoping she wasn't misinterpreting the words he left unsaid.

Roman nodded and said, "It's not home."

"If you consider this a nice place, I can't imagine what sort of hovel you live in back in Loxley!" Moira teased with a smirk, hoping she might dig Roman out of the somber mood he suddenly descended into.

Roman didn't say anything, but he lifted the blanket edge near him and straightened his legs out underneath it. His calf touched hers, but she didn't move away, and neither did he.

202

They sat in silence again. Moira couldn't help but notice it wasn't strained or uncomfortable. For whatever reason, she did not feel compelled to fill the quiet space between them. She reflected on her short time at court and how much emphasis was put on what she said and how she said it. Moira realized a lot more could be learned about someone by what they did with silence rather than what they said to fill it.

"It's nice being here of my own free will," Moira said, attempting again to lighten the mood.

Roman's face was still half covered in shadow, but the part she could see in the firelight lost the dour look from a moment ago. She wanted to bring the mischief out in him again, not sit in a melancholic reverie brought on by a simple question.

Roman gave her a devilish smile and said, "When Gwin gave me the update from Hanna, I did seriously consider taking you by surprise again. Just for the sake of consistency." His eyes twinkled with merriment. "I would have used a cleaner sack than Pewsey used last time, I swear!"

Moira huffed and leaned forward. She suppressed her delight at his turn in mood, and pointed an accusing finger at Roman and said, "You utter ass! Of course, that was your original plan. What swayed you to allow me to come here invited and of my own free will?"

She sat back and crossed her arms, doing her best to keep her expression annoyed rather than show her amusement.

Roman cleared his throat a little and said flippantly, "I like Amis too much to abduct him."

Moira balled up as much of the blanket as she could and threw it at Roman's face. He held up his hands as the wadded-up blanket flew toward him. He caught it easily and tossed it aside.

Moira, laughing despite herself, said, "You are unbelievable, Roman Loxley."

She sat back with a sigh, and before she could stop it, a huge yawn escaped.

Roman turned serious and said, "We need to get you back to the castle. It's later than I should've allowed."

Moira shrugged and said, "It's going to be tough to go back."

With his hand on his heart, Roman replied in mock surprise, "I'm shocked, Beastie. That sounded like it was definitely almost a compliment."

"'Definitely almost'?" Moira asked with as much derision as she could work into her voice.

Roman shrugged but didn't answer. He didn't appear to be in any hurry to get up. Neither was Moira. She wanted desperately to ask him what happened in the Crusades but wasn't sure if that question would be met with an answer or with deep offense at her asking. Although she felt entirely comfortable with Roman, despite their short time knowing each other, she wasn't sure if that comfort level was the same for him.

Instead, she said, "I saw a rather interesting notice posted when I was in Ivywood."

Moira raised an eyebrow, taunting Roman. She couldn't believe she forgot to bring it up earlier. Before leaving the castle, she remembered to grab the rolled-up parchment to bring along to show him.

"Oh?" Roman said as he watched her get up and walk to the large wooden table on the other side of the room.

Moira grabbed the satchel she brought with her and walked back over to her spot on the floor. Gwin must have brought it inside for her after they arrived. She sat with her legs crisscrossed and pulled the bag onto her lap.

She dug out the parchment and held it to her chest, setting the bag off to the side by her teacup. "I brought this to show you, but you must promise not to destroy it," she said seriously.

Roman gave her a skeptical look and leaned forward a little, crisscrossing his own legs.

"Do you take me for a fool, B? I can't make a promise like that until I know what on earth has you so excited."

Moira shrugged and made a pitying face. "That's a shame, outlaw. I'll just have to put this away…," she let the sentence hang for a moment as she slowly reached for her bag again.

Roman made to snatch the parchment from her, but she expected this and quickly held it up and away from his grasp. Now, however, Roman's face was inches from hers as he leaned forward even further, balanced on both knees and one hand, with his other hand reaching toward the parchment. She gasped at the proximity as Roman's eyes locked with hers. He slowly lowered his hand and rested it on the spot where her neck met her shoulder. She inhaled sharply at the unexpected contact. His hand was warm. His thumb stroked her neck twice, leaving her slightly breathless. She let go of the parchment, which dropped onto the lounge cushions behind her, and she reached forward. Her heart pounded wildly, and she could barely form a coherent thought as she stretched out her hand to touch Roman's cheek. Their eyes remained locked as Roman started to move his face closer to hers. Moira closed her eyes and tilted her head. She could feel Roman's breath as he drew closer.

The door to the cabin crashed open, and Wilhelm shouted, "Oy, Ro, we need you -"

He stopped mid-sentence and froze as he stepped into the room and caught sight of them. Roman withdrew his hand from Moira's neck and straightened, sitting on his knees as he glared at Wilhelm.

"What do you need me for?" Roman asked through slightly clenched teeth.

Moira's face flushed, glowing bright red. She was so entirely caught up in the moment that she forgot there were even other people with them. Suddenly, she was thanking the Gods it hadn't been Amis who interrupted them.

Wilhelm had the biggest grin on his face. "Oh, I wager we don't actually *need* you for anything." He waggled his eyebrows. "We were wondering when you wanted us to escort Moira and Amis back to the castle. That is if they're even going back?" More eyebrow wiggling made Moira homicidal.

"Wilhelm?" Moira said murderously.

He grinned even larger, which she hadn't thought possible, and turned toward her. "Yes, Lady Moira?" He said with insincere formality.

She gave him a mocking grin in return and said, "Go to hell!"

Both men burst out laughing. Roman rocked back onto the floor and said, "Yeah, I have to second that."

Amis came in and looked curiously at the three of them. Moira, still glaring, and Roman and Wilhelm, still laughing.

"Oh, I've walked into something, haven't I?" Amis said rubbing his hands together with too much excitement.

"Never mind, Amis. We were just discussing the many ways in which Wilhelm can go to hell," Moira said, standing up from the floor. It suddenly felt a lot less cozy than when it was just her and Roman in the cabin.

Roman stood, too. Then said, "Not to detract from the very important topic of Wilhelm's imminent death, courtesy of Moira, I do have an important question." He looked sternly at Amis and Wilhelm before turning to Moira. "Before we get you back to the castle, may I *please* see what's on that damned parchment? I cannot live with two unresolved and disappointing situations in one night." He held Moira's gaze for an extra moment.

"What parchment?" Wilhelm asked.

Moira broke away from Roman's gaze to turn and grab the parchment. She held it up and said, "This parchment. It is currently my most prized possession." She waved it in front of her, teasing Roman.

"This I have got to see!" Amis exclaimed, and Wilhelm nodded.

Wilhelm and Amis stepped further into the room and were now also standing where moments ago Moira and Roman had been about to kiss. She stifled her sense of renewed annoyance at the loss of that moment. She sighed and looked at Roman, who had such an impossibly eager

208

look on his face that she realized she couldn't leave without showing him the wanted poster with his face and crimes printed on it.

Without any further fanfare or delay, Moira unfurled the wanted poster that she'd taken from Ivywood Village. She held it up so it faced the three men. From the printed words to the slightly off but still accurate depiction of Roman, they all stared for several seconds before bursting out in renewed laughter.

"Debauchery?!" Wilhelm roared.

"I need more information on the public indecency charge!" Amis nearly shouted, bent over and laughing.

"I think you two are focusing on the wrong things!" Roman scolded, grinning from ear to ear.

He stepped forward and Moira backed up defensively. She pulled the parchment closer to her and gave Roman a warning glare. He held his hands up and stepped back.

"I'm not going to take it, B. I'd never come between you and your most prized possession," he said. Moira relaxed a little. Roman leaned in and said quietly, "How flattering for me, by the way, that your favorite thing happens to be a drawing of my face." He gave her a wink and then turned back to Wilhelm and Amis while pointing at the reward amount. "Did you two miss this? My head happens to be worth not one but *two* tower pounds. That right there is a large fortune, lads!"

Wilhelm rolled his eyes, and Amis clapped. Roman pointed at the sum again and then gave a dramatic bow.

"Surest sign of an outlaw's success, gentlemen. You are in the presence of greatness!"

Moira couldn't help but roll her eyes.

"Only you, Roman Loxley, would find immense pleasure in your own 'wanted' poster. I should have known!"

With a shake of her head, Moira rolled the poster back up and handed it to Roman. He looked at her, clearly confused.

Moira explained, "I can't keep it at the castle. You'll have to keep it safe for me."

Roman grinned and accepted the parchment. "It would be my pleasure!"

"I hate to be the messenger of such a logical statement," said Amis, "but I do think it's past time for us to be on our way back to the castle."

He looked at Moira as if he was just as disappointed to leave as she was. She gave a small pout but nodded and gathered her bag and empty teacup off the floor.

Roman grabbed the cup from her and walked over to set it on the large dining table. Moira pulled her cloak out of the bottom of her bag and slung it over her shoulders. She sighed and let Amis lead her out of the cabin.

As she walked toward the door, she looked over her shoulder and asked Roman, "Pewsey isn't taking us back, is he?"

"You two really do dislike each other, don't you?" Roman asked, sounding somewhat surprised.

"Unexplained loathing passes between us with the ease of a knife through butter!" Moira responded acrimoniously.

He looked a little taken aback, but Roman recovered quickly and said, "Wil and I will be the ones getting you home. I'm honestly not sure where Pewsey is, but I'll be sure and extend your best wishes when I see him next."

"Please don't," Moira responded, following Amis and Wilhelm out of the cabin with Roman close behind.

Moira was relieved Roman did not waste any breath defending Pewsey. They walked rather solemnly toward the horses, saddled and ready. Moira felt her heart sink but knew there was no realistic way she could stay here, so she heaved herself onto the horse and let Wilhelm lead her back to the castle.

Chapter Thirty-Three

As they approached the edge of the forest, Moira had to force herself to keep moving toward the castle. In her opinion, the return ride through the Blackwood went too quick. The group kept up a light flow of chatter between them but also enjoyed several moments of companionable silence. Moira was relaxed and happy with their travel quartet, so she felt the sting of disappointment even stronger once the castle came into view through the trees.

With an audible sigh, Moira dismounted and looked at Amis. He gave her an understanding smile, his own features mirroring Moira's; neither of them was in any particular hurry to return to Ivywood Castle.

"Moira, wait," Roman said, lightly touching her arm as she turned to walk back toward the castle.

Amis was already a little farther ahead, and he paused, waiting for Moira to catch up. She looked at Roman expectantly.

Roman hesitated ever so slightly. He squared his shoulders, as if steeling his resolve and said, "I'll see you at the Archery Tournament in just a few days, alright?"

Moira's eyes widened, and she stepped closer. She forced herself to keep her voice low and said, "What do you mean you'll see me at the Archery Tournament? Have you managed to forget, again, that you're a literal outlaw? Please explain to me how on earth showing up at a very public event is a good idea." Moira's voice shook. She couldn't contain her distress and frustration.

Roman flashed his catastrophically mischievous smile and said, "Did I not tell you? I'll be competing."

She stared, blinked a few times, rubbed her forehead and looked heavenward.

"You'll be competing?" Moira asked, still staring at the sky, beseeching the stars to grant her patience.

"Yes."

"Yes?" She snarled, finally bringing her gaze back to the man standing in front of her.

"In disguise," he added.

Moira shook her head.

"You'll be competing at the Archery Tournament in disguise?" She hoped that her continued questions would inspire Roman to share real details.

He simply nodded in response.

Moira rolled her eyes and let her string of criticism loose.

"Unless this disguise includes a way to entirely change your stature and appearance, I think you'll be discovered mighty quick, outlaw. Did you forget the wanted poster already? They have you pegged, wild hair and all! Not to mention the fact that you're a well-known member of the nobility, outside of your more infamous persona. But yes, let's blunder forward and flash your archery skills for all of Anglia to see."

Moira's chest heaved as she worked to get her temper back under control. Try as she might, she couldn't imagine any disguise that would adequately change Roman's appearance enough to avoid detection. She shook her head again, at a loss.

"Don't worry, B. It's going to work out," he said comfortingly as he reached out and touched her in that spot where her neck and shoulder met. He caressed her throat with his thumb while holding her gaze. Roman removed his hand and got back on his horse.

Moira's breath caught in her throat, and she found herself unable to speak. Roman waved to Amis, nodded to Wilhelm, gave Moira one last reassuring smile, and turned his horse toward the hideout.

With a huff, Moira turned and caught up with Amis. Unable to stop herself, she said, "That hardheaded jackass is going to get himself captured."

Amis laughed but said nothing as they continued to walk back toward the castle and return to their regular lives. Moira couldn't help but feel as though a lot was suddenly left hanging between her and the outlaw.

Chapter Thirty-Four

Moira was enjoying her final morning of freedom with a visit to Ivywood Village. Prince Lyric and his accompanying lords were due to return to Ivywood Castle later that afternoon. She was doing her absolute best to squelch the feeling of dread settling into her gut at the thought of their return. The days without Lord Leofwin had been glorious and opened Moira's eyes to just how sheltered her life in the castle had become. She was tired of walking on eggshells and trying to navigate the complicated nature of the men who currently ruled her life. Something needed to change for her, and soon.

Before coming down to the village, Moira strolled through the library in blissful solitude. She originally went in search of the large text on estates and families that she'd found weeks ago, but Amis failed to return it to the correct shelf. She vowed to herself that she'd talk to him about it later and hopefully locate the book. There was a lot more reading she wanted to do about the royal bloodlines since it turned out there was a lot going on that was connected with nobility. She found several other books of interest in her search and spent the morning perusing *A Treatise on Health.* As she wandered out of the library, she found a text titled *Head Wounds: Stop the Bleeding,* which she honestly couldn't ascertain as satire or not, but she did skim some of the pages.

As Moira wandered down the main road of the village, she saw Meggy walking toward her with the town friar. Fleetingly, Moira considered finding an excuse to avoid the interaction, as she dreaded religious debate. Something, in her limited experience, every town friar seemed to thrive on. It was too late, however, as Meggy had seen her and was waving excitedly. Moira decided she would just have to keep the interaction short, which wouldn't be too difficult as she needed to get back to the castle soon.

"Moira!" Meggy called boisterously. "I am so happy to see you! Can I introduce you to the town friar?"

Meggy gestured to the man next to her, clothed in a deep brown robe. The robe went all the way down to the ground, kissing the gravel and weeds under the friar's feet. Moira looked at the friar and couldn't help but smile as the man beamed at her. She begrudgingly noted he possessed a kind, open face with the most bizarre facial hair she'd ever seen. He had a thick but trimmed beard everywhere except for his chin. She wondered if he shaved his chin or if he just couldn't grow hair there. Whatever the cause, his chin was as naked as the top of his head, which was completely bald. The friar had the pale skin of one who rarely sees the sun and his shoulders were permanently slumped forward.

"I am Friar George Carlton Harold Tucksen, but most people call me Friar Tuck or just Tuck," he said, still looking like the most genial man she'd ever met. "I understand we

216

have a certain friend in common," he whispered while taking a conspiratorial step toward her. He gave her a gentle nudge with his elbow and then stepped back again.

Moira was confused, but only momentarily. Meggy was nodding at her with such vigor that she realized they must be talking about Roman. She raised her eyebrows at Friar Tuck and glanced around as inconspicuously as she could before saying, "Is that right? Perhaps we can go somewhere else to discuss this? I can't say I'm entirely fond of talking about our *friend* out in the open like this, but you've piqued my interest, Friar Tuck."

The friar nodded vigorously.

"Follow me!" Friar Tuck said jovially. He turned around and walked quickly for a man his age; leading them to the town parish, which was down the road from where they stood.

Moira groaned inwardly, knowing her father would have lectured her for visiting a parish of the new religious order when her family never gave up the old religion. She reasoned her father would undoubtedly understand that going into the church to chat was not the same as going into the church to worship...or so she told herself. In all honesty, the family practiced their religion in a very lax manner, so she was a little rusty on what the rules were. Not to mention the important detail of her father's disappearance. The likelihood of him lecturing her about anything was next to nonexistent.

Regardless of this internal debate, Moira followed the friar without question, far too curious to turn down the opportunity to chat. The church was not large. It was made of weathered gray stone with a thatched roof and looked as if it served the town well. There was a small addition of sorts around the back, which the friar explained was his residence. He led Moira and Meggy inside. Moira balked ever so slightly at the harsh interior. The furniture was sparse, and the friar appeared to live in one room, with a small cot in one corner and a table with four plain chairs in the other. There was no decoration or frill in the space. It was austere and simple, absolutely nothing like the castle.

Friar Tuck looked at Moira and nodded as he said, "Do not fret over my living conditions, m'lady. A friar takes a vow of poverty. All is as it should be."

She smiled softly and said, "I did not mean to offend."

He shook his head as he reached out and patted her arm. "No offense taken. It must come as a shock for someone who currently lives within the grandeur of Prince Lyric's court."

Friar Tuck gave her a long look, which she did not understand, but she guessed it was a pointed look meant to make her think differently about the prince and his lifestyle. *Not to worry,* she thought, *that thought process started to change a while ago and not in the prince's favor.*

Meggy appeared to be bursting at the seams and unable to contain herself any longer. She squealed, "It's him, Moira!"

Moira looked at Meggy in confusion. "It's who, Meggy?"

Meggy gestured at Friar Tuck in a spasmodic manner that gave away her excitement and frustration.

"It's *him*! He is the one who gets the coppers and silvers from Roman's gang and gives them to the people of the village. Friar Tuck has been leaving coins for Alaine's family. Her Gran wasn't lying!"

Despite her attempts to keep up her manners while in the presence of the friar, Moira found herself turning to him in shock and saying, "Holy shit!" She cringed and flushed as soon as she said it. Her hand flew to her mouth, and she was about to apologize, but the friar was laughing with merriment.

"'Holy' shit is my favorite kind," he joked, with a booming laugh. "Do not worry about the language, m'lady. I may be a friar, but I've lived in this world long enough to have heard much worse than that!"

"I'll do my best not to worry about my divine expletive if you'll agree to call me Moira."

Friar Tuck managed to smile even broader before nodding his head in agreement. "Moira, lady of sacred swears, I think we shall get along resplendently!"

Meggy clapped her hands and sat down in one of the chairs at the table. Moira and Friar Tuck followed once their laughter abated.

Moira glanced out the window and said, "I do have to return to the castle somewhat soon, I'm afraid. Friar Tuck, do you truly do what Meggy claims?"

"Excuse me. You have no reason to doubt what I've said," Meggy said with a pout.

"How foolish of me to doubt you, Megs. You're right. I'm sorry!" Moira responded with as much sincerity as she could while looking at her pouting young friend.

"What Meggy says is true, as she's just caught me doing it," said Friar Tuck cheerily, as if being caught leaving money from a known outlaw was nothing abnormal.

Meggy nodded zealously, then said, "I sure did! I was taking over a book to leave for Alaine in our secret spot when I spied the friar sneaking out the back door. I hollered at him - sorry about that, friar - and asked what exactly he was doing behaving like a man of dishonest intentions - again, friar, sorry - which he found very amusing, and we had a nice long chat about how he helps people in ways that can't always be known."

A small chuckle escaped Moira at the way Meggy interacted with the friar, but she knew already that there was no upset from the friar over Meggy's words and actions. In fact, it seemed like the friar was quite pleased to have been caught. Moira knew firsthand that it was a lot more fun when one had friends in on the secret with you. Perhaps the friar had been intentional with the timing of his discovery.

Meggy continued, "I told him I knew someone who had a recent chat with Roman Loxley, and then poof, as we walked down the road, there you were!"

Here was where Moira wasn't sure what to do. She had never divulged to Meggy her true involvement with Roman's band of fugitives. There were thoughts shared and allusions made, maybe, but even that wasn't concrete evidence that she knew Roman. All Meggy was basing her assumption on was the chat Moira told her about at the Autumn Ball. Moira wanted to have an open discussion with Friar Tuck, but she stumbled over how much to say in front of Meggy. She was hesitant to put Meggy in any danger by divulging too much.

Friar Tuck looked at Moira with an air of understanding and said, "If you have the means to help someone without causing any harm to yourself or others, you should do so. That is what our friend believes. It is what I believe. However it is you may know him, I can trust that it is also something you believe."

He gave Moira a wink, and she returned it with a smile and sigh of relief. It looked like Friar Tuck wouldn't be pressing her for details today, which she was immeasurably grateful for.

With another sigh of regret, Moira announced it was truly time for her to go. She gave Meggy a quick hug and turned to Friar Tuck, who stood up when she did.

Moira started, "Thank you, Friar Tuck. I-,"

He interrupted and said, "You may just call me Tuck. Those who truly know me call me Tuck."

Tuck raised his eyebrows as if asking her for acknowledgment. Moira bobbed her head. The old man guided her toward the door, his robes dragging softly on the stone floor.

"No one likes a lingering goodbye, Moira. Come back soon, and we can chat."

Moira couldn't help but laugh and let herself be gently pushed out the door. She started walking quickly back toward the castle. It was chilly, and she didn't want to waste any more time outdoors. As her boots crunched on the gravel of the road, she realized with surprise that she really did want to visit the friar again. He was not at all what she expected.

Chapter Thirty-Five

Prince Lyric along with Lords Maddicot, Leofwin, Godberd, Owen and Dayben all returned as planned. The prince and his escorts arrived first, followed shortly by the others. Moira wondered where they went and what they did, but none of the men acted as if anything out of the usual happened. Although it bothered her to do so, Moira followed their lead and behaved as if Leofwin never left.

The day of the Archery Tournament arrived. Ivywood Village and castle were close to bursting with fanfare and frivolity. Meanwhile, Moira was certain she had never felt so anxious in her entire life. There was so much depending on this annual event and without any intimate details of the outlaw's plan, Moira was a tangle of nerves. Any time she thought of Roman competing in disguise, she immediately broke out in an anxious sweat. She didn't know what the disguise would be, but she still had a hard time imagining such a large and distinctive man blending in and not standing out.

"What's got your head in the clouds this morning?" Hanna asked with concern as Moira sat in her chaise.

Moira held her book but hadn't been actively reading for several minutes now.

"My mind has run away with me, Han. Just sitting here and imagining the competition, I guess."

Moira hoped she sounded at least half convincing since it wasn't an outright lie. She was unwilling to discuss just how anxious she felt.

"Wishing you could compete yourself?" Hanna asked.

"What?" Moira asked distractedly, half her mind still lost in her worries. "Oh yes. Yes, of course."

In truth, Moira had not really thought about competing. Although she was an ace shot, there was too much on her mind lately. Ladies of the court were not invited to participate.

"I do wish I could compete," Moira clarified. "I think a couple of the lords around here could benefit from a lady knocking them down a peg or two."

She'd love to see the faces of Prince Lyric, Lord Maddicot, and Lord Leofwin when they saw what a decent marksman she was.

"Things are always changing around here, girl. Maybe next year you can join and whoop them all!" Hanna said with a comforting pat on Moira's arm as she walked toward the door. Before she walked out of the room, she turned to Moira and said, "It's perfectly acceptable to worry about a certain fugitive of the law who may or may not have a reckless plan for today's tournament." Hanna gave Moira one last meaningful look before she walked out and shut the door behind her.

"Ugh!" Moira said to no one but herself.

She tossed her book aside and threw her head back onto the cushion behind her. *Damn Hanna's constant intuition and attention to detail,* she thought before picking her book back up and attempting to read.

Chapter Thirty-Six

Despite her efforts, Moira never got back into her book. Eventually, she gave up and meandered down to the archery pitch. It was normally a large, empty field adjacent to the castle gardens; however, in preparation for the big event, it was transformed into the competition arena.

Moira sat in the King's box - well, currently the *prince's* box - trying not to wring her hands while scanning the crowd. She was shocked by how many people were already milling about. Thankfully the prince's box was raised off the ground, giving her a good view over the heads of the gathering masses.

The arena was rectangular in shape, with the attendees lined up on either side and the royal box on end, behind where the archers would stand. At the far end of the field were the targets. Purple flags flapped in the gentle breeze, indicating where the field was for anyone who was unfamiliar with the grounds.

A man's hand covered hers, stilling them. Moira looked up and saw Leofwin. She managed to suppress the groan that threatened to leave her throat at the sight of him. Leofwin gave her a smile and a pat on her hands before removing his.

"No need to be nervous. I shall win this competition, and we may celebrate my victory this evening," Lord Leofwin stated, puffing out his chest as he tended to do when speaking importantly of himself. It was the first time he'd spoken to her since returning from his trip.

Moira did not have the open malice within her to tell Leofwin that she expected him to come in dead last. She witnessed him practicing on accident once and noticed his skills were merely passable. It was a surprise to know he was competing at all. Moira chose to stay silent, as there was absolutely nothing nice she could say in a convincing manner.

Prince Lyric arrived in the box and abruptly banished Lord Leofwin to the competitor's tent. This worked nicely for Moira, who realized Leofwin was staring at her, most likely awaiting an encouraging response that she did not have to give.

"Excited, my dear?" Prince Lyric asked her, leaning toward her from his large throne-like seat.

What is it with the endearing nicknames? Moira wondered to herself. She still stifled rage every time Leofwin called her "pet," and now here came Lyric with "dear." The oddest part was that Prince Lyric was Leofwin's age or maybe a couple of years older. He was no old man, so the endearment was extra strange. Although now that she was thinking about it, Leofwin had not used his nickname for her since before the incident…

Shoving aside her distracted train of thought, Moira said, "Yes, quite excited, your Highness. I am an avid archer myself, or at least I was back home."

As she spoke, Moira could tell Prince Lyric looked at her without listening. His eyes grew unfocused, and his head tilted ever so slightly, as if his mind was somewhere else. She tamped down her irritation and kept her answer short. The sooner Lyric moved on from their conversation, the sooner she could return to her search for Roman.

"How lovely," Prince Lyric said half-heartedly while already starting to turn toward someone on his other side.

A petite woman with long, voluminous, and tightly curled black hair arrived and sat next to Moira. Try as she might, Moira couldn't place who the woman was. If they stood next to each other, Moira guessed that the woman wouldn't even reach her shoulders. The stranger appeared to be in a dress that was not her own, as it dragged on the ground as she walked. Moira was certain she had never seen her before, and she tried not to stare. Instead, she smiled politely but did not engage in conversation. There were honestly too many women in and out of the court for Moira to keep track of them all, and she assumed the woman felt the same about her.

A trumpet played and a court crier announced the competition was due to begin shortly. Moira listened as the man explained the competition, even though she'd heard the rules countless times before. He explained that each archer was given the same type of bow and the same arrows in order to keep the competition as fair as possible. There would be two rounds of competition, with archers shooting at the butts (mounds of earth covered with turf first, then covered again with a rough canvas-like cloth that had the bullseye painted on). Round one would have the butts placed twenty yards away. Round two would have the butts placed thirty-two yards away. Each round would include two shots per archer.

Moira turned and noticed Prince Lyric was no longer seated on his throne. She felt an irresistible urge to figure out where he'd gone, so she excused herself and left the box.

Finding him was easier than expected, as he stopped just outside the box entrance and was having another heated conversation with Lord Maddicot. Moira stopped at the bottom step of the platform and listened. The prince's back was to Moira, and Maddicot was so engrossed in the prince's words that he failed to notice her.

"He will be here, Maddicot. Undoubtedly in some masquerade, but he will be here, and he will be the best," Prince Lyric snarled and started to turn back to the entrance of the box. When he saw Moira, she quickly started moving again, trying to appear as though she had not been listening.

The prince said, "Ah, the maid Moira! I assume you've come to let me know the games are due to begin any moment. Do excuse us, dear. We are just discussing the rascal outlaw. Not to worry, the competition will not be interrupted! Return to your seat."

Moira kept her courtier's smile plastered on her face. She realized Prince Lyric was forcibly ushering her back to her seat, but she couldn't manage to form a coherent word. She allowed him to push her back to her seat next to the mysterious woman.

Once she was seated, Moira let her mind run free. They were going to capture Roman. They knew he was here. Moira's palms began to sweat, and she was frantically scanning the crowd again, searching for any sign of Roman. Every so often a bearded man would snag her gaze, but after closer examination it was never who she was so desperately searching for. She knew she had to warn him. Although she didn't know the plan, she knew that getting caught could not possibly be a key component.

"What happened?" asked the petite woman next to her. She was leaned over very close to Moira and whispered in her ear.

Moira jumped a little.

"Pardon me?" Moira asked, astonished this stranger realized something was wrong.

The woman looked at Moira in annoyance.

"What happened when you followed the prince?"

Moira stared dumbly at the woman, increasingly concerned about how attentive she'd been.

With an exaggerated huff of annoyance, the woman explained, "I'm Bobby. Roman sent me to stay with you in case something goes wrong. Naturally, he didn't tell you this plan, the knave. Tell me what happened, Moira."

The woman who claimed to be Bobby, a member of Roman's band of outlaws, was looking at her expectantly. Bobby clearly expected Moira to trust her instantaneously.

No matter what the woman expected, Moira was completely bewildered. Roman talked about Bobby but not once did he mention Bobby is a *woman*. Moira did not have the brain capacity for this right now.

"It's short for Roberta," the woman expounded. "Gods above, stop focusing on the wrong thing. I'm sorry my arrival has come as such a shock, but I assure you we can spiral endlessly about me being a woman if we all survive this. Now tell me what happened."

Moira blinked a few times and took a breath. She was somewhat relieved Bobby was so direct; a quality Moira desperately needed right now.

Moira said, "Right, sorry. Just a lot to take in." She looked directly at Bobby and said, "I'll be pissed at Roman later if we can figure out how to save his sorry ass."

As much as she hated to keep focusing on the wrong thing, it would have been nice to get to know Bobby before she was in a compromising situation.

"Prince Lyric knows Roman is here. He doesn't know where or who he is pretending to be, but he knows. The prince plans to capture him." She spoke softly but swiftly.

"Well, that's not ideal. We need a plan. Immediately."

Bobby gripped Moira's arm, which she did not particularly love, but she wasn't sure how to break free without being rude to the person who may or may not be able to help her. They were still barely speaking above a whisper.

"Not ideal, for sure," Moira said. She paused a moment and voiced the first thought that came to her mind, "I must enter the tournament. I need to compete. I need to in order to get into the competitors' tent."

There was very little thought behind this plan. Once Moira got to the competitor's tent, she had no idea what to do. She figured it would all unfold once she got there.

"Yes!" Bobby said, surprising Moira with her immediate agreement. She expected some sort of argument to unfold.

"Yes, that's brilliant. The utter distraction and failure of you competing will offer the perfect diversion!" Bobby nearly clapped, then caught herself and put her hands in her lap.

Moira went from being concerned about her plan and worrying over Roman to being completely annoyed with Bobby.

"Sorry to disappoint you, Bobby, but I'm an experienced archer. I'm hoping the fact that I'm a woman competing and *winning* will be the diversion we need." She glared a little at Bobby, unable to stop herself. "What will you do?" She asked. She tried not to sound accusatory, but she couldn't help but wonder what this tiny woman could accomplish. There was zero discussion of her skills or abilities when Roman and Wilhelm talked about her. Moira sincerely hoped that Bobby's plan would include tailing her all day.

"I'm staying here. Someone needs to keep an eye and ear on the royal usurper," Bobby responded with a somewhat chilling grin.

Moira wasn't sure yet if she wanted to like Bobby, but in this moment, she was forced to at least trust her. She pulled herself together, stood up, and once again excused herself from the box, noting that Prince Lyric was engrossed in a whispered conversation with one of his guards.

As quickly as she could without drawing attention, Moira walked to the competitor's tent. She noticed fewer people were milling about, and she assumed they were all getting settled in to watch the tournament.

Moira strolled straight through the opening of the tent and came to a dead stop. All the men waiting to compete were staring at her, including Amis, Lord Leofwin, Lord Maddicot, Lord Dayben, and one other man who looked vaguely familiar. The rest of the competitors were unknown to her. She held no one's gaze but looked around for someone in charge.

A rather small man with a stack of parchment came up to her and asked, "May I help you, miss? My name is Rolf, and I'm in charge of the Archery Tournament."

"I wish to compete. In fact, I demand it. I will require a bow and arrows. Thank you," Moira stated authoritatively.

Moira clasped her hands and felt that she managed to speak in her best impression of Prince Lyric - full of confidence and the expectation that her demands would be met.

The man named Rolf sputtered and said, "Well, miss. That's unheard of, I'm afraid. There is no precedent for a lady to compete...," he trailed off rather suddenly as Moira glared at him with her arms crossed over her chest. She was making sure to use her height to her full advantage and was looking down her nose at Rolf.

Lord Leofwin, the oaf that he was, chose to interject, "Now, Lady Moira. Let's not make a stunt out of the tournament. I shall teach you to use a wee bow and arrow another day. No need to interfere with a man's competition!" He chuckled and looked around for support.

Moira glanced at Amis, sending him a desperate look. He must know she wasn't throwing herself into the competition for no reason.

Amis spoke up, stating loudly, "I can vouch for her! Moira is my sister and is a skilled archer. I say we let her compete!"

There was no response from Rolf or the other competitors. Amis grabbed Leofwin and motioned to Rolf, who walked over and started to argue with both men. Maddicot walked over to listen but seemed to keep half his attention on the other competitors.

Moira used the opportunity to take a closer look at the man standing off to the side on his own, the one who seemed obscurely familiar to her. He was a large man, maybe an inch or two taller than her, and had closely cropped hair, a clean-shaven face, and a rather rotund stomach. Moira noticed his stomach looked a bit odd compared to the rest of the man, which appeared muscular and sturdy. Not at all in tune with his gut. She continued surveying the man. Her gaze traveled up to his face when she couldn't help but notice his eyes, which were dancing in barely contained amusement. She nearly flinched. *Roman?* He gave her the smallest of nods and looked away, confirming it was him. She admitted the hair alone was a hugely successful disguise, but the clean-shaven face really made Roman look unrecognizable. She stared at him, questioning who she saw, and knew the court would have a hard time connecting this well-kept lord to the scruffy, disheveled outlaw that he had become. The wanted poster she found was no longer remotely accurate to his current appearance.

Moira gathered her thoughts, looked away from Roman, and approached the still-arguing group of men.

She demanded, "A bow and arrows if you please. Or shall I borrow someone else's when my turn arrives? I do not need my brother to get me in, nor do I need my betrothed to grant me approval. I shall compete."

Moira reminded herself she was here to turn all attention to her and remove any potential spotlight from Roman. Prince Lyric was banking on Roman being the best archer here. She needed to win, and she needed to do it in a grand, possibly obnoxious manner. If she couldn't win, she still needed to keep all possible attention on her.

Amis clapped Rolf on the shoulder and led him over to a corner of the tent. She told herself she needed to thank him later for blindly following her lead in this sudden change of plans. Amis grabbed Moira a bow and arrows from a pile of equipment and supplies.

"Good man!" Amis cheered as Rolf did nothing to challenge him.

Moira noticed Rolf scurry out of the tent, undoubtedly to tell Prince Lyric of the latest development in the competition. Moira fervently hoped the prince would be too curious to force her out of the competition.

Amis gave Moira a squeeze on her shoulder and went back to speaking with several of the other lords, dragging Lord Leofwin, who still looked flabbergasted, with him. As casually as she could manage, Moira walked over to the freshly cut and shaved Roman to whisper, "They're onto you. Leave the competition. Let me win."

Roman studied her, a look of surprise flashing on his face before he glanced away. Moira could tell he was deep in thought.

He looked at her again and said, "Is that why you're here and insisting you be allowed to compete?"

She held his gaze. "Yes, you witless criminal. Prince Lyric is certain you will take the victory by a landslide, which is how they will identify you, and then they plan to capture you." She could barely keep her voice to a whisper. Why was he not turning and running back to the Blackwood hideout right this second? Did he not understand?

Roman smiled at her, his head tilted endearingly.

"You are worried about me."

Moira seethed.

Before she could speak, he leaned down and said quietly, "I have one thing to say to you, my dear, concerned Beastie."

"And what is that?" She said through gritted teeth.

Moira noticed that the other competitors were starting to leave the tent.

"Let's see what you've got." He gave her a wicked wink and followed the rest of the men out of the tent and into the arena.

Chapter Thirty-Seven

Moira stood frozen in astonishment and frustration. Did Roman just taunt her? What on earth was she doing risking her neck for this brainless outlaw when he wasn't even going to take advantage of the distraction she created?

Rolf popped his head back into the tent and asked, "Coming, my Lady? You were quite insistent a moment ago, but if you've changed your mind, it isn't too late." The poor man sounded like his dearest wish was for her to withdraw.

Moira refocused, took a breath, and told Rolf, to his visible horror, that she was still going to compete. She walked confidently out of the tent, the flap held open by Rolf and entered the archery arena. The other competitors were lined up to the side. She saw Lord Leofwin, Lord Maddicot, Amis, and Roman. Many of the other competitors traveled from other villages to be here, and the majority were strangers to her. This was a mild comfort, as she felt she was about to cause significant embarrassment, so it was nice most people didn't know her.

As she looked around, Moira became acutely aware of the silence permeating the arena. The audience surrounded them on two sides since the archery arena was a long rectangle. She hoped the lull was due to the shock of a female competitor and nothing more significant. That was the plan, after all. She gazed in Bobby's direction and got a slight nod of approval. Moira was careful not to look at Prince Lyric.

She remained hopeful her distraction would work, even if Roman refused to cooperate.

Since the competition was broken out into groups of three, the competitors who were not actively competing were sent to stand off to the side as men were called up to shoot. After every three men fired, the marks were recorded, the second shot was made, then the arrows were removed, and the canvas bullseyes were replaced before the next trio of competitors was drawn forward. Moira counted and realized there were sixteen archers competing. She cringed, realizing she would quite possibly have to go up and shoot on her own since she had thrown off the evenness of the original fifteen. She stood a little taller, rolling her shoulders a couple of times. She had not shot since the day she and Amis spent in the forest, but she'd have to pull it together quickly. There was absolutely no time to warm up or practice.

Rolf was suddenly in front of her, motioning for her to go up to the shooting line. Moira went up with Lord Maddicot and the barely disguised Roman. Moira looked to Amis for support, and he gave her a big grin and one solitary clap in encouragement. She returned the smile, took another deep breath, and walked up to the designated area.

On the short walk to the shooting line, Moira told herself she was not allowed to spiral into panic. Roman may not take this seriously, but she would. No matter how long it had been since she last practiced, she'd been shooting a bow and arrow most of her life. She could do this.

Maddicot shot first, and Moira nearly scoffed at his inadequacy. He barely hit the target at all and quickly stepped back after shooting, as if he did not care how he'd done at all. This behavior made Moira wonder if Maddicot had his own ulterior motive. Was he intentionally shooting poorly? Moira assumed most of the competitors were strangers to Prince Lyric and Lord Maddicot just as much as they were to her. After a year in the court, Moira noticed that the prince preferred to keep himself sequestered with a collection of similar faces; however, the outer circles of the court seemed to have a constant flux. Lesser favored lords seemed to always change who they brought to court, allowing their decisions to be based purely on who would return the favor most substantially. Prince Lyric kept his usual group of lords close, and everyone else stayed at arm's length. It was no wonder Roman's questionable disguise was working - they did not actually *know* him. Other than the wanted posters she'd seen around the village, Roman had gone unknown to the prince and his lords for several years now.

After some polite scattered applause from the audience after Maddicot's second shot, it was Moira's turn. Her thoughts distracted her from seeing how Maddicot fared with his second round. The scattered, quiet clapping from the audience made her think his second shot went just as well as his first.

Moira stepped forward a little and adjusted her stance, with her left foot in front and her right in back; her toe pointed slightly outward. With a flutter of annoyance, she brushed aside her nerves. She nocked her first arrow and raised the bow. One deep breath. Two. With her second breath, Moira shut out all other sights, sounds and distractions. This was one of her favorite things to do and she let that happiness wash out her anxiety. It was easier to block everything out than she thought it would be.

Moira pulled back on her bowstring and was immediately annoyed to realize her dress did not allow her the range of motion she needed. She froze briefly, her arm stuck mid-draw, unsure how to proceed if she couldn't pull her arm back all the way. There was only one thing she could think to do. Moira took another breath and then gave one heaving pull with all her might. She pulled the bowstring back and heard a loud rip down the right side of her dress. Relief washed over her now that she now had the bow fully drawn. A familiar strain in her shoulders, chest and back took over her senses as she held the bow drawn, not yet ready to fire. Hanna would be annoyed with her over the ripped dress, but Moira knew she would understand.

Although Moira heard some initial tittering from the crowd as her dress audibly ripped down one side, they were all silent once again as she prepared to take her first shot. With one last breath, Moira took aim and let the arrow fly.

Moira didn't want to watch, but she knew she had to. Her arrow sliced through the air with the precision she trained for. It landed nearly dead center on the bullseye. Moira let out an enthusiastic *whoop*, unable to hide her excitement. The crowd erupted into a shocked outpouring of support, starting with several gasps of surprise and quickly followed by clapping and cheering. Moira smiled and waved. She waved her right arm -the side where her dress ripped, but attempted to hold the fabric together with her left hand. This proved difficult as she still held her bow, but she did her best.

Without any more fanfare, Moira nocked her second arrow and pulled the bow back with ease. Her muscles ripped with anticipation. Fueled by the confidence of her first shot's success, she took a single breath before aiming and firing her second. The arrow flew just as straight and true, hitting the target dead center of the bullseye. Unable to contain her excitement, Moira leapt into the air and let out a second *whoop* of excitement. The crowd cheered even louder than her first shot, and she waved again, this time not caring how much the side of her dress gaped open.

Rolf stepped forward, a look of pleasant surprise on his face, and motioned for her to step back and stand next to Maddicot. With one last smile to the crowds, Moira stepped back where Rolf indicated she should stand. Moira gave

Roman a rather cocky, taunting smile, but she suppressed the urge to stick out her tongue. If he wasn't going to get out as he should, she would have to soundly kick his ass.

"I see your brother was not lying," Lord Maddicot said, leaning toward her.

Moira was still beaming and settling into the fact that she belonged in the competition, distraction or no. She did her best to pretend that it did not bother her to have any kind of praise or attention from Lord Maddicot.

She held her ground and kept her gaze forward as she said, "Amis does not lie. He and our father taught me well. I've always been an excellent shot."

Lord Maddicot huffed. "I see no one taught you any humility." He lowered his voice even more as he got closer to her. "It's too bad we'll still capture the fiendish criminal Roman Loxley, despite your best efforts at a diversion, m'lady."

Moira froze. She gulped audibly and clenched her jaw. Her ears began to buzz, and she missed Roman's shot as she turned to look up at Maddicot's face. "Excuse me, m'lord?" She maintained her stare, forcing a look of innocence. and continued, "I'm not sure what you're talking about." She feigned confusion as best she could, but she knew Maddicot realized she was eavesdropping on them earlier, after all.

"I haven't figured you out yet, *Maid Moira*, but rest assured I will. For now, I'll keep your possible betrayal to

244

myself. I do love a challenge," he said sycophantically. He gave her a truly maniacal grin and held her stare.

Moira knew this was a situation where saying nothing did her more service than responding. So, she stayed silent, but held her innocently confused expression while she kept her gaze on the threatening lord.

Maddicot merely held his smile and turned away from her, walking back down the slight slope to the waiting area for the competitors. Thanks to their interaction, she missed both of Roman's shots. Their trio was done with round one, and it was time to allow the next three up. Moira glanced around, wondering if anyone overheard what Maddicot said to her. Thankfully, they were not the center of attention. As she started walking back down the slope, she wondered how Roman had done. The crowd was boisterous, so she assumed he shot well.

Amis was up next. Moira noticed Roman was talking animatedly with one of the men she didn't know. *Damn him*, she thought. She needed to let him know what Maddicot said to her. Roman needed to leave the competition now or he would be captured.

Chapter Thirty-Eight

Moira stood with the other competitors, clutching the side of her dress together and feeling less and less like a successful diversion. Although she shot well, Amis and several other men also hit direct bullseyes in round one. The second round was about to begin, and the points were even higher due to the longer distance, but she was awash in doubt that she would be able to win the competition.

In all honesty, after her chat with Maddicot, she was entirely unable to focus on the competition at all. She couldn't take her eyes off Maddicot. He said he wouldn't tell anyone about her involvement with Roman, but she didn't trust him. His threat about Roman rang in her ears and she couldn't help imagining Maddicot detaining Roman as soon as he stepped up for round two of the competition. As the prince's closest companion, Moira didn't believe Maddicot would just keep this development to himself. Moira broke out in an anxious sweat, and she could feel her heart pounding in her chest. A wave of crushing inadequacy washed over her as she realized she had no idea what she should do.

"Where's your confidence gone, B?" Roman whispered coyly from behind her.

Roman caught her by surprise, and she strained to stop herself from whipping around. She looked casually over to Amis, chatting with Leofwin - who was willfully ignoring her. After noting that no one in particular, was watching her, Moira turned around and said vehemently, "I'm suddenly wondering why I entered the tournament in the first place." She spoke barely above a whisper but knew Roman could hear her.

Roman's brow furrowed as he looked at her. "What do you me-?"

Before Roman could finish his thought, dozens of the prince's guards stormed into the arena. Moira stared, mouth gaping, unsure of what changed to cause the sudden arrival of so many sentries. The crowd erupted into angry shouts of disappointment - the second half of the tournament had barely begun before the interruption. Moira looked around frantically, registering in the back of her mind that Roman touched the small of her back quickly before stepping away from her. She closed her eyes, then opened them again and looked for Amis. He was walking toward her with a wild look of confusion. She stayed planted where she was. The guards continued to line up on the field, parallel to and in front of the archery targets. It looked as if no one would be finishing the competition.

Chapter Thirty-Nine

Prince Lyric stepped dramatically onto the field. He walked to the center and spoke loudly and clearly, declaring, "I apologize for the interruption; however, it appears we have a traitorous outlaw in our midst." He paused for effect, looking at the competitors who had been pushed and shoved up to the field and were all standing in line. There were gasps of surprise from the crowd, who all quieted down to hear the prince speak. "One of these men is Roman Loxley," the prince announced while gesturing grandly at the line of competitors. More gasps rang from the crowd, including a few melodramatic screams.

It took all of Moira's self-control not to look right at Roman, who stood just a few feet to her right. Amis and one other man were in between them. She kept her gaze on the prince and did her best to look shocked and upset, as she knew she should. Amis gave her an almost imperceptible shake of his head while side-eyeing her. She gave the smallest bob of her head possible, trying to reassure him that she wouldn't do anything. Moira snuck a quick peak at the prince's seating box and noticed Bobby was gone. She sent up a prayer to the old Gods and the new ones that the mysterious woman had run to get help.

The prince started to pace, a few steps one way, a few steps back, while glaring at the archers lined up in front of him. The intimidating lineup of guards stood behind him, waiting for their orders. Prince Lyric stopped, looked at each of the lords in the lineup, and gave them each a nod. Every single one gave him a slight bow in response and walked out of the competition area. On his way, Lord Leofwin grabbed Moira roughly by the arm and jerked his head at Amis, indicating he, too, should leave the field. Moira felt a fresh wave of annoyance at Leofwin, knowing he bruised her again with his harsh grip. The last marks had finally disappeared just days ago. He held her left arm in an unyielding grip and pulled her while Moira held her bodice together and tried to keep up.

When they reached the edge of the arena, they stopped just in front of the crowds, who were still watching with rapt attention. Leofwin let go of her with a slight shove. Moira rubbed her arm tenderly, and Leofwin gave her a sneer before focusing again on the prince. Amis, following behind Leofwin's hasty retreat from the field, walked over to stand next to her. He draped his cloak gently around her shoulders. Moira didn't notice where he grabbed the cloak from, but she was grateful. Holding her bodice together was getting annoying and she sensed she would need the use of both arms soon. Moira stepped away from Leofwin as much as possible while still watching what was unfolding.

Now that she was off to the side and no longer under the direct scrutiny of Prince Lyric, Moira dared to look at Roman. The outlaw looked at the prince as though he was

249

bored. Moira watched him, incredulous. She wanted to give Roman a swift kick in the shin and tell him to act right, which in this case meant to *act like the scared subject of an unstable ruler,* not like someone who was disgruntled at the interruption of his impending victory. Even though the disguise was minimal and almost lazy, Moira realized amidst her panic, she had still been foolishly hopeful things would work out in Roman's favor.

Prince Lyric gave a final cursory glance at the remaining eleven men and then turned to command, "Bring him out."

Moira couldn't tell who the prince spoke to, but she knew things were about to get even worse.

The prince shouted, "For those of you who are not Roman Loxley, rest assured no harm shall come to you." He paused, and Moira watched several of the men on the field literally deflate before her eyes. Clearly, there was uncertainty about what would happen to everyone, even those truly innocent men who had just come for the tournament. "It seems the outlaw had someone in his camp who could not be fully trusted. Especially when caught sneaking into *my* castle and attempting to steal something from *my* trophy room," Lyric sneered with palpable, malicious excitement.

Amis inhaled sharply, and Moira closed her eyes. She reached out to Amis for support and held onto his arm as though her life depended on it. He placed his own hand over

250

hers and gave her a tight squeeze. Moira felt grounded by Amis's touch, but her heart continued to beat ferociously and the knot of anxiety in her stomach grew. The crowd remained eerily silent. Moira could barely hear anything over the sound of her own raging heartbeat and erratic breathing. She took one deep inhale and, as she exhaled, said, "fuck!" in the quietest whisper she could manage. Amis's mouth twitched ever so slightly, and he gave her another squeeze. She was at a loss for what else she could say. Her favorite expletive seemed all-inclusive at this moment.

Moira looked at Roman again. For the first time since she met him, she thought he looked nervous. He hid it well, she reasoned. His anxiety on display, no matter how subtly, sent her nerves back into overdrive. Moira's mouth went dry, and she realized her plan to cause a successful distraction had failed. No matter what she did, as soon as Roman refused to leave the competition, this was always going to be his fate. She wracked her mind for something, *anything*, that she could do to take away the danger Roman faced.

"Ah, here is my new friend now!" Prince Lyric said with a sneer as he held his arm out toward none other than Pewsey.

The sniveling, grubby, weak man was being led out in shackles. Moira noted Pewsey didn't struggle at all. His hands and feet were bound in chains, but he walked well enough with small, careful steps. He did not look up as he walked out but kept his gaze on the ground in front of him. The crowd remained silent, and Moira could hear the *clink, clink, clink* of the heavy chains as Pewsey slowly walked across the field. For the first time since she'd met him, Moira had more than enough reason to hate this man with every fiber of her being. The prince reached out and took the lead chain from the guard who escorted Pewsey across the field. Prince Lyric gave an unfriendly tug, which caused Pewsey to stumble forward on his last few steps. He fell to his knees, and the prince laughed.

Roman's face turned to stone. Moira had not seen his initial reaction to Pewsey's appearance, but now he looked as though he held no emotion within him. There was nothing but cold, hard hatred seeping from his being. Roman's eyes were slightly narrowed, but the rest of his features remained stiffly neutral. The only tell of his most certainly roiling emotions was his tightly clenched jaw, which Moira caught flexing twice as she looked at him.

"This unfortunate creature is Marcus Pewsey. Lord Owen caught him in my trophy room mere moments after the tournament began, snooping about where he doesn't belong." The prince gave Pewsey a swift kick to the ribs, forcing him to fall to his side. The chains clinked again as Pewsey moved, rolling slightly and attempting to catch his breath. Moira was surprised Pewsey didn't shout or groan.

The violence made Moira flinch, and Amis put his arm around her, pulling her into his side. She never liked Pewsey, but she suddenly felt ill over what she expected might happen to him next. Despite her hatred of the man, she never wished to be part of the spectacle of watching him suffer.

"I have decided to forgive this sniveling creature because he gave me what I've been after for quite some time. He has given me Roman Loxley," Prince Lyric said as he drew his sword and pointed it right at Roman. The prince looked back down at Pewsey and said, "Unfortunately, my forgiveness does come with an additional price. Politics and reputation come first, I'm afraid," Prince Lyric smugly explained.

Lyric shrugged and plunged his sword into Pewsey's stomach.

A guttural, wet sound escaped Pewsey's lips as a look of confused outrage crossed his face. Moira nearly screamed but put her hands up and covered her mouth as Amis reached up to tuck her head into his shoulder. His arm wrapped tighter around her as he pulled her in close. She let him comfort her for just a moment before she pulled away, unable to hide from whatever horror was about to happen next. Pewsey lay on his side, still awkwardly bound by the chains as blood gushed out of his stomach and flowed from the corner of his mouth.

"It will not be quick, the poor bastard," Amis said quietly to her.

Meanwhile, Prince Lyric started to walk slowly toward Roman. He drug his bloodied blade behind him.

"Everyone get out of the way, dammit!" The prince shouted madly, raising and waving his sword at the men still lined up next to Roman. One man to Roman's right gave him a pitying glance before turning and running toward the exit. Roman held Prince Lyric's stare unflinchingly, even as everyone around him fled.

Moira glanced wildly around, searching for Wilhelm or Bobby, but saw neither of them in the crowd. She realized with a jolt that she wasn't even sure if Wil had been present for the tournament. If Pewsey was caught inside the castle, perhaps that's where Wil was, too. Never mind Bobby, who would likely be unable to offer much aid. Moira's mind raced as she remained frozen and unable to act.

"Your days of stealing from me are over," Prince Lyric seethed at Roman as he came to a stop a few feet away from the outlaw.

Moira heard Amis's breath hitch again as they both stared in petrified silence at Roman and Prince Lyric. They stood mere feet away from each other. Roman's hands were tucked neatly behind his back, that fake gut still sticking out in front of him. The prince kept adjusting his grip on his sword. He had a manic look in his eyes, and Moira could sense the intensity roiling off his body as he prepared for whatever was about to come next.

To her total surprise, Roman smirked at the prince before saying, "I doubt it."

Prince Lyric tilted his head back and let loose a disturbing howl, his shoulders went back, and his torso arched backward as he screamed. With heavy breathing and a clear tension to his demeanor, the prince straightened and stood there panting. He glared at Roman for several beats but said nothing. Roman maintained his look of curious indifference, with one eyebrow raised at the bizarre behavior, as the prince began circling him, dragging the tip of his sword on the ground. The sound of the sword dragging through the dirt and grass put Moira even more on edge, almost as if it was counting down the seconds until it was buried in Roman.

As Moira watched, she heard Pewsey take one last loud, wet breath before going silent. His body slumped into the grass, the chains clinking one more time with the final moment. It seemed like no one else took notice of his death – not when a much more exciting interaction unfolded at the other end of the field. Several tears ran down Moira's face before she realized she was crying. She used the edge of Amis's cloak to dry her face discreetly, not wanting to draw attention to herself. The entire arena remained engrossed in the scene before them. Prince Lyric and Roman continued their stare-down, neither of them speaking. Moira wondered if anyone had left to ensure their safety or if everyone was simply too entranced to leave.

After several uneasy minutes passed, Prince Lyric abruptly stepped closer to Roman, causing several people in the crowd behind Moira to gasp. Lyric slowly brought up his sword and held the tip to Roman's neck. Moira trembled but remained silent. She knew any intervention on her part would only make things worse, and yet she continued to try and come up with a plan to make it all stop. Her mind, despite her efforts to get the wheels spinning and ideas flowing, remained painfully blank. Amis still had his arm around her, but he seemed to be struggling with his own self-control. Moira's mind wandered again to Wil and Bobby, but she couldn't bear to look away from Roman.

Prince Lyric now stood inches away from Roman's face. Moira saw his lips moving, but whatever he said was indiscernible to her and those around her. She heard someone behind her say quietly, "What's happening? What did he say?" The woman was promptly shushed and didn't speak again. Whatever the prince said, Roman's smirk returned, but he didn't respond. The bloody sword remained pressed ominously against his neck.

Moira glanced at Amis, who returned her look with one of anguish and worry. His face was warped in a way she had never seen before. Amis was typically care-free and frivolous - she realized she preferred him that way. The day was not at all what she expected. She had known that Roman competing came with risks, huge ones even, but this far exceeded her worst expectations. Primarily because even her worst outlook earlier in the day had not included a betrayal from Pewsey and the clear failure of whatever mission had him inside the castle. The double failure hit hard, especially as Pewsey now lay dead and Roman was being threatened with the sword that killed him.

Another wave of tremors ripped through Moira's body from her head down to her toes. She turned away from Pewsey's body to look again at Roman and Lyric, who seemed to be locked in a battle of wills. Moira suddenly found herself wondering what the cause for King Leo would look like without Roman Loxley as their leader. She felt a vice-like grip around her heart at the actual thought of Roman dying and immediately banished that path of thinking. No matter how bad things seemed right now, she refused to entertain a future that did not contain Roman.

Without any warning, Prince Lyric slammed his crowned head into Roman's face. Moira was unable to stop the cry that tore from her throat at the extreme change in behavior. One moment the men were glaring silently at each other. The next, Roman's nose was gushing blood and a large gash appeared just between his eyebrows. Although the blow initially made Roman bend backward at the waist and lift his hands to his face, he did not remain in that awkward position for long. He shook his head slightly and stood straight again with his hands once again clasped firmly behind him. Moira stared at Roman, who managed to appear nonchalant despite the blood now running down his face.

Under her breath, Moira beseeched, "Do something, you ass!"

Prince Lyric turned to the guards behind him and said, "Come, have some fun, men! My only rule: *leave him alive....*" He gave Roman one last vile glare before turning to walk off the field. Almost as an afterthought, Lyric shouted, "If anyone interferes, I'll have their head on a platter before they can say 'Roman Loxley.'"

Lord Maddicot rushed to the prince's side and escorted him back toward the castle. The prince shoved the sword into Maddicot's hands and stomped up the path without looking back once. The guards were slowly walking toward Roman, who remained standing where he was.

"Roman!" Moira shouted as loudly as she could. His head snapped to her, and she desperately yelled, "Don't die!" She realized as soon as she'd said it that what she meant and what she said were quite possibly two different things.

Roman gave her a hasty, mischievous smile and then looked at the guards walking toward him as he drew his bow and arrows from his back. The smile combined with his bloodied face created an intimidating, uncomfortable combination. For whatever reason, the guards were moving toward Roman in some sort of controlled march. This seemed bizarre to Moira and Amis, who looked at each other in confusion. Roman started to fire his arrows at the approaching lines, which spurred them into a less tactical approach. Roman managed to take down five of the guards before they scattered and ran at him. He tossed his bow to the side but kept his arrows. Using two arrows held in his hand to defend himself, he punched his right fist forward and drove the arrows into a guard's throat. He pulled the arrows back out, blood gushing and spurting in their wake, and stepped forward to repeat the maneuver on the next closest man.

Amis started to pull Moira back, attempting to get her to leave. She fought against him, unwilling to abandon Roman, who was still fighting even though the guards were now swarming him.

"Amis, no -," Moira cried, attempting to pull away from his grasp.

Lord Leofwin appeared in front of Moira, blocking both her path and her view of the fight. Frantic, she attempted to look around Leofwin, but he grabbed her chin and forced her to look directly at him. She nearly screamed, but before she could, he said, "This is not for a lady to witness." He looked to Amis and said, "Get her back to the castle. Now. Before I carry her back myself."

"Sorry, Moi," Amis grunted as he lifted her over his shoulder and carried her back toward the castle. Unwilling to injure Amis, Moira put up no fight.

The last thing she saw was Roman thrown to the ground by one massive guard. As he fell, the other guards converged upon him. Moira closed her eyes and let the tears flow, finally accepting that there was nothing she could do.

Chapter Forty

Moira paced the length of her living room, too agitated to sit down with Amis and Hanna. She felt an insuppressible urge to go back down to the archery pitch and find out what happened to Roman. Amis had carried her the entire way to the castle and back up to her rooms, not daring to set her down.

"Have you got anything else to drink up here?" Amis asked, holding up his empty glass to no one in particular.

Hanna scowled at him and said, "You finished off the whiskey we had at an alarming rate, Amis."

"Yes, but what you had left was not nearly enough. Have you already forgotten what we just witnessed?" Amis asked, adding an extra air of melancholy to his tone. "Not to mention the fact that I carried Moira the entire way back to the castle. I'm simply parched!"

Hanna arched her brow and said, "No problem was ever solved with an excess of whiskey, Amis." She paused, then leaned forward in the chaise and said, "We've already got one nightmare on our hands. The last thing we need is another. Riles McDougal once drank too much whiskey, and do you know what happened to him?" She stared at Amis, who clearly struggled to suppress a grin but shook his head in response. Hanna glared and said, "He fell out a window, lost consciousness, and woke up the next morning to find he'd married a statue."

Amis let out a contagious burst of laughter that had even Moira pausing in her fret-fest to laugh along.

"Good Gods, Hanna, that cannot be true!" Amis nearly shouted as Hanna sat on the lounge, still glaring daggers at him.

"It is entirely true, you rascal!" Hanna scolded, then sat back into the cushions behind her with a sound *harumph*.

The laughter successfully brought Moira out of her fog of frustration and worry. She was finally able to sit down at the small dining table near her window, which was a serious improvement from her constant pacing. More time passed than she wanted to admit - time in which anything could have happened to Roman. One thing was for certain, the awful events of earlier opened a maw of raw emotion within Moira, one she had done her best to ignore despite the fun banter and almost-kiss that happened between her and Roman. Now she was forced to admit to herself that she had - entirely by accident and very inconveniently - fallen in love with Roman Loxley. It was an aggravating development that she would have to fully address later if he was proven to have survived the onslaught from the guards.

Amis jumped up from the couch suddenly, pointing at Hanna and saying, "That's it! Hanna, you're a genius!"

Hanna scoffed and said, "Clearly."

Moira rolled her eyes and said, "Care to explain *why* you're making this proclamation?"

"Intoxicated people do the dumbest things!" Amis exclaimed, starting to search through the cabinet in Moira's room where Hanna usually stashed a small supply of liquor. He gave up quickly, though, having already finished off the only bottle of whiskey that had been in the cabinet. "I need to appear intoxicated…," he half mumbled as he turned to look at them again.

With an eyebrow arched, Moira said, "Mission accomplished, Amis. You appear intoxicated at this very moment." She turned to Hanna and asked, "How much was left in that bottle, Han?"

Hanna shrugged and started to speak, but Amis interrupted. "You're not following at all, Moi!"

"What am I supposed to be following exactly?" Moira asked while looking at Amis in exasperation.

"The plan!" Amis exclaimed and then promptly ran out of her room.

Moira looked at Hanna in alarm. "Truly, what was in that bottle?"

"Maybe two fingers of whiskey, not much at all. Even you wouldn't be drunk off what was left," Hanna said with a wave of her hand, dismissing Moira's concerns.

"We really don't have time for whatever he's got -," Moira said as she started to stand up, but she was cut short by Amis's return to her rooms. He barreled back in just as quickly as he'd left, but this time he was brandishing a much fuller bottle of whiskey.

"Had this in my room. I, unlike you lot, like to have emergency stock of the essentials." He popped off the top, took another swig, wiped his mouth, and said, "Now, for my plan, I just need to -." But they never heard the first version of Amis's plan.

At that moment, Wilhelm came tumbling in through Moira's door, practically flinging it off its hinges when he entered and causing Moira to squeal in surprise.

He threw off his hood and said, "I love it when the ladies can't contain their excitement to see me!" Then he gave a dramatic bow, shut and latched the door behind him, and went over to the chaise where Hanna lay. He lifted her feet, sat down, and plopped her feet down in his lap.

Everyone in the room stared at Wilhelm in shock. Moira stood up and walked over to slap him on the shoulder, saying, "Where the hell have you been? We are stuck up here, worried sick about what the hell is happening, and you swish in here like nothing's going on." She was fuming and had to return her manic pacing, much to Amis's visible annoyance.

"No need for further violence, *m'lady*," Wil started, a little too sarcastically for Moira's taste at the current moment. "I come bearing information, thanks very much. I had to 'swish' in here since I'm a little bit banned from this castle, or have you forgotten?"

Moira stopped dead in her tracks and turned to face Wilhelm. Hanna removed her feet from Wil's lap and got up from the chaise. As she stood, she said quietly, "I want no association with you right about now, lad."

With a finger pointed at Wilhelm, Moira snarled, "Despite the fact that you and Roman insist on showing up here constantly, no, I've been rather unable to forget that you're a wanted fugitive. In case you haven't noticed, my entire existence recently has been based entirely on the fact that you're an outcast on a mission." She glared at him, channeling all the built-up apprehension and anguish into her eyes in the hopes she'd get through to him. "I went from reading about adventure - in that chaise, you're sitting on, by the way - to being thrown headfirst into it." She took a breath, releasing the last bit of tension within her, plopped into the spot on the chaise vacated by Hanna, and said quietly, "At least tell me he's alive."

Amis and Hanna were both seated at the small table now, but they leaned forward imperceptibly. Moira sat on the chaise sideways, next to Wilhelm, who craned his neck to look at her. His expression softened from one of self-defense to one of understanding. He nodded slightly before saying, "He's alive, Moi. But he's not in good shape."

The use of her nickname and the almost positive news made Moira's throat constrict. She gave Wil a small nod before looking down at her hands and taking a moment to collect herself. There was a lump forming in her throat and she knew if she spoke now, it would come out as a sob. No one else spoke, but she heard Amis give a sigh of relief, and she heard the chair creak as Hanna settled into it.

"Where is he?" Moira eventually managed to ask, voice cracking.

"He's in the dungeon. Alone, except for one guard down the hall from his cell," Wil responded, his head still turned to look at her.

"Then we get him out," Moira responded decisively.

Wil gave her an answering grin. "I was hoping you'd say that."

Moira returned the smile, albeit a little weakly. Although her initial concern had been addressed, she was momentarily frozen by the weight of the latest development. She looked at Amis and asked, "Any chance your whiskey plan can be revised to work for this new development?"

With a sly grin and arch of his brow, Amis replied, "Hell yeah, it can!"

Chapter Forty-One

The plan lacked finesse, but Moira felt it stood a chance of working since Prince Lyric seemed confident Roman was secure in the dungeons. Or at least incapable of escaping, even if he were to get out of his cell. They were using that assumption to their advantage...or so she hoped. Amis's plan was to douse himself in the whiskey - "without too much waste, of course!" - and appear as though he was absolutely blinkered with drink. With the guard posted at the exterior dungeon entrance fully distracted by Amis' intoxicated antics, Wilhelm would swoop in and "dispose" of him. Moira chose not to get into the details of whatever that meant. During this time, Moira would go down the back steps to the dungeon, located near the kitchens inside the castle, and break into Roman's cell. "Break in" was a generous term, seeing as Wilhelm reported the cell was not locked due to the condition Roman was in when placed inside. Prince Lyric's over-confidence was going to be their best means of escape tonight.

When Moira questioned him, Wil replied, "The Prince is clearly blinded after the successful beating on the archery range." He shrugged and said, "We've benefitted from this sort of behavior before. Lyric feels undefeated, acts foolishly, and pays the price. He never learns."

Amis gave her a shrug, and they ran through the plan one more time before deciding there was nothing else they could do besides act. *Acta non verba,* as Roman told her not so long ago. If everything went right, Amis and Wilhelm would meet back up with Moira and Roman at the edge of the forest, in the usual meeting place. If anything went wrong, Moira was to hide a little deeper into the forest, hopefully with Roman, and wait for Hanna, who would remain in Moira's rooms until dawn and ideally be able to get more information from inside the castle.

Without further delay, Amis gave Moira a quick hug before they all set out for what was quite possibly the most precarious plan they could come up with.

Chapter Forty-Two

Despite all her doubts, Moira made it into the cell almost as easily as Wilhelm predicted. The castle corridors were deserted. Anyone who was awake at this hour was part of the boisterous celebrations happening in the Great Hall. Moira passed the empty kitchen, the warmth of the room briefly called to her as she shivered in the dark hallway. She resisted temptation and continued past the kitchen and around the corner to the dungeon stairs.

While the cell was not locked, there was a bar pushed through to secure the door, which would have been nearly impossible to remove from the inside. Prince Lyric attempted to keep Roman inside but clearly did not expect someone from inside the castle to come down to help him get out. It was obvious the prince's priority lay in celebrating his perceived victory tonight.

Once in the cell, Moira crouched next to Roman's head. He was lying on his side on a stone bench in the corner, unmoving other than the inconsistent rise and fall of his chest. One arm dangled over the side of the bench, and the knuckles on his hand dripped blood onto the dirty stone floor. It was dark and damp, without any windows or airflow. A shiver rushed up Moira's spine as she took in the horrible conditions. There was nothing down here for comfort. Everything was made of stone, wood or metal. Moira trembled and realized it was near freezing, in part thanks to the season inching closer and closer to winter. As quietly as possible, she set down the small lantern she carried and reached out gently to touch his face. Roman startled awake and looked around wildly, his breath coming in loud gasps and gulps.

"Shh, it's ok. It's me," Moira whispered calmly but firmly. She hoped her tone was reassuring without belying her true feelings of dread, concern and fear.

Roman closed his eyes again and winced. He groaned loudly, and Moira tried to hush him without being insensitive. By the looks of him, he had plenty to groan about. He had a gash between his eyebrows from the prince's headbutting him, along with another gash under his left eye; his face and neck were covered with blood, and she could see dark bruises blooming all over him. Both eyes would most likely be black and blue for quite some time. It looked like his right eye might be swollen shut entirely, but in the dim light, Moira couldn't tell. There were multiple rips in his tunic, but she couldn't find any obvious major wounds on his arms. She shivered and wondered what other injuries had been inflicted that she couldn't even see. She hoped his legs were not badly injured since she needed him to walk out of here. There was no way she could carry him. Roman gritted his teeth and pushed himself up, breathing heavily as he moved painfully slow.

"Roman, please be quiet. I know you're hurt, but we can't be heard. Amis and Wil managed to take out the guard who was posted, but his replacement could be due at any moment. I need to get you out of here," Moira hissed urgently and remained crouched, looking up at him slightly now that he was sitting up. He didn't respond, and her worry grew. "Roman?" she asked tentatively.

"A moment, B." His voice was rough, gravelly, and dry. He had a look of pure suffering on his face, which she could see more of now that he didn't have his unruly beard.

It was the wrong time, but Moira found herself hoping he would grow the beard back. She wasn't sure she liked clean-shaven Roman nearly as much.

"Where are the others?" Roman croaked in a barely audible whisper.

"I'll explain everything as soon as we get you out of this dungeon. I need you to walk, outlaw. I need you to summon that hard-headed bravado from earlier," she teased and paused, hoping she might get a small chuckle out of him, but he remained silent. She pursed her lips before saying, "You can lean on me, but we have to get you out of here *now*." Moira grabbed the lantern, stood, and reached out to him, hoping silently that she could support him.

Roman nodded and took a deep breath, which invited a new round of grimaces. "Fuck," he said with a growl as he reached toward her. She put her hand out, clasped his, and heaved. Finally, he was on his feet. It had only been a matter of minutes since she arrived in his cell, but to Moira it felt as if hours had passed.

"I hate to be heartless, outlaw, but is there any way you could speed things up?" She hoped that the snark might distract him while also conveying they really did need to get moving. Moira had no experience with someone who was so severely beaten, but she was starting to get a little frustrated with Roman's lack of urgency.

Roman leaned on her, his right arm draped heavily over her shoulders. He looked sideways at her and said, "Please tell me Hanna is available for medical aid. I have a feeling I will not survive if you are in sole charge of taking care of me."

She grinned, maybe a little too broadly, and said, "I'm all you've got. Your scene earlier resulted in an uproar, I'm afraid." She wrapped her arm a little firmer around his torso and said, "Let's go, outlaw. No time to be a lazy clout." She started to move slowly, with a gentle tug at his middle to get him moving.

"Gods save me," he mumbled as he started moving with her.

After what felt like approximately six hours, they finally stepped out of the cell and into the main corridor of the dungeon. Moira paused and took a moment to listen. There was no guarantee Amis or Wil would be able to find her after they dealt with the guard, but she remained hopeful one of them would. As the seconds ticked by, and the dungeon rang with silence, her hope was dwindling. Roman's head started to loll to the side, and she turned to him in panic.

"Roman? No, please. No, no! You must stay awake," she said. Her voice was pitched, and she spoke a little louder than she should have. If he passed out fully, she would not be able to move him on her own. She took a shuddering breath and gave him another soft shake, and said, "Talk to me, outlaw. Tell me something I don't know."

Roman moaned a little but did give her a weak smile before he said, "Everything hurts."

"I said something I *don't* know." She closed her eyes for a moment, took a calming breath, and said, "Come on, let's keep moving. We just need to get out of the dungeons, and then I can come up with a plan. Talk to me, Roman, please. I can't do this without you."

His arm around her shoulders tightened a little. "You came down here without a plan?" Roman mumbled. He continued to move as she did, albeit much slower than she wanted. They reached the stairs, and Roman hadn't said another word.

"Dammit!" Moira exclaimed under her breath.

The stairs would be a huge hurdle for Roman. Once they were out of the dungeon and in the main castle, she had no idea what to do. This was where she realized just how shallow their planning was. Neither she, Amis nor Wilhelm considered what it would take to get Roman out of the dungeon and to the forest. She cursed her own stupidity. Getting Roman into her rooms on the second level of the castle would be impossible and unhelpful. He was far too injured to go up a second larger set of stairs, and the risk of being seen would grow the farther she pulled him along. She cursed Wilhelm, Amis, and herself again for foolishly failing to come up with an in-between plan.

"Can I rest?" he asked. His eyes were shut and he probably thought they were at a good stopping place since she hadn't made him move in several seconds.

"No, outlaw. I'm sorry. We've got to get up these steps. Let's start one at a time, okay? I'll help you." She took the first step, hoping it would be easier to pull him up toward her rather than shove him from behind. Steely determination took over, and she knew their escape was all on her. There was no time to waste wondering about Amis and Wilhelm or beating herself up over their lack of planning.

Sweat gathered on her forehead, slipped down the back of her neck from her hair, and started to trickle between her shoulder blades. They progressed slowly up the stairs, with Moira heaving Roman up each step, then pausing to listen for anyone coming. It was late, well past midnight, so she was comfortable with the slim chances of being caught. However, the fact that the most wanted fugitive of the country was kept in the palace dungeons might change the overall atmosphere of royal security, and that's what kept her on high alert. After what felt like two millennia, she heaved Roman to the top step and let him lean against a wall while she stepped around the corner to assess what to do next.

Her own breathing was labored, and her arms and shoulders were on fire from the effort of pulling Roman up the steep steps. Despite her exhaustion and physical discomfort, Moira felt a small surge of relief and pride that they'd made it to the main level of the castle.

The castle halls were dim, with only one or two torches lit every so often. It gave a flickering and ominous look to an already stressful stretch of corridor. Moira took a second to breathe. She knew she needed to calm her thoughts, slow her breathing and gather her wits before deciding on the next step of the plan. Amis and Wilhelm had overseen the guard on duty and were seemingly successful, considering Moira met no one down in the dungeons. If needed, he or Wil would tackle the next guard as well to ensure Moira and Roman made it out in one piece. So far, there was nothing specific about this part of the plan that had gone wrong, but Moira couldn't help the gnawing feeling in her gut that something happened to Amis and Wilhelm. She shook off the feeling of dread as best she could and focused on her immediate problem. Roman was clearly in no condition to get straight to the hideout. She wasn't even sure she could get him to the forest right now. The pressing need was to take care of the obvious injuries, clean him up and let him rest. Even if the rest was minimal, she knew it would make a world of difference.

While it was a risky choice, to be sure, Moira felt the most attainable option right now was the kitchen. Rather than question herself further, she turned back and went around the corner to retrieve Roman, who, thankfully, was still vertical. He leaned against the wall with his eyes closed, his breathing was labored and heavy. She approached, and he opened his eyes.

"This is all backward, you know?" he said quietly.

She cocked her head a little and said, "What's backward?" Moira didn't say it out loud, but she suddenly worried Roman had sustained a far worse head injury than she originally thought. She looked closer at his eyes - well, the one that was fully open - and was immediately relieved to see they looked normal. Exhausted, hurt. But normal.

"I think I'm meant to be the one who rescues you. By my count, you've saved my ass at least two times," he said with a lopsided grin.

The gash under his eye was still bleeding, but not much. All the other blood he seemed to be covered in appeared dry. Moira wondered how much of it came from the guards he fought earlier and how much was his. She sincerely hoped most of the dried blood did not belong to him. Moira was grateful Roman didn't seem to be leaving a blood trail behind them, which would've been an added complication she didn't particularly want to deal with.

Moira gave him an exaggerated look of sympathy as she reached out and placed his arm back around her shoulders before tucking her arm around his waist. "It's definitely been more than two times, Roman. And I specifically recall you telling me to stop rescuing you, so clearly, I have issues following direct orders." She answered as she pulled him gently away from the wall, which he'd still been leaning against heavily, despite his arm around her shoulders. She continued, "I'm no physician, but I have to assume your injuries aren't life-threatening if you're over here grumbling about your masculine image being damaged." Another light tug got him moving again, blindly following her wherever she led. She looked at him sideways as they moved and said, "If you'd like, I can leave you here to find your own way out. I would love nothing more than to go to my room and curl up with a book. Getting yourself out of the castle might build your credibility back up."

Roman groaned and said, "Don't start worrying about my image now. You are clearly the superior person in this equation."

Moira stopped their progress and turned to stare at him. He looked down at her, surprised they'd stopped.

"What?" he said, with a tone of mild alarm.

"I just really wonder how hard they hit your head, that's all." No matter how she tried, she couldn't keep back her teasing tone.

Despite his facial injuries, Roman managed to give her an excellent glare. She smiled at him and said, "Enough with the flattery, you fool. Let's get you to the kitchen, so I can clean you up and let you sit for a minute or two."

Neither of them spoke again as they navigated the short distance from the dungeon stairs to the kitchen. Moira was relieved but was beginning to wonder when their luck would run out. How many more times could Roman sneak through these castle halls before he was caught and locked away so securely that they'd never be able to get him out again? It would have been all too easy to spiral into that open pit of despair within her, but she forced herself to hold back and continue to take the night one step at a time.

As usual, the kitchens were pleasantly warm. During midday, they could reach stifling temperatures as meals were made, but right now, it was comfortable. The coals in the large fireplace were still white and smoldering. It would only be an hour or two at most before the kitchen maids came in to get the early morning chores done, so she needed to work quickly. Roman found a wooden chair to sit in next to the large range. Moira set the lantern next to him, then gathered some supplies. There was a barrel of water in one corner and a pile of folded rags in another. She grabbed a wooden bowl off the open shelves, filled it with water, and carried everything over to Roman's side. He was still awake and watching her. Almost as an afterthought, she went over to grab a goblet, filled it from the barrel, and handed it to Roman.

She looked at Roman, pausing for a moment before she got to work. "I'm not good at this kind of thing...," she said as she let the thought hang, somewhat unfinished.

"That's perfect because my standards of care at the moment are very low." He grinned at her with a mix of playfulness and kind understanding, which she appreciated. The fact that he could still banter took a lot of pressure off her for some reason.

"Just talk to me while I work, alright? Distract both of us a little." Moira dipped one of the rags in the bowl of water. She winced a little, surprised that the water felt so frigid. "It's a little cold, okay? Summon that swagger I know and love and brace yourself." She started to gently dab away the blood from Roman's neck and ears, starting where there was no obvious injury.

Roman flinched slightly at the initial contact with the cold rag but otherwise remained motionless. He cleared his throat a little and began to talk. "I was twenty-three when I left for the Crusades." Moira stopped for a second, surprised at his choice of topic, but resumed her ministrations without making eye contact. She didn't want him to stop the story before he even started. Roman tilted his head back, closed his eyes, and continued. "I hadn't been the Lord of Loxley for very long when it was time for me to serve King Leo in the fight for the Holy Land. I left my father behind to run things at the estate. He wasn't terribly fond of the idea. Not only was he disgruntled at having to step back into the role he so recently vacated, but he was truly upset about me going to fight. I was the sole heir, after all."

Moira looked at Roman, his head still tipped, and his eyes still closed. If not for the bruising, swelling and blood, he might have looked peaceful. She said quietly, "I imagine he was upset at the thought of losing you because he loved you, not just because you were his only heir." She dipped the rag into the bowl again, causing the water to turn pink. She rang it out between her hands and set to work on cleaning the wound under his eye. Before she touched the rag to his face, she touched his arm gently with her free hand and said, "Let me know if it feels like I'm peeling your face off." Then she got to work gently cleaning the laceration.

He let out a small groan but otherwise didn't complain. He continued with his story, barely moving his mouth as he spoke, which she was grateful for. "The crusades were…unimaginable. It was an obvious campaign of insanity, and I had a hard time believing that we fought to regain the Holy Land because it felt more politically driven. King Leo may have wanted to protect the Old Religion and honor the Gods, but I believe once he was in battle and recognized what could be won, he became blinded by greed. Greed for land, greed for the expansion of his rule, and greed for glory. He - ahh, shit!" Roman jerked away from her violently.

Moira cringed and pulled her hand back. "I'm sorry! I was hoping to get this bit done while you were distracted." She found bits of dirt and debris in the cut on his face. Although she felt terrible about doing it, she knew the wound needed a more thorough cleaning. "I think I've just got one more obvious little bit to get out, and it's over." Before he could respond, she pulled out a small pebble and placed the rag back on his face with a little extra pressure to stop the fresh flow of blood. She grabbed his hand and pressed it to the cloth. "Hold, please." He probably needed stitching on that wound, but there was no way she was doing that, and not just because she lacked supplies.

He looked at her skeptically and said, "What happened to the Moira who could barely be bothered to talk to me while I cleaned myself up? Who are you, and what have you done with her?!" He raised his voice just a little in mock alarm that dripped with sarcasm.

She rolled her eyes and got up to get a fresh bowl of water. She plopped a rag into the bowl as she returned to Roman's side. "Tilt your head down a little." He complied and didn't say anything further as she started to gently peruse his scalp with her fingers. "This is much easier now that your hair isn't so mangy and long. I don't see any grievous cuts, so that's a relief. There is a spectacular bruise blossoming on the back of your head, though."

"You're going to ignore my teasing then?" He asked, looking up at her.

She lightly grabbed the sides of his head and tilted it back down so she could get one final look at the back of his head. "I'm not done here, outlaw. You're still behaving as though you're suffering a serious head injury." She smiled, knowing he couldn't see her face.

He scoffed, "I hear you smiling, you know."

"Alright, now I know something is wrong if you're claiming you can *hear* a smile!"

He reached up and pinched her side. She yelped a little and stepped back, surprised. She put her hands on her hips and mustered a glare, "Is that any way to treat the person literally cleaning blood off of you?" He shrugged. A little haughty, she replied, "For your information, I've done some reading in my spare time. And I've chatted with Hanna about basic wound care. I figured if I was going to aid and abet an infamous outlaw, I better be more prepared. Now, can I please finish here so we can get you out of the castle before someone discovers us, or have you forgotten the fact that I just hauled you out of the dungeon?"

Roman's features softened ever so slightly before he nodded. "I should've known you'd turn to the books," he said.

Moira smiled in return, took yet another deep breath, and said, "Stand up and remove your tunic." He raised his eyebrows in response. "Do you have broken ribs again? I'm guessing yes, based on the way you've been breathing and the way you're stifling any laughter." She crossed her arms and stared at him. "Your wrist is swollen, too. Do you think it's broken? I think I can fashion a brace, if needed."

"You're very imperious today," he said, still sitting.

"And you're surprisingly cavalier for someone who recently received a very public pummeling and had to be busted out of a dungeon," she responded loftily.

Roman chuckled, grasping his side, and said, "Well, that's because when you're in my line of work, you tend to be on a first-name basis with the afterlife."

She kept her arms crossed and started to tap her toe, just to highlight her impatience. "I'm wondering what part of this situation you believe grants us the time to chit-chat with each other without moving." She pursed her lips, suppressing her smile.

Roman reached out a hand in a silent request for assistance. Moira grasped it and started to heave Roman up and out of the chair just as Wilhelm stormed into the kitchen, startling them both. As Moira gasped in surprise, Wilhelm

283

turned quickly in her direction, causing him to trip over his own feet as they attempted to keep him moving, despite the direction in which his head and torso turned. The effect was a loud, resounding crash as he slammed into a cook's table and caused several large pots to tumble to the floor. Wilhelm regained his footing quickly, popping back up with surprising agility. He chased after one of the large pots that continued to roll and clang on the stone floor. Moira and Roman stood frozen, hands still clasped from her effort to help him stand.

Wilhelm wrangled the rogue items, set them loudly on the table, and said, "We need to get out of here!" His eyes were wild, his blonde hair was practically standing on end, and he had a thick sheen of sweat covering his face and neck.

Moira looked at him incredulously, "No shit, Wil! Would you like to try and make a little more noise?"

Roman let go of Moira's hand and stepped toward Wil, saying, "Where is Amis?"

Moira stepped forward, eager to hear an update on her brother. She felt almost ashamed that she hadn't realized Amis should be with Wilhelm but wasn't. The fear from earlier settled back into her gut, heavy and roiling.

Wilhelm looked at Moira and said low and fast, "He's going to meet you in your rooms. We took care of the second round of dungeon guards - two this time - but then Maddicot showed up, and we had to split up. It was obviously important that Amis not be seen in the dungeons, so I sent him out and handled the situation myself." He turned to Roman and said, "They know you're out, Ro. We have to run. And I do mean that literally."

"Shit!" Moira exclaimed venomously, and both men paused to look at her, but she focused on Roman. "Maddicot knows I am involved with you. I'm not sure what he knows specifically or how much, but he said something to me earlier at the tournament. With everything that happened, I completely forgot." She looked at Wilhelm and said, "Thank you for making sure my brother got out. I don't need Maddicot breathing down both our necks."

Roman continued to stare at her as if searching for something. He was about to speak when Wilhelm grabbed him by the elbow and started to pull him toward the back door of the kitchens, the door Moira usually used to sneak out and go down to the village. Moira followed, wishing she had more time to clean Roman up. It still looked as if every movement caused him severe pain.

They reached the door, and Roman turned around and looked at Moira again as Wilhelm let go of his arm. She couldn't quite tell what expression he wore, thanks to his swollen eye and bruised features. He said quietly, "I'm sorry." His voice hitched, and Moira had to blink away the sudden welling of tears in her eyes. Roman cleared his throat and said, "Be safe. Wait for word from us before you do *anything*. Lay low. Do not act until I contact you." He reached out with a dirty, bloody hand and touched that spot where her shoulder and neck met, caressed her throat with his thumb, then turned and stumbled after Wilhelm.

Chapter Forty-Three

Moira stood in the doorway and watched Roman and Wilhelm until they faded into the darkness. She shook herself out of the reverie she was in, then ran back to the hearth where Roman had sat and gathered up the supplies she used. It took all her self-control to work quickly and quietly. Both bloodied rags were shoved into the pocket of her dress as she ran back to the door to toss the dirty water outside. As silently as possible, she set the bowl back onto the cook's table, not caring where it had been originally. She blew out the lantern and shoved it into a cabinet, not wanting to risk the light getting her caught in the still-dark castle. With one last cursory glance at the kitchen, she turned to leave.

Once out of the kitchen door, Moira realized she should have used more caution. The noise from Wilhelm's fall should have drawn a surge of guards, but no one came running. She ardently hoped that the continuing festivity in the great hall meant very few people heard the clatter, but the lack of response was suspicious.

She continued into the corridor when an unusual instinct told her to freeze. Her heart slammed in her chest as she saw an arm reach out for her in the shadows. A large male body was attached to the arm, but she couldn't make out who it was, which made her extremely hopeful that whoever it was couldn't tell who she was either. The corridor just outside the kitchens was black, the one torch previously lit had been extinguished. Working on that same burst of instinct, Moira ducked swiftly, and she heard the arm swing in the empty air above her. She remained crouched on the ground, unsure of what to do next when she heard the doors to the Great Hall slam open, and the prince bellowed, "Greggory!" in his imperious voice.

Her heart pounded even heavier at the confirmation of who stood before her. The light spilling out of the Great Hall's doorway did not reach Moira, and she was able to do an awkward bear crawl back into the kitchen as Lord Maddicot was distracted and turned away. Moira remained crouched as she inched back into the kitchen. Once inside, she flopped in an exhausted heap to the floor and leaned back against the wall while she tried to calm her breathing. From across the room, she heard a small gasp, and Moira turned to see a young kitchen maid.

Moira held a finger up to her lips, indicating to the girl that she needed her to be quiet. The girl gave a faint nod, and Moira whispered, "I cannot be found here. Lord Maddicot might be searching for me."

The girl's eyes grew wide, but she stayed silent. Moira recognized the girl from all the times she'd come through the kitchens on her way to the village. She had copper-colored hair and was so thin Moira guessed that her family was struggling. Without a sound, the girl stepped closer.

"You bring the books to Meggy Taylor, don't you?" she asked, almost inaudibly.

Moira couldn't help the smile that came to her face. She said just as quietly, "Yes, I do."

"I'm Alaine. I've never met you because my Gran reckons reading is evil, but Meggy always shares what you teach her and the books that you bring." She whispered rapidly, almost in one breath.

"Alaine!" Moira felt a surprising wave of relief wash through her as she realized this girl was not going to bring further danger to her. "Yes, Meggy has mentioned you. I'm so sorry to ask this of you, but is there anywhere you can hide me?" Moira was trying to keep the desperation out of her voice, but that nagging instinct told her Maddicot would return, and soon, to search for her.

Alaine's face turned serious for a moment before she said, "There's a priest hole up inside the fireplace. Hanna said it was created to hide the Old Religion priests from the crusaders when the fights first started. She said King Leo still supported the old ways, so the castle was used to hide them." As she spoke, she walked over to the large fireplace, where the coals were still a grayish white. "The only challenge is, I don't know how we'd get you back out. Especially if a fire gets lit."

Moira's heart continued to hammer in her chest as she followed Alaine over to the fireplace. She felt stale with sweat from all the stress of the night. The chair where Roman sat mere minutes ago was still there, and she wondered how on earth things could change as quickly as they had.

Moira took a breath and said, "Forget getting me out. How on earth will you get me *in*?"

Alaine looked at her nervously. She half shrugged and said, "Far as I know, it's a small chamber of sorts just off the main chimney. If we put the stool in the embers, maybe you can stand on that and then you could see it?" As she finished speaking, she walked over to a three-legged stool in the corner, grabbed it, and set it in the coals of the fireplace. She looked at Moira expectantly. "Begging your pardon, but I do think you said we were in a hurry, m'lady."

Moira grimaced. She was suddenly faced with the rush of an entirely new fear - that of crawling into a chimney without a clear exit plan. Of course, she'd read about priest holes. They came in many shapes and sizes all throughout Anglia manor houses and castles. Some were not as safe as others, as they'd been built in a hurry at the onset of the Crusades. Ideally, King Leo would have ensured that any priest hole he added to the castle would be safe...or so she wanted to think. There were many horror stories of priests being trapped inside and dying of starvation. The worst stories were those priest holes in chimneys, just like this one, where priests had died due to lack of oxygen once a fire was lit and fresh air disappeared.

Moira gulped audibly and said, "Are you quite certain the priest hole isn't built into the paneling over there?" she said, gesturing vaguely to one of the large cabinets.

Alaine shook her head, "Quite sure, m'lady. The women in the kitchens only ever talk about this one spot, and only Hanna knew what it was for."

Without another word, Moira steeled her nerves, hiked up her skirt, ducked a little, stepped onto the waiting stool, and stood up in the chimney shaft. She remained bent slightly, mostly due to discomfort, but stood slowly and looked up. Sure enough, off to the left was an obvious cavity.

"I see it," she said to Alaine.

Alaine stuck her head into the hearth near Moira's legs and said, "I can hear someone coming. You must hurry!" There was a terror-filled urgency in her voice, and Moira knew she couldn't delay any longer. The hole was right at her eye level, maybe a tiny bit above. She put her hands on the ledge and gave a great heave while also pushing off the stool. After a brief moment of struggle, Moira pulled and climbed until she was sitting in what had to be the smallest priest hole this side of Gallya. She dusted off her hands, which proved foolish as the entire space was coated in soot and dust. Moira was able to sit straight up, but her head grazed the ceiling of the hole. She wanted to see how far she could scoot away from the opening, so she started to scoot further to the left. Unfortunately, she slammed into the opposite wall all too quickly and was able to lean over and reach the edge easily.

Do not freak out, dammit, she said to herself.

There came a loud crash from the kitchen below her. Moira gave a jolt and shuffled back toward the ledge, hoping to hear what was going on. Another resounding crash rang up through the hearth. It sounded as though someone was ransacking the kitchen. She heard Alaine give a faint squeal, but she couldn't tell if any words were exchanged. With an acute swell of dread, Moira realized that the turmoil in the kitchen was most likely Lord Maddicot searching for her or taking out his frustrations on Alaine and the pots and pans. Possibly both. A feeling of guilt settled into the pit of Moira's stomach, leaving her feeling ill. She should have known better than to climb up here and leave Alaine alone to face the angry lord. Now she was most likely stuck up here until someone could give her the all-clear and put the stool back in place for her to get down safely.

Several pots and pans rained on the stone floor, creating a thunderstorm of clanging. Moira covered her ears, and she wondered how loud it must be for Alaine. She broke out in a roiling sweat, and not just because the priest hole was a stifling temperature. Her mind reeled over the fact that this cavity was created with the sole intention of hiding fully grown men for unknown amounts of time. Mere minutes had passed since she climbed up here, and already she was desperate to get out. A fresh burst of panic settled in when she entertained the pure hell of being up here when a fire was fully lit. Her breath started to come in gasps and uneven pulls, which only broadened her panic. She closed her eyes and forced herself to take several deep, measured breaths.

There was the unmistakable sound of muffled talking, which pulled Moira back out of her spiral and into the reality of the moment. She leaned toward the edge of the hole, but try as she might, Moira couldn't make out who it was or what was being said. If she had to wager a guess, she would have said the voice sounded male, but whoever spoke was not standing close to the fireplace.

The room below grew quiet. No one lit a fire, and there were no new crashes reverberating through the space. An indiscernible amount of time passed in total silence. Moira leaned her head back against the brick, deciding she didn't care how much soot got in her hair. She wondered if daylight was breaking and when the kitchen would come to life. The room had a large range where most of the cooking was done, but never once had Moira stepped foot in the kitchen and not seen this fire lit.

She passed the time with thoughts about Roman. Her chest hurt at the sight of him stumbling painfully through the castle grounds. Moira found herself seething over Bobby's sudden appearance and even more unexplained disappearance. She wanted to believe Bobby fled the

Archery Tournament to get help, but she didn't know the woman well enough to assume much of anything.

Moira was just beginning to entertain the idea of jumping down into the cinders and hoping for the best when she heard Hanna's whispered voice carry up to her.

"You about ready to get down from there, girl?"

"Hanna, you have no idea how happy I am to hear your voice right now," Moira said with a sob. "Is Alaine alright? What happened?" Moira shuffled and turned, so her legs hung over the edge, waiting for the stool to appear. She sniffed and did her best to hold onto her emotions for a bit longer.

The stool swung into the fireplace below her, and Moira wasted no time lowering herself down onto it. She crouched down with both feet on the stool, arms braced on the inside ledge of the fireplace, and looked warily into the dimly lit kitchen. There were several kitchen maids hustling about, picking up the scattered mess left behind by Lord Maddicot. Ceramic cookware lay in shards all over the stone floor. Pots and pans lay strewn about, left where they landed after being thrown. The chair Roman occupied as she tended to his injuries lay in pieces. Moira grimaced at the damage done.

Hanna bent down and reached a hand out to Moira, which she gladly accepted as she hopped from the stool. Moira immediately wrapped Hanna in a fierce embrace. From one of the windows, Moira saw dawn was breaking.

The night was over, and she had yet to make it back to her room.

Hanna broke the hug and said, "Servant's stairs. Now. We must get you to your rooms before any fresh hell breaks loose." She pulled Moira toward a narrow door in the corner of the kitchen.

"That's not a staircase!" Moira said, shocked at the size of the doorway.

Hanna opened it and gestured inside. Moira was surprised to see it was a very narrow set of stairs leading to the second floor of the castle. Moira stepped closer and looked closer at the space, then looked back at Hanna.

"I just crawled out of a space smaller than a chicken coop, and now you want me to go up the narrowest staircase known to man? I don't think so." She crossed her arms for added effect.

Hanna gave her a look filled with so much annoyance that Moira decided not to push the issue and instead opted to sprint up the stairs as quickly as possible. In all fairness, there really was no point in getting caught now after everything they'd been through. Moira poked her head out of the door on the second floor and saw no one around, so she and Hanna made the short walk to her room without any further excitement.

Chapter Forty-Four

Moira was walking into her bedroom with Hanna close behind her when someone knocked at her door. Moira paused, immediately wary of who would be at her door at this hour. She turned and looked at Hanna.

Moira's brow furrowed as she stood in the doorway to her bedroom and stared at the still-closed door leading out to the castle hallway. "Wouldn't be Amis…who I thought was supposed to be in here waiting for me?"

Hanna shook her head and said, "I sent him to his own room to rest. Get into your bedchamber. I'll answer the door." She gave Moira a slight shove and then walked to the door, where someone gave another knock. "Impatience is rude," Hanna mumbled as Moira stepped into her room and shut the door most of the way, leaving it open just a crack so she could listen.

Moira heard her door opening. Hanna said in a surprisingly polite and chipper voice, "Good morning, what can I do for you?" Since she was alone, Moira let her eyes roll so dramatically that she felt a weird satisfaction from it. Hanna's formality indicated whoever was at the door was not a casual friend. Unfortunately, whoever it was spoke too softly for Moira to hear them properly.

Hanna spoke again, saying, "I'm afraid Lady Moira is not prepared to take breakfast in the Great Hall this morning. She plans to dine in her rooms, as usual."

Since moving into the castle, Moira almost never ate breakfast in the great hall. It was the one meal she was guaranteed to enjoy in her room, away from the courtiers and their gossip. More muffled speaking came from the person at her door. The tone changed somewhat, a little louder than before, which set Moira's nerves on edge.

To Moira's surprise, Hanna gave a sigh before she responded a final time. She said, "Very well. If Lord Leofwin insists, I shall get Lady Moira ready and send her down to breakfast as soon as possible." The unmistakable sound of the door's latch slid into place, and Moira stepped out of her bedroom.

"You have got to be joking," she whined without attempting to hide her exhaustion and frustration. "Look at me, Han! I'm filthy! I spent the night spiriting away an outlaw and then I sat in a fireplace, and you can absolutely tell!" Moira gestured to her body, a quick up and down motion, then pointed at her head before giving a melodramatic twirl to ensure Hanna got the point.

Hanna shook her head and rubbed at her temples, a rare show of emotion for her. The last few weeks were starting to take their toll on everyone, it seemed. "I know precisely how you look, Moira, having dug you out of that fireplace mere

297

minutes ago. In case you weren't eavesdropping -," Hanna said pointedly and gave Moira a look. She continued, "I tried to get you out of breakfast in the Great Hall, but your betrothed sent his most determined servant, and there was absolutely no way to get out of it." Hanna sighed, gave Moira a once over, grimaced, and said, "To the bathing room. And quickly. We haven't got much time to get that soot out of your hair. I suppose if we don't get it wet and try to shake it out, that might work best...?" she trailed off while waving Moira into the adjoining room.

Moments later, Moira cringed at the sight of herself in the looking glass that was mounted to the wall. She looked like an ashen, manic apparition that appeared from another universe. At a minimum, she would need an hour to get presentable, but she knew she wasn't going to get that much time. A loud groan escaped her lips, but she found that Hanna only nodded in agreement rather than scolding her for it. Further proof that the events of yesterday and last night had pushed them both to their limits.

"We'd better not waste too much time with lamentations, girl. I would like to avoid a visit from Leofwin himself," Hanna groused.

Moira nodded solemnly and began peeling herself out of her dress as Hanna loosened it from behind. In her year at the castle, Moira survived some truly miserable meals, but she had a feeling this was about to make the top of that list.

Chapter Forty-Five

There was not enough tea or coffee in the castle to wake Moira up, but she was determined to guzzle it down anyway, figuring it couldn't hurt. Her head pounded with a fierceness she'd never experienced before. The pain started at the front and radiated back until it settled right where her head and neck met. Although she and Hanna worked quickly and done a fair job cleaning her up, Moira still felt downright filthy and depleted of all energy. All she could smell was soot, no matter how many times she blew her nose. She was crammed into a simple forest green frock, and Hanna braided her hair in one easy plait down her back. The dark circles under her eyes from lack of sleep were impossible to hide, as was her overall ashen complexion.

Lord Leofwin sat next to her in an obnoxiously cheery manner. She knew he spent the night celebrating, and she could not for the life of her understand how he put forth such a sunny disposition. *He must still be blinkered*, she thought to herself. The lords and ladies in the Great Hall were all going on about the Archery Tournament and the evening's more substantial events. Some people were learning for the first time that Roman had made an impossible escape, despite being detained in the dungeons. Moira listened to them all in a detached manner, sullenly wishing she was upstairs in bed. Somewhere deep in her tired mind, she knew she should be playing along and act excited about the gossip; however, she could not muster any interest.

"Lady Moira, I had no idea you were such a keen archer!" Lady Lucia said to her from across the table. This effectively pulled Moira from her sulking inner diatribe, which she was sinking further into the longer she listened to everyone around her. She looked up at Lucia in mild surprise and noticed the lady wore a blunt expression as if she was intentionally pulling Moira out of her own head.

Moira sat up a little straighter and smiled at Lucia, making sure to put on her best courtier's face as the question caused several heads to turn their way. "Yes, my father taught me, and I grew up practicing with Amis and several other children in Huntsley," Moira responded in her most animated voice.

Leofwin was side-eyeing her with a skeptical expression that made her skin crawl. During the competition, he had determinedly not addressed her, and now she wondered what sort of retaliation she would be forced to endure for daring to enter the competition in the first place. Leofwin held his knife in one hand, fork in the other, both frozen in midair as he listened to their conversation.

Lucia pointedly ignored Leofwin, who sat just to Moira's right. She held Moira's gaze with a little too much intensity and said, "I think that's simply marvelous! It certainly provided a little excitement in an otherwise traditionally dull tournament."

With an audible grunt, Leofwin said, "I think we can all agree that Lady Moira managed to present a rather shallow experience compared to the real excitement of the day."

Moira stared down at her plate of mostly untouched food. She felt as though Leofwin were baiting her with that comment and could find nothing in her knackered mind that would be safe to say.

"If you're referring to the excitement with Roman Loxley, then I am afraid I must politely disagree," Lucia said in that courtly angelic voice she used, "I rather preferred watching the competition and Lady Moira than the eventual violence and upheaval that tore the rest of the event apart. I'm afraid I don't have the disposition to enjoy that sort of entertainment." There was the faintest edge to her voice at the end, as if she wasn't entirely able to hide her disgust over the day's events and Leofwin's obvious enjoyment of them.

Rather than respond to Lucia, Leofwin mumbled something under his breath and set his utensils down with an air of frustration. He looked at Moira fully and said, "I think it's time you and I take a morning stroll through the gardens."

He started to stand and offered his hand to Moira. There were only two things Moira wanted to do, and those things were to take a bath and go to bed. In that order. She couldn't rally any sort of interest in a walk with Leofwin but knew she no choice in the matter. With one last smile for Lucia, Moira stood up and let Leofwin take her hand.

****

Moira walked along at Lord Leofwin's side, wondering if he really wanted a quiet walk through the gardens. He said nothing since leaving the Great Hall, which suited her perfectly. The less she had to say, the better at this point. Her exhaustion was settling in fully, and she worried that her limited social filters might break down entirely if pushed any further.

Leofwin's hand over hers suddenly tightened as he held onto her wrist and shoved her into a corner of the castle's exterior wall. She gasped in surprise, taken aback by the sudden change in direction and his overall demeanor.

"You're hurting me, Conor," Moira scolded. She hoped the use of his first name might bring him to his senses, but his grip only tightened as he stepped closer to her.

"Who is he?" Leofwin asked her through gritted teeth as he pressed his body to hers, effectively rendering her almost immobile as she was crammed further against the castle wall.

She looked at him in honest confusion before she asked, "Who is who?"

"Don't play the fool with me, *pet!*" Leofwin replied, snarling. He hadn't called her pet since before he assaulted her, and now he said it with raging animosity.

Alarms were going off in Moira's head. While he had yet to mention Roman's name, Moira knew better than to assume that was who Leofwin asked about. Better to have him explain what exactly he was after rather than try to fill in the blanks and possibly dig herself a new hole to get out of.

"Since I'm not *playing* the fool, I guess it's safe for us to assume I am one," Moira responded with a little more spite than she should have.

Leofwin scoffed and sneered at her, "I loathe that mouth of yours, constantly dripping with a smart answer or some low-brow mockery. You do well to hide it most of the time, but far too often, you can't keep that wickedness under control. It's the first thing I'll make sure to beat out of you once we are finally married."

Moira's face turned to stone, and she remained silent. There was nothing she could say at this moment that would prove helpful to her, and she knew it.

With that evil sneer still in place, Leofwin continued, "Now, in my usually respected opinion, the only answer for your increased erratic behavior is that you have taken a lover. Tell me. Who is he?" His grip was still tight on her wrist, and he started to twist it in an unnatural direction.

Before she could prevent it, a small yelp escaped Moira's lips, which only made Leofwin grin a little wider. His face grew red, and he broke out in a heavy sweat from the exertion. Leofwin stopped his twisting but held her wrist where it was while he trapped her other hand with his. "I think we are well past the time to show each other our true colors. You've started to get a glimpse of mine, and I have certainly started to get an idea of yours."

"If you don't like what you see, why are you upholding the engagement?" Moira spat, refusing to give him any more satisfaction about how much he was hurting her. His face was so close to hers that she could smell the stale alcohol from last night and some of his breakfast from this morning. It took all her willpower not to gag on the scent of him. She tucked away his stench and that sharp pain in her wrist into a far corner of her mind and focused instead on how much she loathed the man before her. She let all her hatred seep into her eyes right where he could see it.

"I would have thought that was quite obvious," he taunted, still holding her wrist in that twisted spot.

She cocked her head and gave him a questioning look, truly not sure what was meant to be so obvious.

"Your father arranged an impressive dowry for you, *pet*. Perhaps you really were unaware of that?" He gave her a searching look, and she knew he had caught the real surprise that she couldn't disguise. "I would have thought you knew since there is no other reason for someone of my stature and position to remain engaged to marry a gangly and unbecoming rag such as yourself. If it wasn't for your dowry, I would find a much more suitable woman to marry. One who wouldn't cause me such constant embarrassment." He gave her wrist a little more of a twist, and she knew that if he went much further, he would cause break it.

"Take the dowry and let me go. I don't want anything but my freedom," she said, maybe a little too hopeful that he would agree.

"Oh, if only I could! Trust me. I have explored that option; however, there are strict laws in the land that Prince Lyric refuses to overlook. Even for me," he said with a clear tone of bitter frustration. Moira found it mildly fascinating that Prince Lyric would deny Leofwin anything, particularly something that seemed eerily similar to what he did to his people on a regular basis - swindle them out of their money.

Leofwin pressed his body into hers more aggressively and said, "Who is your lover?"

Moira looked at him without breaking his gaze and said, "I have no lover." She almost added "here" but realized that tidbit of information really wouldn't do her any favors. Besides, whatever happened back in Huntsley happened to an entirely different version of herself, and that young man could barely be called a lover.

Their eye contact remained unbroken as Leofwin held her in that awkward and uncomfortable position. His body pressed against hers, smashed against the castle wall, tucked into a corner of the gardens. One hand he held tightly while the other was held out at an uncomfortable angle. She noticed the increasing sheen of sweat on his face and couldn't help but get a small ounce of satisfaction from knowing that whatever this interaction could be called, it was taking a lot out of him. Moira kept her face neutral, almost uninterested, but also withheld her earlier look of defiance. There was no lover to hide from him, but if this was his best guess on what she'd been up to, she wouldn't waste a lot of energy trying to persuade him that something else was going on.

With an odd growl of sorts, Leofwin gave her a weak shove and let go of her while moving away. Moira let out an audible gasp of relief at having her wrist returned to its normal position. She cradled it in her other arm and rubbed it slightly while attempting to calm her breathing.

Leofwin turned away from her, stared in silence at the surrounding gardens, then said, "Lover or not, eventually I will find out what is going on here. You and your entire deportment have changed in the last several weeks." He turned to look at her again. "If you continue on in this manner, I do believe we may not both survive our impending marriage."

With one last jeer in her direction, Lord Leofwin walked off stiffly toward the castle. He gave her no opportunity to respond, nor did she want one. Once he was out of earshot, she said quietly, "It is you who would not survive, you slimy bastard."

Chapter Forty-Six

After the altercation with Leofwin in the gardens, Moira immediately returned to her rooms, where she collapsed on her bed without taking the bath she previously longed for. She did not wake until the following morning when Hanna woke her with the scent of coffee and pastries.

Moira luxuriated in a long morning bath, finally ridding herself of the residual fireplace grit and grime. After a full hour passed, she felt like she was finally able to begin to process the events of the last few days, along with everything that happened with Leofwin. There was nothing on her agenda today other than the inquisition she planned to lead, so she tossed on a tunic and trousers rather than a dress.

Moira walked into the main room of her suite and noted that Hanna was not on the settee with her usual mending. She briefly wondered where she could be and realized that not too long ago, she began wondering what Hanna did during the day. There had been the smallest window of time where Moira was mildly suspicious of Hanna's activities, and she was still surprised that they were both secretly working for the same cause.

Moira shook her head and plopped down onto her favorite chaise lounge. There was a book on the armrest, waiting to be picked up and read, but Moira found herself unable to immerse herself in someone else's world when her reality seemed overwhelming. Typically, she loved to ignore her own reality in favor of escaping into another, but at this moment, her entire being was occupied.

In the past year and a half, Moira had lost her father, allowed herself to be engulfed in grief, been summoned to court by her betrothed (whom she had never met), adjusted to court life (sort of), and then through some unexpected turn of events she found herself completely submerged in a secret cause to get King Leo back on the throne. That last one was a real doozy considering she believed, like the rest of the kingdom, that King Leo was killed in the crusades. Top off everything with the fact that she had very annoyingly fallen for the leader of the cause, who may or may not be alive after a severe public beating and midnight flight for his life.

"Ooof," Moira said out loud to no one but herself. She stared unseeing at the rug on the floor in front of her. Moira sat like this for quite some time, allowing her mind to ebb and flow through the myriad of events that recently transpired. After the chaos and upheaval of the last month or more, she was grateful for the unexpected time to sit and mentally sift through everything.

****

Hanna and Amis broke Moira's reverie, entering her room abruptly but carrying platters of food. She looked up at them from her spot on the lounge and smiled. Amis returned her smile easily, but Hanna gave her a look of suspicious curiosity.

They both set down the trays they carried; Amis having brought his over to the small, low-legged table in the center of the living room area. His tray contained beverages, which Moira leaned forward to grab greedily.

"Thanks, Amis! Tea sounds perfect right now," Moira crooned happily.

Hanna continued to look at Moira skeptically. Finally, Hanna stepped around the chaise and stood in front of Moira, and said cautiously, "What happened?"

Moira looked up at her and gave her an even bigger smile. "Oh no, Hanny. I get to ask the questions today, and I assure you that I have had plenty of time to create quite a list for you to answer."

Moira gestured back toward the small dining table on the other side of the room. She and Amis had eaten many meals at this small table, but Hanna had never sat and dined with them before.

"I want us all to sit down, share a meal, and talk. Please," Moira said.

Hanna looked at Amis and said, "Has she been given some sort of mood-altering substance? Perhaps Leofwin managed to slip her something…," she trailed off a little as Moira started to laugh.

"Hanna!" Moira said, with the hint of her laughter still in her voice, "I have most certainly not been given anything!"

With a fierce look of doubt, Hanna said, "Then what in hell has given you this oddly tranquil attitude as you make casual demands? I am legitimately concerned!"

Amis continued to watch the two in rapt attention. Moira had laughed off Hanna's concerns, which seemed to only make the latter even more concerned.

"Good Gods, am I not allowed to finally be relaxed after some decent rest and reflection?" Moira asked, exasperated.

Hanna and Amis replied in unison, "No!"

"Ha!" Moira said, standing up and walking over to the table. She held her teacup in one hand and motioned for the others to join her with her other hand. "I am not under the influence of any sort of mood-altering herb. I simply had time to sit here by myself for the first time in ages. Believe it or not - and you do look inclined toward disbelief - the time to reflect did wonders for me. Now. Sit, please. Both of you. We have things to discuss."

Amis and Hanna shared another look. With an easy shrug, Amis walked over to the table and sat down. He said, "Sit with us, Hanna. Not as a servant or lady's maid, but as our co-conspirator!" He gave her a wiggle of his eyebrows and patted the chair next to him. Moira beamed and hoped that Hanna would set aside her usual grip on formality when they were in the castle. So far, Hanna only dropped the stiff structure when she absolutely had to, but Moira wanted

311

Hanna to loosen up more easily as they continued to work with Roman.

"Hanna, you dug me out of a priest's hole in the wee hours of the morning just yesterday. I do believe that sitting down at my dining table will be the least of your sins this week," Moira pointed out while giving Hanna's seat another pat.

With a sideways bob of her head and a little shrug, Hanna acquiesced and sat down with Moira and Amis. Plates were quickly doled out, all loaded and heaped with food. Amis made sure to serve Hanna, who seemed secretly pleased with the arrangement.

After a few moments passed in companionable silence while they ate, Moira set her utensils down, wiped the corners of her mouth, and said, "Why the *hell* did no one tell me Bobby is a woman?"

There was an initial pause as Hanna and Amis processed the sudden question, but both recovered quickly. Amis simply laughed and said, "*That* is your first, most pressing question, Moi?"

"Yes, it definitely is!" Moira answered indignantly, crossing her arms over her chest.

"I think we may need to work through your priorities," Amis said, still holding onto some of his laughter over her question.

"Nobody was hiding the fact that Bobby is a woman," Hanna said, looking rather aghast at Moira.

"Well, that's the thing, Han," Moira said, tiptoeing into the realm of utterly dramatic, but she didn't care. She waved her cup around as she spoke, keeping her voice reasonable but still feeling quite strongly about the situation. "Maybe nobody was hiding that fact, but I've racked my brains and realized that none of you used feminine pronouns or descriptive words when discussing her. It was all irritatingly vague. 'Oh, Bobby isn't in camp tonight!' and 'Bobby might be the least merry of us all!', blah blah blah! How convenient that I somehow remained in the dark about this rather significant detail," Moira ranted.

Amis was smirking at her, entertained by her rant, and even Hanna had a suppressed grin hiding behind her usual stern exterior. Moira didn't quit, instead, she continued in a somewhat deflated manner, "I was going insane looking for help in the crowds the day of the Archery Tournament, but because I didn't know who would be there or what Bobby looked like, I wasted precious time searching for help when she was there the whole time. I wasted even more time wrapping my mind around the fact that she was sitting next to me and the fact that she is a woman." Moira took a huge breath, exhaled, and sat back.

Hanna set down her utensils, pursed her lips while looking at Moira, and said, "I'm sorry, I just want to make

313

sure what you're upset about. It bothers you that Bobby is a woman?"

Moira rolled her eyes, exasperated. She rested her elbow on the table, placed her head in her hands, and said, "No, Hanna. It's bloody fantastic that Bobby is a woman. What I'm frustrated about is the fact that nobody thought it was an important detail to share with me! I met what felt like half the bloody crew that night when Amis and I visited the hideout, and still, it never came up!"

"Well, Bobby wasn't in the camp that night," Amis pointed out with an ill-hidden mischievous grin bursting from his face.

Moira ground her teeth and looked up to glare at Amis. She gave him her best smile imitation and said, "Yes, Amis. Thank you." Growing up with him had taught her when she was being baited, and this just happened to be a time when she didn't want to put up with it.

"Enough!" Hanna said, tossing her napkin onto the table in a gesture Moira knew went against every rule of etiquette she knew. "Moira, you are focused on the wrong things, as usual. Bobby is a woman. It was not intentionally hidden from you, and I know that for a fact. Please refrain from wasting any more time on this trivial nonsense. I'm not sure the extra minutes of knowing Bobby's identity ahead of time could have made much of a difference that day. Prince Lyric knew Roman was there, Pewsey was still caught and betrayed us, and Roman was still beaten in front of everyone. Bobby or not, that happened. Woman or not, that happened."

Amis swallowed audibly. Moira sat a little straighter and looked at Hanna. She nodded, realizing that she had indeed been focusing on the wrong thing. Even if Bobby was a man, nothing that day would have changed. Moira would still not have known that a friend sat next to her, and she would have had to make the same decisions that she'd made to begin with.

"You're right, Han," Moira said quietly.

"I know I am," Hanna responded, not unkindly.

"There is something I'd like to know," Amis announced as he started to stack their plates back onto the serving tray. "Where did Bobby go amidst the chaos?"

Hanna eyed him warily. Amis was stacking dishes rather precariously, and Moira could sense that Hanna was dying to fix the work he'd done, but she refrained.

"She fled, of course. It does the cause no good if every single person is clustered together in terrified, useless solidarity," Hanna responded as if this much should be obvious.

"There's no code?" Amis asked, incredulous.

"Code for what?"

"For not leaving a man behind or some such thing. Moira reads constantly, isn't there usually some sort of code between the brotherhoods of the world that says nobody gets left behind?" Amis turned to Moira expectantly.

Moira swayed in her seat and bobbed her head back and forth as she thought. "Generally speaking, yes. However, I think that may be a more militaristic approach to a 'brotherhood' rather than a realistic one, Amis."

"It isn't practical," Hanna jumped in before Amis could argue. His brow furrowed, and he looked like he was about to defend his point further. Hanna said, "You two could bring down the entire monarchy by driving everyone insane with these odd points you refuse to drop. Bobby did what she was supposed to do - she attempted to finish Pewsey's mission, and once that was done, she made it back to the hideout as safely and quickly as possible."

"What was Pewsey's mission?" Moira asked.

"That I cannot tell you," Hanna said.

"But -," Moira started to argue.

"I cannot tell you because I do not know, so don't go jumping down my throat about it," Hanna responded in annoyance. Moira noticed that her planned-out inquisition had veered entirely off track from what she mapped out in her mind earlier.

"I do suspect it's a situation where you wouldn't want all the eggs in one basket, so to speak," Amis said to the sudden silence filling the room. "It's smart of Roman really to keep his team diversified in their pursuits."

Moira looked at Amis skeptically and said, "Right...Speaking of our foolish leader -"

"Perhaps you mean fearless?" Amis interjected.

"I do not," Moira continued, "Our *foolish* leader. The one who challenged an entire group of royal guards to combat. Has anyone heard from him?"

There was a brief pause, which evaporated Moira's earlier tranquility. She looked between Amis and Hanna a little desperately, wanting to know what they were hiding.

Hanna shook her head and said, "I have no word. Everyone is lying low right now. Gwin may not come for supplies for several weeks. It could be much longer until we get any meaningful news." With a despairing look on her face, Hanna continued, "It is time for us to lie low as well. There is no greater mission right now than going on with castle life as if nothing happened."

"I can confirm that he is not back in the castle dungeons, which means he at least escaped the castle grounds. Where he and Wilhelm - and that rotten *woman* Bobby," Amis said with a wink, "- ended up, nobody seems to know."

A rush of emotion swept through Moira, and she could do nothing but look down at the table. She twisted her fingers in her lap and attempted to adjust to the idea that after several weeks of being entirely inundated with the outlaw and his cause, she might now suddenly go weeks with no word. There would be no information on his condition, no surprise banter in the castle gardens, and no one to spy for. All too suddenly, she felt the oppressing feeling of Leofwin and his new insistence they marry weighing down upon her. This time, she wouldn't ignore the crushing feeling. This time, she would push back.

With a burst of conviction, Moira looked up and said, "I cannot do that. I cannot return to castle life as it was before. Just because Roman may have to hide indefinitely, it doesn't mean we have to. He's the outlaw, after all. We aren't."

Amis gave her a huge grin and slapped his leg, "I do love this new Moira! She's got all the foundations of the old one, but she cares a lot less for the rules!"

Meanwhile, Hanna looked at them both as if their heads were on fire. "You two are about to become one of my cautionary tales."

Chapter Forty-Seven

Autumn was evaporating as the usual winter chill crept into Ivywood. Moira worried about the impending weather and what it might mean for Roman and his men. A week passed without any additional contact or information, just as Hanna predicted. Without a clear direction or plan in mind, Moira and Amis followed Hanna's wishes to return to castle life as if nothing had happened. They both did their best to stay engaged in the courtly gossip; however, Amis was more successful than Moira, as usual. Initially, it bothered her, but then Moira realized she had never been as good as Amis when it came to courtly intrigue.

A return to a routine meant Moira had ample amounts of library time once again, which she loved. At least in the library, she didn't need to pretend to be anyone she wasn't. Her time among the books recently was spent continuing her research on various estates in northern Anglia, but so far, she hadn't learned anything new and exciting. It turns out the most momentous thing to happen was not yet recorded in the history books, which was unfortunate since it was exactly what she wanted more information on – the Crusades. Moira briefly considered asking Prince Lyric outright about the transfer of the Loxley estate to the commoner-sheriff, but realized that was her worst idea yet.

Moira stumbled upon a floorplan for an estate in Gest, which showed the many priest holes hidden throughout the large manor. The estate belonged to the Nefren family, but it was a lineage she was unfamiliar with. As she perused the floor pan and the various hiding places, Moira was struck with an idea. For the briefest moment, she sat frozen as her mind ran wild. Then, she slowly closed the book, added it to her towering stack, and left the library immediately. Normally she would work on reshelving the books she'd taken down, but there was no time.

Earlier in the day, she left her room without shoes again, which was a horrible habit she needed to break now that the castle's corridors were getting colder. The chilly stone under her feet sent a shiver through her soles all the way up her back. While the main rooms of the castle were heated with large fireplaces, the hallways always remained cold and drafty this time of year, or so she was told. Moira cursed herself for her stupidity but hurried toward the kitchens without wasting time to go up and get her shoes.

Once Moira entered the kitchen, she took a moment to enjoy the warm stones under her feet. She gave her toes a grateful wiggle as she looked around at the women who were responsible for keeping the castle running. There were several women kneading dough and more chopping up vegetables and meat. Two large pots hung over the massive hearth and several sat on top of the wide range, simmering a stew that Moira knew would taste delicious. She didn't let her gaze linger on the fireplace, as all she could think about was the smothering feeling of the small hiding place inside. As she continued to gaze around the room, one of the women approached her, a questioning look on her face.

Moira smiled at her and said, "Sorry to be a bother, but I was just wondering if Alaine is here today?"

The woman wiped her hands on her apron and said in a quiet, steady voice, "Alaine is normally only here in the morning, m'lady. She will be back early tomorrow. Can I help you with something?" She smiled at Moira kindly, and Moira realized that in all the time she whipped through this room of the castle to escape, she had never paid much attention to the women who worked here.

Moira returned her smile and said, "No, but thank you. If you could let her know I'd like to chat with her that would be appreciated." She started to retreat when the woman stepped closer and shook her head ever so slightly.

"M'lady, I would be willing to assist you with *whatever* you may need," said the woman as she gave Moira a very pointed look. "My name is Sigrid."

Sigrid spoke in a conspiratorial tone, making Moira wonder if she was offering a little more than just the usual kitchen services. There was a slight pause in her answer as Moira struggled internally with what should be said. Clearly, some women in the kitchen were in on the cause, given that Hanna met Gwin down here several times a month; however, Moira had never thought to ask who else in the castle knew or worked for Roman. She found herself wishing, not for the first time, that there was some clear way for her to know who was a friend and who was a foe. Despite her reservations, Moira decided she felt comfortable trusting Sigrid with at least her immediate question.

With a steadying breath, Moira said, "Actually, Sigrid, there might be something you can help me with. I was just in the library, doing some reading when I happened upon some material that discussed priest holes." She stopped here and looked directly at Sigrid, trying to gauge if the woman showed any outward reaction to the term. Moira was in luck, for her new companion gave her the smallest smile and nodded, encouragement to continue. "This, of course, got me thinking, as I'm a curious sort, about whether or not this castle has any priest holes or things of that nature?"

Although Moira clearly knew firsthand that there was a priest hole in the very room they spoke, she had been in and out of that hiding spot before the kitchens were up and running. She also had no idea which in this room could be fully trusted. Even though they were speaking in a near whisper, Moira did not want to divulge too much.

Sigrid looked around the room quickly before she answered Moira. She gave her an intense but fleeting look, then said, "I'm afraid I won't be able to help you with that today, m'lady. Shall I let Alaine know you're looking for her?" Although she had kept her voice low, Moira wondered if the intense look meant she needed to merely play along and not push for any additional information.

Moira nodded and said, "I would appreciate that, Sigrid. Thank you!"

Without any other reason to stay in the kitchen, Moira gave an odd sort of curtsy and turned to leave. She felt as though the interaction had a glimmer of hope before it took a turn and ended abruptly. There were still so many questions left unanswered and Moira was beginning to wonder just how she was going to continue without Roman's direct influence.

Chapter Forty-Eight

Moira and Amis had just finished breakfast and were chatting amiably when a timid knock sounded at her door. Moira looked at Amis questioningly. Hanna had left ages ago without returning, and she wouldn't have knocked before entering.

"Why does a knock always elicit such intrigue?" Moira asked Amis as she stood and went over to her door.

"Because, dear sister, until very recently, no one actually knocked at your door," Amis answered snarkily.

Moira rolled her eyes but didn't offer a smart retort since what Amis said was technically true. She opened her door and let out a small gasp of surprise when she saw Alaine standing there, wringing her hands and looking wildly up and down the hall. Moira motioned for the girl to come inside, then quickly shut the door.

"Alaine, I was going to come down to the kitchens in the hopes that you and I could chat. Did Sigrid let you know I was looking for you yesterday?"

Alaine stood just inside the room, it was clear she felt uncomfortable and out of place. Moira gestured for her to take a seat, but Alaine shook her head.

"We don't have much time, m'lady," Alaine said quietly while glancing nervously at Amis, who still sat at the small breakfast table.

"Much time?" Moira asked, stepping around Alaine to sit back down at the table. "This is my brother, Amis. He's alright once you get past the garish outfits and exasperating behavior. Also, please call me Moira," she said with a smile.

Alaine nodded slightly at Amis as he raised his teacup toward her in greeting. "M'l -, erm, Moira, Sigrid did tell me you were looking for me. And she did mention what you were asking about." Alaine took a breath and then stepped a little closer to the table before saying, "There are many priest holes in the castle, but the thing I think you'll find far more interesting is a secret passageway to the prince's trophy room."

Moira stared at Alaine. Her jaw dropped, leaving her mouth agape as she processed what was said.

Amis spoke up first, asking, "Pardon my dimwittedness, but did you just say there's a secret passageway leading into the prince's beloved trophy room?"

Alaine bobbed her head up and down, so aggressively it was comical.

"Does the prince know about it?" Moira asked as she stood and slipped into her nearest boots. If they were going on some sort of adventure, she was not about to repeat yesterday's barefooted mistake.

"No, m'lady," Alaine said as she shook her head. "There are very few who know about this particular passageway."

"But how do you -," Amis started to inquire, but Moira interrupted him.

"Let's save some of our questions for later, Amis. Alaine said we don't have much time, and I get the feeling we've already squandered a good chunk of it." Moira looked at Alaine, who shrugged a little but nodded, confirming what Moira suspected. "Why are we almost out of time, Alaine?"

"Oh, you're allowed to ask questions, and I'm not, is that it?" Amis asked petulantly from his seat, still at the table.

Moira rolled her eyes and turned her back on Amis. "Never mind. Let's go!"

"Hold on! First, I'm denied questions, and now I'm denied the excitement and adventure of witnessing the passageway itself?" Amis said, finally standing.

"Fine, Amis. Come along," Moira said impatiently, but then paused and asked Alaine, "Is there room in this passageway for three?"

Alaine already started toward the door, and she did not stop as she said, "There is room as long as the three are quiet."

There was no way not to laugh at Alaine's comment, so Moira did so as she followed her toward the door. Without any further discussion, the door was opened, and they all proceeded down the hall. Moira made sure to give the corridor a quick glace before leaving her room. Thankfully it was one of the usual times of day when foot traffic on the second floor of the castle was rare. People had already eaten breakfast and had now moved on to a late-morning activity of some sort.

The trio walked in near silence, with Moira feeling particularly surprised that Alaine seemed to glide silently rather than walk. Dressed like most young kitchen maids, Alaine was wearing a simple brown dress and apron. The fabric looked worn, but soft. Moira attempted to replicate the girl's silent and graceful stride but failed almost immediately and stumbled over her own feet. Amis was walking behind her, so he was able to reach forward and catch her before she fell. He was clearly suppressing his laughter over Moira's behavior, but he managed to level her out and keep moving without missing a single beat. Moira straightened her shoulders and decided her usual walk would work fine for the time being.

Alaine led them past the kitchen without pause. She continued walking, took them around a bend and down a narrow, dark hallway until she reached the rarely used stairwell to the dungeons. Moira's breath hitched, and Amis nearly walked into her as she stopped suddenly.

"What's happened? Where are we?" Amis asked in a whisper, leaning around Moira to look at Alaine.

"We're at the dungeon stairs," Moira answered quietly, noting her voice sounded a little faint. Since helping Roman escape, Moira had been very careful to avoid this hallway and staircase.

With a little bob of her head, Alaine took a breath and explained, "Getting to the secret passageway is not pleasant."

Moira couldn't hide her skepticism as she looked back at Amis, then at Alaine again. She blinked a few times before saying, "I have a feeling 'not pleasant' is the mildest way you could possibly describe *anything* in those dungeons, Alaine." She looked directly at Amis again and said, "My limited experience has taught me that the dungeons are dank and vile in a way that only a dark collection of sewage in various stone cells can be."

Amis threw her a look of sheer horror as he said, "I could have done without the descriptive language, Moi. I was down here that night, too."

Alaine turned away from their chatter and started to make her way down the narrow and uneven stairs. Moira gave Amis a shrug of apology - which made him roll his eyes - and then began to follow their young guide. Moira was unexpectedly flooded with the same adrenaline she felt the last time she was on this staircase. She had to remind herself that she was not sneaking a severely wounded fugitive out of the dungeons. *No*, she said to herself, *this time, you're simply going down into the dungeons to crawl into some sort of secret passage, totally normal.*

As they continued down the stairs, Moira noticed it quickly got much gloomier. The limited light from the corridor above was almost imperceptible now, and they were only halfway down the stairs. She wished desperately that there was a railing or something to hold on to, but there was not, and she was revolted by the urge to put her hand onto the wall to steady herself. There was clearly years' worth of muck and grime on the walls. The further down they went, the more they noticed a significant stench rising from the dungeons. Despite her vivid memories of getting Roman out of the dungeons, Moira realized that her senses that night must have blocked out the unpleasantness she now registered. She had seen and acknowledged the filth of the dungeon, but the stench and squalor had felt like far away details compared to right now.

"Gods above, it's rank!" Amis said in a loud, hissing whisper.

"Plug your nose and breathe through your mouth," Moira responded with a quick glance over her shoulder at Amis. She heard him take several big gulps of air through his mouth, but then he made a sudden retching sound.

"Thanks a bloody tower pound for that one, Moira," he snarled at her. "Breathing through your mouth only means you can *taste* the putrid air."

There was no stopping it, Moira let out a giggle and immediately clamped her hand over her mouth. While that had not been the intended result of her suggestion, she had to admit it was a little funny. On the night of Roman's escape, Moira was too distracted to fully register just how awful it smelled down here. She was grateful that her adrenaline had blocked that much, and she wished she had a little more of it now. Blocking out the foul odor would make this journey far more pleasant.

"I'm sorry!" She said once she regained her composure.

Other than a muffled grumble, Amis remained silent behind her, and Alaine continued to ease them slowly down the dark dungeon steps without uttering a sound. Moira felt like their progress was just as slow, if not slower, than when she was dragging Roman. A swift sense of urgency descended upon her. Why had Alaine not brought along a lantern? And why were they going so slow, just on the stairs?

Just as she was about to point out their need for light, they reached the bottom of the stairs. It appeared rather suddenly, causing Moira to stumble when her feet hit even ground and not another step. They were standing in the main long, narrow hallway. Down at the far end was a pinpoint of bright light, which Moira knew was the one barred window. There was no other fresh air or natural light down here, and most of the cells were entirely underground, which accounted for the musty, mossy smell that sat on top of the sewage odor. Alaine motioned for Moira and Amis to stay put, then she disappeared around a corner to the right, which Moira had failed to notice until this moment.

From somewhere in the distance, Moira heard a faint groaning. She looked back down the hallway toward the window and wondered who was imprisoned down there right now. As far as she knew, the dungeons were almost always empty, wasted space. It was one of the prince's big points of proof that they were living during *peaceful times.* An empty dungeon meant there were no criminals in the land, which Prince Lyric claimed was a sign that all his people had exactly what they needed. There was no need to be a criminal if you had everything to sustain yourself and your loved ones. Moira rolled her eyes, unable to stop herself as she thought of the prince's flawed logic. She wondered what Roman Loxley, an infamous criminal, meant to Prince Lyric in terms of his peaceful kingdom. Probably just a hurdle to overcome on his way to the throne.

"Where did she go?" Amis whispered to Moira, leaning into her slightly.

Moira shrugged. "I don't know, but I hope she comes back soon. I hate it down here."

Amis nodded vigorously, which made Moira smile. They stood in silence for another minute or two. Moira looked around in the dim light, taking in more of the dungeons than she had the last time. She noticed a metal frame hanging on one wall and wondered what it was for. She stepped closer to it and noticed there were evenly spaced holes punctured into the metal. Moira pointed at them and looked at Amis.

Amis squinted slightly as he stepped closer to her and then grimaced. "Wall stocks," he explained. "Prisoners are hung by their ankles and left."

Moira took a step away from the wall stocks, shuddering over the brutality of it. She and Amis stood next to each other in silence until they heard the quiet steps of Alaine as she returned. She held a lantern so dimmed that it was barely even lit, and her face looked strained.

"Follow me," she said and turned right back around.

"I haven't been down this way, Alaine. I've only been down here once, and I was in a cell not too far from the stairs. Where are we going?" Moira asked, still whispering.

Alaine paused and turned around. She motioned for them to move in closer. Amis stepped up next to Moira, and they stood there, hunched together.

"We are going to the pit," Alaine said, with a tremor in her voice.

Amis gulped audibly.

"The pit?" Moira asked, unable to contain the dread in her voice.

With a deep breath and a small move of her head, Alaine said, "Yes. The pit. It is where the worst of the prisoners were taken and forgotten. It has not been used in many years, thankfully. But we must go down into the pit, and then we can get up through the secret passage."

A small, indistinct squeak escaped Amis. He looked like he was going to say something, but then he quickly shut his eyes and shook his head and made a sort of convulsing gesture with his shoulders.

"Are you quite sure it hasn't been used in many years?" Moira asked, noticing a tremor in her own voice. Her hands were also shaking, and she'd broken out in a cold sweat at the mere mention of the pit.

"I am certain," Alaine said, squaring her shoulders, "I checked just now to make sure that no one was recently tossed in."

A near hysterical laugh came from Amis, who whispered, "Tossed in!" He shook his head once more before mumbling, "Bloody hell."

"There is a reason not many people know of this particular passage, M'la – Moira," Alaine stated. "There is also a reason that even fewer use it. Do you wish to continue, or would you like to return to your rooms?"

Moira squared her shoulders and said, "We must continue. It would be foolish to give up such an opportunity because the circumstances are unpleasant." Moira turned to Amis and asked, "Are you going to come with us or not?"

333

All three looked at each other, and Amis winced and nodded. Alaine turned around again and continued down the narrow hall until they reached the end. She stopped and turned slightly to her left, then pointed downward. Moira and Amis squeezed into the corner of the dead end. They stood next to her, and both looked down at a narrow hole in the ground, tucked into a small carved-out space in the otherwise solid wall to their left. There was a metal grate over the hole, which appeared to be on hinges with a spot on the front to lock it. Alaine crouched down and slowly lifted the metal grate, which surprisingly made no noise as it moved.

"The pit," Alaine muttered, with a wave of her hand toward the dark hole.

"Lovely," Moira responded, suppressing the gag threatening to burst out of her at the smell emanating from the hole. Despite the awful odor of the main dungeons, the smell of the pit was far worse. The mix of long rotted flesh, damp earth, and something Moira couldn't identify rose from the pit to assault her nose. It was an overwhelming stench that nearly sent her running back to her room to bathe.

"Now that is the pungent odor of decaying flesh if I've ever known it!" Amis exclaimed while holding a hand over his nose and mouth.

"It is technically the smell of long-decayed flesh. Alaine did say it hadn't been used in a long time," Moira pointed out.

Amis simply glared at her as if the details of when the flesh decayed couldn't have mattered less to him. Moira chuckled softly. despite their awful circumstances and said, "Semantics, Amis." Try as she might, she couldn't hold back a tiny smirk as she thought back to her similar interactions with Roman.

Despite her young age, Moira admitted Alaine was much tougher than she expected. She was beginning to wonder why Sigrid hadn't been the one to bring them here, but then realized it was probably much easier for a young kitchen maid with fewer duties to bring them rather than one of the women who ran the kitchens. Moira was also astounded the smell rising from the pit wasn't bothering the girl more, but she decided not to make an issue of it.

"Lead the way, Alaine," Moira nudged, hoping her voice didn't betray just how much she did not actually want to go into the pit.

Chapter Fourt-Nine

Moira learned quickly that the best way to enter the pit was to sit on the edge of the hole and give a strong shove, allowing her body to just drop down through the short tunnel and into the bottom. Alaine did this almost gracefully and looked as though she had shoved herself into the pit many times before. Amis gave Moira a pointed look with an arched eyebrow before motioning for her to go next.

"I think I may need you to shove me, Amis," Moira told him in a hushed voice as if she was embarrassed to admit it.

"Oh, I'd love nothing more, trust me," Amis quipped.

Moira lowered herself to the floor, her feet entering the hole before her. She looked up and behind her to glare at Amis before saying, "No one forced you into this!"

"Hush and shut your mouth, who knows what you'll land in down there!" He commanded as he crouched down next to her.

Almost as an afterthought, Moira crossed her arms over her chest. Alaine hadn't said to do this, but Moira had no idea how long or narrow the hole actually was, and she would hate to injure herself right now. Moira gave a nervous nod and felt Amis's hands on her back right before he gave her a gentle but firm shove. The rancid air rushed past her as she slipped into the pit. Her skirts flew up a little, but not much, as she briefly free-fell into the open air of the pit. Her feet crashed into the ground just as she caught sight of Alaine's dimly lit lantern. Moira almost landed on her feet, but the surprise of the landing caused her knees to buckle, and she lost her balance before she toppled right into the damp earth...or what she sincerely hoped was earth.

As fast as she could, Moira jumped up and brushed herself off. Amis made his own appearance, agile as an acrobat, just as she finished getting the rest of the muck off her chin. He managed to land on his feet in an offensively gallant way that left Moira gaping at him.

"I feel a fool for asking this now, but how the bloody hell do we get *out*?" Amis asked.

"The getting out comes later," Alaine replied enigmatically. An ominous shadow was cast upon her small face from the lantern she held. She turned abruptly and walked over to the far wall of the pit, which Moira noticed did indeed have a large stone removed.

"This is the passage?" Amis asked.

Moira scoffed a little and said, "What else would it be? Honestly, why waste breath with that question?" She followed Alaine, who stepped onto a large stone on the ground and started to climb into the hole.

"Don't be cruel, Moi. I'm simply trying to follow this scheme," he responded, his voice a little shakier than normal. "I am learning rapidly that I don't like being underground in a cramped, dark space. Particularly one that smells of fetid flesh."

With that, Moira's annoyance faded. She remembered how claustrophobic she felt in the fireplace priest hide and immediately felt sympathetic. Not wanting to waste any more time with words, she gave Amis an apologetic smile and a light squeeze on the shoulder. His expression softened, and he gave her a tilt of the head, indicating she was forgiven and should follow Alaine.

Now crouched up in the entrance to the passageway, Alaine said, "That stone I used as a step is the one that usually blocks the passage. We must remember to return it to its spot when we come back, lest someone find it and discovers this passageway."

Amis looked at the stone, then turned to look back around what little they could see of the pit. He said, "Right, I'm not willing to believe this place gets the foot traffic to warrant concern of discovery; however, we shall return the stone if we ourselves return."

With an exasperated shake of her head, Moira stepped up onto the stone and climbed into the passageway. Alaine moved out of the way, but Moira could not see where she went. Once she shimmied in through the narrow opening, Moira saw a very narrow, incredibly steep staircase; Alaine stood on the third step to allow room for the other two to enter behind her.

"This doublet will never be the same," Amis lamented as he dragged himself through the hole and into the passageway on his stomach. "I wish I had time to change prior to leaving." He stood up in the narrow space, dusted himself off, and looked up. Alaine and Moira were both looking at him. "What?" He shot at them accusingly, feeling antagonistic over their expressions.

Neither Alaine nor Moira deigned to answer, instead, they both turned and started to walk up the treacherous-looking staircase. Alaine adjusted the lantern to allow for a slightly brighter light and walked determinedly upward. Moira had to catch herself from face-planting several times. The stairs were steep and uneven, creating a perilous path for someone with her coordination challenges. At one point, she caught her toe so unexpectedly that she pitched forward and was only saved from disaster by Amis's quick reflexes. He grabbed the back of her gown and heaved, stopping her forward momentum and only causing a slight scramble as she worked to regain her balance. The one true positive of climbing the staircase was the slightly improved air quality. As they moved up, the putrid smell of the pit quickly faded.

Just as Moira was about to ask how much further they needed to go, the staircase veered slightly to the side, and Alaine disappeared around the corner. Moira hiked her skirts up higher and hurried to follow her with Amis close behind. They very nearly slammed into Alaine as they rounded the corner and found her standing in a very small alcove of sorts. The stairs ended, and there was nowhere else to go that Moira could see.

"We must be quiet," Alaine whispered urgently as she once again dimmed the lantern to a barely visible glow.

"I thought you said this tunnel would lead us to the trophy room?" Amis asked, clearly piqued over being misled.

Moira looked around the small space in confusion, uncertain where they were. The walls were made of the same stone as the rest of the castle. There was no doorway or clear indication that they were anywhere near the trophy room. She started to imagine the route they'd taken through the castle walls as they'd climbed the hidden stairs, but her mind struggled to comprehend it all. She tried to picture a map of the castle; where the pit was located in the dungeons, where the secret tunnel was and where the stairs led them, but her mind failed her.

Alaine stepped over to one of the walls in the small nook. She removed a rectangular stone from the wall, which caused a narrow shaft of light to shine into the space. Alaine pointed at the hole and said almost inaudibly, "Look through here, Moira."

A little hesitant, Moira stepped forward. She wasn't entirely sure why, but very suddenly, her heart rate spiked, and that antsy feeling crept back in. Not wanting to waste the journey after they'd finally reached their destination, she stepped up to the empty space left by the stone. It was almost at eye level; Moira had to stoop just a little.

"What am I...?" Moira started to ask but then trailed off. At first, it was difficult to know what exactly she was seeing. Her view through the hole in the wall showed slats and gloom. Once she focused a little more on the space beyond the slats, she realized she was looking into the trophy room, as Alaine had indicated earlier, but Moira saw the room through a suit of armor. Specifically, through the removeable mouth portion in the suit's helmet.

Excitement replaced her earlier feeling of apprehension, and Moira turned around to look at Amis and Alaine. "It really is the trophy room! Am I looking through a suit of armor? It's hard to tell."

"Yes," Alaine breathed. "The armor is a curiosity in the trophy room because it's mounted to the wall in a manner that makes it look as though the armor is stepping out of the stone. Which was done specifically for this passageway, although I don't believe many still alive today know that."

Once Alaine confirmed Moira's suspicions, she knew precisely where they stood. On her recent escapades into the prince's beloved trophy room, she had taken note of the mounted suit of armor behind the writing table, but not once had she given it more than a fleeting thought.

"I've always wondered why on earth it was like that! It struck me as a very odd design choice in an otherwise suit of armor-less castle," Amis exclaimed, stepping forward and motioning for Moira to step out of the way. As Amis looked through the slot, he bounced up and down with excitement. "Oh, this is excellent! Minus the utter horror you go through to get here, of course."

"It really is a shame the entrance is located in the pit," Moira agreed. "Why on earth was it put there in the first place?"

Alaine shrugged. "I don't know who built the passageway. I assume the same king who built the castle. It is possible King Leo built the tunnel when he had the priest hides added, but the structure of all this makes me think it existed prior to his rule."

"You're very bright, Alaine. Who told you about this?" Moira asked in a whisper; she was beginning to miss speaking at a normal volume.

With pursed lips, Alaine shook her head. "Sigrid told me I shouldn't tell you how we know about the passageway."

This irked Moira to her very core, but she didn't want to push the subject when they were still concealed within the castle walls. While it probably didn't matter in the grand scheme of things, Moira was very curious to know what other passageways like this existed, if any. The women in the kitchens and the men who served elsewhere in the castle probably held more secrets than Prince Lyric would ever be comfortable with. All the possibilities jolted Moira's mind into overdrive, and she wished desperately that she had an active connection with Roman. He would have been in a frenzy to get into this passageway and be able to spy on Prince Lyric.

"Shit! Shit, Moira, get over here!" Amis hissed under his breath.

Without hesitation, Moira stepped over to Amis, and he practically shoved her up against the wall and put her face at the peephole. She attempted to whip around and ask him what the hell his problem was, but as he held her face toward the gap in the wall, she realized what had him so riled up. Prince Lyric, Lord Maddicot, Lord Dayben, Lord Leofwin, and Lord Owen were all settling themselves into the trophy room.

Chapter Fifty

"*Shit!*" Moira muttered mostly to herself before briefly turning to gawk at Amis. A beat later, she was back to looking through the slats in the armor's helmet. As she spied on the prince and his usual group of lords, she heard Amis whispering behind her, most likely catching Alaine up on what was happening. Nobody in the trophy room had spoken yet, and Moira was very curious about how well they'd be able to hear the men in the room. She worried the acoustics through the suit of armor and then through the stone separating them might make auditory spying rather difficult.

The suit of armor she spied through was located behind and slightly to the left of the large writing table. Moira watched as the prince settled himself at the desk while the lords found places at the other end of the room. From where Moira was positioned, she could tell that the prince had an ornate wooden box out on the desk - the same one she'd seen during her earlier foray into the trophy room - but she could not tell what the prince had taken out of it. He must have opened the box in the brief moment she had turned to look at Amis. Whatever was pulled out of the box now sat directly in front of Lyric on the desk, which meant his body effectively blocked Moira's view. Across the room from her was the roaring fireplace, which Lord Dayben leaned against casually while the other lords relaxed on the lounges and chairs.

"Did we lock the damned door?" Prince Lyric barked at no one in particular.

Moira stopped herself from squealing with joy. She heard the prince almost perfectly, if not without a slight metallic echo to his words.

"It's locked, Your Highness," Lord Maddicot said wearily.

Moira smirked from her hiding spot as she watched Maddicot get up from his seat by the fire and go over to tug on the doors. He held the prince's gaze as he gave the door a light pull, verifying that they were indeed secured. After her fake drunken intrusion, it seemed the group had upped their security efforts.

"Thank you, Greggory," The prince mumbled, almost inaudible to Moira.

Although she didn't want to miss anything, Moira turned around to Amis and Alaine just long enough to say, "It's a bloody shame that this is not a better setup. I have to choose whether I look or press my ear to the slot. Major design flaw!" She hardly took a breath as she whispered to them before turning back around to continue her spying. As an afterthought, she turned again and said to Alaine, "Best thing ever in the world, of course. You have no idea how grateful I am." She trailed off at the end, as she turned back around and saw Prince Lyric stand up.

"*Shit!*" Moira said excitedly under her breath, speaking to only herself. Her wasted time turning around had cost her the chance to see what was on the table. Out of the corner of her available, but limited vision through the armor, she saw Prince Lyric return the ornate wooden box to its usual shelf. Although she didn't see the shelf, she knew which one it was from the last time she spied on this group. Damn her excited verbosity. It had cost her both the opportunity to see what was taken from the box and the chance to see where Prince Lyric kept the key, assuming it was somewhere in the trophy room.

"Where is Fitzroy with our drinks?" Leofwin moaned. He appeared to have draped himself lazily across one of the lounges closest to the fire.

"The man has gotten sluggish in his old age. I may have to send for him a second time," Lord Owen said rather sadistically. Moira wondered what on earth Fitzroy had done to elicit such animosity from the lord.

"He is not your man to send for, Clarence," Prince Lyric snapped from his chair. He had returned to his throne-like seat after putting the box away. "He may be old, but he's also deaf. Deaf is my favorite type of servant. Do you know why *Lord* Owen?" The prince stood as he spoke, stepping around the desk to lean against the front edge, arms crossed. There was a mocking tone when he switched back to the lord's official title, which seemed to put all the men on edge.

346

Moira could not see his face, but she would have bet her entire (slightly stolen) book collection that Lyric had a sneer on his already pinched and narrow face.

To his credit, Lord Owen looked as if he inadvertently stepped into the lair of a wild animal and now wondered how he would safely get out. Although he was across the room from Moira's hiding spot, she saw a slight sheen appear on the lord's significant forehead, which he dabbed at with a handkerchief before speaking.

"No, my prince," Lord Owen said, "I do not."

Moira turned her head to the side so she could cram her right ear into the slot, attempting to hear the men across the room a little easier. The distance created a muffled sound effect.

There was a sudden shuffle in the room, which caused Moira to quickly change tactics and return to looking rather than listening through the spy hole. Prince Lyric had practically run across the room and stopped at Lord Owen's side. He was standing too close for the lord to stand, which made Lord Owen visibly panic. Moira had to shift a little left and right just to get a full view of the scene in front of her. *Damn these slats in the helmet*, she thought to herself. Just as she looked back at Prince Lyric, his hand swung out and grabbed Lord Owen by the ear. Lyric gave a great heave and stepped backward, dragging the lord along by his left ear. The entire sequence of events was violent and pathetic, as

Lord Owen crawled along, unable to stand, while the prince drug him back toward his writing table.

Prince Lyric came to a stop just in front of the table but kept a firm hold of the lord's ear as he bent down and shouted into it, "I LIKE A DEAF SERVANT BECAUSE HE CANNOT SPY ON ME, YOU DAFT WEASEL!" With that, the prince let go of the lord's ear and walked around his desk to sit back down. He straightened his shirt before saying, "Do not call me 'prince'. I am king in every way but the legal formalities that we are striving to correct."

Lord Owen sat in a kneeling position, rubbing his now bright red ear. Moira glanced at the other lords, who were all pointedly looking anywhere but Lord Owen or Prince Lyric. The more she spied, the more Moira witnessed this unpleasant and erratic behavior from the prince. More of what the courtiers said to her in her early weeks in the castle was finally making sense. Many women warned her to avoid the prince entirely; some had warned of his frequent outbursts, but until very recently, Moira had been lucky to avoid all of it. This, she reasoned as she stared at the now silent room, was most likely due to the fact that her first year at court had been spent hermitted in the library as much as possible.

Moira didn't hear it, but there must have been a knock at the door because Lord Maddicot sprang from his chair and went to unlatch and open it. The subject of the prince's

348

outburst, a frail old manservant named Fitzroy, lurched into the trophy room with an uneven gait. He carried a tray laden with drinks, which Moira expected to fall at any moment. To her surprise, and Lord Dayben's by the expression he wore in the corner, Fitzroy set the tray down smoothly onto the low table in the middle of the sitting area. Fitzroy was bald except for about twelve white hairs on the top of his head, which wobbled as he bent at the waist in a bow to the prince.

Prince Lyric lazily waved at hand at the man, then said rather loudly, "Be gone, you old bastard. We have no more need of you!"

The cruel words made Moira cringe. Fitzroy might be deaf, but Moira was sure he could read lips, which meant he knew exactly what was yelled at him. Lord Godberd, to his credit, quickly hid his own expression of astonishment at the prince's words. This was the first glimpse of his face Moira had since he was in a chair facing away from her. He stood the moment Fitzroy walked in with the tray, which was oddly courteous of the lord. Before she could soften toward the man, Moira reminded herself that Lord Godberd was involved with Lyric for a reason, and standing when a servant entered the room did not erase whatever atrocities he had already committed and was most likely willing to commit for the prince's twisted cause.

Each man slowly stepped forward after Fitzroy left and claimed a drink. Moira felt a light tap on her shoulders, which caused her to jump. She turned swiftly and hissed, "You just scared my fucking soul from my body!"

Amis smirked and said, "You're hogging the spy hole! I want to see it! We can barely hear anything from back here. Just muffled sounds at various volumes."

Moira glared at her brother, took one last glance through the peephole, and said in a whisper, "Fine, but pay close attention. We're still spying, whether Roman is around to hear what we learn or not!"

With a wave of his hand as if brushing her off, Amis practically leapt forward to look through the gap in the stones. Rather begrudgingly, Moira stepped back closer to the steps where Amis had been. It was tough to hand over the opportunity to get some information, but at least for the moment, it seemed like the men were taking the time to regroup after the unexpected violent paroxysm from the prince. Moira trusted Amis to pass on anything she missed.

For the first time in what felt like ages, Moira looked at Alaine. She stood pressed against the wall; the dim lantern forgotten at her feet. Her thin arms were wrapped around her torso, and every few seconds, a fresh tremor radiated down her body. Alarmed at the state of the young girl, Moira stepped in front of her and bent down to look her in the eyes.

As quietly and gently as possible, Moira asked, "Alaine? Are you alright?" She put her hands on the girl's shoulders and gave her a gentle rub, hoping that she was comforting and not frightening.

Alaine nodded, looked down a little, and leaned her forehead against Moira's. This surprised Moira, but she managed to stop herself from jerking back at the unexpected contact. Alaine only held her head there for a moment before straightening back out and saying, "I did not expect there to be people in the trophy room. Sigrid said I could show you the passageway and then return to the kitchens."

"Ah," Moira breathed, understanding now why the girl had such a strong reaction. "If the prince does not know of this passageway, I cannot imagine we will be caught. It will all be fine. Even if they heard us, imagine the time it would take them to muddle through where we are and how we got here. Do you want to head back to the kitchens on your own? I'm sure we can find out own way out."

Alaine vigorously shook her head. "I promised Sigrid I would get you in and back out safely." She wore a confident look as she straightened up and uncrossed her arms. The expression of sheer determination and control that she had earlier reappeared as she looked Moira in the eyes.

"Alright, Alaine," Moira said with a nod. She understood that sense of duty, even if there was no real logic within it. She knew she and Amis could make it out of here safely, but she would not steal that point of honor from Alaine, not after she had so bravely led them here through the dungeons and the pit.

When Moira turned around, Amis was motioning silently for her to return to the spy hole. His face remained glued to the spot, but his arm was reaching out behind him and waving at her to step forward. Moira hustled forward, standing right next to Amis and attempting to get back into the prime spot.

Amis stepped out of the way and let her look back into the room. He moved to stand directly behind her and said quietly into her ear, "They are discussing the king."

Chapter Fifty-One

If Moira could have wedged herself into the suit of armor itself, she would have in a heartbeat. While she wouldn't go so far as to say she was ungrateful for this windfall of an opportunity, she was mildly annoyed with the man who came up with this concept, for it left a lot to be desired in terms of ease of spying. It looked like nothing visually exciting was happening, so Moira turned her head to the side and crammed her ear as far into the space as possible.

" -get that the dosage cannot change," Lord Dayben said.

Moira was frustrated with Amis once again. Thanks to his insistence that he get a turn, she had missed the beginning of the conversation.

"Nobody said anything about changing the dosage, Noll," Lord Maddicot responded testily. "We all understand the dosage is important, so you can quit harping on it at every damned meeting."

"I will not quit 'harping' on it, as this entire bloody operation depends on that man having the proper dosage applied via tincture twice a day at the exact same times. No more, no less. Any more and we kill him -," explained Lord Dayben, but he was interrupted as the other lords spoke in unison.

"- any less, and he gets away."

"Yes, we know the drill, Noll. As I said," Maddicot carried on, now glaring fully at Dayben. "Let us return to the original reason we called for this meeting. The village witch who prepares the tincture for us is running low on supplies."

"How is that possible?" Prince Lyric asked, still seated at his writing table, with his hands steepled together in front of him as his elbows rested on the padded edge of the armchair.

Moira glanced around the room and noticed Lord Leofwin was staring blankly at the ceiling while Lords Owen and Godberd seemed to hang on Lord Maddicot's every word. How typical of Leofwin to not even be engaged in the secret plot he willingly took part in.

"She claims that the place in the forest where she usually picks the flower is now bare. She has taken all she can and is unable to find more," Maddicot answered.

Moira cursed them all for not using the name of whatever it was they were talking about. What did the village witch harvest from the forest to turn into a tincture that was then used on King Leo? She wondered if Amis caught the name of whatever it was when they first started speaking; however, she was not about to turn around and ask him. Not when she risked missing new and vital information.

Prince Lyric sat in silence for a moment before saying loudly, "I do not want her excuses! The purple poison is one of the most common in Anglia. If she cannot find it, I will have her executed and find a different woman who can do what she cannot." The prince stood and threw his cup across the room, shattering the glass in the back of the fireplace. All four lords who were seated near the still roaring fire flinched and shielded themselves from errant glass shards. His tone held no room for disbelief - he would do exactly as he threatened, and everyone there knew it. The prince's shoulders rose and fell dramatically as he stood there breathing heavily after his second outburst of the evening.

Lord Maddicot held the prince's gaze and gave a small bow. He said almost too quietly for Moira to hear, "I will let her know."

"Good. Now all of you, get the hell out of my trophy room," shouted the prince, sitting back down in his cushioned chair.

"Yes, Your Highness," they all answered in almost perfect synchronization.

Lord Maddicot stood first and opened the doors. He held them as the other lords filed through, each one bowing at the waist to the prince as they passed him. As far as Moira could tell, the prince did nothing in return. Lord Maddicot gave a deep bow, and then he closed the doors behind him as he left.

Moira waited with bated breath, staring at the back of the prince's head and wondering what he would do now that the room was his. Amis tapped on her shoulder again, to which she held up a finger behind her, attempting to indicate that she needed just one more moment. Unfortunately, Amis did not agree with her desire to continue watching, as he grabbed her shoulder roughly and turned her around.

"We need to go," he said with quiet urgency. "Alaine insists we leave now."

Alaine gave Moira a vigorous nod when she turned to look at her. With one last longing glance back to the spy hole, Moira nodded in agreement. They had already stayed here for too long. There was no hesitation in Alaine as she bent down to grab the stone and replaced it silently to its original place. The pinpricks of light that shone through from the trophy room disappeared.

Chapter Fifty-Two

Leaving the passageway itself was quick and easy when compared with the absolute torture of stepping back into the pit. The smell assaulted all three of them as they approached, and Moira felt her skin crawl with a deep desire to be above ground and out of narrow, dark spaces.

Moira and Alaine weaved their hands together to create a boost for Amis after deciding that he should be the first one out of the pit. This was primarily because he was the only one who would be strong enough to lift anyone up and out of it. Amis stepped onto their hands, apologized for his filthy boots touching them, and sprung up into the dungeon with his usual graceful ease.

"It is going to take every ounce of my self-control to stop from sprinting back to my room," Moira said, slightly out of breath, once they were all out of the pit and Amis was closing the grate behind them. "I am also really looking forward to speaking above a whisper!"

Alaine nodded fervently and said, "That was much more of an adventure than I anticipated. I am extremely late for my duties in the kitchen."

"I'm so sorry about that, Alaine," Moira said, truly feeling a little rotten that they had kept her from anything. "I will say that staying was entirely worth it in terms of everything we managed to overhear."

"Agreed!" Amis said as they started to walk down the dungeon hallway. "Now for part two - returning to our respective places in the castle without arousing suspicion."

****

Despite Moira's concerns about being intercepted (which manifested in the form of a dry mouth and sweaty palms) as they walked through the castle, they were not stopped by anyone. The weather gifted them an oddly nice day for the time of year, which meant the majority of the courtiers were outside. Moira and Amis escorted Alaine back to the kitchens since it was on their way back to Moira's room. They said a quick "thank you" but didn't delay her any further than they already had.

As they slowly ascended the stairs, Moira realized just how much time had passed since they left her room. Their usual midday mealtime had come and gone, leaving Moira to wonder what Hanna thought of their absence. She'd soon find out, as she and Amis reached her room after what felt like an interminable amount of time.

The second they were inside, Moira started speaking. "What is the 'purple poison' that the prince mentioned? Do you think the man they spoke about was King Leo? Wait, you overheard the beginning of that conversation, which means you know if it was King Leo…did you tell me they were talking about the king? It all happened so quickly and so unexpectedly that the tiny details of it all are now blending together. All I can recall is the big stuff...pit, outburst, drinks...poison reference...What?" She stopped suddenly as Amis grabbed her by the shoulders.

"You are ranting and pacing, a combination I do not have the energy for at this particular moment. Can we please sit down and talk before I flee in search of peace?" Amis begged her while motioning to the comfortable seating options in her main room.

With an impatient eye roll, Moira acquiesced and sat down. As she settled in, she begrudgingly admitted to herself that Amis had a point. A comfortable seat after their foray into the pit and secret passageway felt like exactly what she needed. Before he sat down, Amis made sure to visit the recently restocked alcohol cabinet and poured himself a generous-looking goblet of whiskey. He motioned between Moira and his goblet, offering to get her some, too. After a moment of thought, Moira nodded. She decided that she needed a dose of liquid stamina after the morning they had.

Amis handed her a second goblet, filled slightly less generously, she noted, before perching on the settee. He took a large drink of his whiskey before setting it on the small table in the middle of the room. With a sigh, he said, "Yes, they were talking about the king. I believe 'purple poison' is another term for Monkshood."

"Believe it or not, that doesn't entirely answer my question," Moira responded, sipping her own whiskey and

359

appreciating the comforting smolder she felt at the back of her throat.

Amis cocked his head and said, "Here, I thought you were an avid reader!"

"Believe it or not, you churl, my usual reading doesn't often bring me into direct contact with detailed litanies on various poisons," Moira fired back. "As I'm not a complete dolt, I already deduced that the 'purple poison' is a poison, so calling it by another name without any further information does not answer my question in any way."

With a chuckle, Amis grabbed his goblet from the table and gave her a sort of solute with it before taking another long drink. He smacked his lips appreciatively and then said, "Fair enough, Moi. You've got me there."

Moira gave her brother a self-satisfied smirk and then took another sip of her own drink before setting it down and relaxing back into the chaise. She pursed her lips in thought and then asked, "So, do you actually know anything about Monkshood? I have to admit, calling it the 'purple poison' feels far more covert. No wonder they don't say its real name."

Amis scoffed and looked skeptically at her. "Do you honestly believe the prince uses that term just to sound more covert?" Moira shrugged and nodded. "How sweetly naive of you!" Amis teased. "I would imagine he uses it because that's what the woman in the village who makes the tincture

360

calls it. Purple poison is its common name because the poison itself comes from - are you ready for this?"

This time Moira scoffed and said, "Out with it before I lose my patience and go look it up myself in the prince's own library!"

With a flourish of his hand, Amis said, "A purple flower."

Moira's brow furrowed as she stared at Amis. "The poison is a purple flower?"

All Amis did was grin at her and take another gulp of his swiftly diminishing whiskey.

"How do people discover these things?" Moira said with an exaggerated sigh. "I mean truly! Who first came upon the flower and decided that eating it was the right call, only to then be proven monstrously wrong when he died? Or suffered whatever ill effects came from ingesting the damn thing?" She huffed in exasperation.

"The human experience is a wondrous thing, is it not?" Amis said with an air of delighted sarcasm. "Do you think the smell of the pit will ever fully leave our nostrils?" Amis asked as he gave his doublet a good sniff.

There was a lull in conversation while Moira let her roiling thoughts reconcile. She went to stand up, ready to pace as she talked through the rest of her tangled thoughts, but Amis put his hand on her knee and shook his head sternly.

"I really cannot fathom your need to move while you work through things. Normally I can put up with this unique quirk, but not today. I am exhausted in both mind and body." Moira gave Amis a pointed look while gently removing his hand from her knee. She sat back into the cushions as belligerently as possible, just to make sure he knew she was willing to comply but not happy about it. Amis relaxed as well and said, "Thank you! Now let's have it."

"A tincture is some sort of salve, right?" Moira mused out loud, not entirely sure if Amis could answer.

"A tincture is distilled alcohol mixed with herbal extracts. Commonly taken orally to relieve various ailments," Hanna said from the doorway.

Moira jumped, startled by Hanna's sudden appearance. Amis gave his biggest grin and finished off his drink.

"Try making a noise sometimes, Han. It would be great to know when you enter a room from time to time," Moira scolded, unable to keep the bite from her voice when she was trying to recover from the scare.

"I would rather you learn to pay a little more attention to your surroundings, girl," Hanna said while very pointedly latching the door.

"What do you know about tinctures, Hanna dear?" Amis asked jovially as he meandered back to the alcohol cabinet. Hanna stepped further into the room to stand in front of the cabinet, effectively barring Amis from his intended goal. He stopped and looked down at her, pouting.

"I can tell from your tone that you've had enough for now. Sit," Hanna said, waving Amis back toward the settee. Surprisingly, Amis did as he was told. Hanna folded her arms across her chest and said, "Moira Ellyn Finglas, why are you asking about tinctures? And why does this room smell like an upturned cemetery? I assume it has something to do with your failure to attend the midday meal."

The use of her full name always made Moira squirm, whether she misbehaved or not. She scrunched her nose at Hanna and said, "I'm happy to answer your questions, Hanna...Ashdown..." Moira paused, finger tapping her chin, and said, "Hanna, what *is* your middle name?"

Hanna did not answer but instead continued to stand with her arms crossed while she stared at Moira.

"Oh, do start tapping your foot, Han!" Amis cheered from his spot on the sofa.

This seemed to break the spell of frustration between Hanna and Moira, as both burst out laughing.

"We are co-conspirators now, you know. I don't need to be lectured for my behavior or glowered at until I provide a sufficient answer," Moira said in an even tone. She really harbored no animosity toward Hanna, but she knew a little less parenting would be necessary for them to work together.

For whatever reason, this comment seemed to give Hanna indigestion, or so her expression indicated. Her gaze fell to the floor. When she finally spoke, there was the faintest edge to her voice. "I know where you have been, as Sigrid told me when I went looking for you in the kitchen," Hanna said. She paused, and Moira sensed she was not meant to fill this silence with any of her own interjections, so she sat quietly. Finally, Hanna looked directly at her again and said, "I know Roman told you not to act. Told you not to do *anything* until he sent word. Why are you disobeying his orders?"

Moira's brow furrowed, and her voice dropped as she asked, "Why am I *disobeying* his orders?"

"Uh oh," Amis muttered under his breath.

"Roman Loxley is leading this operation, in case you have forgotten," Hanna started, but Moira interrupted her.

"I never agreed to obey Roman Loxley, so you'll have to toss that notion out the window, Hanna," Moira snarled, unable to hide just how much that word irritated her. "I did agree to be his spy. To help him in the cause. All in exchange for a better life for Amis and me." Moira paused, catching her breath. She was more annoyed than she should be and knew she should calm down before she continued, but she kept going anyway. "I haven't seen Roman around lately," her voice hitched a little, but she pushed through the emotion, "Regardless of his absence, my goal remains the same. I will continue to work toward a better life. My focus might be narrow and selfish, but it stands to reason that if Amis and I are living better, that must mean something for everyone else, too. King Leo is alive...and whether Roman is around to continue to lead the fight to bring him back to the throne or not, we know that the king is alive. That knowledge is worth *disobeying orders*."

There was complete silence, apart from the sound of elevated breathing. Moira stood up at some point during her speech. She found herself suddenly drained of all energy, and she fell back into the comforting embrace of her chair. Amis lifted his glass in a toast but abandoned the gesture when he remembered it was empty.

Hanna, meanwhile, turned around and crouched down in the liquor cupboard behind her. She pulled out a goblet and a bottle of whiskey. With a heavy sigh, she walked across the room and set her glass next to Moira's and Amis's. The pop of the cork from the bottle felt louder than normal in the absence of any other noise. Hanna poured herself a few fingers of the amber liquid before moving to Amis's glass. He made sure to give the end of the bottle an extra tilt as she poured, earning himself an endearing glare from Hanna. With an assessing look first at Moira's glass and then at her face, Hanna wiggled the bottle slightly, asking if Moira wanted more. Moira shook her head and picked up her glass, which still contained enough whiskey in it to satisfy her for the time being.

Hanna returned the whiskey to the cabinet and then pulled over a chair from the small dining table and sat down heavily. "Gods help us if you are as assiduous in this compulsion as you are in every other." With that, she raised her glass before tossing back the entire measure of liquor. "Now, tell me everything and do so without embellishment. I've got to get you ready for dinner in an hour."

Chapter Fifty-Three

Despite the now chilly temperatures, Moira found herself walking down to Ivywood Village to see Meggy. Not only did she have a few books to share after many weeks without visiting, but she also wanted to talk to her friend and see if she knew anything about the woman who was helping Prince Lyric repeatedly poison King Leo – the village witch. Moira was extremely curious if the woman knew how her tinctures were being used. Although several days had passed since her foray into the secret passage - with no desire to return any time soon - Moira had not worked out how the prince managed to poison the king on a regular basis while keeping him alive. There had been at least two late nights spent in the library researching the purple poison, Monkshood, *aconitum napellus;* but so far, Moira found no answers to her ever-growing list of questions. Part of the challenge Moira faced while doing research in the castle library was the fact that there was almost no organization system; or at least not one she could easily discern and follow. If she ever had the chance and the time (permission not required), Moira decided she would reorganize the entire library to something far more logical and easier to track.

The companionship of her thoughts kept Moira entertained and distracted her from the bite of the air as she entered the outer limits of the village. Houses, crofts, and farmsteads started to appear, all bringing the familiar noises of rural life. Moira found herself humming as she picked up her pace, suddenly very excited to see Meggy for the first time in what felt like years. She reached the Taylors' cottage in record time and eagerly knocked on the door. There was no sound within the cottage, and the chimney only had a faint wisp of smoke coming from it, making Moira wonder if anyone was home. At this time of year, there would normally be a roaring fire in the kitchen and smoke in the chimney to show it.

Moira opened the door a crack and called out for Meggy, but the cottage remained silent. She felt a surge of disappointment and wondered if she should leave the books for Meggy. After a quick glance around she abandoned the idea. Since she couldn't risk leaving the books out in the open, Moira wasn't sure where she could hide them. With one last call for Meggy and no response, Moira hoisted her book bag back onto her shoulder, closed the door, and turned to leave.

With her head low and her mind elsewhere, Moira walked back down the pebbled path toward the village's dirt road. She was so deep in thought that she walked right into a large, brown object standing at the end of the Taylors' path. A squeak of surprise escaped her, and she put her hand up to her chest as she skirted back a few steps.

"Oh, Friar Tuck!" Moira exclaimed as she saw his friendly, beaming face looking at her. "You nearly scared the soul out of me!"

The friar made a small bow and said, "My sincerest apologies! I would never want to frighten the soul out of a new friend." The corners of his mouth twitched as he smiled at her. She noted the light breeze made the bottom of his long beard dance along his belly.

Moira smirked facetiously and asked, "What about the soul of an old friend?"

With a wink, the friar responded, "Ah, now that is different. The soul of an old friend is better known to me. I would know whether there is one to scare or not!"

Moira laughed, delighted, and her previous sullenness melted away, despite her disappointment over not seeing Meggy.

"It is splendid to see you, Friar Tuck. Especially knowing my soul is safe and sound," Moira said warmly.

"Excellent! Now, let us get somewhere either warmer or far more interesting where we may talk. The temperature does not yet warrant snow, but it does seem as though my fingers and toes may fall off at any moment." The friar held out his robed arm to her, and Moira took it with a smile.

"Where are we going?" She asked.

"That is entirely dependent on what you need to talk about," Tuck responded cryptically.

Moira stopped walking and looked skeptically at the friar. "You're a mysterious man, Friar Tuck."

With his usual beam, Friar Tuck nodded sagely and said, "A man of the cloth must be many things."

With an amused scoff Moira asked, "Have you heard anything from our mutual friend?" She tried to keep the longing out of her voice and felt she'd done a reasonable job at it, considering the friar did not know her well.

For the first time since she met him, the friar's face fell. He looked up at the sky, eyes squinting, and said, "It has been weeks since I heard from anyone connected with our friend." He looked back at Moira with sympathy and said, "My only comfort is knowing that if something truly awful happened, we would know because the prince would be spreading word with reckless abandon."

Moira nodded and tugged gently on the friar's arm, indicating they should start walking again. The fabric of his robe was rough, but warm. She wondered if he had any comfort in his life.

Once they were moving at a slow pace, Moira said softly, "After the Archery Competition and the disaster that unfolded, our friend told me he would be unavailable for a long stretch of time. I am attempting to carry on as best as I can without him."

Friar Tuck kept his gaze forward, but Moira saw the corner of his mouth curve upward as he said, "I imagine you've been triumphant."

Moira was tickled by his response, and she couldn't help but ask, "What makes you say that?"

With a shrug, the friar explained, "After my many years on this earth, serving all kinds of people, I've come to learn that there are people who do great things. Make things happen. Whether through backbreaking hard work or through sheer force of will, maybe a little of both…things happen around them and for them. Call it my intuition, or simply an old man's ramblings, but I know such things."

"And you believe I am one of these people?" Moira asked curiously.

"Oh no, my new friend!" Friar Tuck said, his smile returning, "I *know* you are one of these people." He gave her hand a gentle squeeze and said, "Tell me what brought you to the village today. Remember, I know everything, so there is nothing I cannot help you with."

Moira laughed generously. Something about Friar Tuck brought out a more carefree atmosphere, and she found it freeing. There had been too many hard days recently. Although she and Amis could always joke and find laughter along with plenty of sarcasm, there was always a weight to it that had never existed before. This darker overture was thanks to their new objectives in life, but it was still a shadow of the merriment they used to share. Moira felt lighter as she let her laughter flow naturally and enjoyed not having to cut it short to remain hidden or avoid detection.

Once she regained some composure, Moira said, "I should come to talk to you more often, Friar Tuck."

"If you do, you'll have to remember to call me Tuck."

"Right, of course. We are almost old friends now. I need to remember that," she said in a chipper voice she hardly recognized. "Let's keep walking, and you tell me what you know about the purple poison."

Tuck's steps faltered imperceptibly, but he kept walking at their current relaxed pace as he said, "I know the flower grows in certain areas of the Blackwood Forest. Rather abundantly, last I knew. There is another name for it, which escapes me now."

"Monkshood?" Moira whispered questioningly.

With a flick of his eyebrow and a sideways glance, Tuck said, "Ah, I see you may already know a few things yourself. Why don't you ask me your real question, Moira."

They continued to walk at a snail's pace down the main road of the village. People passed and smiled or gave the friar a friendly doff of their hat, but no one interrupted them or seemed to care what they were doing. It was a nice change from the constant watchfulness and intrigue of the palace. Moira assumed they would end up at the chapel again, but the friar seemed to be walking without a clear purpose. Her mind was working furiously on whether she should tell Tuck the full story or just ask him a few specific questions without the supporting details. Ultimately, she decided she would ask her questions and only provide further details if the friar inquired.

"Could someone be given small doses of the purple poison and survive?" Moira asked softly.

Tuck cleared his throat before speaking barely above a whisper. "There were experiments done once, not long ago, by an evil group of men." The friar swallowed audibly and glanced around as if checking to ensure they weren't being watched. This made Moira nervous, but she remained silent, unwilling to interrupt the story. She began looking around tentatively. She was trying to give the impression they were just out for a walk, while also gauging if anyone was eavesdropping.

Tuck pulled Moira's arm tighter into his, ensuring she was close enough to hear him. "The men started with very small doses of the poison, almost nonexistent amounts, simply to see what happened. The victims of their practice experienced a variety of symptoms ranging from numbness in their limbs, tingling of their whole bodies, nausea, violent and prolific vomiting, and difficulty breathing. Some people reacted within moments, while others took longer to show any sign of the poison. All of those forced into this endeavor were kept under lock and key for observation. Their doses were increased with regularity, and they were constantly watched. Some of the victims survived, but barely. Many of them eventually died as the poisonous concoction was altered and increased. Several of them experienced worsened symptoms when they were taken *off* the poison, which was probably the most shocking result. Those who survived lived a ghost life. A half-life. They were wholly dependent on their captors who kept them alive just to continue to poison them."

Moira's throat went dry, and she found that while her mind raced, she couldn't form a coherent response to the horror she just heard. Is this what the prince was doing to his brother? She knew the king was not likely to be kept in comfort, but to imagine that he might be held in some heinous cycle of poisoning just to control him? Poisoned just for the sake of easily keeping him imprisoned? Or was there another motive to the poisoning? Moira didn't know what to think. The concept made her stomach churn, and she sucked in several gulps of air before she felt like she wouldn't vomit right there on the side of the road.

"That's fucked - uh…I mean, that is incredibly wrong…" Moira trailed off, feeling her face flush at her use of language.

The friar chuckled good-naturedly. "Not to worry, my dear. Unless you plan to call me a Gallyan, you cannot offend old George Carlton Harold Tucksen."

Moira let out a tentative chuckle, thankful again that the friar maintained open expectations from the people around him. She found it vastly amusing that the worst insult he could think of would be associated with the territory to their south, Gallya. It was not uncommon to feel strongly about the southern territory, as it was the country that started the Crusades. Arguably, it was the country whose existence and war put her in the exact position she was in now…it was the reason she did not have her father here with her to help navigate through this immense moral and honor-driven thicket she found herself entangled in.

They were still walking slowly and without direction through the village, which suited their daunting conversation topic. Moira wasn't sure she could manage to sit still even if they'd gone inside.

"When you say these experiments happened 'not long ago,' do you mean within the last few years?" Moira asked.

Tuck turned his head toward her slightly and looked at her from the corner of his hazel eyes. "These experiments started immediately after King Leo's departure for the Crusades."

Moira gasped as she felt her stomach drop. King Leo left to fight in the Crusades, leaving his younger brother to rule in his stead, unknowingly leaving his people in the hands of a monster. It seemed Prince Lyric had been waiting for the right opportunity to complete these experiments and the

Crusades gave him what he needed. Moira stopped walking and turned to look directly at the friar. Her arm hung loosely at her side, no longer tucked into the warmth of his side.

"Did Prince Lyric fund these experiments?" She asked, unable to keep the tremor and rage from her voice. The longer she was involved in this twisted cause, the more she realized that none of the events of the last few years were happenstance. It was much worse - the horrors were planned, plotted in secret, and clearly thought out before they were executed.

With a sigh, Tuck said, "He funded and led these practices. From the moment he took over as temporary ruler of this country…In secret, of course, but the type of secret many people knew about, but no one spoke of openly. The lords that he keeps so close to him now were instrumental in the poison experimentation, and they all brought in victims that were used in the testing. They called it *Venenum Hortus.*"

"The poison garden…." Moira mumbled. She could feel her heart slamming in her chest as she stood on at the outer limits of the village. Her mind raced in different directions, and she wasn't sure which thought to follow. She felt ill at the thought of Leofwin, the man she was meant to marry, dragging some poor man away from his life and family just so the prince could execute a vicious and cruel procedure on him. There was absolutely no way her father and mother had known about this. If they had, Moira knew without a doubt that they would have ended the engagement. She reminded herself that the terms of her betrothal had been worked out in her childhood, years before the nefarious behavior began. Moira told herself that much to try and quell the rising feelings of rage and nausea that threatened to overwhelm her.

"What was it all for?" Moira asked, her voice heavy with stifled rage.

Tuck's shoulders sagged sadly, and he shook his head. "I do not know, my dear new friend."

Moira sniffed, pushing down her building emotions and nodded at the friar.

"Are you meant to be anywhere today?" Tuck asked her, effectively breaking the spell of her spiraling negative thoughts.

She blinked a few times and wiped away an errant tear. With a few swift blinks, she cleared the remaining excess moisture from her eyes and responded. "I have no obligations at the castle until this evening when I must attend dinner with Lord Leofwin." Moira couldn't conceal the animosity that crept into her voice at the mention of his name.

Friar Tuck's face erupted in a mischievous but non-threatening smile. A slight breeze ruffled the trailing edges of his robe, and the tips of his substantial beard were blown toward her slightly. He smoothed down his facial hair, twisting one side around his pointer finger and said, "There is somewhere I want to take you."

Tuck bobbed his head toward the road and started to walk, but this time he moved with a determined gait and a clear purpose. Moira looked back toward the village but decided there was no reason to rush back to the castle, especially not when she had no idea how to behave around Prince Lyric and Lord Leofwin, knowing what she now knew.

With a small sigh, she hefted up her skirts and followed the friar, wondering where in Anglia he could be leading her when nothing existed in this direction for miles.

Chapter Fifty-Four

Moira's breathing was embarrassingly labored as she followed along behind Friar Tuck. Nearly an hour had passed since they started their journey. She started to wonder, once again, where he was leading her. They no longer walked along the road but veered into the hilly terrain that existed southeast of the village. They walked in the direction of the town of Gest, but Moira knew they couldn't get there by foot and certainly not by leaving the road. She was long past enjoying the scenery. Initially, it was pleasant to see a little more of the open pastures as she knew from her childhood in Huntsley; however, the charm had worn off quickly. She no longer felt chilled as she labored to keep up with the shockingly agile old man.

"Friar, where are we-," Moira started to ask.

"Tuck, my dear. Call me Tuck. You and I are old friends now!" He said, merrily turning around to shout at her as he continued walking. "It's just over this last hill, you cannot miss it!"

Moira decided to preserve her limited air supply and not respond. All that time living in the castle and doing nothing but reading had finally caught up with her, just as Hanna had once warned her. Despite her habitual time spent reading, Moira felt like she had taken every opportunity to be active that she could, it was just that opportunities were few and far between for a lady of the court. Even if said lady worked as a rebel informant in her spare time.

Amidst her internal ramblings, Moira managed to crest the final hill. She bent forward, hands on her knees and sucked in as much air as she could while vowing never to admit to anyone else just how winded this altogether short journey had made her.

"There it is!" Tuck said, filled with ebullient pride.

Moira looked up finally and cocked her head. "There…" she trailed off. Not entirely sure what it was she saw.

"The Crooked Church!" Tuck nearly shouted.

"The Crooked…" Moira shook her head, wondering if she was about to faint. "Tuck, did you just say The Crooked *Church?*"

Tuck continued to beam at her, which she realized was often just the man's natural facial expression. He nodded so aggressively that his jowls wiggled under his chin, which she could see through the parting in his beard.

With a hand shielding her eyes from the sun, Moira asked, "What exactly makes it crooked?"

He answered her question loudly as he walked toward the building, full tilt down the slight slope. "The inside, of course!"

"Right, the inside," Moira commented to herself as she made a slightly slower and more controlled descent than her companion.

As far as she could tell, Moira was looking at an old, but ordinary building. It had definitely seen better years, as the stone facade was crumbling. There was a thick layer of green overgrowth inching its way into the front door, and a rather impressive vine was snaking its way around the building. The stone was a dark gray color, with a small bell tower on each side of the entrance. It appeared that both bells were gone, leaving the openings empty to the sky. The shadow of an old path still wound up to the front door, but it, too, was covered in overgrowth.

"Tuck, pardon my ignorance, but I'm still failing to see what is crooked about this church. Given your divine background, I'm assuming you haven't brought me to a location where a crooked religion was practiced...have you?" Moira asked tentatively.

Without any significant thought, Moira realized that she blindly trusted Friar Tuck because he was a man of the cloth and an alleged friend of Roman's. She never verified this relationship, but that was mostly due to the time constraints that seemed to dictate every interaction she had with Roman. Not to mention the fact that Roman had recently gone to ground without a single indication of his whereabouts. Moira told herself that it was too late to worry about Tuck now as she already let him lead her to a secluded and abandoned building without any fuss or fight. If he killed her, she felt quite honestly like she deserved it. When it came down to it, she did not have a bad feeling about the friar at all, which made her decide he was very unlikely to murder her.

Moira realized Tuck was looking at her with an odd expression, one of fascinated concern. He finally spoke up after a few seconds of staring and said, "I imagine your mind is a wondrous place to be, Moira Finglas. So many emotions play across your face, but none of them seem to fully betray your thoughts."

"Erm, thank you," Moira responded, unsure of what else she could possibly say.

"There was no 'crooked religion' practiced here. This church, if you choose to step inside, was built crookedly. Some of the men with a unique sense of humor who practiced the old religion built it. They told a tale of a man who survived a fight with a devil. When the man came to worship the following day, the devil followed him and made the structure increasingly complicated to navigate in an attempt to trick and capture the man. The fearless man persevered and evaded the devil, thanks to his devout determination." The beaming grin was back on his face as he motioned for her to step inside. "As someone of the Old Religion, I thought you might like to see it. That and I know of certain things kept here that I did not want to be found."

He shrugged as he said this as if it were common for a friar of the new religious order to store contraband items in a church belonging to the old religion.

Once Moira gathered her thoughts on both the bizarre origin story and her curiosity over what Tuck was hiding here, she said, "I'm sorry, I was just struck by how unusual this whole situation is and how much my father would have loved it." She took another breath and then added, "Oh well, minus the part where I followed someone who is essentially an acquaintance. A friend of a friend, really. Apart from that, though, I think he'd enjoy how you've repurposed what is possibly the most peculiar structure in all of Anglia."

"Does that mean we can finally go inside?" Tuck asked excitedly and with a hint of sarcasm.

Moira chuckled and nodded before she stepped through the doorway. She brushed past the old, deteriorated wooden door hanging limply on its hinges at a very odd angle. As she stepped in, she stumbled slightly but did not fall. It took her a moment once she was inside the building for things to register. Her body, without her consciously realizing it, had compensated for the tilt of the structure, and she found herself standing at an angle. Everything was slightly off. Crooked, just as Tuck said. Moira was standing but with a backward lean and slight arch that was required to stay up and not fall forward. She was astounded, even though Tuck warned her. Her head began to pound as she attempted to make sense of the tilted and distorted way the interior walls were built and the confusing slant of the floor.

"What the hell is happening?" She asked, a little loudly and with a worried pitch.

Tuck walked in and moved past her with far too much confidence. He, too, was tilted backward, with his rounded belly protruding in front of him much more than normal, but he moved as if nothing was awry. He turned a little, angling his body to the right but still backward, so he could look at her. "I told you. It's crooked."

Moira simply stared at him in dumbfounded silence. She blinked several times. Tuck started to move further into the church, and Moira noted the farther he got, the more he tilted to the right.

"I think 'tilted' might have been a better word," Moira mumbled mostly to herself as she precariously followed the surprisingly nimble man.

Just as the friar tilted more to the right, Moira found herself doing the same. There was no rhyme or reason to the building, and she grew increasingly frustrated. Her mind struggled to understand what was happening as she attempted to navigate a space that appeared straight but was actually anything but. The friar practically pranced up a short flight of stairs and then off to the left, disappearing into a room. Moira attempted to follow but found herself slamming into the stairway's railing simply because she'd failed to adjust properly, and the tilt of the staircase was the opposite of what she expected.

"For fuck's sake," she groaned under her breath as she clutched her undoubtedly bruised ribs. There was a faint ache in her side as she drew in a few deep breaths just to test things out. "Why is it always the ribs?" She wondered out loud with a grumble.

From the room ahead, she heard the friar call out, "If you can make it in here, the room is normal, I assure you!"

Unladylike as it was, Moira opted to crawl up the remaining two steps and round the corner in the same manner. It was easier to adjust her weight when she was on all fours versus when she was on her unreliable legs. Her head felt like it was spinning, which grew old with each passing second. She practically threw herself into the room ahead and was immensely relieved when she realized it was indeed a normal room. No tilt or shift or oddity that she could detect.

"Thank the Gods!" Moira said as she lay on the floor.

Tuck appeared above her, standing with his hands on his hips. He clicked his tongue and said, "Thank the Gods indeed, for it is their house of worship!" He looked mildly disappointed as he said glumly, "I expected you to enjoy the Crooked Church!"

Moira scoffed and said, "I'm afraid this proves that we are indeed only *new* friends, my friend. Unfortunately, I am

385

not gifted with the balance and grace you seem to possess. I struggle to find my footing in the straightest, most even-footed spaces, let alone in a building such as this."

Friar Tuck nodded sagely, a now familiar gesture. "Proof once again that no matter where you go, you're still yourself." He sighed and turned back around to rummage in a corner cupboard.

Brows furrowed over the friar's comment, Moira decided it was probably time for her to rise from the floor. Her heartrate had slowed, and she no longer felt like the world was tilting out of control. She sat up slowly and then stood up even slower, not wanting to go lightheaded before she needed to get out of this damned church.

As she stood, Friar Tuck handed her a small pouch closed tightly with a bit of twine. The satchel was light in her hand, nearly weightless, and she stared dumbly at the dark brown fabric. It looked like an oversized tea sachet, but it was made of thicker material. Eventually, she looked up with a questioning look, but she didn't speak. Moira's mind felt like mush. She was too drained to begin to guess what she held in her hand.

"There is no antidote for the purple poison," Tuck began, with a look of remorse upon his aged face. "However, this is something that can help off-set some of the more violent symptoms. If someone has been given increasingly large doses of Monkshood, he will be suffering greatly...if he is alive."

Moira looked intently at the friar. She was breathing so little that she was almost holding her breath. The stakes of her existence seemed to continue to get steeper and steeper with each new thing she learned.

"I am not an incredibly smart man, but based on your earlier questions, I have deduced that the cause our friend fights for...the individual he is hoping to find might be a victim of purple poison."

"Tuck, I imagine we can speak freely here, can we not?" Moira asked anxiously.

"Hmmm," Tuck looked thoughtful. "I do hate to remove the mystery of it all...but I suppose you are right. Although, I do not want you to tell me why you asked your earlier questions."

Moira agreed it was a very curious request, but she did not argue.

"In that pouch is a mixture of herbs that will off-set the immediate symptoms of the purple poison. Please do not misunderstand me - *this will not cure King Leo*." There was an intensity to Tuck's voice Moira had not heard before. She did not break his serious eye contact and listened intently. Tuck continued, "If he truly has been kept this long and poisoned the entire time, he will be facing lifelong residual effects from the poison." Friar Tuck paused as he gave Moira a stern look. She bobbed her head in acknowledgment. "These herbs, if ingested, will hopefully give the king enough improvement to escape wherever they are keeping him."

"Etheldred," Moira whispered.

The friar shook his head vigorously. "The less I know, the better, Moira. I mean that quite seriously."

Moira gulped and nodded. "Sorry, Friar."

With a change in tone and attitude, the friar clapped his hands together and said, "The time to leave has come!"

"Wait!" Moira protested.

"Are you suddenly keen on staying here longer? I would love to show you the rest of the church, but based on earlier, I fear it may cause you to projectile vomit. A sight I do not wish to see," Tuck said teasingly, but it still made Moira flush in embarrassment.

"No, I assure you that I do not wish to stay. It's just that I have so many questions, still...." Moira said, trailing off as she saw the friar turn to leave, sliding a little as his feet hit the slanted floor outside the room.

"It is a fair walk back to Ivywood Village, my newish old friend. There is no better time to talk than when one is enjoying a walk!" Tuck hollered as he scurried down the hall and turned to go down the warped steps.

Moira shook her head and gave in to the friar's unusual ways. She knew she wouldn't be able to persuade him to stay any longer. She tucked the brown pouch into the small drawstring bag she kept tied at her belt. She would have to find a safe place for it as soon as she returned to her room. With a sigh and a fortifying breath, Moira stepped out into the lopsided church hallway once more.

Chapter Fifty-Five

Moira made it out of the Crooked Church, although she felt like leaving was far worse than entering. Even though she knew what to expect, she still found herself unable to accurately judge which way the floor tilted until she was moving in the wrong way and falling to her knees. It took one stumble to realize she needed to lean forward on the way out, not backward like she did upon entering. Once she was out in the sunshine again, standing on normal ground, she felt immense relief.

"Not to be rude, but I can understand why that building is entirely abandoned," Moira said with a backward glare at the structure.

"It is not abandoned. It's minimally utilized," Tuck corrected her sternly.

Moira eyed the back of the friar's head as if he were crazy. "Right…," she said, unable to find any sane answer to the oddly forceful argument.

"Ask your questions now, my dear. I will not be able to speak openly once we are near the village. I believe we should neither dilly nor dally since you have a dinner to prepare for this evening. Too much time has passed since we left the village, and most of that was spent on the journey to the Crooked Church," Tuck lectured from a few steps ahead of her.

With a little hustle in her step, Moira jogged up to walk next to the friar. She wanted to be able to see his face, even from the side, when they spoke.

"Are you able to tell me why a sort of antidote - I know it isn't curative - was hidden in a back room of a neglected and very odd old church?" Moira asked. "Also, while you're in a testimonial mood, can you explain to me how it was discovered in the first place and how you came to know of its existence?"

With a chuckle, the friar jumped right into his answer, wasting no time at all. "An inquisitive mind is an excellent thing! I am certain you remember my explanation of the horrific studies performed using the purple poison?" Moira nodded, but she wasn't sure if the friar looked at her, for he plowed right on. "There was another element to that experiment, which included testing various antidotes. Of course, as we now know, there is none. However, some of the men responded well to various herbal concoctions." Tuck gestured to the pouch at her waist. "The herbs were not entirely restorative, but they did provide enough relief that the vile men performing the experiment were able to benefit substantially. By concocting the right mixture of herbs, they were able to force the poisoned men to recover quicker, thus allowing them to continue their experimentation all the faster. No more waiting for certain symptoms to subside when they could make it happen on their own timeframe."

"That's atrocious!" Moira exclaimed.

"Cruel!" The friar agreed.

Moira smirked. "Immoral!"

Tuck caught on quickly and said, "I'd go so far as to say it was even sinful."

"Sinful, for sure. Vicious as well," Moira said with a dramatic frown.

"Entirely iniquitous," Tuck fired back.

"Ignoble, really. Considering who conducted the experiment!" Suddenly Moira paused, realizing that she had inadvertently created a game based on a terrible situation. "Shit, I suppose this is wrong of us. I do love a good vocabulary battle, but perhaps it's insensitive here?"

"I don't believe finding something lighthearted amidst the depravity and darkness is wrong," Tuck said comfortingly. "Humor is curative in its own way, after all."

She didn't want to keep continue their impromptu game, but Moira gave the friar a small smile of thanks. The moment of levity made her feel better, even if briefly.

"How did you know the parcel was at the Crooked Church?" Moira asked again, not wanting to be pushy.

"I told you," Tuck said, turning to her with his beaming smile. "I know everything!"

Moira let out a generous laugh, although she cut it short, they reached the outer limits of the village. Tuck seemed to notice, too, for he cleared his throat and continued his story.

"Moira, I cannot tell you the full story, for it is not my own to tell. Please be satisfied knowing that a fellow friar learned what was happening. He risked and lost his life to end the experimentation and take as much of their material as possible. He was able to steal several parchments of notes and that one pouch I've given you. Nothing more. If that satchel is lost or damaged, we have the notes to look back on, but gathering the necessary herbs and mixing the right concoction for a remedy may be a significant challenge, so I shall beg you here and now to keep great care of that pouch."

They were still walking toward the village at a steady pace. Cottages came into view, and Moira's shoulder started to ache from carrying the book bag all day. Upon running into Tuck, the bag had been forgotten. She wished she had left it somewhere rather than carrying it this entire journey, continually shifting it from one shoulder to the other.

"I understand, Tuck. Of course, I will protect it," Moira said solemnly. She grabbed the friar's elbow softly, urging him to stop for just a moment. "Thank you," she said, mustering the utmost sincerity she could.

The now-familiar face of the friar looked at her in a gentler version of his usual smile as he said, "I cannot wait to see what you do, Moira Finglas!"

Chapter Fifty-Six

Moira parted with Friar Tuck as they passed the chapel. He proved once again that he was not a man for lingering goodbyes and made short work of his farewells before ducking into the main entrance of his church. She smiled and shook her head slightly, still somewhat unsure of the man but willing to trust him entirely. Without wasting any further time of her own, Moira began her return trek through the village, somewhat slower than before now that she didn't have the spritely old man to keep up with. As she meandered down the main road, she saw Meggy sitting on the front step of her cottage with Alaine.

"Meggy!" Moira called out excitedly. She waved gleefully, unable to hold back her elation at seeing her friend and new accomplice.

With an expression of excited surprise, Meggy looked up. When her eyes met Moira's, she whooped, jumped up off the step, and pelted down the walkway. She reached the road before Moira reached the gate, and Meggy half-leapt into Moira's arms and gave her a rib-cracking hug. Leaning full tilt into the moment of joy, Moira gripped Meggy tightly and spun them both around in one big circle before plopping Meggy back onto the ground. They both giggled playfully, and Moira attempted to tone down her laughter but found she could not. It had been entirely too long since she had seen her friend. In that moment, Moira decided to forego her earlier plan to question Meggy about the village witch. There would be time for official discussion another time.

In a surge of affection, Moira placed her hand on Meggy's cheek and said, "You look well, my friend!"

Meggy beamed and leaned into Moira's hand before saying, "You look sweaty, but it's lovely to see you regardless!"

Moira feigned offense but did take her sleeve and wipe it across her forehead. She had paid so little attention to her general existence today that she failed to realize the journey to and from the Crooked Church had taken a lot out of her.

"It's been one of those days, I'm afraid," Moira sighed before she looked back to the doorway where Alaine still sat. She hollered, "Hello, Alaine!"

Alaine gave her a grimace that looked as if she attempted to smile but failed. Moira looked anxiously at Meggy and asked, "Is Alaine well?"

Meggy looked down at her feet as she scuffed them around in the dirt. "Alaine's been let go from the castle kitchens. She's afraid to go home and tell her Gran on account of them needing her wages. With Roman gone to ground and his men with him, there's been no extra coin in the village for weeks."

Moira closed her eyes and momentarily wallowed in the deeply uneasy feeling that hit her when she realized that

Alaine most likely lost her job because of her and that damned day in the hidden passage. Moira glanced over to Alaine, who suddenly appeared incredibly small and vulnerable as she perched in the doorway of the cottage. Moira felt her face start to crumple, but she pulled herself together swiftly. It was not her position that warranted tears right now. Moira was determined to help, no matter how little.

Without further thought, Moira pulled two coppers from the purse at her waist. She was careful not to remove the pouch that Friar Tuck had given her as she retrieved the coin. Full of sympathetic resolve, Moira walked up the Taylors' path and crouched down next to Alaine.

"Meggy told me what happened, Alaine. I'm sorry. So genuinely sorry. I know you must have been let go because of the time you spent away from the kitchen helping me," Moira paused. She looked at Alaine closely before daring to ask, "Was there nothing Sigrid could do to protect you?"

Alaine sniffled and said, with her head hung low, "Sigrid tried, but she is not the head of the kitchen, so she was unable to prevent my dismissal. Please don't apologize, Moira. I knew the risks when I took you to the passage and I have no regrets. I am proud that I could help you." Alaine raised her head and jutted her chin out slightly as she finished speaking. Moira suppressed a smile; she suddenly felt a kindred spirit in Alaine. The determination and pride were something she could relate to.

"As you know, Roman has gone into strict hiding for the time being," Moira started and was pleased to note she spoke Roman's name without being swamped with emotion. Perhaps what she perceived earlier as love had simply been a passing infatuation, and now that Roman was no longer physically present, she might be able to move past the annoying emotion. She smiled to herself and then looked at Alaine. She held out the coppers and said, "These are for you and your family. Amis and I will be working with Friar Tuck to do our best to make sure that the village does not suffer too much in Roman's prolonged absence. I know this does not cover everything, but it's a small start."

Alaine stared at the coins in Moira's hands, and for a split second, Moira feared she had said or done something offensive. She knew that most villagers were proud and only took money from Roman because he and his men took it straight from the prince and his noblemen, who took it from the people in the first place. The prince like to steal from his subjects in the form of increased taxes and other political contrivances. To the villagers, Roman was simply returning money that was rightfully theirs.

Thinking quickly, Moira said, "Do not worry, this came directly from Lord Leofwin's own purse. He'd combust if he knew I was giving it to you."

A sweetly wicked grin appeared on Alaine's face as she reached out and took the money from Moira's palm. Meggy, who stood behind Moira as she crouched, put a hand on her shoulder. Moira looked up at her and gave Meggy a warm smile.

"Alright, Moira. Enough uprising business," Meggy scolded good-naturedly. Moira must have looked like she was going to argue because Meggy exclaimed, "No point trying to pretend otherwise. We are too far into this, and Alaine has already told me everything." A knowing smirk played on Meggy's freckled face as she looked down at Moira.

With a slight groan, Moira stood from her crouch and looked down at Meggy as she said, "Alright, Megs. You win. I'm done scheming for today."

Meggy smiled broadly as she reached out and took the book bag off Moira's shoulder. "Let's get to the good stuff!"

Moira laughed and decided that she could delay her return to the castle by a few minutes…Leofwin could wait, couldn't he?

Chapter Fifty-Seven

After spending what felt like mere seconds with Meggy and Alaine talking about books, Moira rushed back to the castle. Hanna was openly irritated with her for cutting it so close, but she had Moira ready for dinner in record time. The meal was blissfully uneventful, but Moira detected a certain undercurrent radiating from Leofwin as she sat next to him. Amis and Lady Lucia were across the table from her, and based on the concerned looks Amis kept throwing her way, he was picking up on something as well.

"Tell me, Lord Leofwin," said Lady Lucia in her singsong voice, "What are your plans for the Winter Festival?"

Moira paused in her eating and looked sideways at Leofwin, who seemed surprised to have been addressed by Lucia at all. He recovered quickly, dabbed at his mouth with his napkin, and then spoke.

"I plan to remain at court, as I do every year," he responded in a clipped but not directly rude tone.

"You do not wish to see your family?" Lady Lucia inquired, keeping her voice sweet and her face neutrally interested. Moira wondered what Lucia was up to. She always seemed to intercede at the exact right moment, but Moira didn't know if it was conscious or just part of her deeply ingrained courtier training.

Leofwin looked somewhat annoyed. His gaze shifted to his plate, and there was a ripple of annoyance before he answered. "No, Lady Lucia. I have never gone 'home' for the Winter Festival. My parents died long ago, and I have no desire to interact with my older brother."

Moira kept her gaze as neutral as possible while watching Leofwin. She had not known his parents were dead. And he had an older brother? Moira was surprised, but she remembered that she was just as disinterested in her betrothed as he was in her. In all honesty, she didn't even know where he came from, so it shouldn't shock her to learn he had a brother.

"I'm so sorry to hear that. It must be dreadful to be so disconnected from family," Lucia said, with so much genuine concern that Moira very nearly scoffed at her, but she stopped herself in time.

Leofwin, it seemed, decided he was done with the conversation. He gave Lucia a lingering look of distaste before rising from the table without excusing himself. Without a backward glance, he strode out of the Great Hall. Moira raised her eyebrows and turned to look at Amis and Lucia, who also wore expressions of mild shock.

"Seems his family is a sore subject," Amis said flippantly before returning to his meal.

Lucia snorted in the most unladylike manner Moira had ever witnessed from her. Lucia looked back and forth between Moira and Amis, seeming baffled at their expressions.

"Well," Lucia said, "Naturally it's a sore subject. His brother inherited the family estate and expelled Conor at the first opportunity. No notice, no warning, nothing. Their father passed away one night, and by morning, Conor was homeless."

Moira looked at Amis and asked, "Did you know this?"

"No, of course not. I barely remember the bloke's first name, let alone anything about his personal life," Amis responded.

"You were going to marry him, and yet you did not know this?" Lady Lucia asked in amazement.

Moira was about to respond when Lucia's word choice suddenly caught up with her. "'*Were* going to marry him'? I'm still engaged to marry Lord Leofwin," she said, oddly defensive. Although she really did not want to marry Leofwin, it was a huge concern that Lucia spoke of their engagement in the past tense.

Lucia had the good graces to flush and look down at her plate.

"Why did you use the past tense, Lucia?" Moira asked through gritted teeth while attempting to keep the edge from her voice. There was only so much she could hold back, and it was dwindling quickly as a knot of nerves settled in her stomach.

"Yes, Lucia," crooned Amis, with his own sharp inflection. "Do tell us what you mean by that."

With her hands held up in surrender, Lucia spoke low and fast, "I meant nothing by it; however, it seems that Lord Leofwin may be courting another lady from Gest. I overheard my father mentioning it the other day. It could be nothing, and since I do not know of any actual details, I should have been more careful with my words."

No ready response came to Moira's mind. Her gaze drifted to stare unfocused at a spot in the middle of the table. If Lord Leofwin ended their engagement, she would be free to do as she pleased. There would be no further betrothals arranged without her direct involvement, and since she sincerely hoped to remain unmarried for quite some time, there was no sadness over the way this might unfold. Although it may stain her reputation, it would not bring any lasting effects that she could bring herself to care about. The only downside would be the possible loss of her position in the court. She was summoned here by Leofwin as his betrothed, and as far as she knew, he paid her room and board. Technically, Amis was the lord of their family estate in Huntsley, and they could return any time they wished. Leaving the castle would bring no particular hardship to Moira, despite the fact that it would change her usefulness when it came to Roman and the fight to return King Leo to the throne. Despite this small potential downfall, she found herself nearly buoyant with hope at the thought of no longer being tied to Lord Leofwin in this sham of an engagement. He must have decided her dowry wasn't worth the trouble after all.

Moira's reverie was broken only by the sound of clattering plates and utensils from the other side of the hall. She glanced up to see a commotion building in the far corner of the room. Rather than attempt to figure out what was going on, Moira looked pointedly at Amis and stood from her place at the table. Amis rose from his seat and bobbed his head toward the door. Lucia stood in order to better see the violent-sounding events unfold at the opposite end of the Great Hall.

There were several things Moira needed to do tonight, and she may have already missed her opportunity for one of them. Without glancing back at the ruckus, Moira left the hall and headed toward the prince's beloved trophy room.

Amis caught up to her in the corridor and grabbed her elbow, stopping Moira in her tracks and forcing her to turn around. He gave her a searching look and said, "What's got your knickers in a bundle tonight? I am shocked the news from Lucia didn't elicit a more positive reaction from you."

Moira grinned wickedly. "Not to worry, dear brother! That news put some fanciful thoughts in my mind, to be sure," she said excitedly. Before continuing, Moira lowered her voice conspiratorially. "It's just that now I'm apparently running a certain mission once led by a notorious outlaw who is now utterly useless, I've got a few things to accomplish tonight." She pointed toward the Great Hall, wiggled out of Amis's grasp, and said, "That brawl just so happens to be the distraction I didn't know I needed. Now, you may join me, or you may carry on with Lady Lucia. Up to you." With that, Moira returned to her brisk pace down the corridor.

"You know that I'm joining you!" He huffed, hurrying to catch up to her. "As if I want to miss out on all the entertainment. What do you need from me?" Amis asked eagerly, rubbing his hands together.

Moira smirked as she watched him out of the corner of her eye. He kept up with her fast pace, and they neared the trophy room without further delay. She whispered, "Just play along."

The doors to the trophy room were wide open as the usual band of lords lazed about in the overly warm room. Moira was relieved; clearly, they were not taking part in any wrongful trickery tonight. There was a faint fog of cigar smoke, but otherwise, the room looked as it always did: ominous and quite cozy. Moira stopped in the doorway briefly, locating Leofwin in one of the armchairs next to Lord Dayben by the fireplace. She approached Leofwin as though she was on a mission, which seemed to alarm him and Lord Dayben. Both men straightened in their seats as she approached.

"My lord!" Moira said as loudly and as dramatically as she could manage. "I beg of you, please grant me an allowance to have a new dress made for the Winter Festival! I do not ask for much from you, but I know all the women of the court will be dressed so finely while I shall have to wear a dress that is practically a rag!" Moira wailed and made sure to blink a lot in the hopes that it gave off the impression she was on the verge of tears.

Leofwin blinked dumbly at her, clearly at a loss. His mouth opened and closed several times, but he never spoke. Her arrival and outburst had taken him by surprise.

"Conor, surely you aren't denying your betrothed the allowance and wardrobe she deserves?" Inquired Lord Dayben, openly offended at the thought of such an atrocity.

Leofwin blinked and said, rather confusedly, "Well, no. Of course, she has a clothing allowance..." He trailed off rather weakly.

"I have a pittance!" Moira wept; hand thrown over her forehead as she closed her eyes. She wondered what Amis was making of this from the doorway but didn't dare risk looking at him. He would break her concentration.

"A pittance, Conor?" Lord Dayben raged, glowering at the still seated Leofwin.

Moira didn't expect to receive so much support from Dayben, but she was immensely grateful to have it. Either he didn't believe in the new courtship he'd mentioned around Lucia, or he felt Moira was owed more respect as Leofwin's *current* betrothed. Regardless, Lucia was always finely dressed and seemed to have new gowns monthly, so it made sense that Dayben might have that standard for all ladies at court.

Leofwin looked at Moira with sudden clarity. It was as if he caught on to the fact that a game was unfolding, even if he could not yet identify the parameters. He spoke clearly and firmly then, saying, "Maid Moira wants for nothing. She has never asked me for a copper more than her allowance."

"Until now, that is," Amis piped up and stepped further into the room. "If you intend to marry my sister next spring, as planned, then you better start treating her as your wife and not some lady you're stringing along for frivolity."

Moira had to give it to Amis. He jumped in at the exact right time and with the perfect amount of defensiveness. As far as she knew, there had never been a wedding date even loosely planned, let alone a date next spring, but she thought adding in that fake detail was an impeccable touch. Moira practically beamed at Amis but remembered her own role in this.

"I would ask for some funds to build upon my wardrobe, m'Lord," Moira said sweetly, eyes downcast in a false show of submission.

"What on earth is happening here?" Prince Lyric boomed from the doorway. "Conor, you insufferable coxcomb. Is it true you've been depriving your future wife of a proper monthly allotment?" He stared Leofwin down as though he were a naughty child. "I should have known just by the look of her. Shameful."

Moira let the sting of that last comment roll off her back. Fancy new dresses would never fix the fact that she did not fit in with this court. With a dramatic flick of his hand, Prince Lyric motioned Moira over to his writing table. She hesitated, looking first at Leofwin and then at Amis. Neither seemed to give her any indication of what she should do, so she slowly approached the table. She did not want to incur the prince's wrath; having seen how he behaved in this room all too recently. Her plan had been to pressure Leofwin into money, but that was suddenly unraveling wildly.

As Moira stood at the front edge of the writing table, Prince Lyric turned around and retrieved a familiar ornate wooden box from the shelves behind his throne-like chair. He pulled a key from the inner pocket of his doublet and unlocked the box. It took every ounce of self-control Moira had not to run around the desk to investigate the box as he opened it. She was also giddy over the unexpected knowledge of where Lyric kept the key. Without seeing him, Moira knew that Amis was bursting with excitement behind her. She tried to subtly crane her neck and look into the box, but she couldn't get a good angle. The prince acted swiftly and pulled out a leather drawstring pouch before immediately closing the lid of the box.

As if he could not bother to care more than he already did, Prince Lyric dropped the leather pouch onto the table in front of Moira. It made a very heavy thud as it landed.

"That should make up for Lord Leofwin's pathetic first year as your host at court," Lyric said, almost sweetly. Then he looked at Leofwin with a spark of danger in his gaze as he said, "See to it that she is not underfunded again, Conor."

Moira picked up the small bag and was alarmed at how heavy it felt. She held onto the pouch delicately, as if holding it too tightly would show someone her true intentions, and they would snatch it away. She closed her eyes and tried to gather her thoughts while barely able to believe her luck.

"You," Prince Lyric said, pointing at Amis. "And you," he said to Moira, causing her to open her eyes. "Leave."

"Yes, your majesty," Amis and Moira said in perfect unison. Amis executed a handsome bow while Moira attempted something similar to a curtsy before leaving the room in a barely contained hurry. The doors were practically slammed shut behind them, but they didn't slow their pace until they rounded the corner.

"What in the name of all that is unholy do you plan to do with that weighty sack of coin?" Amis asked her eagerly.

Moira slowed her pace, glanced around to make sure they were alone and said, "Don't get too excited, Amis. I'm slowly but surely going to fill the gaps that Roman has left behind. This money is for the villagers. Do you think you can get it to Friar Tuck tomorrow for disbursement?"

Amis grinned widely at her as he took the leather pouch. "Oh, you are clever!"

Moira gave him a self-satisfied smile in return.

Chapter Fifty-Eight

The following morning, Moira was up before the sun. She dressed in the dark, pulling on a black tunic that used to belong to Amis (and still would if she hadn't nicked it) and black trousers. On her feet was her usual pair of comfortable black boots, which suited her perfectly as she tiptoed down the castle stairs. Normally, the second she made an actual effort to be quiet was also the moment she knocked something over or fell flat on her face. Thankfully, the fates seemed to be on her side today, and she made it to the kitchen without a sound or a new injury.

When Moira stepped into the kitchen, there was a barely detectable lull in the sound of work and the soft sound of women's chatter; however, the usual noise resumed easily once everyone saw her standing in the doorway.

Moira walked over to Sigrid as she was kneading dough at one of the massive worktables in the center of the room.

"Good morning," Moira said softly with a smile.

Sigrid returned the smile but did not stop working. "Good morning, m'lady. What can I do for you at this early hour?"

Moira thought maybe she detected a second message in that question. Something along the lines of *I am very busy, and it is very early for you to be bothering me.* She looked at

Sigrid and nodded, trying to let the woman know she understood and that she would not be a pest for long.

With a conspiratorial look, Moira stepped a little closer to the woman and whispered, "Would it be possible to cook a few extra things a couple of times a week?"

Sigrid paused her kneading and looked intently at Moira. "For what purpose?"

"I want to continue to aid the villagers of Ivywood as much as possible -," Moira caught herself before she said too much. She knew better than to ramble out loud, even if she was in one of the noisiest rooms of the castle and surrounded by who knows how many co-conspirators. Shaking her head while scolding herself, Moira started over. "I believe the villagers might need some additional support as we move into the colder season. With the Winter Festival coming up, I would like to be sure every family has food on their table."

There was a small smile tugging at Sigrid's lips, but she kept her gaze on her work. "I assume this philanthropic endeavor does not have approval from the prince?" She asked as she side-eyed Moira. Her subtle grin remained.

Moira paused and said, "The prince has always encouraged a philanthropic nature in everyone but himself; however, you are correct in your assumption that he does not know about this particular request."

"And you have arranged for someone besides the women of this kitchen to get the extra food down to the village?"

Sigrid inquired as she moved the lump of dough into a wooden bowl and reached for another. As she did this, a woman from another table turned and grabbed the bowl with the recently kneaded dough. Moira was silently impressed at their coordination.

"Yes, I have arranged that," Moira answered, feeling her neck flush just a little over the lie. She had not technically thought of this but knew that she or Amis could get the food to Tuck easily enough, and the friar would handle things from there.

Sigrid nodded and said, "Then it can be done."

Moira smiled even wider before returning her face to a more neutral look. No need to get gossip stirring what they might have discussed today. Without another word, Sigrid gave Moira a look of farewell and returned to her work with full focus once more.

Chapter Fifty-Nine

A full two weeks had passed since Moira successfully arranged for extra food for Ivywood Village. Friar Tuck shared the coins she got from Prince Lyric, and he was delivering bundles of food every other day as well. Moira swore she had never seen the man smile as wide as he did the first time, she brought extra food to pass around.

"You're an angel!" Tuck said, beaming. Then he turned to Amis and asked, "Don't you agree?"

Amis replied in his usual smart-ass manner and said, "Afraid not. I've known her longer."

This earned Amis an elbow from Moira and a *tutting* from the friar as he waggled his finger good-naturedly.

Today was the first day of winter, and Moira was spending it in the most relaxing way possible: with a book in her chaise as Hanna mended yet another item of her clothing. Although this arrangement used to be their weekly norm, Moira found herself somewhat giddy over the novelty of it now.

"I've missed this, Han," Moira said wistfully.

Hanna scoffed and then quickly tried to cover it with an aggressively fake cough.

"What exactly was that?" Moira asked accusingly as she sat up straighter and tossed her book to the side.

Hanna smirked and said, "Nothing at all! I was just momentarily amused over your nostalgia. I typically get more done when you are not lounging around me while I work."

Moira bristled a little but also got the feeling Hanna was teasing her. "Well, I find that downright offensive, Hanna. I never interfere with your work!"

"Of course not, m'lady," Hanna said in mock seriousness. "Except, of course, when you do."

"I am outraged!" Moira attempted to sound outraged, but instead, she fell short and sounded amused.

Hanna laughed and shook her head in exasperation. Moira settled back into her cushions and stared at the ceiling for a moment.

"Do you know what I can't figure out?" Moira asked Hanna.

"How to sit quietly?" Hanna asked, definitely teasing this time.

Moira rolled her eyes and said, "No!"

There was a moment where all Moira could hear was the sound of Hanna's needle and thread passing through the fabric she was mending.

"Well, out with it then!" Hanna said a little irritably.

"Oh, do you suddenly wish to hear my thoughts?"

"Gods, I honestly do not know. Has anyone ever told you that you're impossible?" Hanna asked with a shake of her head.

"Regularly!" Moira said proudly. "Anyway, returning to the point. Me and my never-ending thoughts."

"Yes, out with it before I need to move on to other tasks."

"What I can't figure out is why Prince Lyric would be keeping King Leo alive if what he wants is the throne," Moira mused. She let the thought hang, unsure of how to elaborate.

Hanna set down her mending a tad roughly and stood up from the settee. She stomped over to the door determinedly, and Moira almost called out to her in offense, thinking that she was leaving without a word. Instead, Hanna latched the door and then walked to the window and did the same. She closed the door to Moira's bedroom and tossed another log onto the fire before settling back down in the same spot as before.

"Continue," Hanna said with a wave of her hand, getting back to her mending.

Moira blinked a few times and then said, "I only ask because the easiest route to the throne is through King Leo's death. Is it not?"

"As far as I know, yes," Hanna answered.

Slightly annoyed at Hanna's unhelpful answer, Moira decided to plow on with her musings. Talking out loud was sometimes helpful, she reminded herself. "Then why keep him alive? And why keep him *barely* alive at that? Is there a reason they are poisoning him while keeping him captive?" Moira had filled Hanna in on what she learned from Tuck, but otherwise, they had not explicitly discussed the fact that Leo was most likely living through hell.

"I have no -," Hanna started.

"And what on this Gods-damned green earth happened in the Crusades? I mean, I *know* what happened in the Crusades, but *what happened in the Crusades*, Hanna? How did Roman get thrown out of the Loxley Estate? Why did Lyric give his estate and land to a Sheriff? Was it because Roman aided the king somehow and that aid interfered with whatever Lyric had planned? What is Lyric's end goal besides ascending the throne? I can't imagine his plans end there." Moira paused for dramatic effect, staring intently at Hanna. "These are just a few of the things that keep me up at night. Or interrupt my ability to enjoy it when I'm finally sitting down and relaxing."

Hanna merely looked at Moira in silence. When she finally spoke, she said, "I can answer part of one of those questions."

416

Moira threw her hands up dramatically and said, "Oh, thank the Gods! I will take even one-half of thought off my mind. Anything helps!"

With an inelegant snort, Hanna looked at the ceiling in exasperation. Finally, she looked back at Moira and said, "The Sheriff of Ivywood was 'gifted' the Loxley estate because Lyric was desperate to get rid of him."

Moira sat with her mouth open for several seconds before saying, "Sorry, what?"

"I have only heard this in bits and pieces of gossip, so bear that in mind," Hanna said while she looked at Moira sternly. "From what I understand, the sheriff was becoming a little too insistent when it came to something the prince was hiding. I cannot be sure what, but after your chat with Friar Tucksen, I would wager the sheriff was getting close to discovering the poison experiments that Lyric was having done. The families of the test subjects were hounding the sheriff to find answers. Lyric had to do something."

"Why not just kill the sheriff?" Moira asked, feeling like that was the obvious and easiest option for someone as violent and unscrupulous as Prince Lyric.

Hanna glowered at her.

"What?" Moira asked defensively. "It just seems to me like maybe Lyric is working much harder than he has to when it comes to his nefarious plotting." She added a shrug to show Hanna she did not personally think murdering people who inconvenience you is a good idea.

With a sigh, Hanna said, "The sheriff was beloved by the villagers, and with his plan to keep raising taxes, I believe the prince chose a political move over a practical one."

"Funny how those two are never united options," Moira muttered.

Hanna grinned and said, "Indeed."

"Thank you for admitting that killing the sheriff would have been the practical move, Hanna."

The glare returned, along with an eye roll, and Moira smiled widely in return.

"On top of that," Hanna continued, determined to prevail despite Moira's interruptions. "Roman had become one of King Leo's right-hands in the Crusades. Since the prince received regular reports from the front lines, he knew that Roman was heavily involved with the king and completing missions that went against what Lyric wanted."

"What missions?"

"Have you been able to find anything about the inner-workings of the Crusades when researching in the library?" Hanna challenged.

Moira was slightly taken aback by her tone but responded simply, "No."

"Precisely. I'm not sure there's a better-kept secret in all of Anglia. Nobody who returned will speak of things in detail. Nobody who was here but connected to the Crusades will talk, either. Prince Lyric has made sure that it is legitimately impossible to know what happened unless you were there."

"Well, that's bullshit!" Moira exclaimed.

"Agreed," Hanna said with a chuckle that seemed to ripple through her whole body.

Moira was about to continue her endless questioning when someone abruptly tried to bust through her door. Whoever it was, they were stopped by the latch Hanna had put in place. It sounded as though the latch was unexpected as the person slammed into the door heavily. Moira and Hanna both heard an "oof," followed quickly by a muffled string of curse words.

"Amis," they said, looking at one another.

Moira stood and hurried to the door to let Amis in. As she opened it, Amis pushed past her, breathing heavily.

"Bobby," he said, gasping.

Hanna stood. The forgotten mending in her lap fell to the floor. "What about Bobby?"

"Here," Amis rasped. "Bobby. Is. Here." He spoke between heaving breaths, and Moira wondered how far he'd run to get here.

"Here *as* Bobby or…?" Moira felt lost, unsure if Bobby was here to see them or if Bobby had shown up for other purposes.

Amis bent at the waist and put his hands on his knees. Then he stood up and put his hands behind his head, back arched, as he gulped down air. Hanna started to speak again, but Amis held up one finger, indicating he needed more time to compose himself. After what felt like an eternity, Amis seemed to gather himself enough to speak.

"Bobby is here, but not as Bobby. She was introduced to me as Lady Jocelyn of Gest." At their continued looks of confusion, Amis said to Moira, "I believe she may be the woman Lord Leofwin is secretly courting behind your back."

Moira's brows drew together, and her mouth dropped open.

"What the actual hell?"

Chapter Sixty

Moira spent the rest of the day and the entire evening in a fit of frustration. She went down to the dining hall with Amis, but Bobby and Lord Leofwin were nowhere to be found. Dinner passed without a single sighting of them, and to top it off, the other favored lords were also missing.

"Obviously, they are having a secret dinner with only the prince's trusted band of blockheads," Moira grumbled while shuffling food around on her plate.

Amis reached over and took the roll off her plate while saying, "Oh good Gods above, don't act as if you're heartbroken that you might actually get out of the engagement."

"If you think that's what's bothering me, you have not been paying the slightest bit of attention," Moira replied acerbically.

"Do enlighten me, then," Amis said while shoving large bits of bread into his mouth. "Or would you rather continue moping in an enigmatic manner? I know that ladies do love an air of mystery," he said with his mouth full.

Moira turned and smiled at Amis, despite her sour disposition. "You do know how to pull me out of a mood, Amis," she reached out and snatched back what remained of her bread. She started to tear it apart in a similar manner to what Amis had been doing. After a few bites, she finally spoke again. "I'm upset because it seems as though Bobby was planted in this new role, and I...well, I just would have expected to know about it. I'm certainly not opposed to manipulating Leofwin out of our engagement, but it would have been nice to be part of that plan. It's a good idea, really. Making sure he's the one who ends things would make our lives much easier afterward."

Amis considered her for a moment. As Moira picked at her food after voicing what was on her mind, she was starting to feel slightly better. There was the usual consistent but low hum of everyone around them. Although the group in the smaller, less grand dining hall was not as substantial as usual, it was still a decent-sized gathering. The overall atmosphere seemed to be more relaxed than on other nights, thanks to the absence of his prince and the strict lords who usually surrounded him.

"Roman should have told you," Amis said quietly with a slight tone of irritation.

Moira looked at him and nodded. "Yes," she agreed, "He should have."

"Your relationship with him is different than everyone else. I would have expected him to share more of his plans with you," Amis said, still looking at her intently.

Moira thought briefly about arguing with Amis about the difference in her relationship with Roman, but she wasn't sure what her relationship with him was. Especially not now, not after this prolonged absence, and not after she learned he had been doing some secret planning and plotting that would affect her.

"Don't do that," Amis whispered. He reached out and pinched her on the arm. She glared at him in surprise. "Don't be all 'woe is me' and start to doubt the spark between you and Roman."

With a groan, Moira looked up at the ceiling. "Please don't say spark, Amis. Don't make it ostentatious. I'll vomit, I swear!"

Amis grinned wickedly. "What then? The scintillation? The little glow and flare you both get when you banter? Honestly, it's amazing to think everyone around you has refrained from vomiting."

Moira scrunched her nose and shook her head. "No! Conversation over." She went to stand, but Amis pulled her back down into her seat. He draped his arm around her shoulders and added a little pressure, making sure she stayed put.

"Here's my theory, Moi. From the second Leofwin hurt you, our merry friend began working on the best way to get you out. His intentions are good, even if you do not love his methods." Amis gave her a swift squeeze before he removed his arm from her shoulders. "I think we can also cut him some slack when you consider the typical window for talking when he's around is very slim."

She nodded and tossed the last bit of bread onto the table. "Let's go have a drink or two too many in the comfort of my room."

"I do love where that mind of yours goes sometimes!" Amis cheered. He offered Moira his hand, and they left the hall.

****

"You know what?" Moira asked boisterously, moving to a kneeling position on her chaise.

"What?" Amis asked as he leaned forward excitedly.

"I'm going to go and find her!"

Amis paused and looked incredibly confused. "Find whom?"

"Bobby!" Moira nearly shouted in answer; frustrated that Amis hadn't known immediately who she spoke of. "Or shall I say, 'Lady Jocelyn of Gest'?" She asked in a tone that dripped with false sophistication.

"Just how blinkered are you, Moi?"

She scowled at him before saying, "I'm not blinkered at all, and I'm rather offended you'd think that! I've had just enough to drop my usual veil of restraint."

Moira felt certain that what she said was mostly true. She was definitely not completely drunk, although she was easily tiptoeing closer the more she sipped on the beautiful amber liquid in her glass. For a moment, she looked longingly at it, but decided she'd better call it quits for the night. One must know when to stop drinking when one is plotting spontaneous escapades. She passed the glass to Amis, who made sure it was gone in a matter of seconds.

"You might not be completely inebriated, but I can assure you I am. This means I am all in favor of this out of plumb plan. Onward!" He stood dramatically; hand outstretched before him as if he carried a baton, and started walking toward the door.

"Huzzah!" Moira shouted in response and hopped up from the chaise to follow him.

They were both out in the hall and walking down the corridor before Moira remembered that she ought to close her door rather than draw attention to her absence by leaving it hanging open. She dashed back, pulled it shut quietly, and then rushed to catch up with Amis, who continued to teeter down the hallway toward the stairs. Moira stifled a laugh at the slanted way Amis was moving, and she ignored a small voice in the back of her mind that pointed out that this may not be her brightest idea.

Moira caught up to Amis and looped her arm through his, hoping to steady his gait a bit. She really did not want it to be obvious that they were walking drunkenly through the castle at night. It was still early enough that many residents were still awake, but late at the same time.

"Do you know where she is?" Amis asked, still jovial, but he was beginning to slur his words.

Moira arched an eyebrow and glanced sideways at her brother, wondering if she should get him up to bed instead of dragging him on this misguided adventure.

"Erm...No, I have no idea, actually," Moira finally answered after deciding, against her better judgment, to continue her search for Bobby despite Amis's condition.

"Well, crack on!" Amis rallied.

"Shhhh! I don't fancy getting caught just now, you drunken dolt!" Moira scolded quietly.

Amis merely smiled at her as they continued down the hallway. There were many mounted flames flickering, but some had already been extinguished for the night. Moira realized with a slight jolt that they were heading directly toward the trophy room. While there was a small chance Bobby was in that exact room, she would be there surrounded by several men that Moira did not want to interact with in her current state. Although she felt she had most of her faculties under her control, she knew she bore the faint smell of booze, and she had left her room barefooted once again. And there was Amis, entirely intoxicated and humming as he meandered along next to her.

Moira stopped with a light tug on Amis's arm. Just as they stopped, Prince Lyric's favorite servant stepped out of the room and shut the door behind him. Fitzroy turned and

426

seemed startled at the sight of them but recovered quickly. He grinned at Amis and started walking toward them.

"Oh no," Moira whispered to herself.

"Fitzroy!" Amis called out a little too loudly.

Despite his lack of hearing, Fitzroy smiled genially at Amis, and Moira wondered if they knew each other. Amis disentangled himself from Moira's steadying grasp and stepped toward the man with his arms wide. They embraced with multiple slaps to each other's backs, and then they stepped away from each other.

Fitzroy did not look at Moira, but gave Amis a sort of shrug and tilt of his head, almost as if asking what they were doing here.

"Ah, my friend. We are on a nocturnal expedition!" Amis explained cheerfully.

The old man nodded again, still smiling. Moira continued to watch in spellbound fascination.

"There is a new lady at court. Someone my sister may know from our previous life, you see. She is quite anxious to speak with her but would like to do so without the prying eyes of the court. You know how ladies are," Amis said conspiratorially. Moira noticed that his speech slowed, and he no longer slurred. She assumed her brother was speaking slowly and carefully to ensure the butler would be able to read his lips. They most definitely knew each other. Their interaction was seamless and easy.

Fitzroy nodded sagely and then made a series of gestures. He motioned upward, then hooked his thumb toward the left while also flashing four fingers on his other hand. Amis nodded enthusiastically and clapped quietly, clearly having understood the message.

With a clap on the man's shoulders, Amis said gratefully, "Thank you, my friend! I appreciate you immensely. Shall we have a pint in that dreadful apartment of yours soon?"

A soft chuckle left Fitzroy's throat, which surprised Moira. She immediately felt foolish for assuming the man couldn't laugh and scolded herself silently for her ignorance.

Moira reached forward, offering her hand to Fitzroy. He looked mildly surprised but eventually placed his hand in hers. She said quietly but with clear enunciation, "Thank you for your kindness and help." After a light squeeze, which Fitzroy returned, Moira let go of his hand and turned to Amis. "Where are we going?"

"Up the front staircase to the guest quarters. The 'lady' is staying in the room fourth down on the left," Amis responded assuredly.

The servant's hand gestures suddenly made complete sense, and Moira turned around to continue toward the front of the castle. Fitzroy silently returned to his post outside of the trophy room door. He gave Amis one last bob of his head before staring down at the floor.

"Is there anyone that you aren't friendly with?" Moira asked incredulously.

"Oh, certainly, Moi," Amis said with a scoff.

"Let me guess…you stay away from the wrong sort but befriend everyone else?"

"On the contrary, my innocent sister. I befriend everyone immediately and then wait to find out what sort they are. After that, I simply wait to see how things unfold," he answered with a shrug as if this was everyone's method of interacting with the world.

Moira rolled her eyes and looked at Amis for a beat before responding, "You definitely come in handy!"

"You'd be entirely lost without me!" Amis responded tauntingly.

Although Moira was ready with a snarky response, she paused and looked sideways at her brother as they reached the bottom of the grand staircase in the front entryway of the castle.

"Yes," she finally said. "I would be."

Chapter Sixty-One

"I'm afraid I'm rather intoxicated," Amis slurred as he wobbled in front of the door that would allegedly lead them to Bobby.

"I know you are," Moira responded a bit resentfully. It was her fault for even coming up with this poorly designed adventure, and now here she was with her drunk brother, standing outside the room of a woman she wasn't even sure she wanted to speak with. All the while, her own head was starting to feel more and more like it was stuffed with cotton.

"I'll knock then, shall I?" Amis asked, reaching out with his hand fisted.

"No -," Moira started to say, but Amis had already started knocking.

"Are we not here to see her?!" Amis whispered, exasperated.

Moira sighed and started to speak, but the door began to open slowly. Once it was cracked just enough to look through, she saw Bobby's distinct blue eyes and tightly curled black hair appear. Bobby's eyes went wide at the sight of the two of them and she quickly opened the door fully as she motioned for them to enter the room.

"Lovely, thanks!" Amis slurred happily.

Bobby's brow knit together at the clear indication of Amis's intoxication, and she turned to throw an accusing look at Moira. Although it was a fair place to toss the blame, Moira couldn't help but glare back at Bobby. She was strongly aware of the fact that she had not yet decided to like this woman, whether or not she was in Roman's cadre.

"What in the four hundred hells are you two doing here?" Bobby hissed as she closed the door behind them. There was the distinct sound of the latch sliding into place, which Moira was grateful for.

"This room is beautiful!" Amis exclaimed as he looked around. He bent to touch an ornate bobble that rested on a shelf next to an austere armchair but knocked it over and barely managed a fumbling catch before it shattered on the floor. "Not to worry!" He exclaimed as he placed it gently back on the shelf.

"Amis, why don't you sit down?" Moira asked as she shuffled him toward one of the opulent chairs in the room.

"Lovely!" Amis exclaimed as he threw himself down.

"Yes, yes," Moira said impatiently. "Everything is lovely." She turned to look at Bobby, who appeared more amused than annoyed now.

"You two are such a unique addition to the party," Bobby said.

Moira was about to bristle and defend her and her brother, but she realized Bobby had not sounded mean or sarcastic. She was still smiling in a rather bemused fashion, which was surprising. Rather than take on the defensive, Moira decided to give a tight-lipped smile in response. She knew the smile didn't reach her eyes, but it was the best she could do.

"We don't know each other yet, Moira, but I do suspect that we will become fast friends. Our interactions thus far have not been wholly indicative of who we are as people, you know," Bobby said while lightly crossing her arms and leaning against the wall in a casual, yet confident manner.

Unsure of what to say, Moira simply responded with, "Mmmm..."

As she stood there looking at Bobby, Moira found herself abruptly feeling far more intoxicated than she was. She blamed it on the fact that Bobby put her on uneven footing. In order to buy herself some time, Moira started to look around the main room of Bobby's suite. She was loath to admit it, but Amis was right - the room was indeed lovely. Everything was elegant and pristine. In the corner was a grand fireplace with beautiful carvings at the sides. The carvings were some sort of vine that crawled all the way up and across the mantle before cascading down the other side. Two large windows occupied the wall opposite the main door, which probably created a scenic entry if one were to enter the room by the light of day. She wondered if she could ask to see the bedchamber without sounding ill-mannered, but decided against it. Maybe on the second visit...or one that included her being invited rather than showing up in the middle of the night with her intoxicated brother.

"I hear Leofwin is courting you," Moira said and immediately wished she started with a softer topic.

Bobby arched an eyebrow and lifted her chin. "No, he's not courting *me*."

Her brows drew in as Moira looked at the other woman in confusion. Just as she was about to ask what on earth Bobby was doing as a guest in the castle, Bobby continued to speak.

"He believes he is courting Lady Jocelyn of Gest. He has no idea that he is toting around Roberta Wakefield. Lady of absolutely nothing," she explained with a delightfully wicked grin. "So technically he's courting someone who does not exist. He is not courting *me*."

Despite herself, Moira returned the smile. "Damn," she said in mock exasperation, "I do think I'll like you."

Bobby smiled and said, "I know. Now, I wager you want to know what the hell I'm doing here, who came up with this plan, how it unfolded..." Bobby started waving her hands around vaguely as she said, "Things of that nature?"

A loud snore suddenly arose from the chair behind Moira. It startled her, much to her annoyance, but she was relieved Amis fell asleep. How he managed to get comfortable in the formal, stiff looking chair, she'd never understand. For reasons she couldn't quite pinpoint, she felt more at ease knowing this conversation would be between just her and Bobby.

"That's exactly why I'm here, actually," Moira smiled sweetly, picking the conversation back up after her moment of distraction. She settled herself onto one of the unyielding, rigid chairs, tucking her bare feet up underneath her. "Why is all of your furniture far more beautiful, yet significantly more uncomfortable compared to what I've got in my rooms?" She asked curiously.

Bobby laughed and said, "That's easy, Moira. Leofwin is courting me. He already has you."

Moira's face crinkled in offense before she realized what Bobby said was both true and hilarious. It was obvious that Leofwin was trying to impress the woman he believed was a high-ranking lady from Gest. Meanwhile, Leofwin had been engaged to Moira before he even met her. There really was no point in him ever trying to impress her. Moira let out a soft laugh and shrugged one shoulder; a gesture to show Bobby that she had a point.

"So why are you doing this?" Moira asked, motioning vaguely around the room and hoping that she kept any accusatory undertones out of her voice.

Bobby was about to speak shoved away from the wall and found a seat across from Moira. Bobby looked briefly at the still softly snoring Amis before she settled into her chair with her legs stretched out in front of her. The position was masculine and sloppy, but it made Moira smile.

"I'm doing this because Roman asked me to, of course," Bobby finally said. She said it as if it was the most obvious answer in the world.

Moira looked at Bobby - curiosity nearly bursting out of her - but the other woman remained infuriatingly silent after her short explanation. Moira forced herself to remain silent for just a few moments longer just to see if the lack of commentary motivated Bobby to say more. As a child, Moira had experienced her own father using this tactic on her and she wondered if it worked on everyone or only guilty children. Moira felt her irritation grow with every passing second. Bobby sat across from her without saying another word.

"Pardon me but fuck off if that's the only explanation you've got for me," Moira scoffed while leaning forward slightly. She didn't say it with any animosity, but she was wildly frustrated, and she knew she made her point well.

There was a smile tugging at the corner of Bobby's mouth, giving her the sly expression of a spider who was enjoying her web of secrets a little too much.

"I'm being vile, I apologize," Bobby said, still wearing her half smile, but sounding genuine. "Up until you appeared in the castle, Roman was adamant about no new members in our group, no breaking our focus from King Leo, on and on…there was nothing that could break his focus from what he saw as the *only* priority. The closest people to him were trusted implicitly and everyone else that was not in that innermost circle was depended upon exactly as much as Roman needed and not a smidge more."

Moira realized she was still leaning forward and tried to subtly adjust her position without interrupting her companion. Now that the story had begun, Moira was intent on hearing everything Bobby had to say. She watched Bobby with rapt attention, but the other woman turned to stare out one of the windows. There was nothing to see, of course, but Moira assumed Bobby was gathering her thoughts, so she remained quiet.

"You changed almost everything, Moira," Bobby said, returning her gaze to Moira. "You proved useful and trustworthy, of course. But…," Bobby took a deep breath before she continued. "Suddenly Roman had an obvious distraction. I'm not sure why he decided to approach you in the first place, but you and Amis were both suddenly considered part of our inner workings. The core mission remained the same, naturally. We were still attempting to find where King Leo is hidden and you were an exceptional spy, despite some reservations certain people had about you…But the second Roman knew that Leofwin was harming you and using you for his own financial gain, there was abruptly a second focus. A slight shift. Everyone was shocked, but most of all me. I had never seen Roman Loxley change his focus. Ever. We grew up together in Loxley and I have to say, even as a child he existed with an odd affinity for singular focus."

There was another pause in Bobby's story and Moira wasn't sure what to do. She was doing her best to refrain from fidgeting with her hands, but the battle was quickly lost. Bobby kept looking at her with an intensity that she felt in her core. Those piercing blue eyes bore into her. Moira could tell Bobby was assessing her. This was their longest interaction to date, so it made sense. Maybe Bobby was wondering what on earth was so special about her that Roman would change his focus from King Leo to her...Moira wished she knew the answer to that question.

All the while Bobby was judging her, Moira was doing the same thing. Despite their rocky start, Moira found that she liked Bobby's directness. Her loyalty to Roman was obvious. Moira looked forward to the day when she could ask Bobby about Roman's childhood. Try as she might, she couldn't picture the hard, lean and wild figure of Roman as a little lord growing up in Loxley.

"I resented you, at first," Bobby continued. "When I thought Roman abducted you for his own curiosity and nothing more, it seemed foolish. Dangerous and reckless, too. I was relieved when I learned there was a real purpose and that Wilhelm was on Roman's side. It was difficult to acknowledge each time I returned to the hideout, I had to hear about the information you gathered and the success you were finding as a spy in the castle. You were hidden in plain sight and not a single person questioned what you were doing. I initially thought you had the easiest possible job, but I misjudged it, I think." Bobby gave Moira a weak smile, as if she was uncertain. "Roman asked me to continue my work in Gest, but he also wanted me to begin a new assignment. One with a longer endgame that may or may not be necessary. One where I was to pretend to be a high-ranking lady and entice Lord Leofwin into leaving his engagement to you."

"But how have you accomplished that?" Moira asked, unable to hold back the question. Impersonating someone of wealth was no easy task. The lords and ladies of Anglia were usually well known unless the town or estate was remote. Gest was not far enough away from Ivywood, to Moira's knowledge, for someone to spring up and claim to be a lady.

Bobby grimaced. "Well, that's the rather fascinating part. Lady Jocelyn *did* exist."

Moira opened her mouth to speak but found she had no words. What the hell was Bobby telling her? Did she murder a woman to impersonate her? Roman might have some extreme ideas, but Moira knew he was incapable of murdering an innocent woman to serve his own purpose.

"I can see your mind running away with you," Bobby said with an honest smile. "Nobody murdered Jocelyn, if that's what you're wondering. We do what we must, but in this case it wasn't necessary. Lady Jocelyn was born to a rather eccentric lord. Her mother died in childbirth, so Jocelyn was sequestered by her father for most of her life. People knew she existed, but most never met her. Unfortunately, the sweating sickness that swept through Gest earlier this year took her from this world. My work in Gest is often aided by her father, the mercurial, but brilliant Lord Nigel Nefren. He allowed me to take on his daughter's identity for the purposes of furthering Roman's agenda."

Although Moira arrived in Bobby's room somewhat inebriated, she felt stone sober now. There was far too much information to take in at once and despite her desire to know everything she was learning, she found herself almost resistant to it all. The fact that Roman executed such a plan simply to get her out of a bad engagement was enough to make her feel both incredibly grateful and also intensely angry at the waste of precious resources. She and Amis had discussed the potential need to escape both Leofwin and the castle, if things came down to that, but neither of them had considered going to such preposterous lengths to find a way that meant Leofwin ended things rather than her. Moira knew there was a lot to focus on, but there was one remaining question that she felt they were moving further and further away from.

"So, who are you really?" Moira asked, legitimately curious.

"Roberta Wakefield. A literal nobody, before you interrupt to tell me that my name does not answer your question," Bobby hurriedly said, already knowing that Moira would want more information. "I'm an orphan originally from Fenfoss. I ended up serving the Loxley family after the last of my relatives sent me to Ivywood as a child. They couldn't care for me, and it was their hope that someone would take me in. Roman's mother and father found me and took me to the estate to be a kitchen maid. Roman and I grew up together, in the sort of tangential way that a future lord can grow up alongside a kitchen maid."

Moira looked down at her hands in thought. She was content with what she had learned so far, considering that she arrived unannounced in the middle of the night.

"I'm impressed with what you've done in Roman's absence," Bobby admitted quietly.

"How do you know -," Moira started.

"Friar Tuck," Bobby answered before Moira could finish asking her question. "I managed to escape the clutches of Leofwin long enough to chat with the friar." Bobby looked at Moira in obvious assessment once again, but this time

440

with a definite air of appreciation. "What you've done…it's impressive."

Despite herself, Moira sat up a little straighter. She said a simple, "Thank you," in response while internally feeling almost buoyant over the compliment. It was considerable work to continue to get food and money to the villagers. Recently, she had been attempting to figure out how to aid other villages as Roman had done, but her net of connections was not far reaching yet.

"Things are about to happen, Moira," Bobby said with a note of sudden and severe seriousness. "Roman is healed. He is done lying low and he is ready to act again."

Moira's breath hitched and she had to remind herself to continue breathing. She felt idiotic for her reaction, but she was too afraid to ask about Roman and his condition. After all the weeks that passed with no word, she convinced herself that he fled to some far away location to recover and might never return. It was a foolish thing, but it gave her comfort when she felt abandoned and ignored.

"What do I need to do?" Moira asked.

"Nothing except what you've already been doing," Bobby replied. "Steer clear of me publicly, alright? I honestly have no idea what game Leofwin is playing by bringing me here, but I cannot imagine he wants us to meet. I am only here for one more night before I return to Gest."

"I understand," Moira said with a dip of her head. "I'll wake Amis and leave, but there's one more thing." Moira trailed off, unsure if she really wanted to say it. She took a steadying breath and decided if she didn't say it, then she was a total ass. "Bobby, thank you. I am certain what you are doing is not easy. As someone who has been on Leofwin's arm more times than I can count, I know it is not a pleasant place to be. Even if you're only allowing him to court a fake version of yourself, I appreciate it. My betrothal and subsequent time in the castle have been," Moira paused, her voice beginning to break. She was determined to get this out without showing too much emotion, despite the burning in her eyes and the pressure she felt in her throat. She suppressed her building emotions and said flippantly, "Let's just say the idea of flinging myself from the nearest turret has crossed my mind more than once."

To Moira's utter relief, Bobby laughed and nodded as if she understood completely. With a sigh and a bit of effort, Moira was able to heave herself out of the comfortable chair and began the unpleasant task of waking Amis.

Chapter Sixty-Two

The following morning found Moira ensconced in the prince's library, surrounded by manuscripts, books and loose papers related to her continued research on the purple poison and the Crusades. At the edge of the table was a growing stack of books she wanted to read for pleasure. She glanced longingly at the future to be read pile; daydreaming of the time she would be able to spend curled up reading with nothing else more pressing to do.

"I wish someone would look at me the way you look at books," Amis moaned as he threw himself into the chair across from her.

Moira shrugged and continued scanning a loose piece of parchment as she said, "No truer love exists, I'm afraid, than the love between me and books."

"Disgusting!" Amis replied with a smile.

Moira returned the smile and went back to reading the line of text her finger rested on. "Did you know that some studies of botany state that the smallest dosage of Monkshood can actually be used therapeutically instead of harmfully?"

Amis looked over at the parchment curiously and said, "No I didn't, but I'm quite certain by now that your knowledge of the poison far outweighs mine."

"It just makes me wonder -," Moira stopped mid-thought as a guard stormed into the library and began shouting.

"The prince commands everyone to return to their rooms. Members of Roman Loxley's company have been sighted in Ivywood Village and the prince is putting the castle in isolation!"

"Isolation?" asked Amis with a look of incredulity.

"What does that mean exactly?" Moira queried, unwilling to abandon her current research unless she absolutely had to. "Couldn't I isolate myself in the library?"

"No, m'lady. Absolutely not." The guard spoke sternly. He looked around Amis's age, but plumper around the middle and thoroughly annoyed they didn't jump up immediately to follow his commands. "The prince has ruled that everyone is to return to their rooms. No exceptions."

There was an ominous boom of thunder just outside the library, making the thin panes of glass rattle in the wooden window frames. Moira looked outside with alarm; thunder in the winter was a bizarre occurrence. The sky was dark with thick, heavy clouds rolling in over the castle.

"What on earth?" Amis exclaimed, also looking through the window. "I'll be damned. I've heard of winter thunderstorms, but I've never actually seen one!"

"I will escort you both. Now," the guard bellowed; apparently no longer willing to entertain their lack of urgency regarding his orders.

Realizing that she might not be allowed back in the library anytime in the near future, Moira scrambled to pick up as much of her research as possible to take back to her room. She did not bother asking for permission, as she had an inkling the guard would have said no. Amis jumped in to help her and grabbed several rolled and ancient smelling parchments that she pulled from the shelves in the furthest reaches of the library several days ago but had not yet read. The guard was visibly growing impatient but did not attempt to stop their frantic gathering of reading material.

Huffing a piece of hair out of her face as she readjusted the books overflowing in her arms, Moira gave the guard a small nod as she started to leave the library. Amis followed behind her, complaining that the stack of material he grabbed smelled like "old dirt". Moira rolled her eyes and said nothing as she walked through the ominously empty corridors of the castle.

"Where is everyone?" Moira asked, turning around to look at Amis and the guard, who followed them closely.

"Most residents followed the isolation orders without as much discussion as the two of you," the guard responded with frustration. "I don't believe anyone else felt the need to pack along half the library, either."

Moira scowled at the guard and said, "If you believe this is half the library then you haven't paid any attention to that room."

"Let's bond with the guard later, Moi, eh?" Amis said, nudging her to turn around and continue walking.

With a final glare thrown at the guard, Moira continued toward the stairs with Amis shuffling along next to her. Now that they were clearly cooperating, the guard seemed to back off slightly. He was still following behind them, but not nearly as close as he had been. Moira rounded the final corner; the staircase leading to their rooms in sight, when she heard a shout down the hall.

"Oy, get back here!"

Amis and Moira both froze in their tracks, unsure of where the commotion originated. The shout was nearby, but clearly around a corner because they couldn't see anything from where they stood.

"Support needed! Guards to the trophy room! Guards to the trophy room!" The same unidentified voice shouted from the direction of the library.

With a frantic gleam to his eyes, their guard yelled at them, "You two go straight to your rooms and do not leave under any circumstances!" Then he turned and ran back down the hallway.

"Best wishes with the insurgents!" Amis hollered after him.

Moira giggled at Amis, who managed to sound sincere while also conveying nothing but delight over the guards' current situation. He turned back toward Moira, grinned impishly and then gave a little shrug of his shoulders before continuing toward the stairs. The parchments he carried were haphazardly stacked in his arms and Moira wondered how he managed to keep them all from falling.

"Agh - 'scuse me!" mumbled a large form as it smashed right into Amis and bolted for the stairs.

The precariously stacked parchments no longer remained in Amis's arms as he stumbled. Every single document flew through the air as Amis worked to regain his balance and flailed about.

"Gods damn it all!" Amis exclaimed.

The enormous figure paused halfway up the stairs and turned. Moira stared at the sprawling mess of parchments and then glared at the man who ran into Amis. Her expression changed quickly from one of rage to a look of total surprise as she realized she was throwing fury at none other than Wilhelm.

"Wil!" Moira started, a bit breathless with surprise.

Wilhelm merely beamed at her, tapped his forehead in greeting and said, "Gotta go! Great to see you, Moi!" He turned to dash up the stairs and was gone before Moira had time to say another word.

Moira stood there blinking and Amis started the tedious task of picking up the documents that were knocked from his grasp.

"Fucking Wilhelm," Amis mumbled as he bent down.

Six guards came running around the corner, all breathing loudly and with their armor clanking. The two in the lead came to a stop at the sight of Moira, still standing and holding her stack of books; and Amis, who was crouched over picking up the last rolled parchment. Their original guard stepped forward out of the group and crossed his arms in front of his chest as he scowled at them.

"I distinctly remember telling you two to get to your rooms," he shouted.

"We were on our way when I stumbled," Moira said, thinking as quickly as she could. "I fell into Amis and we both dropped everything we carried. As you can see, Amis just managed to collect the last of the loose parchments. We were just about to go upstairs when you lot came blundering round the corner." Try as she might, she was unable to keep the snark and derision from her tone. The longer she was in the castle and part of Roman's cause, the more she realized just how ineffective the guards really were. Wilhelm had come and gone with plenty of time to spare before these fools finally arrived.

"Did you see anyone while you cleaned up your mess?" asked the guard with his own note of scorn.

"No," said Moira.

"No?" asked another guard.

"What do you mean, 'no'?" A different guard at the very front of the group argued.

"Sorry, I didn't realize I'd spoken in such a confusing manner," Moira sniped. Amis gave a subtle cough behind her, a warning sign. She cleared her throat and continued in a softer manner than before. "Amis and I did not see anyone."

The guards turned to look at Amis then, as if Moira's word could not be trusted.

"Is this true?"

Amis cleared his throat dramatically, which Moira knew was a sign of frustration more than actual necessity. He looked pointedly at the head guard and said, "What my sister said is true. We saw no one."

The guards nodded at Amis, which infuriated Moira for reasons she wasn't even sure she could explain. She took a calming breath and decided she'd settle for being grateful that they were dropping the idiotic issue.

The original guard who found them in the library stepped forward again and pointed at Amis while he said, "Get the lady back to her rooms and stay with her. The isolation orders are still in effect."

Before Moira could say anything in response, Amis stepped in front of her and said, "You have my word, good fellow."

Amis turned around, gave Moira a look that indicated she needed to leave without saying another word, and lifted his chin toward the stairs. She summoned her most withering stare before she acquiesced and turned around. She practically stomped toward the steps. Moira did not want to spend an extra second near the guards, so she moved as quickly as she could without running and practically bolted up the stairs to the second level of the castle. Her face was flushed from holding back her frustration, but she decided she wouldn't let it boil over onto Amis. Although he had not directly defended her, he had done what he needed to in order to keep the interaction from blowing up into something more and once she cooled off, she knew she would be grateful for that.

Chapter Sixty-Three

Upon entering her room, Moira was not surprised to see Wilhelm lounging on the floor, his feet raised and resting on the edge of her settee. Bobby; however, was a surprise, as Moira watched her leave the castle in an obscenely ostentatious carriage earlier that very day. Moira walked into her room with a little huff, attempting to cover her jolt of surprise at the sight of Bobby. She set the books unceremoniously onto the table in front, then turned to Wilhelm with her hands on her hips.

"Is my furniture not good enough for you anymore, Wil?" She asked exasperatedly.

Wilhelm looked at her from the floor with his head tilted all the way back so he could see her. Even from the odd upside-down angle he looked gleeful. Despite her attempt to remain stoic, Moira felt her own smile spread in response. His hair was longer than ever and his red beard looked tangled; all of him needed a serious washing.

"Damn you, Wilhelm Clarke," Moira said, still smiling.

"Missed you too, Moi!" Wilhelm exclaimed as he flipped onto his stomach with surprising speed and then bounced up onto his feet.

"Dreadfully fun to find you here!" Amis enthused as he adjusted his armload of parchment and shook Wilhelm's hand.

Moira rolled her eyes at Bobby, both found amusement in Amis's greeting. Just as she was turning back around to take a seat on her favorite chaise, Moira let out a small gasp of surprise as Wilhelm scooped her up into a backbreaking embrace.

"That's quite enough!" Moira said, whacking him on the arm as Wil let go with a laugh.

"Not a hugger?" Wil asked with a wicked, amused glint in his eyes.

"I'm Anglian. Of course I'm not a hugger," Moira responded as she dramatically straightened her skirts before taking a seat.

"I was straight disappointed that we didn't scare the shoes off you when you came in, Moi. What's up with that?" Wilhelm asked as he sat at the table across from Bobby, propping his feet up on the tabletop and leaning back.

Moira held her legs out straight and wiggled her bare toes as she retorted, "No shoes to scare off!"

Wilhelm snorted and waved her feet down. Moira complied, settling back into her seat as she did.

Amis still had the parchments grasped in one arm, having freed his right hand earlier to shake Wilhelm's. He looked around the room briefly, then shrugged before letting all the documents fall to the floor. A few rolled away but several stayed where they landed, all in a heap.

"Amis Wright Finglas, what the fuck is wrong with you?" Moira blurted as she leapt up to collect her texts from the floor.

With a shrug Amis said, "They'll keep!"

"On the fucking floor, Amis?!" Moira shrieked in exasperation as she grabbed the last parchment, stomped to her bookshelves and tossed the stack onto a shelf with a little more aggression than she meant to. Several parchment rolls bounced off the shelf and fell once again to the floor. Moira grumbled and ignored the titters of laughter from behind her as she placed the straggler documents onto the shelf and made sure they all stayed put.

Moira turned to glare at her audience. Bobby held one hand over her mouth, but Moira could see the merriment dancing in her eyes. For whatever reason, Wilhelm left his seat at the table and settled on the floor once again. Amis was ensconced in the whiskey cabinet, as usual. Moira sighed and sat on her chaise once again.

"Why the floor, Wil. Seriously?" Moira asked, wanting to change the focus from her outburst over the reading material.

"Been too long in the forest. Can't get comfortable on that squishy couch of yours," Wil responded, rubbing his back into the rug to scratch it. "Might not be good enough for your precious scrolls, but I quite like it."

Wil gave Amis a wink as the other raised his glass with a wide grin.

"You haven't been staying in the cabin?" Moira asked, choosing to ignore the comment about the parchment.

"Nah, Ro was worried that Lyric would have men infiltrating that general area of the forest. He thought it was best to leave the cabin empty in case they stumbled upon it. We've been camped at the opposite edge of Blackwood, near the foot of the Maddock Mountains. Damned cold there this time of year," Wilhelm explained. His hands were tucked behind his head now and his eyes were closed.

"Sounds bloody awful," Amis mumbled as he settled into the settee, next to where Wil rested his feet.

"Ah, not bad, really. Better'n bein' dead!"

Amis made a sound that made Moira think he would disagree with that statement. Nobody talked for several moments as they all eased into the comfort of the room. Moira was listening to the sound of the fire crackle when she caught the sound of raised voices outside her door.

All four heads turned in unison to look. The latch had not been set and Moira screamed at herself internally. When was she going to learn to latch the damn door when she had fugitives hiding out in her room?

The door opened slightly, and everyone watched with bated breath. Wilhelm rolled over silently and was now crouched and ready with a hand on his sword. Moira had never noticed that he even had a sword strapped at his hip, but there it was. Amis set down his whiskey glass quietly and was perched at the edge of the couch. Moira and Bobby gave each other a quick look, but then went back to watching the door, which stayed half open, while blocking whoever had started to open it.

"I'll be sure to let her know," said Hanna, speaking to someone in the hallway.

Everyone visibly relaxed as Hanna bustled into the room, closed the door and then turned around. She looked somewhat startled, but then glared at Moira as she pointedly turned back around and slid the latch into place.

"Fabian Drachenburg couldn't be bothered to lock his door either and he was murdered in his sleep by a band of traveling miscreants," Hanna scolded, continuing to stare directly at Moira.

"Yes, Han," Moira managed to say as she stifled her laughter. Amis allowed a small squeak of amusement out, but remained mostly silent as he shook in his seat.

"You're late, Hanna," Bobby said as she leaned forward in her seat. Her elbows rested on the table in front of her with her chin on her left hand.

"I was given about two seconds' notice, so I'm here exactly as soon as I can be. Factor in the debacle with Wilhelm," Hanna turned to stare at Wil with an eyebrow cocked. "Thanks to Wil being seen, the castle corridors are swarming with guards. It's a miracle I'm here at all."

"That was an honest mishap, Hanna," Wilhelm started to explain. "I slipped on the corner of a rug and sent a suit of armor flying. You cannot fathom the cacophony that rang through the damn halls! I just about shit myself - sorry! Inappropriate detail, I suppose – I had to recover my composure and then get to safety," Wilhelm finished his story quickly, apologizing only when Hanna shot daggers at him across the room. He was still crouched and seemed to realize he could relax only once he'd given Hanna an apologetic nod.

"I didn't hear anything," Amis said comfortingly, patting Wil on the shoulder.

Wil sat back on the floor, this time with his back resting against the couch. He gave Amis a grateful smile.

"We were pretty deep in the library, though," Moira chimed in. "I've noticed that the acoustics in that part of the castle are different, thanks to all the books, I imagine."

Wil scrunched his face and turned to Moira, giving her a glare as if she'd taken away the small comfort Amis had given him. She made a grimace-like smile and a quick shrug.

"Wilhelm, you're nearly as clumsy as Moira and I do not say that lightly," Hanna mused as she sat at the table with Bobby.

"I would argue that while I may have a higher frequency of accidents, Wilhelm seems to have far more extreme moments of clumsiness…he comes in with a bang at the worst possible times!" Moira said a little defensively. Although Wil's accidents had thus far caused her some trouble, she found them very entertaining. He was a large man who fell like a tree in the forest.

"Let's just get to the point, shall we?" Wil said with a petulant undertone.

"Yes, let's!" Bobby said with a clap. "I'm not one for this idle chit chat. I am damned close to just climbing out this window and letting you lot wrap it up."

"That window is better for climbing in rather than climbing out," Moira said casually, pointing to the window in her living room. "The one in my bedchamber is much easier as an escape route."

"Digression!" Wilhelm shouted from the floor, raising one fisted hand into the air for emphasis.

"Shush!" Hanna scolded.

"How do you accomplish anything?" Bobby wondered aloud as she looked around exasperatedly.

"I will do the talking now," Wilhelm said, raising both arms above his head. "Here, from this comfortable floor, I am going to divulge the plan and then Bobby and I shall leave through Moira's bedroom window, which is apparently ideal for escaping. Alright?"

Everyone nodded, afraid to break the flow of focus by speaking.

"Roman is ready to act," Wilhelm started with a quick glance to Moira. "We thought we'd wait a few more days, let Bobby get back to Gest and continue her work there; however, our fearless leader is impatient."

"Would that be Roman?" Amis asked sarcastically before draining his glass of whiskey. There were a few stifled giggles from everyone except Wilhelm, who simply turned to glare at Amis.

"Yes," Wil grumbled.

"Well, get on with it!" Bobby growled with impatience.

"What's the big plan, Wil?" Moira asked, leaning forward slightly. A sudden feeling of trepidation crept into her gut. She was bubbling with impatience and anxiety.

As if the mere thought of the plan exhausted him, Wilhelm shifted and said casually, "Roman wants to abduct Prince Lyric."

Chapter Sixty-Four

The quiet that followed Wilhelm's declaration of the plan was the loudest silence Moira had ever heard. Outside her room, the winter storm continued to rage and the sound of sleet hitting the castle could be heard clearly. The wind raged on. Not a single word was said for several minutes as Amis, Hanna and Moira digested the news.

"Let's skip the questions of confirmation," Bobby said sternly. She rose from her chair at the table and took an authoritative stance in the middle of the room. "Roman wants to abduct Prince Lyric. Full stop. No clarification needed." Here she looked specifically at Moira, somehow knowing she was going to ask Wilhelm to repeat his statement.

"Right," Moira mumbled with a nod. "How?" She asked, looking between Wilhelm and Bobby, unsure of who would continue.

"As carefully as possible," Bobby replied with a teasing tone. Moira threw her an impatient glare. Bobby continued, "Ideally, no casualties, but Ro has made it clear that the usual cluster of lords around the prince would be no great loss."

"That's the plan? 'Ideally no casualties'?" Moira asked as Wilhelm gave her a shrug. "That is *not* a plan."

"It is according to Roman," Wilhelm said.

"There will be more to it, but you don't need to worry about it," Bobby said to patronize Moira's growing frustration.

"I won't be part of it?" Moira nearly shouted but found her voice dropping lower instead. "Get Roman *fucking* Loxley here and he can tell me to my face why I won't be involved."

"Moira's got a point, despite her choice in language," Hanna said. "Why are you bothering to tell us the plan if we aren't to be part of it?"

"You won't be a part of the abduction, but Roman is hopeful all of you will leave the castle and go to the cabin. Right now, actually," Bobby said, gesturing toward the door.

Amis held up his hand and started speaking before Moira could. "After everything Moira has done to support the villagers and continue to gather information while Roman has been gone, she's now expected to flee to the cabin and wait it out while all the action unfolds here?"

Both Wilhelm and Bobby had the good sense to look contrite as they bobbed their heads in confirmation.

"No," Amis said firmly as he stood. "Total bloody bollocks. Do you see all the research she's been doing?" He gestured angrily toward the table where the books rested and then to the shelf full of parchment. "You don't even know what she's learned while you've been gone. You have no idea what she's gone through! No clue as to the literal filth she has crawled through to get important information for this gods-forsaken cause. I ruined my best doublet for this group. No, we aren't bloody leaving. Not until Roman shows his godsdamned face and tells us exactly why we aren't staying."

Amis paced and rubbed his chin. His breathing was heavy as everyone watched him in stunned silence. It was unusual for him to take such a serious, aggressive stance, but Moira was grateful for his support. Wilhelm was now standing, watching Amis with a look of concerned curiosity on his face. Bobby had taken a few steps back, allowing more room for his pacing.

"Have we done something to lose Roman's trust?" Amis asked, his demeanor slightly calmer as he paused to look directly at Wilhelm.

"Gods, man! No. Of course not," Wilhelm replied vehemently.

"Then why?" Moira asked, now also standing. She heard her own heightened emotions come through in the question, even though she tried to maintain a level tone.

Wil cringed and closed his eyes. "This wasn't meant to be a fight," he said faintly as he opened his eyes and looked between Moira and Amis. "Roman wants you to leave so you don't complicate the mission or inadvertently betray the fact that you've been involved with us." He held his hands out, palms up in supplication. "He wants you to disappear in the night, no word, no trace. Ro believes the ambiguity of this plan will be beneficial later."

Moira snorted and said derisively, "Yes, because my sudden disappearance on the same night Prince Lyric gets taken and held captive would look like a coincidence?" Wil gave a shrug and opened his mouth to speak but Moira shook her head and continued. "Might I remind you that Lord Leofwin already suspects me. Of what, he's clearly not smart enough to figure out, but the suspicion is there. Dim witted churl that he is, I'm fairly certain he would make the connection."

"We had not considered that," Bobby said in an acquiescing tone.

"Odd, since you're currently in a fake relationship with the man," Amis pointed out.

Bobby threw a glare at Amis for the jab about Leofwin, but she didn't argue.

"Here's the new plan," Moira said calmly, already feeling better after voicing her frustrations. "You two return to whatever temporary hideout Roman is currently using. You share everything we discussed here tonight and then come back to us with a new offer. I'm happy to leave the castle, with Prince Lyric in tow or not, but I'm not going to do it in such a shameful, cowardly manner. I won't flee while the rest of you attempt a high-stakes mission."

"Agreed," Amis voiced with enthusiasm.

Hanna, who watched the discussion unfold as she sat in silence, stood and joined the group in the center of the room. "I have a message for Roman, too."

Irritated, Wilhelm drug his hand down his face and said, "Yes, Hanna?"

"I expect more respect than that," Hanna scolded. Wil looked at her sheepishly, but she continued speaking instead of waiting for an apology. "You tell Roman it's about bloody time he acted. You tell him Moira has more than filled his place while he's been gone, and you let him know that she has damned important information to share when he deigns to show his face. And lastly," Hanna glared at Wil and Bobby in turn, "You tell him I'm not leaving the castle without my things, so I will need adequate time to pack and sneak things out."

Soft laughter erupted as Hanna made her last demand with a smile.

"I mean it!" She said, slightly less intense than before. "You two can disappear as you like, but I'm in no hurry. I'm too old and I've been here too long to flee in the middle of the night with no notice."

"Han, did you ever know someone who abandoned their home in a hurry and in doing so, left behind important, irretrievable objects?" Amis asked with mock curiosity.

"As a matter of fact, I do."

Laughter broke out in full force. Amis, Moira, Wilhelm and Bobby laughed freely, unable to stop themselves. Amis was bent in half, clutching his stomach and laughing in short bursts. Moira had fallen back on her chaise and buried her face in her pillow, attempting to stifle the sound of her loud giggling. Wilhelm laughed more stoically, standing straight with one hand clapped over his mouth as his shoulders shook. Meanwhile, Bobby had the loudest laugh of them all, carrying on shamelessly and ensuring that the others could not regain composure.

"Now really!" Hanna scolded, hands on her hips. "There is an isolation order, in case you've all forgotten! Do you think an outburst like this won't go unnoticed?"

This reminder killed off their laughter almost immediately.

"Fair point, Hanna," Bobby said as she used her sleeve to dab the tears that ran down her cheeks. "I have to say, I don't believe I've laughed that hard in literal years."

"Me either!" Moira exclaimed.

Amis and Wilhelm nodded in agreement, both still looking jovial and lighter than Moira had seen in a long time. Amis especially.

"I'm still trying to figure out what was so funny," griped Hanna with her arms crossed defensively.

"We'll be going, then," Bobby said, deflecting. She nodded toward the door to Moira's room.

Moira stuck out her tongue at Wilhelm in farewell. He returned the gesture.

She stepped closer and asked softly, "I know you have about eighty messages to pass on, but can you manage one more?"

Wilhelm scrunched his face and said, "It's not a mushy message, is it?"

Moira rolled her eyes and crossed her arms. "No," she said crossly. "Tell Roman I'll be waiting."

Wil's face relaxed, but his mouth turned down in confusion. He nodded at Moira and then walked toward Bobby. "Let's do this. Sounds straight terrible out there and I don't expect it's going to get any better."

Hanna harumphed and crossed her arms. She scrunched her face, sour over the fact that no one was answering her earlier question.

Bobby gave a farewell nod to everyone before opening the door to Moira's room and walking straight to the window. She undid the clasp and opened the window before looking outside. Moira, Amis and Hanna all watched as first Bobby and then Wilhelm climbed through. With a sigh, Hanna stepped into the room after they disappeared to close and lock the window. She paused for a moment, hand on the glass, eyes shut before she nodded to herself and stepped back into the main room.

Chapter Sixty-Five

The wind was still howling, and an icy sleet was falling. Every so often there was an ominous flash of lightning followed by a heavy boom of thunder. As the wind shifted, Moira could hear the sleet as it hit the windows; it made a distinct rat-a-tat sound. All things considered, it sounded to her like a brutal night to be outside and she was grateful to be tucked in her bed with her book. Amis and Hanna had long since returned to their own rooms, ignoring the isolation orders by being in the castle halls unescorted.

Moira's room was furnished very simply, but she was fortunate enough to have a small fireplace that kept the space warm on nights like these. Embers glowed and cast odd shadows throughout the room. Although she only wore her chemise, she was comfortable tucked into her blankets. On her bedside table was a small lantern, which she'd lit earlier and brought in so she could read in bed.

In an effort to take the night off from her constant sleuthing and plotting, Moira had come to bed with a book of fiction. The story was suspenseful and so far, it took Moira out of her own head, which was exactly what she'd been hoping for.

She was still attempting to learn more about the Crusades (very little luck there as it seemed the prince refused to entertain the Crusades as a literary subject), while also doing as much research as she could into Monkshood. While she still had the pouch from Friar Tuck, which may be all she needed, she felt a nagging urge to learn more about the poison firsthand. While she now knew a fair bit about the poison, none of it was specifically helpful to her circumstances. Despite all the books that she borrowed from Prince Lyric's library, it seemed that she was doomed to never quite find what she was looking for.

As Moira started to doze off, her book slowly slipped from her hand with each deepening breath she took. Just when she was giving in to the siren call of unconsciousness, there was a subtle thump in the living room, causing her to wake with a jolt. She sat upright in bed, heart pounding and adrenaline coursing through her body, even though she still felt half asleep. Moira rubbed her eyes and listened intently, wondering if she would hear the noise again. Her ears strained to catch the sound of any movement in the front room, but all she could hear was the wind and sleet outside. As quietly as possible, Moira pulled her covers back and slid out of bed. She held her book aloft as if it were a weapon. Her toes curled as her feet met the cold stone floor, but she didn't have time to find stockings and her shoes were all tucked away in the wardrobe.

With a fortifying breath, Moira went to her bedroom door and flung it open. The outer room was dark and silent aside from the raging weather outside. She stepped forward, despite the trepidation she felt and looked carefully into each

468

corner of the room. The fire out here was smoldering even lower than the one in her room, so it gave off very little light. This was probably a blessing, she realized, because otherwise she'd be jumping at shadows. Her heart pounded in her ears as her gaze ripped through the room. As she stood there surrounded by silence, book aloft and wearing nothing but her nightclothes, Moira suddenly felt ridiculous. Her living room was not large and there was no easy hiding place. If someone was there, she would have seen them by now. She lowered her book and quietly snorted at herself. With one more cursory look at the furniture, bookshelves, small dining table and the main door (latched), Moira turned decisively back to her bedroom.

Her reading lantern was dimming slowly as it ran out of oil to sustain the flame and she watched as it took one last dancing flicker before going out. Moira tossed her book gently on the bed beside her as she settled back into her covers with a sigh; she was happy to feel the foot of her bed was still warm.

"You really should be more aware of your surroundings," admonished a figure standing in the darkest corner of her bedroom.

"Ahhhhh," Moira screamed, somewhat stifled as her vocal cords seemed incapable of fully functioning. She grabbed her book, leapt out of bed and chucked it as hard as she could end over end at the form in the corner. She heard a satisfying thud as it made contact.

"Fuck!" the figure groaned. "Who throws a book at someone, B? That is substandard behavior!"

A gasp of surprise left Moira as she scolded, "You scared the soul out of me, outlaw!" She stared at the corner in disbelief as none other than Roman Loxley emerged from the shadows, clutching her book in his left hand while rubbing a spot on his shoulder with his right. The dimming light from the fireplace cast an ominous glow on one half of his face.

After a moment to gather her wits, Moira dropped her hands and smiled. "People underestimate books," she nearly whispered. "They can be a weapon in more ways than one." She felt rather idiotic for saying this and loathed how breathy she sounded.

Overwhelmed by the sheer amount of emotion she was feeling, Moira couldn't believe the fright he'd given her. As she stood there, attempting to get her breathing back under control, Roman remained where he was, still rubbing the spot on his shoulder. There was tension in the air between them; something crackled after being apart so long.

With a smirk, Roman said, "In other words, I scared you so much that you were willing to sacrifice a book in order to save your own neck?"

"I wouldn't say 'sacrifice'," Moira retorted defensively, a little affronted over his word choice.

This elicited a generous laugh from Roman as he stepped out of the shadows. He stood at the foot of her bed and tossed the offending book onto the blankets. "Semantics, B."

Moira couldn't help but smile even wider. With an air of dignified superiority, she replied, "I've said it before and I'll say it again, outlaw. Word choice matters." She shrugged with one shoulder and put a hand on her hip, easing into the conversation now. Unfortunately, this stance reminded her that she was standing in nothing but her nightgown. She quickly grabbed the housecoat Hanna always draped at the foot of her bed and threw it on.

"I find it truly comforting that some things never change," Roman replied, still smiling at her and making no comment about the addition of her robe. She noted his hair had grown out a little and he was clearly working on growing the beard again. Moira was surprised at how quickly it had grown but remembered that a good chunk of time had passed since she watched him run out of the kitchen. It felt like years, if she was honest. Despite the fright and the frustrating way he chose to reappear, Moira felt a sudden tension ease out of her that she hadn't realized she'd been holding on to.

"Like you lurking in the shadows? That seems to be one thing I can count on," she said sarcastically. "Although, shadow stalking me does not actually provide me with much comfort."

Roman rolled his eyes and said, "It should. Clearly you could use someone watching out for you." He took one small step closer and continued in a softer tone, "Watching you always brings me great comfort, but I am willing to acknowledge that it might come across as a little unsettling."

Moira's forehead creased as she gave Roman a look which she hoped conveyed that she believed him to be disturbed. "Unsettling? I think I'd die of shock if you ever arrived to see me in a normal fashion," she teased. Moira tilted her head toward the bedroom door and said, "Let's go to the living room. I can build the fire back up and pour us something to sip on while we talk."

Roman arched his brow and said, "What? Don't trust yourself with me in your bedroom?" He gave a pointed glance toward her bed, which looked pleasantly rumpled from her manic escape moments ago.

"Oh yes, that's it. I often find myself dying to bed the man who just scared the soul out of me after lurking Gods know how long in the shadowy corner of my bedroom," she said cynically.

He didn't speak, but Roman tilted his head and gave her a knowing look. This ruffled her, but she decided not to take the bait.

"Believe it or not, I've got a lot to tell you," Moira said with a sigh.

He smirked, and she shook her head, attempting to keep her face stern and serious.

"Let me guess," he mused in a tone that suggested he was not guessing at all. "You ignored my request to *wait* to act upon *anything* until hearing from me?" He made sure to put extra emphasis on the words wait and anything.

"I think we both know the answer to that," Moira started to argue, but shut her mouth before she could get into the swing of her rant. She ignored Roman's self-righteous grin and said, "I couldn't stop certain events from unfolding just because you needed time to heal."

"Not only heal, B. I had to let some of the heat die down. Might I remind you that I was in the prince's clutches before I escaped?" He asked, still baiting her.

Moira scoffed and said, "And whose fault was that? Maybe you're the one who needs reminding, since you only escaped that dungeon thanks to me. Which was me failing to follow your orders once again, since I distinctly remember you asking me to stop rescuing you." She crossed her arms and stared at him, her eyes alight with challenge. "Besides, we both know Wilhelm and Bobby scampered out of here earlier tonight, tails between their legs, to return to you with details of all my misdeeds." If Moira could have suppressed her cocky smirk, she would have.

Roman gave her a grimacing smile in return and said, "They did, indeed. You opted, again, to ignore my request - the request that you leave the castle tonight - and instead demanded that I come speak to you. Here I am, Beastie." He stepped one foot back and gave her a dramatic and flourishing bow; both arms stretched out as he tilted and kept his eyes on her.

"Well, it's nice to know one of us is capable of following orders," Moira jabbed arrogantly.

Roman's smile grew as he said gently, "I missed you, Moira."

"Obviously, I'm very missable," Moira responded smartly before she could stop herself.

Roman gave a soft laugh, but the merriment in his eyes was quickly overshadowed by something much darker. A look that made Moira's breathing hitch crossed his face as he stepped around the bed and came to stand directly in front of her. Moira gulped audibly but kept her eyes on Roman's as his hand came down to rest on the spot where her shoulder and neck met. Just as he'd done before, his thumb rubbed the front of her throat softly. Moira took a steadying breath as Roman lowered his head and placed his lips softly on hers. Hesitantly, Moira reached her hand up and placed it on his chest. Something akin to a moan rumbled deep in Roman's chest as he pressed the length of his body against Moira's. Her hands moved up to wrap around Roman's neck as she opened her mouth to deepen the kiss and give in to the sensations running away with her. His hand snaked through her hair and tilted her head back further. All coherent thought left Moira's mind as she held on tightly to Roman, silently hoping the moment would never end.

Moira would have happily continued if Roman had not pulled away. He put his forehead against hers with one hand in her hair and the other wrapped around her. He sighed as he said, "Tell me something I don't know, B."

She grinned as she pulled back slightly, wanting to look at him. With some annoyance, Moira admitted, "I'm fairly certain that I've fallen in love with you."

Roman chuckled softly, leaned in, and gave her a gentle kiss before pulling back and saying, "I said something I don't know."

Moira scrunched her face in false outrage as she lightly smacked him on the chest. "You did not know that! I've kept my emotions under lock and key, thank you very much."

"Ha!" Roman exclaimed as he grabbed her hand and turned. He gave her a gentle tug as he led her out into the living room.

Moira followed without protest and let go of his hand as she walked to the fireplace. She wanted a moment to herself to calm down. The kiss had consumed her, and she was grateful Roman pulled back before things went any further. Although she was not opposed, there was too much happening right now. Maybe naively, she hoped that their first time together might be spent without a plot to abduct the prince looming over them.

All that remained of the earlier fire in her living room was some lightly smoldering ash and coal. She pulled another log from the basket next to the fireplace and tossed it onto the embers. With the tools kept next to the fireplace, Moira gave the coals a few pokes, blowing on them as she did, coaxing the fire back to life. She struggled and was about to give up when Roman sighed behind her. He gave her a gentle nudge and set to work on the fire while she turned around and went to the liquor cabinet.

With whiskey in hand and a fire crackling, Moira settled into the cushions on her chaise while Roman perched on the edge of it. He pulled her feet into his lap and took a long drink before he said anything.

"You shouldn't have called them 'misdeeds,'" he said quietly.

Moira furrowed her brow and looked at him, unsure of what he was referring to.

"Everything you've done," Roman said, gesturing vaguely at her. "You shouldn't call what you've accomplished 'misdeeds.' What you did in my absence it was…," he paused, searching her face. "It was brave, Moira. Not to mention impressive, clever, and incredibly frustrating."

Moira started to grin as he spoke, right up until he said frustrating, which sparked a scowl and something like a snarl to escape her mouth. "Frustrating for you, maybe!"

"Yes, frustrating for me!" He agreed sharply but was also amused.

"Oh," she said, somewhat surprised that he hadn't argued the point.

"I don't need to increase the size of that ego with commendations on every little detail. From my perspective, I was equally frustrated and impressed with what you were accomplishing. I'm not exactly used to my orders being ignored."

Moira scoffed a little and said, "I'm not good with orders, outlaw. Especially ones that make no sense. All I did was take advantage of the opportunities that presented themselves. The people here depended on you and the aid you provided. I only wish I could have helped people outside of Ivywood. Before you returned, I was trying to find out how to expand my influence. There was plenty to do. Unfortunately, I think the term 'misdeeds' might be what people outside this particular group call what I've done."

Roman shrugged and took another sip of his whiskey. Moira followed suit but kept her gaze on Roman, curious about what he expected out of their current conversation. The winter storm seemed to have died down a little. There was no longer the constant background noise of sleet hitting the windows, and Moira couldn't hear the roaring wind any longer.

"You can't be the hero in everyone's story, B. That isn't how life works. Do you think I am the golden hero in every villager's life?"

Moira scoffed good-naturedly as she said, "I honestly hope no one refers to you as the 'golden hero' in any story! I can guarantee Wil would agree with me on that."

Although he granted Moira a mollifying smile, Roman's face remained mostly serious as he continued. "My embellishment aside, my point stands. I do not earn accolades at every turn. Men have died for the cause. Men who were never part of it, to begin with. My intent is never to end a life, Moira, but plans go awry."

"Moral gray area," Moira responded with a small shrug.

Roman looked at her in surprise and confusion.

Moira sat a little straighter, pulled her legs back toward her, and crossed them as she tucked them under her robe. The room was still a little chilly, despite the fire coming back to life.

"Listen, outlaw. I don't want to downplay the things you've been through and the things you've done. I appreciate and understand that doing the right thing, in the long run, may include alternative choices along the way. No," she said, holding up a hand as Roman looked like he may want to interject. "Please, let me finish?" She asked. He nodded. "There will be time, Roman. Time to talk about everything. To dig into the nastier details, if that's what you want. Tonight is not that night."

Roman cleared his throat and said, "You're right."

Without waiting for further comment, Moira dove into an explanation of everything she learned in Roman's absence. She started where they left off - telling him how she had hidden inside the kitchen's priest hole, how she learned about the purple poison and her adventure with Friar Tuck, and all about how she and Amis followed Alaine to the secret passageway in the pit. She did her best to remain organized in her storytelling, but so much happened in such a small period that certain timelines were fuzzy. Roman listened intently and did not interrupt, despite several times when she knew he wanted to cut in and lecture her. By the time she was done telling him everything she could think of, her throat was dry, and she felt drained, exhausted.

Somewhere along the way, Roman stood up and started pacing while Moira spoke. He ran his hands through his hair a few times and toyed with his beard as he walked. His face remained mostly passive, but she knew he was deep in thought. Even once she was done, Roman continued to pace for several moments before he stopped in front of her. He crouched down so he was eye to eye with her as she sat on the chaise and then grabbed both of her hands in his.

"The time to stay in place and endure is over. I have so much to say, but I fear there just isn't time," he said with an unidentifiable undercurrent of emotion. "Will you help me abduct Prince Lyric tonight?"

"It would be hubris to try," Moira said, looking at Roman intently. His face fell a little at her words, but she kept talking before he could misunderstand her. "Lucky for you, I've been operating on pure hubris lately. I'm in!"

Roman grinned wickedly, leaped up, and scooped Moira off the chaise as he stood. He swung her around once before setting her down. He paused and looked at her. With one hand back in that special spot, he said, "I have fallen for you, too. Just in case I forgot to say it earlier."

"You did forget to say it, as a matter of fact," Moira said with a wide, happy grin playing on her face.

"Well, you weren't particularly effusive with your sentiment, so I felt like maybe we weren't at the declaration stage."

Moira shook her head slightly and said, "I don't know how to talk about it yet. It seems impossible to feel the way I do when we've had so little time together."

"I know what you mean," Roman said softly.

"I do love you," Moira whispered. "If it was insubstantial, maybe I could be more effusive about it."

Roman leaned down and gave her another soft kiss before pulling back and saying, "Ready to storm the castle?" He wiggled his eyebrows a little for dramatic effect.

Moira laughed and rolled her eyes. "Does it count as 'storming the castle' if you're already inside? Might it be difficult to spirit away an important man without any sort of reinforcement?"

"Who said I was lacking support, B? Do you think so little of me?" He held his hand over his heart as if she'd wounded him.

She tilted her head and crossed her arms, asking, "Where are Wilhelm and Bobby?"

"Ah hah!" Roman exclaimed. "They're around. There is more than just the cadre here tonight, my wee beastie!"

"Roman, what is going on? I thought the most important missions only included your most trusted inner circle?" Moira asked as she started to lose her patience. While Roman seemed alight with excitement, she was left feeling somewhat frustrated. She still did not know the full plan.

"Get dressed, and I'll tell you on the way," Roman said as he plopped back down on the chaise and tossed back the last of his whiskey.

"Get dressed?!" Moira nearly shouted.

"Oh, I'm sorry. Did you fancy an adventure through the castle in nothing but your nightclothes? I hadn't factored that in as part of the abduction plan, but I'd be happy to re-work things if you like?"

"Scoundrel!" Moira scolded as she turned dramatically toward her room. She did not want to admit that she'd forgotten she was not fully clothed. While she hated feeling like it was a waste of time, she admitted that getting dressed in actual clothing was obviously necessary. As quickly as she could, Moira threw on an old pair of Amis's trousers that fit her reasonably well, some well-worn but comfortable boots, and a black tunic. Since she wasn't sure she would be returning, Moira tucked the satchel from Friar Tuck deep into the side of her right boot. Before leaving her room, she added a belt around her middle in the vague hope that she'd be able to obtain a weapon to tuck into it. She took a breath and stepped back into the main room, ready for whatever may come.

Chapter Sixty-Six

"What about Amis?" Moira whispered frantically as she held tight to Roman's hand and let him lead her down the steps and through the dark castle hallways.

"Not to worry," Roman said, turning toward her slightly but not slowing his pace in the slightest. "Amis was recruited earlier in the night. Probably around the same time you launched a book at my head."

Moira scowled and sped up. "I have no regrets about defending myself," she responded assertively.

Roman threw her a smile but held a finger to his lips as they rounded the corner and started walking straight toward the trophy room. Moira groaned inwardly, wondering why on earth every monumental moment with Prince Lyric needed to transpire in that one damned room.

"What exactly is our plan, outlaw?" Moira asked with a light tug on Roman's hand.

"The plan is underway, B. Time to play along."

Moira dropped Roman's hand and stopped in her tracks. "You said you would fill me in, and this does not count. What the hell is happening tonight?"

With a slightly frustrated sigh, Roman turned around and took a step back to where Moira stood. She crossed her arms, uncaring of whatever sort of delay she might cause.

"We are partners, Roman, or we are nothing. I will not take anything less, including half-assed answers on what is about to happen."

Roman nodded and said, "You're right. I'm behaving badly."

"You are. Continue," Moira said, gesturing with her hand to speed things up.

"Sigrid, from the kitchens -"

"I know Sigrid, skip the introductions and long-winded explanations, Roman. We don't have time."

With a slight quirk to his mouth and an attempt at a glare, Roman continued his explanation. He spoke quietly but quickly. "Sigrid added a sleeping draught to the wine goblets of Prince Lyric and Lords Maddicot, Leofwin, Dayben, Godberd, and Owen. Since their evening routine is to retire to the trophy room after dinner, the plan was for Wilhelm and Amis to get into the room shortly after the group with the hopes that all the men would have fallen into their drugged sleep. From there, the butler would be dealt with - in a nonviolent manner -," Roman added swiftly at the look on Moira's face. After her last interaction with the man, she knew Amis would be against harming Fitzroy. "Once the butler is gone, they will keep the room locked until we arrive. From there, we ensure the men are unable to follow us as we make away with the dear, sweet prince."

Moira tipped her head right and left in thought and said, "That might work."

Roman sighed but gave her an endearing smirk as he shook his head. He held his hand out to her, and she placed her hand in his without a second thought. With a gentle squeeze, he started walking with determination once again. She kept pace with him and felt a flutter of excitement as they approached the door.

"Roman, wait!" Moira rasped as a sudden realization hit her. She pulled her hand free from his. "Am I staying in the castle or going with you to the hideout?" She scolded herself for not having thought of this important question earlier. Although she defied him about leaving the castle earlier, now that she was included in the actual events of the night, she was not against it. As long as she wasn't treated as some sort of luggage to arrange transportation for, she was open to it.

"It's up to you, Moira," Roman said softly. He looked as if he would say more, but he held back whatever else was on his mind.

"Would it be," Moira paused and took a deep breath. "Would it be alright if I wait to decide?"

Roman nodded and remained silent. Moira nodded in return, and without speaking, they took the last few steps to the closed doors of the trophy room. There was no Fitzroy standing guard as Moira expected, which meant there must have been success with the first stage of the plan. Moira glanced down the hallway toward the library, but everything was silent and almost completely dark.

As she looked down the hall, an ominous feeling threatened to overwhelm Moira. She reached out and grabbed Roman's wrist as he reached for the door handle. She gripped his wrist tightly and attempted to find words to explain the sudden pit in the bottom of her stomach, but instead, she only looked at him. There were no words for it, but Moira knew something was not right.

Roman stared back at her in questioning concern but did not speak. His eyes roved the hallway behind Moira, searching for whatever caused the change in her demeanor. When he looked back at Moira, she gave him an uncertain shrug and whispered almost inaudibly, "Something is not right."

He gave her an understanding nod before saying, "We must proceed. If something is wrong, it involves Wilhelm and Amis. We cannot turn back."

The sinking feeling intensified as Moira realized the fact that even if she turned and fled, she had skin in the game. There was plenty to lose even if she never set foot in the damned trophy room ever again. With a deep breath that did nothing to calm her frayed nerves, Moira nodded at Roman and let go of his wrist.

Roman opened the door slowly at first, but he threw it open violently as soon as he realized the room was dark. The only light came from the flickering fire in the grate, not nearly enough to see anything in detail. As he stepped through the door, Roman started to draw his sword. Moira followed him closely and found herself wishing she had asked Roman for a weapon.

"You're late!" Shouted a gruff voice to the left as a giant form barreled into Roman, knocking him off his feet.

Moira rushed into the room just as Roman was tackled to the floor. There were sounds of a significant struggle, but all Moira could make out were their dark figures on the floor. Someone shut and locked the door behind her, causing Moira to turn around in alarm.

A second tall, dark figure moved toward Moira, but she gave the form a heaving shove before he could touch or grab her. The unknown man stumbled backward, tripping over Roman and the other man as they fought on the floor.

"Run, Moira!" Roman bellowed.

Moira was about to respond when the second man popped up behind her and wrapped his arms tightly around her. He had clearly regained his footing while she was distracted by Roman's shouting. Moira screamed, jumped, and did her best to free herself from his grasp, but whoever he was, his grip was absolute. As he tightened his hold, her ability to take a full breath dwindled quickly, forcing her to stop her efforts to free herself. She was only able to take shallow breaths. Once Moira gave up her immediate escape efforts and focused instead on calming her breathing, she registered the fact that the scuffling on the floor had stopped.

"Roman?!" she shrieked as full panic set in rapidly.

"Hush, pet," Leofwin whispered in her ear as he tightened his grip on her even more.

"No," Moira breathed, unwilling to accept the fact that it was Leofwin who held her.

A flare of light appeared behind Moira and Leofwin. She tried to turn to see what was happening, but Leofwin held her tightly.

"Fuck you, Conor," Moira seethed. She was unable to put all the animosity she felt into her words, thanks to her limited air supply, but it didn't stop her from trying.

A slow clapping noise came from behind Moira and Leofwin. It came from the general area of Prince Lyric's large writing table. More light was slowly springing into the room, and Moira realized someone must be lighting the torches lining the walls and the candles on the shelves. She craned her neck to see and was shocked to see Fitzroy move into her line of vision as he worked his way around the room. The poor man was bleeding heavily from his head and seemed to have trouble with his balance. Surely, he was not the one who clapped. Moira wanted to call out to Fitzroy and tell him to run but she knew it would not do either of them any good.

As Moira watched Fitzroy light the last of the torches and back out of the room, she was nearly crushed by the realization that the entire plan, from start to finish, had failed. Had Amis and Wilhelm ever made it into this room? It was clear the sleeping draught Sigrid was meant to slip to the prince and his lords never made it down their throats. Her mind reeled as she ran through the possible scenarios. Had Fitzroy been able to warn Amis and Wil that the room was not filled with sleeping men, as their plan depended on? Were they caught and held captive somewhere? She held back the tears that were building behind her eyes. Moira told herself sternly that there was nothing she could do at this moment other than focus on her immediate situation and how to get out of it. Panicking about Amis and Wil would not help her escape Leofwin's grasp.

"I do love a good scheme," snarled Prince Lyric.

Leofwin turned, lifting Moira's feet off the ground as he did and turning her with him. Standing behind his writing desk was the prince. He had both hands planted on the tabletop as he glared at the room through his busy, bright red eyebrows. Moira remained silent and looked down at the floor, unsure of what else she should do, but knowing she didn't want to incite any of the prince's rage.

"Too bad this scheme is utter shit," Lyric said with a jeer.

Chapter Sixty-Seven

Try as she might, Moira could not catch her breath. Leofwin's tight grasp around her did not lessen. She was utterly disgusted; she hated his touch. Lord Maddicot was now restraining Roman, who appeared to have ceased his struggle. Moira again wondered where Wilhelm and Amis were. She sent up a silent prayer to the old Gods that both her brother and Wilhelm were not injured or dead.

Prince Lyric was staring alternatingly at Moira and Roman. He wore an expression of sadistic excitement. The prince was enraged, that much was obvious, but at the same time he continued to look wild and gleeful.

"What do you want us to do with this filth?" Maddicot asked, sending a knee into the back of Roman's thigh as he held him from behind. Roman grunted and stumbled forward a little, but regained his balance quickly as Maddicot heaved him back up into a standing position. Roman kept his gaze on the stone floor of the trophy room, his jaw clenched tightly. As far as Moira knew, Roman had not raised his gaze to meet that of Prince Lyric.

"I want you to wait until I speak, dammit! Always impatient, Maddicot. You have never been good at the long game. You are weak!" Prince Lyric spat the last word and turned his back on everyone.

Lyric took a few steps toward the shelving behind his large writing table, but then jerked back around. In a fit of rage, the prince sprang forward and swept all the contents from the desk to the ground. Bits of parchment fluttered to the floor slowly, while heavier objects crashed and clattered. A glass ornament shattered noisily and left a wide radius of shards behind. Lyric continued his rampage by turning and ripping a mounted deer's head from the wall and slamming it to the floor. This was more disruptive than destructive, as the head seemed to be too heavy for Lyric to slam very effectively. There was no visible damage done to the mount, although it made an incredibly loud noise. A guard flung open the door and rushed in, surprising Moira. She wondered where on earth the guard came from when minutes ago, she and Roman had traversed most of the castle without seeing a soul. Regardless of where he came from, the man met the full force of the prince's rage.

"Out!" shouted Lyric, "Godsdammit, I will call you if I need you!" The prince's face was an alarming shade of red and he was nearly incandescent with fury. There was a slight sheen to his forehead from the exertion of his outburst.

At the very least, the interruption ended Lyric's spree of destruction. Moira looked over to Roman and was shocked to see he raised his gaze. There was an unreadable expression on his face as he stared at the prince and the mess surrounding him. Roman's hair was dancing out in all directions, which only increased the dramatic, feral look of him. There was a small trickle of blood coming from his nose, but otherwise there were no signs of his struggle with Maddicot. If Moira did not know him, she would have turned and run the other way.

Moira noticed Leofwin's grip on her relaxed ever so slightly, and she tried to subtly put some distance between her body and his. As soon as she shifted, he snapped out of his reverie and tightened his grip once again.

His mouth pressed against her ear as he whispered, "Do not embarrass me further, *pet*. Remain still."

The feeling of his wet lips against her ear sent her over the edge. Moira could not take it any longer. Without a single thought, she pitched her head forward as far as she could before jerking back and slamming it soundly into Leofwin's nose. The sound of his nose breaking was oddly satisfying, as was the freedom it earned her.

The cost of her sudden freedom came swiftly. Leofwin drew his arm and backhanded Moira. Her head snapped back, and she stumbled into the wall behind her. Moira's head rang, but she didn't feel any bleeding. The side of her face where Leofwin's blow landed seared with pain.

"Bitch!" Leofwin shouted as he clutched his gushing nose.

Moira couldn't stop herself from the small, self-satisfied little giggle that escaped her. Unfortunately, the sound unleashed something in Leofwin, and he lashed out violently, grabbing her with his bloody hands. He pulled her toward him and captured her throat in his right hand while his left wrapped around her waist. Not only was she back in his clutches, but now she was face to face with him as blood poured from his nose. Moira fought against his grip, but her head was still murky from the blow he delivered, and she felt as though she didn't have full control of her limbs. Her arms were trapped as Leofwin squeezed her even tighter with the arm wrapped around her torso.

As Leofwin leered at her, breathing heavily, he also increased his grip around her neck. Prince Lyric started clapping once again. Moira gasped for air.

"Oh, bravo! Excellent. I had no idea our *lady* Moira had so much -," he paused as if searching for the right word. "Spunk. I am not sure you can handle her, Conor." He laughed rather viciously and clapped again.

As Moira started to worry about her air supply, she thought again of Amis. No matter what happened tonight, she hoped he would not appear in this room and see what was unfolding.

"Stop," Roman growled.

Roman's single word broke the silent tension that followed Prince Lyric's laughter.

"What did you say?" Prince Lyric sneered, as he looked at Roman in shock.

"Stop," Roman thundered. "The sniveling, bloody man with his hand around the lady's neck. Make him stop or I will."

Roman stood straight. His shoulders back while his elbows were still awkwardly, but firmly, held behind him by Maddicot. His chest heaved as he looked at Leofwin with nothing but rage and loathing.

Moira noticed that her vision was going black around the edges and blurry in the middle, but despite this new complication she could see the fury radiating from Roman.

Leofwin quit staring at Moira and looked over at Roman, but his hand remained around her neck. He even tightened his grip a little, making her grimace despite her small effort not to. She did not want Roman to do anything foolish on her behalf. Moira knew she could survive this awful situation, at least temporarily. Roman, on the other hand, would most likely be killed at the prince's earliest convenience.

It took every ounce of effort she had, but Moira managed to speak in a raspy whisper, "No, Roman."

Moira was looking at Roman from the corner of her watering eyes, unable to fully turn her head toward him. This glance earned her a violent shake from Leofwin as he attempted to turn her gaze away from Roman. She groaned and wondered for the first time if Leofwin might kill her. She found the thought particularly upsetting. Primarily because

Leofwin was a human rat, and she found the thought of him killing her both abhorrent and embarrassing.

"Release the girl, Conor. I do not want a dead lady on my hands," the prince said in a tone that strongly implied he regretted making the command.

Leofwin did not relax his grip.

"I said release the girl, *Lord* Leofwin. If I must remind you one more time, I shall let the rambunctious maid Moira stab you with the tiny blade I know you have stashed in your boot," Lyric shouted.

Leofwin loosened his grip on Moira's throat and she felt her body take over, immediately gulping in as much air as she possibly could. His hand was still on her neck, but he was no longer restricting her airways. As a few more seconds passed, her vision returned to normal, and her head stopped throbbing as strongly. Her throat felt like it was on fire; each breath raking its teeth down the inflamed tissue.

"Better," Lyric said through gritted teeth. "Now for the love of me and my kingdom, staunch that blood gushing from your mangled nose before you ruin my rug!"

In order to dig out a handkerchief, Leofwin had to release Moira. He gave her a slight shove as he did so and Moira, still shaken and regaining her bearings, fell to the ground. Moira landed on hands and knees as she continued to take deep breaths. She felt weak, momentarily unable to support herself as she collapsed onto the cold floor.

Roman roared. He ripped his arms free from Maddicot with surprising ease; as if he was never actually being restrained but allowed the illusion for the sake of everyone there. He grabbed a large, gold object from one of the nearby shelves and smashed it into the side of Maddicot's head. Maddicot crumpled to the ground like a puppet whose master dropped his strings. Roman stormed over to Leofwin, who just managed to shove the handkerchief into his two gushing nostrils right in time for Roman's fist to hit him square in the nose. Leofwin collapsed to the ground with a yelp of pain.

Moira was attempting to stand when a guard burst backward through the closed door, closely followed by Wilhelm. He appeared to have thrown the guard into the door to open it. Moira rolled her eyes, despite the circumstances. Only Wilhelm would use a man as a battering ram.

"Wil, grab Moira. She's been mistreated," Roman ordered as he turned toward Prince Lyric, who still lurked near his desk.

Before she could argue, Wilhelm scooped Moira up in his arms. Despite the surrounding chaos, Moira marveled at Wil's strength. She was not a small woman and he still managed to hoist her with ease.

"Where's Bob and Amis?" Roman asked over his shoulder. He pulled some sort of nasty looking ax from the wall and pointed it at Prince Lyric. Moira was suddenly thankful for the assortment of random weapons that the trophy room provided them. She noted that the prince wore a sick look of pleasure, as though events were unfolding just as he hoped they would.

"Tying up loose ends, Ro. Leave princey. Let's go before things get worse," said Wilhelm with a slight note of desperation in his voice.

"Take Moira and go. I'm not done here."

"No!" Moira shouted as she began to struggle in Wil's arms. There was no way she was leaving Roman here. She looked at Maddicot who was still out cold, but she heard Leofwin start to shift and move over in the corner. He may have a twice broken nose, but he could still call for help.

"I hate to ruin this marvelous escape attempt, but I assure you no one is leaving this castle tonight. The only place you're all going is to the dungeons and then the noose," Prince Lyric practically sang as he sauntered toward Leofwin's crumpled form. "Get up, you lousy ass! Get up and apprehend this man!" The prince was screaming at Leofwin, but so far, all the lord managed was a constant low moan and very little movement.

"Put me down, Wilhelm Clarke. Do not make me claw your eyes out!" Moira hissed as she slammed her fists into Wil's chest. She wasn't sure she could hurt her friend, but she was not about to play damsel in distress, at least not now that her head had finally cleared. Wilhelm hesitated but set her down.

Moira ran to the other end of the trophy room, behind Prince Lyric, and grabbed the locked wooden box. She tossed it to Wilhelm.

"That's all we need. Let's go. Now, Roman."

Roman and Wilhelm looked at her as if she'd gone mad. She sighed at the waste of time and said, "Grab the key Prince Lyric keeps in his inside pocket and let's go." Moira looked pointedly at Roman and said, "Trust me."

Both men paused and looked at each other. Roman nodded and pressed the pointed tip of the ax to the prince's throat as he ripped open Lyric's doublet and roughly reached into the pocket. He pulled out the key; kept on a short red ribbon, and then stepped back. Roman tossed the ax at Prince Lyric and turned to run out of the room. The odd tactic worked, as the prince was briefly distracted by the ax flying at his face, which allowed them to bolt from the room.

As an afterthought, Moira reached down into Leofwin's boot and pulled out the small knife he kept there. She figured any weapon was better than none at this point.

"Now what?" Moira asked as they ran into the hallway.

With a chuckle and wicked grin, Roman turned to her and said, "You're an outlaw now, Beastie!"

Chapter Sixty-Eight

Wilhelm led the way as the trio fled through the castle halls. Moira kept up, but she seemed to be the only one who repeatedly looked behind them, checking to see if they were being pursued. It seemed suspicious to her that no one followed them in their escape.

"Where are we going? And where is Amis?" Moira gasped through panting breaths, not breaking stride but finally voicing one of her burning questions.

"The kitchen," Wil responded, turning his head to speak to her.

"Why aren't we being followed?" Moira asked, not responding to the answer. The kitchens seemed to be where Roman liked to make his escape, so it made sense to her that they'd go there. She wondered if they would find Sigrid and have time to ask her what happened with the sleeping draught.

"They're following us, B. You can be certain of that," Roman said in an ominous tone.

Wilhelm slowed as they approached the main door to the kitchen. Moira turned to look at Roman, bringing her shoulders up into a frustrated shrug as she said, "What do you mean they're following us? No one is behind us."

They walked through the large kitchen archway and froze. Moira had to remind herself to breathe as Roman grabbed hold of her upper arm and held onto her tightly. Wilhelm seemed to be suffering from similar issues as he stood there, mouth agape, eyes blinking frantically.

"No," Moira said with a moan as she took in the brutal scene in the kitchen.

Her gaze kept scanning the room repeatedly, unable to fully grasp what she was seeing. Sigrid lay across the large wooden worktable, lifeless and with her limbs splayed out in all directions. She looked as if someone tossed her there as an afterthought. A pair of small feet stuck out from behind the table where Sigrid lay. Moira knew without looking that those feet belonged to Alaine. There were pots and pans flung everywhere. A fine dust covered most surfaces and Moira faintly registered the substance must be flour. She wondered if it was flung about carelessly by whoever had done this. The flour gave a ghostly, otherworldly appearance to the already awful scene before her.

Finally, Moira looked over to the large fireplace. The very same one that she'd climbed into and hidden in. There, sprawled on the floor in front of the hearth was Amis. He too appeared as lifeless as Sigrid and Alaine. Roman still had hold of Moira's upper arm, but she jerked herself free from his grasp and rushed to Amis. She kneeled at the floor beside him; cold and jagged stone digging into her knees and shins, but she couldn't bring herself to care.

She was numb. Unfeeling. His hand was limp in hers, but she continued to cling to it. Vaguely, she realized the growing clamor around her. She should stand. She should fight.

All she could do was sit and try to will life back into that beloved face.

Chapter Sixty-Nine

Castle guards rushed into the kitchen, forcing Wil and Roman to jump into action as Moira knelt on the floor.

"Amis," Moira sobbed, still gripping his hand and gently shaking his shoulder.

If not for the unnatural stillness, Moira would have assumed Amis was sleeping. His face looked peaceful, as if he was asleep and having the best dream. The usual mischief was gone from his features, replaced by a slackness that Moira found deeply upsetting. There was no rise and fall to his chest. No breathing that she could detect. She placed her ear against his chest and could not hear the thud of his heart.

There was a light coating of flour covering Amis. Moira gently dusted the front of his shirt, ran her hands through his hair, and softly brushed it from his face. While it did not bring life back his features, removing the flour at least ensured Amis looked less spectral.

"Moira!" Roman hollered from across the room as he fought off one of the guards who stormed into the kitchen.

Although Moira registered somewhere deep in her mind that Roman was calling to her, she couldn't bring herself to respond. He was shouting warning after warning, telling her to stand, to run, to hide...she could not move from her place beside Amis. The hand she held was still warm. How long ago had he been alive? How long ago had Alaine and Sigrid been alive? Roman sounded far away and muffled, as did the sounds of fighting. Nothing in that moment felt real to Moira. Rather than succumb to the building sensation of overwhelming despair, Moira let a comforting numbness take over. It was easier than facing her emotions head-on.

"Such a tragedy," whispered a dark shape next to her. It materialized out of nowhere and placed its hand on her shoulder. With Moira's dimmed senses, nothing could surprise her.

Roman roared incoherently behind her. Something had happened; there was a new edge to his shouting that hadn't been there before.

With a furrowed brow and vague sense of confusion, Moira turned to look at the figure. She came roaring back to life as she realized it was Prince Lyric crouched next to her. The man responsible for Amis's death touched her and whispered in her ear. Not even her deep desire to detach from reality could have kept her numb to the prince's presence. He continued to speak to her, but all Moira heard was the blood thundering in her ears. No other sound permeated the barrier of her own wrath. A violent rage built as she looked back at Amis's motionless form and then returned her gaze to Prince Lyric's false look of sympathy.

Moira closed her eyes and inhaled deeply. When she opened them again, Lyric must have seen some glimpse of her fury, for he quickly removed his hand from her shoulder and left it suspended in the air as if unsure what to do with it. Moira's left hand still held tightly to Amis's, but in her right hand she clutched the small knife she pulled from Leofwin's boot. As swiftly as she could, she adjusted her grip on the blade and then lashed out as violently as she could. Prince Lyric's hand clamped around her wrist, but was just a second too late to save himself entirely. All he did was manage to slow her down. The blade plunged into Lyric's ribs.

"You foul bitch!" Snarled Prince Lyric as he stared at the tiny handle protruding from his side. He kept his tight grip on Moira's wrist.

"Let go of me," Moira screamed at the top of her lungs, leaning toward the prince in an attempt to yell directly into his ear.

As childish as the maneuver was, Moira was pleased when it worked. The prince immediately dropped her wrist as he jerked backward and covered his ear. Taking advantage of his distraction, Moira reached forward and attempted to grab the knife and pull it from the prince's ribs. She wanted her weapon back, but he was slightly faster. Lyric slapped her hand away and bared his teeth at her in some sort of feral display.

"Fucker!" She screamed as she shoved the prince with all her might. Lyric's balance gave way easily enough thanks to his half-crouched position and his concern for the knife in his side.

Moira rose from the floor. She had finally let go of Amis's hand to shove the prince, but she hated that she had to do it.

"Moira!" Roman shouted again as he kept fighting and tried to move closer to her.

Moira turned to look at Roman, breaking her internal debate about whether or not she should try to drag Amis's body out of the kitchen. It was a morbid thought, but she was loath to leave him lying where he was. When she looked at Roman, she realized the large kitchen table was a barrier between them. How had she stepped around it and away from Roman so quickly just moments ago?

Wilhelm was fighting two guards in the opposite corner. He was the closest one to their exit. Several guards lay motionless and bloody on the kitchen's floury floor. Moira's stomach roiled at the realization that the mixture of blood, flour and movement was creating a nasty red paste of sorts.

"Get to Wil, Moira!" Roman roared, shoving back yet another guard before plunging his blade through the man's neck.

Despite every urge to try and bring Amis, Moira turned toward Wilhelm with a broken sob. She would have sworn that she felt her heart shatter completely with the decision to leave Amis behind.

Dimly, Moira wondered where the other lords were. Leofwin and Maddicot were likely still indisposed due to the injuries they sustained in the trophy room. It was clear Lyric left them behind when he pursued Moira, Roman and Wilhelm to the kitchen, but where were the rest? Lords Godberd, Owen and Dayben should have appeared to fight for the prince and finally take down the nefarious outlaw that had caused them years of strife. Since Bobby wasn't lying here lifeless with the others, Moira assumed she escaped. But without knowing anything for sure, she could only hope Bobby was at least somewhere safe. The now constant pit of foreboding in Moira's stomach grew larger as she silently hoped Hanna was not in danger.

"Another half-assed escape attempt," Prince Lyric sneered as he grabbed the back of Moira's tunic and pulled her roughly against him.

Moira heard Lyric pull the knife out of his side. He reached around, pressing the bloody blade against her neck. She held her head as high as she could, attempting to get away from the dripping blade, but he pressed it harder into her skin until she felt the sting of the edge break her skin. A scream escaped her as she kicked backward blindly, but she couldn't make contact with any part of Lyric.

In her panic, a moment of clarity hit. As Lyric held his left elbow high, pressing the knife to Moira's throat, she realized he was leaving his injured side unprotected. With a huge breath in, Moira silently prayed that Lyric wouldn't swipe the blade across her throat once she slammed her elbow into his injured ribs. For the split second her elbow was raised, she felt Lyric freeze in what she assumed was realization of what was about to happen. This time, he was not quicker than she was, and she brought the inside of her elbow down into his injured ribs with a satisfying slam.

The groaning prince dropped the blade and let go of Moira as he hunched to cover his side and cower in pain. Moira decided it was worth the risk and bent to grab the knife from the floor before stepping away from the prince. She grabbed it and stumbled several steps, moving out of his reach. He was laying on the floor in the fetal position as he clutched his injured side and groaned constantly.

As Moira watched the prince writhe, she moved backward until she found herself bumping into the wooden table where Sigrid lay. Even at a quick glance, Sigrid looked just as peaceful as Amis. Her face had a ghostly pallor to it, but Moira couldn't tell if it was from the flour or from death. Moira peered around the corner of the table, daring a look at Alaine and noted that she was also in blissful repose. An unsettling feeling took root deep in Moira's stomach as she continued to look at the unmarried face of the young girl who risked so much to help her. Try as she might, Moira couldn't identify the unsettling feeling. Where it came from or why it was there would have to be dissected later.

A large hand settled on Moira's shoulder. She held the blade and spun around, narrowly missing a swipe at Roman's face.

"Whoa, B! It's me! It's just me!" Roman said as he held his hands up in surrender; stepping away from her as he spoke.

Moira dropped the blade and threw herself into Roman's chest, allowing herself one small moment of weakness. Roman threw his free arm tightly around her while his dominant hand held tight to his sword. Moira gave herself three deep breaths while sheltered against Roman's chest, then stepped away and looked around the room.

Wilhelm leaned against the wall in utter exhaustion. He was covered in blood that Moira hoped wasn't his. The floor was littered with dead or severely wounded guards. Moira did not attempt to count them. She knew more would be on their way. Prince Lyric was still moaning by the hearth, uncomfortably close to Amis's body.

"Amis is dead," Moira said softly, finally looking into Roman's eyes.

Roman held her gaze and nodded solemnly.

"Sigrid and Alaine, too," Moira whispered.

"Yes," Roman responded quietly, gently.

"We need to go," Wilhelm lamented as he threw open the kitchen door and glanced outside. He didn't appear to see anything threatening as he turned around to look at them.

"I know we can't bring him, but please get my brother's body away from that piece of human filth," Moira said with such vehemence that she surprised even herself.

Without a word Roman stepped over to Amis. He looked down at the prince and Moira saw the sword twitch in his hand. Roman brought the blade up with a heaving grunt. The blade came down so swiftly, Moira wasn't sure what happened until the prince was sitting up and screaming in horror as he looked at his right foot, which now lay completely detached from his ankle.

As if he lobbed off limbs on a regular basis, Roman casually wiped his blade on the sleeve of the prince's tunic. Prince Lyric barely flinched, too distracted by his agony. His own blood was now smeared on his ornate sleeve. Once the blade was sufficiently cleaned, Roman sheathed it and turned toward Amis. He crouched down and gently, carefully picked Amis up. The sight brought a fresh wave of tears to Moira's eyes, but she wiped them away impatiently. She did not have time to mourn right now. Roman made sure Amis's head was supported as he stood, but even then, it lolled backward in a way that made Moira feel sick.

"You are right, Moira. We cannot bring him," Roman said with a note of serious melancholy as he noticed the brief

509

look of hope that crossed Moira's face as he lifted her brother's body so easily. "I wish that we could, but he would slow us down and complicate our escape."

Moira gulped down a sob as she nodded. She knew Roman would carry Amis's body as far as he could if she asked it of him, but she couldn't do that. They were barely about to escape as it was, and she could not risk their lives to have the possibility of burying Amis. She could hear Amis in her mind, playfully scolding her for even considering the idea. *Impractical, Moi. Imagine all the whiskey you could carry instead of my heaping corpse!*

"Lay him here," Moira said weakly, gesturing toward the empty space on the large table next to Sigrid. "I don't want him on the floor in a pool of the prince's blood."

Roman nodded grimly and set Amis gently next to Sigrid. He wordlessly stepped around Moira and lifted the tiny form of Alaine. Moira moved Sigrid's arm, making room for Alaine in between the two larger forms.

Wilhelm crossed the kitchen at a sprint and plunged his sword into the stomach of Lord Owen. Moira flinched at the sudden movement and watched with her mouth wide open as Wilhelm leaned into his blade, plunging it further into Owen's abdomen. Roman cursed under his breath. Neither Moira nor Roman heard Owen's approach. Wil withdrew his sword as Owen clutched his stomach wordlessly and dropped to his knees before toppling over onto a lifeless guard. Moira shut her eyes and tried to tune out the wet gurgling sounds of Owen's last breaths.

Wil turned to look at them. Cold fury covered his face as he said through gritted teeth, "We. Need. To. Go."

Roman nodded and gave the prince one last look of disgust. Lyric was still on the floor, rocking back and forth while clutching his leg.

Moira reached out and gave Amis's hand one last squeeze before setting it down gently on the table. As she moved toward the exit, Moira let her tears flow freely. She straightened her back and looked at the door resolutely. Vowing that she would not look back, Moira walked out of the kitchen. Roman was close at her back and Wil brought up the rear.

Chapter Seventy

Moira's feet carried her through the castle grounds easily enough. Although she'd spent countless hours out here, the landscape felt foreign. She stumbled on a few roots and rocks, but she barely noticed as Roman prevented her from falling on her face every single time, just as Amis had done countless times.

As they reached the edge of the forest and stepped into its comforting embrace, Moira wondered how her lungs continued to draw air, how her heart kept beating. She wanted to know how her body continued to propel her forward despite the fact that a large part of her heart and soul was left behind.

Roman threw side-eyed glances at Moira as they moved, but he remained silent. As much as she knew he was dying to speak, he did not poke or prod. She reminded herself to thank him later for that small kindness.

Wilhelm, who was now ahead of them, stopped just inside a small clearing a little way into the forest. He turned and watched them as they approached. Once Moira was in arm's reach, Wil pulled her into the tightest hug she'd ever experienced. Rather than fight the embrace, Moira threw her arms around her friend and returned his squeeze.

"As soon as we reach the hideout, you can let it all out, Moi," Wil said softly as he stepped back a few paces.

Moira nodded but didn't respond as she felt the lump return to the back of her throat.

Roman came up behind them and placed his hand on the small of Moira's back. She leaned into his side, appreciating both men more than she ever had before.

"We can't go to the hideout," Roman said through clenched teeth. It was clear he was still running off the fumes of his adrenaline and panic.

Moira wondered vaguely when they'd all be able to calm down because right now, it felt like it might take years before she felt normal again.

"What do you mean?" Wil asked in shock. "If Bobby truly made it out of the castle, that's where she would have gone, Ro."

"What if we are being followed? You think they would let us sprint away from the castle after that and never try to find us?" Roman spat in return.

"You chopped off the prince's fucking foot, mate. I don't believe he'll be personally coming after us any time soon," Wil said loudly as he stepped closer to Roman. "Not to mention, we took down every guard that came at us, along with that damned sneaky lord. Nobody saw us leave. Nobody came after us once we set foot outside the castle. I'm not saying we stay at the hideout forever, man. But I think it would be foolish to avoid it now when we need supplies before we leave."

"Leave?" Moira asked in surprise.

Roman looked at Moira and then back at Wil. He did not answer Moira's question but said to Wil, "Fine. We return to the hideout, but *only* to grab our supplies and leave. I'm not sure we have enough coin for the journey, but we'll have to make do."

Wilhelm slung a bag off his shoulder and dumped the contents to the ground. The wooden box they'd taken from the trophy room landed with a heavy thunk, along with several leather pouches and a loaf of bread.

Roman looked at the spilled contents and then back up to Wilhelm. A slow smile spread across his bearded face. Moira stared at the wooden box lying on the ground amidst the twigs, dirt, and leaves. She had completely forgotten about their small victory earlier in the night. The victory of escaping the trophy room with both the wooden box and the key to unlock it. At one point less than an hour ago, she had run through the castle halls in elation over these things.

"Wil, are those all pouches of money?" Roman asked as he crouched down and started to pick them up.

"Sure are, Ro! Nicked 'em off that Leofwin git and a couple of the guards in the kitchen. They were all just hanging out in the open, calling to me. You know I can't resist a noble mugging," Wil answered with a shrug and a small glimmer of pride.

"You brilliant bastard," Roman cheered as he poured several coins into the palm of his hand from one of the leather pouches.

Moira gave Wil a weak smile, happy in some distant part of her that he thought to do what she and Roman were too distracted to consider. She wanted to be more involved in the conversation. She desperately needed something to pull her out of this numbness before she settled too far into it and never came out again.

"I need something to do," she said into the excited silence. "We can't stand here talking and not acting. Roman, please. Whether we go to the hideout or dance our way to the Moran Sea, I do not care," Moira begged. She hated how she sounded and the clear hopeless ring in her voice. But her every heartbeat said *Amis is dead. Amis is dead. Amis is dead.* She was desperate for a task, a purpose. Anything that could ground her back in reality.

Roman nodded as he looked at her. He placed his hand on the back of her head and pulled her in for a gentle kiss. He gave her a lingering look of reassurance as he said to Wilhelm, "We go to the Hideout. If things went right for Bobby - and I sure as hell hope they did - she should be there waiting for us."

Wilhelm nodded and crouched down to shove everything back into the canvas bag. He blew on the loaf of bread before dusting off some of the dirt and leaves by hand. For some reason, this display gave Moira a fit of giggles. Wilhelm paused in his work and looked at her as if she'd lost what remained of her sanity. Roman took a step back and stared at her as well.

"Sorry!" Moira said through small fits of laughter. "I'm sorry, now is not the time to laugh. Obviously," she continued, gesturing randomly with her hands and still attempting to regain some of her composure. She felt nearly manic. The laughter kept bursting out of her, despite her attempts to quell it. "It's just that...well, what the fuck happened? We've fled for our lives, leaving behind people we loved, people who helped us, and somewhere along the way, Wilhelm thought with his stomach and grabbed a loaf of bread! He's dumped onto the ground and must clean off before shoving it back into a bag I didn't even realize he was carrying!"

Roman gave Moira a concerned smile, possibly just relieved that she was showing any sort of reaction, even if it was lunacy. Wilhelm meanwhile gave her a massive grin as he wiggled his eyebrows and took a giant bite out of the bread.

"What if this is as good as it gets? What a fucking nightmare!" Moira said, sounding unhinged and more joyful than she actually felt.

Roman looked at her somberly and said, "It will get better, B."

His comment sobered her up, and Moira took one deep, shaky breath as she wiped her cheeks with the backs of her hand. Somewhere during her outburst of laughter, she started crying again, and she hadn't even noticed. As she calmed down, Moira realized that she felt a lot better, despite the awful circumstances.

She gave Roman and Wil a reassuring nod and said firmly, "To the hideout, then."

Chapter Seventy-One

After they reached the halfway point in their journey to the hideout, they were intercepted by Bobby and Hanna. Moira was walking behind Wilhelm, her hand held comfortingly by Roman, when there was a commotion ahead. Moira looked up to see Bobby and Hanna come thundering through the forest on horseback. One extra horse trailed behind; reins held by Bobby. Wil waved and hollered at them as if they had not seen the three weary travelers walking toward them.

"We bloody see you, Wilhelm Clarke," Hanna said exasperatedly.

Both women hopped off their horses as soon as they were a few feet away from the trio. Hanna walked up to Moira and gave her a rib-crushing embrace. Moira leaned into it and wondered briefly if she was always going to need these reaffirming hugs now.

"I'm glad you're alive, girl," Hanna said gruffly. She let go of Moira and looked around before saying, "I'm glad all of you are alive."

"Did you leave through the kitchen?" Moira asked, unsure if Hanna embraced her because she knew of Amis, Alaine, and Sigrid. It was possible the hug was simply because the night had been riddled with risk.

Hanna's stoic face very nearly broke as she looked at Moira and gave a small nod. Her bottom lip quivered, and Moira had to look away before she lost her composure all over again. Roman reached over and took her hand; he'd let go of it when Hanna walked over to hug her.

Moira cleared her throat and asked tentatively, "What happened tonight, Han? Why did everything go wrong?"

"We don't know," Bobby chimed in from where she stood by the horses. "I saw Sigrid put the sleeping draught into the wine for the prince and his lords. Someone must have intercepted it. We will have to find out more later, but as of right now, you lot need to get gone."

Hanna looked at Moira and said, "They were poisoned, Moira. Take some small comfort in that." Moira opened her mouth in shock, offended that Hanna would suggest she take any comfort whatsoever in Amis's death. Hanna shook her head gently and said, "They did not suffer. Amis, Sigrid, and Alaine went peacefully. There was no violent end for them to meet. They were given the tiniest blessing of a peaceful passing."

Moira gulped back the heavy emotion that threatened to overwhelm her. She felt her eyes burn once again with repressed tears, and a knot returned in the back of her throat as she held back her sobs. Rather than argue or say anything, she simply pursed her lips and nodded before staring down at the forest floor. A complicated tangle of thoughts ran through her grief-addled mind as Moira wondered if their passing really had been peaceful. If the prince killed them using the purple poison, the very one she'd spent endless hours reading about, then it was possible they all had a brief and painful moment of realization before they fell unconscious. Rather than linger too long over that heartbreaking fact, Moira opted to believe Hanna's version of events.

Wilhelm walked over to Bobby and took the reins of all three horses. With one arm, he pulled Bobby in for a squeeze. Moira smiled as Bobby half-heartedly leaned into the hug before quickly pulling away and stepping several paces back.

"Glad you made it out, Bob," Wil said softly.

"You should be all packed. Enough food to get you to Gest," Bobby responded curtly, as she gestured toward the horses and their packs.

"I don't have anything," Moira said, looking between Hanna and Roman. Panic built swiftly as she scolded herself for leaving with nothing but that damned satchel in her boot.

Hanna scoffed and looked genuinely offended. "Have you not noticed that I've gone through your wardrobe multiple times and pulled things out that never went back in?"

Moira looked at Hanna in confusion before saying, "Umm, no."

"You know, Gwendolyn Her-"

"I have noticed you sorting through my wardrobe multiple times, Hanna. Never have I paid two seconds' notice to what went in and out of that old thing," Moira said quickly, hating that the beginning of Hanna's cautionary tale caused her to look around for Amis so they could share in the delight. She could not bear to hear the entire story without Amis there to laugh with her.

Hanna looked momentarily insulted, but she did not press the issue. Instead, she said, "Very well then. You have clothing packed, Moira."

"Thank you, Hanna," Moira said as she dropped Roman's hand and stepped forward and surprised Hanna with a second hug. She leaned down and said so only Hanna could hear, "For *everything*."

Hanna gave her an extra squeeze before letting go and walking away while brushing her eyes.

"I'll be returning to the castle. I'll do what I can ensure Amis gets a proper burial, Moira," Hanna told her reassuringly. Moira gave her a grateful smile in response.

Roman motioned Moira over and helped her climb onto the back of one of the waiting horses. He handed her the reins and gave her leg a comforting pat.

"I'll murder you myself if you let anything happen to that girl," Hanna scolded, jabbing Roman in the chest with one finger. He was near twice her height, but she still managed to look terrifying.

With an endearing grin, Roman said, "If I let anything happen to her, I'll make sure to come back just to endure your punishment. I swear it, Hanna."

The twitch of a grin sneaked across Hanna's face as she *harrumphed* at Roman. She jerked her chin toward the horse, indicating clearly that she was done with him. He shook his head and walked over to Bobby.

Roman reached out and shook Bobby's hand before saying, "Thank you."

Bobby nodded and said, "Stay safe. Don't forget what we are fighting for."

Without any further words of encouragement or farewell, Roman, Wilhelm, and Moira continued their journey. Bobby and Hanna turned in different directions and started walking back through the forest to their own destinations.

Chapter Seventy-Two

Moira followed Roman's horse through the forest as they headed southeast toward Gest. They stayed on the outer edge of the forest for as long as possible before venturing out into the open. Wilhelm rode behind her, which she was grateful for. She remained unarmed and planned to change that as quickly as possible.

"I hope they packed enough food. Amis warned me that Moira could really put it away," Wilhelm said in jest.

For the briefest of moments, Moira could feel it in the air as Wilhelm regretted what he said. Moira's own heart constricted at the thought of Wilhelm and Amis discussing her and her habits. Rather than sink into the sadness of it, Moira let the feeling bring a soft smile to her face.

Moira turned her head a little and said to Wil, "You have no idea. It was nice of him to warn you about me, really."

Wil gave a soft laugh in return, and Moira knew he was relieved to know he hadn't upset her.

"So, what's in Gest?" Moira asked, speaking a little louder, so Roman knew she was asking him.

"Supplies and aid. Gest is merely a stop on our journey, B," Roman responded as he slowed his horse and turned in his saddle.

They were still in the forest but a little closer to the outer edge. The trees were not incredibly close, but they were close enough that they couldn't ride side by side yet.

Moira turned to look at Wilhelm, who gave her an enormous and mischievous grin in return. She turned back to Roman and asked, "Then where are we really going?"

Roman stopped his horse so he could turn around further and look at Moira directly. His grin matched Wil's as he said, "It's time for King Leo to come home. We are going to Etheldred."

The End

Made in the USA
Monee, IL
07 July 2023